Benjamin Disraeli

Wit and wisdom of Benjamin Disraeli, earl of Beaconsfield

collected from his writings and speeches

Benjamin Disraeli

Wit and wisdom of Benjamin Disraeli, earl of Beaconsfield
collected from his writings and speeches

ISBN/EAN: 9783744739672

Printed in Europe, USA, Canada, Australia, Japan

Cover: Foto ©Raphael Reischuk / pixelio.de

More available books at **www.hansebooks.com**

WIT AND WISDOM

OF

BENJAMIN DISRAELI

EARL OF BEACONSFIELD

COLLECTED from HIS WRITINGS and SPEECHES.

NEW EDITION

LONDON
LONGMANS, GREEN, AND CO.
1883

PREFACE.

As 'good wine needs no bush,' so words of wit and
wisdom, whether falling from the lips, or flowing from
the pen, of a great man, do not call for a preface—and
no one will gainsay the fact that Benjamin Disraeli, Earl of Beaconsfield, was one of the greatest
men of the century—probably the greatest, when the
difficulties which he had to overcome are taken into
consideration.

It is not given to many to excel either in action
or in thought ; to very few indeed to be *facile princeps*
in both, as was Lord Beaconsfield—a Janus of literature and politics, in the study a Thackeray, a Bolingbroke in the Senate.

But this is neither the time nor the place for
panegyric. The air is still ringing with the voice of
unanimous England, proclaiming the patience and
the patriotism of the great statesman, extolling the
eloquence of the brilliant debater, the sparkling
phrases of the witty writer, who has just passed
away.

This selection does not purport to be exhaustive—very far from it. It would be easy to compile other volumes equally wise and witty. The gold nearest the surface has been extracted from the rich lode, but an ample store of nuggets remains to reward the seeker ; and the object of the present work will be more than accomplished if it induces others to look for further treasure in the writings and speeches of the Earl of Beaconsfield.

It only remains to add that the present work was begun before Lord Beaconsfield's last illness, and that, though the manuscript was never in his hands, he expressed his approval and looked forward to its publication with interest.

CONTENTS.

	PAGE
Ability	1
Absence	1
Abuse	1
Action	1
Adoption	2
Advantage	2
Adventure	2
Adversity	2
Advice	2
Age	5
Agitation	6
Alhambra	7
Alliteration	9
Ambition	9
America	9
Americans	10
Anecdote	10
Anglo-French Alliance	10
Anonymous	11
Anxiety	12
Apologies	12
Archery	12
Architecture	12
Aristocracy	12
Armine (Ferdinand)	13
Art	14
Ashantee	15
Assassination	16
Association	16
Austria	16
Authors	16
Autumn	16

	PAGE
Badinage	17
Balaclava	17
Bar	17
Baronetcy	17
Baths	17
Beauty	17
Bellair (Lady)	18
Bentinck (Lord George)	21
Bishop	21
Blue-stocking	25
Blush	25
Bolingbroke	25
Books	27
Bow	28
Breakfast	28
Brecon (Duke of)	28
Bribery	29
Brougham (Lord)	30
Buckinghamshire	31
Byron	31
Cab	31
Cabal	32
Cabinet	32
Cadurcis (Captain)	33
Calamities	34
Calculation	34
Canning	34
Capital	35
Cards	35
Casualties	35
Catesby (Monsignore)	35
Cause	36

	PAGE		PAGE
Celibacy	36	Corisande (Lady)	66
Chance	36	Corporations	66
Change	36	Country Houses	67
Chapel	37	Credit	87
Character	38	Creed	87
Charity	38	Crimean War	87
Christianity	38	Critics	88
Church	39	Cyprus	88
Circuit	46	Dacre (May)	89
Circumstances	47	D.ince	90
City	47	Dawn	90
Civilisation	47	Day	90
Clergyman of the Old School	48	Death	90
Club	48	Debate	91
Coalition	49	Debaters	92
Cobden	49	Debt	94
Coercion	49	Delicacy	95
Coffee	50	Democracy	95
Colonies	50	Departures	96
Combination	50	Deputations	96
Commerce	50	Derby (Earl of)	96
Commercial Distress	50	Derby Race (the)	96
Commercial World	50	Despair	96
Commission	51	Desperation	96
Committee	51	Destiny	96
Common Sense	51	De trop	97
Complain	51	Development	97
Composition	51	Digestion	97
Conceit	53	Dinner	97
Conciliation	53	Diplomacy	105
Conduct	53	Diplomatists	105
Conference	53	Dissolution	105
Coningsby	53	Divinity	105
Conscience	55	Divorce	106
Conservatism	55	Don Quixote	106
Conservatism in 1834	56	Downing Street	107
Conservative	57	Dress	107
Consols	59	Duel	107
Constancy	59	Duke and Duchess	107
Constantinople	59	Duke of St. James	109
Constituencies	60	Dynasties	110
Constitution	61	East	110
Conversation	62	East India Company	110
Coquette	65	Economy	110

	PAGE		PAGE
Education . . .	110	Formality . . .	133
Egyptian Ornament	111	Fortune	133
Election . . .	112	Frankfort Fair . .	133
Eloquence . .	112	Frankness . . .	135
Emigration . .	112	Freedom . . .	135
Empire . . .	112	Free Trade . .	135
Ems . . .	113	French . . .	135
Endowment . .	115	Friendship . .	136
Endymion and Myra	115	Frill (Count) . .	139
Endymion . .	115	Future . . .	139
Energy . . .	117	Gambling . .	139
England . . .	118	Garden . . .	142
English . . .	118	Gardener . .	146
Enterprise . .	119	Gay (Lucian) .	146
Enthusiasm . .	119	Genius . . .	146
Equality . .	120	Gentlemen . .	146
Estate . . .	120	Geology . . .	147
Eternity . .	121	Gerard (Walter) .	148
Eton . . .	121	Girl of the Period .	148
Eva . . .	121	Gladstone . .	148
Evening . .	123	Glastonbury (Adrian)	149
Events . . .	124	Government . .	150
Everingham (Lady)	125	Grandison (Cardinal)	151
Exaggeration .	125	Granted . . .	152
Expediency . .	125	Gratitude . .	152
Experience . .	125	Greatness . .	152
Explain . .	125	Grecian . .	153
Extreme . .	126	Greece . .	153
Faith . . .	126	Grey (Vivian) .	153
Fame . . .	126	Grief . . .	155
Fane (Violet) .	126	Guy Flouncey (Mr. and Mrs.) .	156
Farewell . .	127	Half-measures . .	157
Fashion . .	127	Hampshire (Marquis and Mar-	
Fate . . .	128	chioness of) . .	158
Feebleness . .	129	Hand . . .	158
Feeling . .	129	Hansard . . .	159
Fenians . .	129	Happiness . .	159
Ferrol (Count of) .	129	Heart . . .	159
Figures . .	131	Herbert (Marmion) .	159
Finance . .	131	Heroes . .	163
Firmness . .	131	History . .	163
Flattery . .	132	Holidays . .	163
Flirtation . .	132	Home . . .	163
Florence . .	132	Hope . . .	163

	PAGE		PAGE
Horse Exercise	164	Localities	192
House of Commons	164	London	192
House of Lords	165	Long-sight	198
Hume (Mr.)	167	Lord Mayor	198
Idea	167	Lord Mayor's Day	198
Ignorance	167	Louis XIV.	198
Imagination	167	Love	199
Imogene	168	Lowe, Robert (Lord Sherbrooke)	204
Imprudence	169	Luck	204
Impudence	169	Lyle (Eustace)	205
Impulse	169	Machine	206
Inheritance	170	Majority	206
India	170	Man	206
Insignificant Beginnings	170	Manners	208
Institutions	171	Manufacturer	208
Intellect	171	Marriage	211
Intrigue	171	Measures	212
Invention	172	Mediterranean	212
Ireland	172	Melbourne (Lord)	213
Irish	173	Memory	213
Isandula	173	Metaphysics	213
Italian Lakes	174	Millbank (Mr.)	214
Jacobin	174	Millbank (Oswald)	214
Jerusalem	175	Millbank (Edith)	216
Jesuits	177	Minister	217
Jews	177	Ministry	219
Jobs	181	Mission	219
Justice	181	Monastics	219
Kitchen	181	Money	221
Knowledge	182	Monmouth (Lord)	221
Land	182	Montfort (Lord)	221
Law	183	Montfort (Lady)	223
Lawyers	183	Moon	224
Learning	183	Morality	225
Lebanon	183	Morley (Stephen)	226
Legislators	183	Morning	226
Leman, Lake	183	Mountain Air	227
Letters	184	Mountain Valleys	228
Lewis (Sir George)	184	Music	228
Liberalism	185	Myra	229
Life	188	Mystery	229
Lineage	190	Nation	230
Literature	191	National Petition	230
Local	191	Nationality	230

	PAGE		PAGE
Nature	230	Petrarch	251
Necessity	230	Philosophy	252
Neuchatel (Adrian, Lord		Phœbus (Mr.)	254
Hainault)	230	Phœbus (Madame)	255
Neuchatel, Mrs. (Lady Hai-		Physician	255
nault)	231	Piety	256
Neuchatel (Adriana)	231	Pigeon-shooting	256
Neutrality	232	Pinto (Mr.)	256
News	232	Pitt	257
Night	232	Pluto	257
Non-intervention	233	Pleasure	258
Nonsense	234	Poet	258
Novel (Receipt for writing a)	234	Poetry	259
Novelty	234	Policy	276
Oblivion	234	Politics	276
Obscure	234	Political Economy	277
Offer	234	Popular Gratitude	277
Old Gentleman	234	Population	277
Opportunity	235	Post Office	277
Opposition	235	Power	277
Orator (Job Thornberry)	236	Practical	278
Oratory	236	Prayer	278
Originality	237	Precedent	278
Ortolans	237	Press	279
Oxford	237	Pretenders	279
Oxford (A Professor at)	238	Pride of Ancestry	279
Palmerston (Lord)	239	Princess Alice	279
Parents	240	Prince Consort	281
Paris	241	Princes	283
Parliament	241	Private Secretaries	283
Party	241	Processions	284
Parvenus	243	Profound	284
Past	243	Property	284
Patience	243	Prophecy (A)	284
Patriotism	243	Prophet	284
Peace	243	Protection	284
Pearls	244	Proverbs	285
Peel (Sir Robert)	244	Prudence	285
Peerage	247	Public	285
People	247	Publicity	287
Perseverance	250	Purpose	287
Personal	250	Queen	288
Personality of Creator	251	Question	288
Personality of Devil	251	Race	288

	PAGE		PAGE
Radical	289	Sensible	313
Raglan (Lord) . .	289	Sentimental . . .	313
Railway Mania . .	290	Sergius (Baron) . .	313
Rank	291	Services	313
Reaction	291	Servility . . .	314
Recess	291	Seville	314
Reciprocity . . .	292	Shower	315
Reform . . .	292	Sidney (Lord Henry) .	315
Religion	295	Sidonia	317
Remorse . . .	296	Silence	320
Republican . . .	296	Sleep . . .	320
Resolution . . .	297	Smile	321
Retirement . . .	297	Social . . .	321
Retrenchment . . .	297	Society	322
Retrogression . . .	297	Sorrow	324
Revolution . . .	298	Southey	324
Ridicule	298	Sovereignty . . .	325
Rigby (Mr.) . . .	298	Spaniards . . .	325
Ritualism . . .	299	Spanish Bull-fight .	325
Rivers	299	Spanish Fan . . .	328
Rodney (Mrs.) . .	300	Special Correspondent .	329
Rodney (Mr.) . . .	301	Speech	329
Roehampton (Lord) .	301	Speed	329
Rome	302	Spirits	329
Routine . . .	303	Spring	330
Royalty . . .	303	St. Aldegonde (Lord) .	331
Rumour . . .	304	Statesmanship . .	332
Russell (Lord John) .	304	Statesmen . . .	333
Russia . . .	305	Station . . .	333
Russian	305	St. Jerome (Lady) .	333
Sacerdotal . . .	305	Stock Exchange . .	333
Sanitas	306	Strength . . .	334
Satiety	306	Sublimity . . .	334
Scepticism . . .	306	Success . . .	334
School	306	Summer Evening .	334
Schoolboy . . .	308	Sun . . .	335
Science	309	Sunday . . .	335
Scotch	310	Sunrise . . .	335
Scrope (Sir Fraunceys) .	310	Superannuation . .	335
Sea	311	Superior Persons . .	336
Season	311	Suspense . . .	336
Sedition	312	Switzerland . . .	336
Self-complacency . .	312	Sybil . . .	337
Self-respect . . .	313	Sympathy . . .	339

CONTENTS.

	PAGE			PAGE
System	340	Unobtrusiveness		357
Tact	340	Vacation		357
Tancred (Lord Montacute)	340	Variety		357
Taste	341	Vegetarian View of Animal		
Taxation	341	Food		358
Temper	341	Vehemence		358
Temple (Henrietta)	342	Venetia		358
Testimonial	342	Venice		358
Thames	342	Vice		364
Theodora (Mrs. Campian)	343	Victoria		364
Theology	343	Vigo (Mr.)		366
Thug	343	Virtue		366
Time	344	Voice		367
' Times' (The)	344	Voltaire		368
Tobacco	344	Volunteers		369
Toil	344	Waldershare		369
Tongue	344	War		370
Tory	344	Wealth		370
Town Houses	347	Wellington, Duke of		371
Trade	352	Whigs		373
Travel	353	Whisper		374
Tremaine, Mr. Bertie	353	Will		374
Truth	355	Williams (Fenwick) of Kars		374
Tu Quoque	356	Woman		375
Turf	356	Wordsworth		378
Tutor	356	Working Classes		378
Unconstitutional	357	World		379
Unfortunate	357	Youth		380
Unhappiness	357			

WIT AND WISDOM

EARL OF BEACONSFIELD.

———◦◦◦———

ABILITY.

I pride myself upon recognising and upholding ability in every party and wherever I meet it.—*Speech at Newport Pagnell (General Election), February* 5, 1874.

ABSENCE.

I believe absence is often a great element of charm.— ('Lord Roehampton') *Endymion.*

ABUSE.

It isn't calling your neighbours names that settles a question.—('Widow Carey') *Sybil.*

ACTION.

Action may not always bring happiness ; but there is no happiness without action.—('The General') *Lothair.*

The standing committee of the Holy Alliance of Peoples all rose, although they were extreme Republicans, when the General entered. Such is the magical influence of a man of action over men of the pen and the tongue.—*Lothair.*

Action must be founded on knowledge.—*Contarini Fleming.*

B

ADOPTION.

The principle of adoption was the secret and endurance of Rome. It gave Rome alike the Scipios and the Antonines.—('Bertie Tremaine') *Endymion.*

ADVANTAGE.

Next to knowing when to seize an opportunity, the most important thing in life is to know when to forego an advantage.—('Tiresias') *The Infernal Marriage.*

ADVENTURE.

How full of adventure is life ! It is monotonous only to the monotonous.—*Tancred.*

Adventure and contemplation share our being like day and night.—('Sidonia') *Coningsby.*

The fruit of my tree of knowledge is plucked, and it is this, 'Adventures are to the adventurous.'—*Alroy.*

ADVERSITY.

There is no education like adversity.—('Sidney Wilton') *Endymion.*

I suppose it is adversity that develops the kindly qualities of our nature. I believe the sense of common degradation has a tendency to make the degraded amiable—at least among themselves. I am told it is found so in the plantations in slave-gangs.—('St. Barbe') *Endymion.*

Adversity is necessarily not a sanguine season, and in this respect a political party is no exception to all other human combinations.—*Life of Lord George Bentinck.*

ADVICE.

Advice is not a popular thing to give.—('Miss Arundel') *Lothair.*

I do not like giving advice, because it is an unnecessary responsibility under any circumstances.—*Speech at Ayles-*

bury (Royal and Central Bucks Agricultural Association),
September 21, 1865.

Be patient : cherish hope. Read more : ponder less.
Nature is more powerful than education : time will develop
everything. Trust not overmuch to the blessed Magdalen :
learn to protect yourself.—*Contarini Fleming.*

A Father's Advice to his Son.—'But to enter society
with pleasure, Contarini, you must be qualified for it. I
think it quite time for you to make yourself master of some
accomplishments. Decidedly you should make yourself a
good dancer. Without dancing you can never attain a
perfectly graceful carriage, which is of the highest importance in life, and should be every man's ambition. You
are yet too young fully to comprehend how much in life
depends upon manner. Whenever you see a man who is
successful in society, try to discover what makes him pleasing,
and if possible adopt his system. You should learn to
fence. For languages, at present, French will be sufficient.
You speak it fairly ; try to speak it elegantly. Read French
authors. Read Rochefoucault. The French writers are the
finest in the world, for they clear our heads of all ridiculous
ideas. Study precision.

'Do not talk too much at present ; do not *try* to talk.
But whenever you speak, speak with self-possession. Speak
in a subdued tone, and always look at the person whom you
are addressing. Before one can engage in general conversation with any effect, there is a certain acquaintance with
trifling but amusing subjects which must be first attained.
You will soon pick up sufficient by listening and observing.
Never argue. In society nothing must be discussed ; give
only results. If any person differ from you, bow and turn
the conversation. In society never think ; always be on
the watch, or you will miss many opportunities and say
many disagreeable things.

'Talk to women, talk to women as much as you can
This is the best school. This is the way to gain fluency

because you need not care what you say, and had better not be sensible. They, too, will rally you on many points, and as they are women you will not be offended. Nothing is of so much importance and of so much use to a young man entering life as to be well criticised by women. It is impossible to get rid of those thousand bad habits which we pick up in boyhood, without this supervision. Unfortunately you have no sisters. But never be offended if a woman rally you ; encourage her, otherwise you will never be free from your awkwardness or any little oddities, and certainly never learn to dress.

'You ride pretty well, but you had better go through the manège. Every gentleman should be a perfect cavalier. You shall have your own groom and horses, and I wish you to ride regularly every day.

'As you are to be at home for so short a time, and for other reasons, I think it better that you should not have a tutor in the house. Parcel out your morning then for your separate masters. Rise early and regularly and read for three hours. Read the Memoirs of the Cardinal de Retz, the Life of Richelieu, everything about Napoleon : read works of that kind. Strelamb shall prepare you a list. Read no history, nothing but biography, for that is life without theory. Then fence. Take an hour with your French master, but do not throw the burden of the conversation upon him. Give him an account of something. Describe to him the events of yesterday, or give him a detailed account of the constitution. You will have then sufficiently rested yourself for your dancing. And after that ride and amuse yourself as much as you can. Amusement to an observing mind is study.'—('Mr. Fleming.') *Contarini Fleming.*

Advice to a Boy going to School.—You will find Eton a great change ; you will experience many trials and temptations ; but you will triumph over and withstand them all, if you will attend to these few directions. Fear God ; morning and night let nothing induce you ever to omit your prayers to Him; you will find that praying will make you happy. Obey your superiors; always treat your masters with respect. Ever speak the truth. So long as you adhere to this rule, you never can be involved in any serious misfortune. A deviation from truth is, in general, the foundation of all misery. Be kind to your companions, but be firm. Do not be laughed into doing that which you know to be wrong. Be modest and humble, but ever respect yourself. Remember who you are, and also that it is your duty to excel. Providence has given you a great lot. Think ever that you are born to perform great duties.—('Lady Annabel') *Venetia.*

AGE.

Age was frequently beautiful, wisdom appeared like an aftermath, and the heart which seemed dry and deadened suddenly put forth shoots of sympathy.—('Mr. Phœbus') *Lothair.*

The disappointment of manhood succeeds to the delusion of youth; let us hope that the heritage of age is not despair.—*Vivian Grey.*

I hold that the characteristic of the present age is craving credulity.—*Speech at Meeting of Society for increasing Endowments of Small Livings in the Diocess of Oxford, November 25, 1864.*

'The spirit of the age is the very thing that a great man changes,' said Sidonia.

'Does he not rather avail himself of it?' asked Coningsby.

'Parvenus do, but not prophets, great legislators, great conquerors. They destroy and they create.'—*Coningsby.*

I look upon the spirit of the age as a spirit hostile to Kings and Gods.—('Saturn') *The Infernal Marriage.*

It appears to me that I should not greatly err were I to describe the spirit of this age as the spirit of equality.—*Speech at Glasgow University, November 19, 1873.*

I would say a knowledge of the spirit of the age is necessary for every public man. But it does not follow, because the spirit of the age is perceived and recognised, it should be embraced and followed, or even that success in life depends upon adopting it. What I wish to impress upon you is that success in life depends on comprehending it.— *Speech at Glasgow University, November* 19, 1873.

AGITATION.

We may visit on the laches of the Liverpool Ministry the introduction of that principle and power into our Constitution, which ultimately may absorb all: Agitation.— *Coningsby.*

Demagogues and agitators are very unpleasant, and leagues and registers may be very unpleasant, but they are incidents to a free and constitutional country, and you must put up with these inconveniences or do without many important advantages.—*Speech in House of Commons (Representation of the People Bill), April* 12, 1867.

There is one feature about the present agitation in Ireland which is most repulsive and I think most dangerous. Agitation in Ireland is not a novel subject. It has taken many forms. It has been led by men of different characters and idiosyncrasies. It has taken the form of Repeal, it has taken the form of Home Rule, and you may observe that all these movements had over them a varnish, no doubt a mere varnish, of what may be called generous feeling. Even a Fenian was a patriot, or thought he was. But if the present agitation is fostered in Ireland by the Government, it is one which will not easily terminate, because it is an agitation addressed to the most sordid character of the Irish people, not to the romantic and imaginative. An agitation conducted by men who have been taught to believe that the property of others ought to belong to them—an agitation conducted in such a spirit and for such a result is one which Her Majesty's Government will find more diffi-

cult to deal with than the agitation of previous years.—
*Speech in House of Lords (Compensation for Disturbance
Bill), August* 3, 1880.

ALHAMBRA.

Let us enter Alhambra !

See ! here is the Court of Myrtles, and I gather you a
sprig. Mark how exquisitely everything is proportioned ;
mark how slight, and small, and delicate ! And now we
are in the Court of Columns, the far-famed Court of
Columns. Let us enter the chambers that open round this
quadrangle. How beautiful are their deeply-carved and
purple roofs, studded with gold, and the walls entirely
covered with the most fanciful fret-work, relieved with that
violet tint which must have been copied from their Andalusian skies. Here you may sit in the coolest shade, reclining
on your divan, with your beads or pipe, and view the dazzling
sunlight in the court, which assuredly must scorch the
flowers, if the faithful lions. ever ceased from pouring forth
that element, which you must travel in Spain or Africa to
honour. How many chambers ! the Hall of the Ambassadors ever the most sumptuous. How fanciful its mosaic
ceiling of ivory and tortoiseshell, mother-of-pearl and gold !
And then the Hall of Justice with its cedar roof, and the
Harem, and the baths : all perfect. Not a single roof has
yielded, thanks to those elegant horse-shoe arches and
those crowds of marble columns, with their oriental capitals.
What a scene ! Is it beautiful ? Oh ! conceive it in the
time of the Boabdils ; conceive it with all its costly decora-
tions, all the gilding, all the imperial purple, all the violet
relief, all the scarlet borders, all the glittering inscriptions
and precious mosaics, burnished, bright, and fresh. Conceive it full of still greater ornaments, the living groups, with
their splendid and vivid and picturesque costume, and,
above all, their rich and shining arms, some standing in
conversing groups, some smoking in sedate silence, some

telling their beads, some squatting round a storier. Then the bustle and the rush, and the coming horsemen, all in motion, and all glancing in the most brilliant sun.

Alhambra is a strong illustration of what I have long thought, that however there may be a standard of taste, there is no standard of style. I must place Alhambra with the Parthenon, the Pantheon, the Cathedral of Seville, the temple of Dendera. They are different combinations of the same principles of taste. Thus we may equally admire Æschylus, Virgil, Calderon, and Ferdousi. There never could have been a controversy on such a point, if mankind had not confused the ideas of taste and style. The Saracenic architecture is the most inventive and fanciful, but at the same time the most fitting and delicate that can be conceived. There would be no doubt about its title to be considered among the finest inventions of man, if it were better known. It is only to be found, in any degree of European perfection, in Spain. Some of the tombs of the Mamlouk Sultans in the desert round Cairo, wrongly styled by the French 'the tombs of the Caliphs,' are equal, I think, to Alhambra. When a person sneers at the Saracenic, ask him what he has seen. Perhaps a barbarous, although picturesque, building, called the Ducal Palace, at Venice. What should we think of a man who decided on the architecture of Agrippa by the buildings of Justinian, or judged the age of Pericles by the restorations of Hadrian? Yet he would not commit so great a blunder. There is a Moorish palace, the Alcazar, at Seville, a huge mosque at Cordova turned into a Cathedral, with partial alteration, Alhambra at Granada; these are the great specimens in Europe, and sufficient for all study. There is a shrine and a chapel of a Moorish saint at Cordova, quite untouched, with the blue mosaic and the golden honeycomb roof, as vivid and as brilliant as when the Santon was worshipped. I have never seen any work of art so exquisite. The materials are the richest, the ornaments the most costly, and in detail the most elegant and the most novel, the most fanciful and the most flowing, that I ever contemplated. And yet nothing at the same time can be conceived more just than the proportion of the whole, and more mellowed than the blending of the parts, which indeed Palladio could not excel.—*Contarini Fleming.*

ALLITERATION.

'Fancy franchises,'—alliteration tickles the ear, and is a very popular form of language among savages. It is, I believe, the characteristic of rude and barbarous poetry : but it is not an argument in legislation.—*Speech in the House of Commons (Representation of the People Bill), March* 19, 1860.

AMBITION.

It was that noble ambition, the highest and the best, that must be born in the heart, and organised in the brain, which will not let a man be content unless his intellectual power is recognised by his race, and desires that it should contribute to their welfare. It is the heroic feeling ; the feeling that in old days produced demi-gods ; without which no State is safe ; without which political institutions are meat without salt, the Crown a bauble, the Church an establishment, Parliaments debating clubs, and civilisation itself but a fitful and transient dream.—*Coningsby.*

AMERICA.

The enterprise of America generally precedes that of Europe, as the industry of England precedes that of the rest of Europe, and I look forward with confidence that the industry and enterprise of America will be productive of beneficial results upon this country.—*Speech in House of Commons (Address in answer to Her Majesty's most gracious Speech), December* 8, 1878.

American ladies—I can never make out what they believe, or what they disbelieve. It is a sort of confusion between Mrs. Beecher Stowe and the Fifth Avenue congregation and Barnum.—(' The Bishop ') *Lothair.*

I have not been influenced by that sort of rowdy rhetoric which is expressed in public meetings and public journals, from which, I fear, in this country is formed too rapidly our opinion of the character and possible conduct of the American people. I look upon such expressions as something like those strong and fantastic drinks, that we hear of as such favourites on the other side of the Atlantic ; and I should as soon suppose that this rowdy rhetoric is a symbol of the real character of the American people as that those potations are symbols of the aliment and nutrition of their bodies.—*Speech in House of Commons (Defences of Canada), March* 13, 1865.

ANECDOTE.

An after-dinner anecdote ought to be as piquant as anchovy toast.—(' Von Königstein ') *Vivian Grey.*

Mr. Pinto would sometimes remark that when a man fell into his anecdotage, it was a sign for him to retire from the world.—*Lothair.*

ANGLO-FRENCH ALLIANCE.

It is the essence of English policy, and not only of English policy, but of French policy also, that there should be an alliance between England and France. It is an alliance founded upon a principle totally independent of forms of government, totally independent of dynasties, totally independent of the character of the rulers of that country. It does, indeed, so happen that the present ruler of France is a man eminently gifted, who from a variety of circumstances naturally exercises a great influence over events. The Emperor Napoleon is not only a prince, but he is a statesman. The Emperor of France is a man who has not only a great knowledge of human nature generally, but he is a man who has a great knowledge of English human nature ; and it is clear that when the ruler of France is not only a statesman, but one intimately acquainted with the character, the laws, the customs, and the whole condition of England, we have a security for the cultivation and maintenance of that alliance which under other and less favourable circumstances we might not have enjoyed.—*Address from Hustings to Buckinghamshire Electors*, 1858.

ANONYMOUS.

An anonymous writer should at least display power. When Jupiter hurls a thunderbolt, it may be mercy in the god to veil his glory with a cloud ; but we can only view with contemptuous lenity the mischievous varlet who pelts us with mud as we are riding along, and then hides behind a dust-bin.—*Attack on ' Globe,'* 1836.

Anonymous writing is not the exception, but it is the rule of the literature of this country. Who wrote 'Thomas à Kempis'? Nobody knows. Who wrote 'The Whole Duty of Man'? Now there is a book which every one of us ought to have studied—which for generations our predecessors have studied—which has had more editions than any book in the world, and which is not a scandalous book, a libellous book, or a political book, but an anonymous book. Who was the author of 'Waverley'? An anonymous writer. Who was the author of 'Robinson Crusoe'? An anonymous writer. Who was the author of 'A Vindication of Natural Society'? Why—one who became afterwards one of the most brilliant ornaments of this House—Mr. Burke. What are the most brilliant performances of political literature ? What are those works that were written by one who in this House occupied the highest post, whose name will ever be remembered, and whose oratory, though a tradition, lives in the memory of the nation? I mean Lord Bolingbroke. What are Lord Bolingbroke's works? All those works which we are continually quoting are anonymous.—*Speech in House of Commons* (*Newspaper Stamp Duties Bill*), *April* 30, 1854.

ANXIETY.

Nothing in life is more remarkable than the unnecessary anxiety which we endure and generally occasion ourselves. *Lothair.*

Nobody should ever look anxious, except those who have no anxiety.—*Endymion.*

People without cares do not require so much food as those whose life entails anxieties.—('Mr. St. Lys') *Sybil.*

APOLOGIES.

Apologies only account for that which they do not alter. *Speech in House of Commons* (*Order of Business*), *July* 28, 1871.

ARCHERY.

We are yet to learn the sight that is more dangerous for your bachelor to witness, or the ceremony which more perfectly develops all that the sex would wish us to remark, than this old English custom.— *Young Duke.*

ARCHITECTURE.

What is wanted in architecture, as in so many things, is a man. One suggestion might be made—no profession in England has done its duty until it has furnished a victim ; even our boasted navy never achieved a great victory until we shot an admiral. Suppose an architect were hanged. Terror has its inspiration, as well as competition.— *Tancred.*

ARISTOCRACY.

There is no longer, in fact, an aristocracy in England, for the superiority of the animal man is an essential quality of aristocracy.—*Sybil.*

I do not understand how an aristocracy can exist, unless it be distinguished by some quality which no other class of the community possesses. Distinction is the basis of aristocracy. If you permit only one class of the population, for example, to bear arms, they are an aristocracy ; not one much to my taste ; but still a great fact. That, however, is not the characteristic of the English peerage. I have yet to learn they are richer than we are, better informed, wiser, or more distinguished for public or private virtue.—(' Mr. Millbank ') *Coningsby.*

ARMINE (FERDINAND).

At ten years of age he was one of those spirited and at the same time docile boys, who seem to combine with the wild and careless grace of childhood the thoughtfulness and self-discipline of maturer age. It was the constant and truthful boast of his parents, that, in spite of all his liveliness, he had never in the whole course of his life disobeyed them. In the village, where he was idolised, they called him ' the little prince ;' he was so gentle and so generous, so kind and yet so dignified in his demeanour. His education was remarkable ; for though he never quitted home, and lived in such extreme seclusion, so richly gifted were those few persons with whom he passed his life, that it would have been difficult to have fixed upon a youth, however favoured by fortune, who enjoyed greater advantages for the cultivation of his mind and manners. From the first dawn of the intellect of the young Armine, Glastonbury had devoted himself to its culture ; and the kind scholar, who had not shrunk from the painful and patient task of impregnating a young mind with the seeds of knowledge, had bedewed its budding promise with all the fertilising influence of his learning and his taste. As Ferdinand advanced in years, he had participated in the accomplishments of his mother ; from her he derived not only a taste for the fine arts, but no unskilful practice. She, too, had cultivated the rich voice with which Nature had endowed him; and it was his mother who taught him not only to sing, but to dance. In more manly accomplishments, Ferdinand could not have found a more skilful instructor than his father, a consummate sportsman, and who, like all his ancestors, was remarkable for his finished horsemanship and the certainty of his aim. Under a roof, too, whose inmates were distinguished for their sincere piety and unaffected virtue the higher duties of existence were not forgotten; and Ferdinand Armine was early and ever taught to be sincere, dutiful, charitable, and just; and to have a deep sense of the great account hereafter to be delivered to his Creator. The very foibles of his parents which he imbibed tended to the maintenance of his magnanimity. His illustrious lineage was early impressed upon him, and inasmuch as little now was left to them but their honour, so it was doubly incumbent upon him to preserve that chief treasure, of which fortune could not deprive them, unsullied.—*Henrietta Temple.*

ART.

Art is order, method, harmonious results, obtained by fine and powerful principles.—*Tancred.*

True Principles of Art.—Aryan principles, not merely the study of nature, but of beautiful nature; the art of design in a country inhabited by a first-rate race, and where the laws, the manners, the customs, are calculated to maintain the health and beauty of a first-rate race. In a greater or less degree, these conditions obtained from the age of Pericles to the age of Hadrian in pure Aryan communities, but Semitism began then to prevail, and ultimately triumphed Semitism has destroyed art; it taught man to despise his own body, and the essence of art is to honour the human frame.—('Mr. Phœbus') *Lothair.*

Greek Art.—In art the Greeks were the children of the Egyptians. The day may yet come when we shall do justice to the high powers of that mysterious and imaginative people. The origin of Doric and Ionic invention must be traced amid the palaces of Carnac and the temples of Luxoor. For myself, I confess I ever gaze upon the marvels of art with a feeling of despair. With horror I remember that, through some mysterious necessity, civilisation seems to have deserted the most favoured regions and the choicest intellects. The Persian whose very being is poetry, the Arab whose subtle mind could penetrate into the very secret shrine of Nature, the Greek whose acute perceptions seemed granted only for the creation of the beautiful, these are now unlettered slaves in barbarous lands. The arts are yielded to the flat-nosed Franks. And they toil, and study, and invent theories to account for their own incompetence. Now it is the climate, now the religion, now the government ; everything but the truth, everything but the mortifying suspicion that their organisation may be different, and that they may be as distinct a race from their models as they undoubtedly are from the Kalmuck and the Negro. *Contarini Fleming.*

In the study of the fine arts, they mutually assist each other.—*Contarini Fleming.*

ASHANTEE.

I am mistaken if these are not feats of arms which will not easily be forgotten in this country. I know it has always been a vulgar error to associate military glory only with armies of magnitude. But that is not a just view to take. Some of the greatest military feats have been performed by small armies. In modern history, nothing perhaps is more illustrative of this truth than the conquest of Mexico by Cortes. So great a result effected by such slight means is not easily matched in the history of man.— *Speech in House of Commons (Ashantee War—Vote of Thanks), March* 30, 1874.

ASSASSINATION.

Assassination has never changed the history of the world.—*Speech in the House of Commons (Assassination of the President of the United States, May* 1865).

ASSOCIATION.

The principle of association is the want of the age.—('Stephen Morley') *Sybil.*

AUSTRIA.

Poor Austria ! Two things made her a nation : she was German and she was Catholic, and now she is neither. ('Monsignore Berwick') *Lothair.*

AUTHORS.

The creators of opinion.—*Speech in the House of Commons (Copyright), April* 25, 1838.

These scribblers are at present the fashion, and are very well to ask to dinner ; but I confess a more intimate connection with them is not at all to my taste.—('Jove') *The Infernal Marriage.*

I think the author who speaks about his own books is almost as bad as a mother who talks about her own children.—*Speech at Banquet to Lord Rector, Glasgow, November* 19, 1870.

The author is, as we must ever remember, of peculiar organisation. He is a being born with a predisposition which with him is irresistible, the bent of which he cannot in any way avoid, whether it directs him to the abstruse researches of erudition or induces him to mount into the fervid and turbulent atmosphere of imagination.—*Speech at Royal Literary Fund Dinner, May* 6, 1868

AUTUMN.

The woods were beginning to assume the first fair livery of autumn, when it is beautiful without decay. The lime and the larch had not yet dropped a golden leaf, and the burnished beeches flamed in the sun. Every now and then an occasional oak or elm rose, still as full of deep green foliage as if it were midsummer ; while the dark verdure of the pines sprang up with effective contrast amid the gleaming and resplendent chestnuts.—*Endymion.*

BADINAGE.

Men destined to the highest places should beware of badinage.—('Bertie Tremaine') *Endymion.*

BALACLAVA.

The fight of Balaclava—that was a feat of chivalry, fiery with consummate courage and bright with flashing valour.— *Speech in the House of Commons (Vote of Thanks to the Allied Armies), December* 15, 1855.

BAR.

The Bar—pooh ! Law and bad jokes till we are forty ; and then, with the most brilliant success, the prospect of gout and a coronet.—*Vivian Grey.*

BARONETCY.

A baronetcy has become a distinction of the middle class : our physician, for example, is a baronet, and I dare say some of our tradesmen—brewers or people of that sort. ('Lady Joan Fitz-Warene') *Sybil.*

BATHS.

Baths should only be used to drown the enemies of the people. I always was against washing, it takes the marrow out of a man.—('The Liberator Hatton') *Sybil.*

BEAUTY.

Beauty can inspire miracles.—*Young Duke.*

His eyes fell upon the outline of a cheek not too full, yet promising of beauty, like hope of paradise.—*Young Duke.*

c

BELLAIR (LADY).

Lady Bellair was of child-like stature, and quite erect, though ninety years of age ; the tasteful simplicity of her costume, her little plain white silk bonnet, her grey silk dress, her apron, her grey mittens, and her Cinderella shoes, all admirably contrasted with the vast and flaunting splendour of her companion, not less than her ladyship's small yet exquisitely proportioned form, her highly finished extremities, and her keen sarcastic grey eye. The expression of her countenance now, however, was somewhat serious.

The Viscountess Dowager Bellair was the last remaining link between the two centuries. Herself born of a noble family, and distinguished both for her beauty and her wit, she had reigned for a quarter of a century the favourite subject of Sir Joshua ; had flirted with Lord Carlyle, and chatted with Dr. Johnson. But the most remarkable quality of her ladyship's destiny was her preservation. Time, that had rolled on nearly a century since her birth, had spared alike her physical and mental powers. She was almost as active in body, and quite as lively in mind, as when seventy years before she skipped in Marylebone Gardens, or puzzled the gentlemen of the Tuesday Night Club at Mrs. Cornely's masquerades. Those wonderful seventy years indeed had passed to Lady Bellair like one of those very masked balls in which she had formerly sparkled ; she had lived in a perpetual crowd of strange and brilliant characters. All that had been famous for beauty, rank, fashion, wit, genius, had been gathered round her throne ; and at this very hour a fresh and admiring generation, distinguished for these qualities, cheerfully acknowledged her supremacy, and paid to her their homage. The heroes and heroines of her youth, her middle life, even of her old age, had vanished ; brilliant orators, profound statesmen, inspired bards, ripe scholars, illustrious warriors ; beauties whose dazzling charms had turned the world mad ;

choice spirits, whose flying words or whose fanciful manners made every saloon smile or wonder, all had disappeared. She had witnessed revolutions in every country in the world; she remembered Brighton a fishing-town, and Manchester a village; she had shared the pomp of nabobs and the profusion of loan-mongers; she had stimulated the early ambition of Charles Fox, and had sympathised with the last aspirations of George Canning; she had been the confidant of the loves alike of Byron and Alfieri; had worn mourning for General Wolfe, and given a festival to the Duke of Wellington; had laughed with George Selwyn, and smiled at Lord Alvanley; had known the first macaroni and the last dandy; remembered the Gunnings, and introduced the Sheridans! But she herself was unchanged; still restless for novelty, still eager for amusement; still anxiously watching the entrance on the stage of some new stream of characters, and indefatigable in attracting the notice of everyone whose talents might contribute to her entertainment, or whose attention might gratify her vanity. And, really, when one recollected Lady Bellair's long career, and witnessed at the same time her diminutive form and her unrivalled vitality, he might almost be tempted to believe, that if not absolutely immortal, it was at least her strange destiny not so much vulgarly to die, as to grow like the heroine of the fairy tale, each year smaller and smaller,

'Fine, by degrees, and beautifully less,

until her ladyship might at length subside into airy nothingness, and so rather vanish than expire.

It was the fashion to say that her ladyship had no heart; in most instances an unmeaning phrase; in her case certainly an unjust one. Ninety years of experience had assuredly not been thrown away on a mind of remarkable acuteness; but Lady Bellair's feelings were still quick and warm, and could be even profound. Her fancy was so lively, that her attention was soon engaged; her taste so

refined, that her affection was not so easily obtained.
Hence she acquired a character for caprice, because she
repented at leisure those first impressions which with her
were irresistible ; for, in truth, Lady Bellair, though she
had nearly completed her century, and had passed her
whole life in the most artificial circles, was the very
creature of impulse. Her first homage she always declared
was paid to talent, her second to beauty, her third to blood.
The favoured individual who might combine these three
splendid qualifications, was, with Lady Bellair, a nymph or
a demi-god. As for mere wealth, she really despised it,
though she liked her favourites to be rich.

Her knowledge of human nature, which was considerable, her acquaintance with human weaknesses, which was
unrivalled, were not thrown away upon Lady Bellair. Her
ladyship's perception of character was fine and quick, and
nothing delighted her so much as making a person a tool.
Capable, where her heart was touched, of the finest sympathy and the most generous actions, where her feelings
were not engaged she experienced no compunction in turning her companions to account, or, indeed, sometimes in
honouring them with her intimacy for that purpose. But
if you had the skill to detect her plots, and the courage to
make her aware of your consciousness of them, you never
displeased her, and often gained her friendship. For Lady
Bellair had a fine taste for humour, and when she chose to
be candid, an indulgence which was not rare with her, she
could dissect her own character and conduct with equal
spirit and impartiality. In her own instance it cannot be
denied that she comprised the three great qualifications
she so much prized : for she was very witty ; had blood in
her veins, to use her own expression ; and was the prettiest
woman in the world, for her years. For the rest, though
no person was more highly bred, she could be very impertinent ; but if you treated her with servility, she absolutely
loathed you.—*Henrietta Temple.*

BENTINCK (LORD GEORGE).

His eager and energetic disposition ; his quick perception, clear judgment, and prompt decision ; the tenacity with
which he clung to his opinions ; his frankness and love of
truth ; his daring and speculative spirit ; his lofty bearing,
blended as it was with a simplicity of manner very remarkable ; the ardour of his friendships, even the fierceness of
his hates and prejudices ; all combined to form one of those
strong characters who, whatever may be their pursuit, must
always direct and lead. Nature had clothed his vehement
spirit with a material form which was in perfect harmony
with its noble and commanding character. He was tall
and remarkable for his presence ; his countenance almost a
model of manly beauty ; the face oval, the complexion clear
and mantling ; the forehead lofty and white ; the nose
aquiline and delicately moulded ; the upper lip short. But
it was in the dark-brown eye, that flashed with piercing
scrutiny, that all the character of the man came forth ; a
brilliant glance, not soft, but ardent, acute, imperious, incapable of deception or of being deceived.—*Life of Lord
George Bentinck.*

BISHOP.

When the duchess found that the interview with the
bishop had been fruitless of the anticipated results, she was
staggered, disheartened ; but she was a woman of too high
a spirit to succumb under a first defeat. She was of opinion
that his lordship had misunderstood the case, or had mis-
managed it ; her confidence in him, too, was not so illimitable since he had permitted the Puseyites to have candles
on their altars, although he had forbidden their being
lighted, as when he had declared, twenty years before, that
the finger of God was about to protestantise Ireland. His
lordship had said and had done many things since that
time which had occasioned the duchess many misgivings,

although she had chosen that they should not occur to her recollection until he failed in convincing her son that religious truth was to be found in the parish of St. James, and political justice in the happy haunts of Montacute Forest.

The bishop had voted for the Church Temporalities Bill in 1833, which at one swoop had suppressed ten Irish episcopates. This was a queer suffrage for the apostle of the second Reformation. True it is that Whiggism was then in the ascendant, and two years afterwards, when Whiggism had received a heavy blow and great discouragement ; when we had been blessed in the interval with a decided though feeble Conservative administration, and were blessed at the moment with a strong though undecided Conservative opposition ; his lordship, with characteristic activity, had galloped across country into the right line again, denounced the Appropriation Clause in a spirit worthy of his earlier days, and, quite forgetting the ten Irish Bishoprics, that only four and twenty months before he had doomed to destruction, was all for proselytising Ireland again by the efficacious means of Irish Protestant bishops.—*Tancred.*

The Bishop was high church, and would not himself have made a bad cardinal, being polished and plausible, well-lettered, yet quite a man of the world. He was fond of society, and justified his taste in this respect by the flattering belief that by his presence he was extending the power of the Church ; certainly favouring an ambition which could not be described as being moderate. The Bishop had no abstract prejudice against gentlemen who wore red hats, and under ordinary circumstances would have welcomed his brother churchman with unaffected cordiality, not to say sympathy ; but in the present instance, however gracious his mien and honeyed his expressions, he only looked upon the Cardinal as a dangerous rival, intent upon clutching from his fold the most precious of his flock, and he had long looked to this occasion as the one which might decide the spiritual welfare and career of Lothair. The odds were not to be despised. There were two Monsignores in the room besides the Cardinal, but the Bishop was a man of contrivance and resolution, not easily disheartened or defeated. Nor was he without allies. He did not count much on the University don, who was to arrive on the morrow in the shape of the head of an Oxford house, though he was a don of magnitude. This eminent personage had already let Lothair slip from his influence. But the Bishop had a subtle counsellor in his chaplain, who wore as good a cassock as any Monsignore, and he brought with him also a trusty archdeacon in a purple coat, whose countenance was quite entitled to a place in the Acta Sanctorum.

It was amusing to observe the elaborate courtesy and more than Christian kindness which the rival prelates and their official followers extended to each other. But under all this unction on both sides were unceasing observation, and a vigilance that never flagged ; and on both sides there was an uneasy but irresistible conviction that they were on the eve of one of the decisive battles of the social world.—*Lothair.*

He combined a great talent for action with very limited powers of thought. Bustling, energetic, versatile, gifted with an indomitable perseverance, and stimulated by an ambition that knew no repose, with a capacity for mastering details and an inordinate passion for affairs, he could permit nothing to be done without his interference, and consequently was perpetually involved in transactions which were either failures or blunders. He was one of those leaders who are not guides. Having little real knowledge, and not endowed with those high qualities of intellect which permit their possessor to generalise the details afforded by study and experience, and so deduce rules of conduct, his lordship, when he received those frequent appeals which were the necessary consequence of his officious life, became obscure, confused, contradictory, inconsistent, illogical. The oracle was always dark. Placed in a high post in an age of political analysis, the bustling intermeddler was unable to supply society with a single solution. Enunciating second-hand, with characteristic precipitation, some big principle in vogue, as if he were a discoverer, he invariably shrank from its subsequent application, the moment that he found it might be unpopular and inconvenient. All his quandaries terminated in the same catastrophe—a compromise. Abstract principles with him ever ended in concrete expediency. The aggregate of circumstances outweighed the isolated cause. The primordial tenet, which had been advocated with uncompromising arrogance, gently subsided into some second-rate measure recommended with all the artifice of an impenetrable ambiguity.

Beginning with the second Reformation, which was a little rash but dashing, the Bishop, always ready, had in the course of his episcopal career placed himself at the head of every movement in the Church which others had originated, and had as regularly withdrawn at the right moment, when the heat was over, or had become, on the contrary, excessive. Furiously evangelical, soberly high and dry, and fervently Puseyite, each phasis of his faith concludes with what the Spaniards term a 'transaction.' The saints are to have their new churches, but they are also to have their rubrics and their canons ; the universities may supply successors to the apostles, but they are also presented with a church commission ; even the Puseyites may have candles on their altars, but they must not be lighted.

It will be seen, therefore, that his lordship was one of those characters not ill-adapted to an eminent station in an age like the present, and in a country like our own ; an age of movement, but of confused ideas ; a country of progress, but too rich to risk much change. Under these circumstances, the spirit of a period and a people seek a safety-valve in bustle.—*Endymion.*

BLUE-STOCKING.

Lady Joan Fitz-Warene only required a listener ; she did not make inquiries like Lady Maud, or impart her own impressions by suggesting them as your own. Lady Joan gave Egremont an account of the Aztec cities, of which she had been reading that morning, and of the several historical theories which their discovery had suggested ; then she imparted her own, which differed from all, but which seemed clearly the right one. Mexico led to Egypt. Lady Joan was as familiar with the Pharaohs as with the Caciques of the New World. The phonetic system was despatched by the way. Then came Champollion ; then Paris ; then all its celebrities, literary and especially scientific ; then came the letter from Arago received that morning ; and the letter from Dr. Buckland expected to-morrow. She was delighted that one had written ; wondered why the other had not. Finally, before the ladies had retired, she had invited Egremont to join Lady Marney in a visit to her observatory, where they were to behold a comet which she had been the first to detect.—*Sybil.*

BLUSH.

Blushing like a Worcestershire orchard before harvest.— *Endymion.*

BOLINGBROKE.

No one was better qualified to be the minister of a free and powerful nation than Henry St. John, and destiny at first appeared to combine with nature in the elevation of his fortunes. Opposed to the Whigs from principle, for an oligarchy is hostile to genius, and recoiling from the Tory tenets, which his unprejudiced and vigorous mind taught him at the same time to dread and contemn, Lord Bolingbroke at the outset of his career incurred the commonplace imputation of insincerity and inconsistency because in an age of unsettled parties with principles contradictory of their conduct, he maintained that vigilant and meditative independence which is the privilege of an original and determined spirit. In the earlier years of his career he meditated over the formation of a new party, that dream of youthful ambition in a perplexed and discordant age, but destined in English politics to be never more substantial than a vision. More experienced in political life, he became aware that he had only to choose between the Whigs and the Tories, and his sagacious intellect, not satisfied with the superficial character of these celebrated divisions, penetrated their interior and essential qualities, and discovered, in spite of all the affectation of popular sympathy on one side, and of admiration of arbitrary power on the other, that this choice was in fact a choice between oligarchy and democracy. From the moment that Lord Bolingbroke, in becoming a Tory, embraced the national cause, he devoted himself absolutely to his party ; all the energies of his Protean mind were lavished in their service ; and although the equitable prudence of the Whig minister restrained him from advocating the cause of the nation in the Senate, it was his inspiring pen that made Walpole tremble in the recesses of the Treasury, and in a series of writings unequalled in English literature for their spirited patriotism, their just and profound views, and the golden eloquence in which they were expressed, eradicated from Toryism all those absurd and odious doctrines which Toryism had adventitiously adopted, clearly developed its essential and permanent character, discarded *jure divino*, demolished passive obedience, threw to the winds the doctrine of non-resistance, placed the abolition of James and the accession of George on their right bases, and in the complete re-organisation of the public mind laid the foundation for the future accession of the Tory party to power, and to that popular and triumphant career which must ever await the policy of an administration inspired by the spirit of our free and ancient institutions.—*Vindication of the Constitution*, 1835.

BOOKS.

Bookworms do not make Chancellors of State.—('Lady Montfort') *Endymion.*

Without books the discoveries of science, the inventions of art, the grand pedigrees and noble precedents of the intellectual development of man, would have no record ; none of those maxims and household words which illustrate, animate, adorn, and cheer life, would exist. Those imaginary characters as they are called, but which are really much more vital and substantial than half our acquaintance, would no longer exist. There would be no Hamlets, no Don Quixotes, no Falstaffs. And therefore I can easily conceive that mankind has instinctively felt how much even those who are unlettered owe to the cultivated record of the impulses of, invention and the discoveries of truth.—*Speech at Royal Literary Fund Dinner, May* 6, 1868.

Consols at a hundred were the origin of all book societies.—('Cleveland') *Vivian Grey.*

Those that cannot themselves observe, can at least acquire the observation of others.—('De Winter') *Contarini Fleming.*

It is difficult to decide which is the most valuable companion to a country eremite at his nightly studies, the volume that keeps him awake, or the one that sets him slumbering.—*Lothair.*

Books are fatal : they are the curse of the human race. Nine-tenths of existing books are nonsense, and the clever books are the refutation of that nonsense. The greatest misfortune that ever befel man was the invention of printing.—('Mr. Phœbus') *Lothair.*

A Remarkable Book, '*The Revelations of Chaos.*'—It explains everything, and is written in a very agreeable style. Everything is explained by geology and astronomy, and in that way. It shows you exactly how a star is formed. Nothing can be so pretty : a cluster of vapour, the cream of the milky way, a sort of celestial cheese. But what is most interesting is the way in which man has been developed. You know, all is development. The principle is perpetually going on. First, there was nothing, then there was something; then, I forget the next, I think there were shells, then fishes; then we came, let me see, did we come next? Never mind that; we came at last. And the next change there will be something very superior to us, something with wings. Ah! that's it: we were fishes, and I believe we shall be crows. But you must read it. —(' Lady Constance') *Tancred.*

Book-making, a composition which requires no ordinary qualities of character and intelligence—method, judgment, self-restraint, not too much imagination, perception of character, and powers of calculation.—*Endymion.*

Bow.

Waldershare's bow was a study. Its grace and ceremony must have been organic, for there was no traditionary type in existence from which he could have derived or inherited it.—*Endymion.*

Breakfast.

Breakfast at Brentham was served on half a dozen or more round tables, which vied with each other in grace and merriment, brilliant as a cluster of Greek or Italian Republics, instead of a great metropolitan table, like a central government absorbing all the genius and resources of society.—*Lothair.*

Brecon (Duke of).

The Duke of Brecon was rather below the middle size, but he had a singularly athletic frame not devoid of symmetry. His head was well placed on his broad shoulders, and his mien was commanding. He was narrow-minded and prejudiced, but acute, and endowed with an unbending will. He was an eminent sportsman, and brave even to brutality. His boast was that he had succeeded in everything he had attempted, and he would not admit the possibility of future failure. Though still a very young man he had won the Derby, training his own horse ; and he successfully managed a fine stud in defiance of the ring, whom it was one of the secret objects of his life to extirpate. Though his manner to men was peremptory, cold, and hard, he might be described as popular, for there existed a superstitious belief in his judgment, and it was known that in some instances when he had been consulted he had given more than advice. It could not be said that he was beloved, but he was feared and highly considered. Parasites were necessary to him, though he despised them.

The Duke of Brecon was an avowed admirer of Lady Corisande, and was intimate with her family. The Duchess liked him much, and was often seen at ball or assembly on his arm. He had such excellent principles, she said ; was so straightforward, so true and firm. It was whispered that even Lady Corisande had remarked that the Duke of Brecon was the only young man of the time who had ' character.' The truth is the Duke, though absolute and hard to men, could be soft and deferential to women, and such an exception to a general disposition has a charm. It was said also that he had, when requisite, a bewitching smile.—*Lothair.*

BRIBERY.

The more I see of these things—and, like many others in this House, I have witnessed the results of many general elections—the more I am convinced that bribery and corruption, although they may be very convenient for gratifying the ambition or the vanity of individuals, have very little effect on the fortunes or the power of parties ; and it is a great mistake to suppose that bribery and corruption are means by which power can either be obtained or retained. In all periods which have been characterised by very great corruption, it will always be found to have been caused by some new class forcing itself into a position in society, and that it was not due to the effects of rival parties. Of this I am convinced myself, that bribery and corruption affect very little the course of public affairs.—*Speech in House of Commons (Representation of People Bill), May* 30, 1867.

Whenever a very powerful and wealthy class arises in this country, nothing can prevent it asserting a claim to the possession of political power ; and whenever a new class of that kind arises, you always find that bribery is rife when an election is held. It was so in the time of Sir Robert Walpole, when there were the Turkey merchants, men who had made great fortunes ; they attacked all the boroughs and turned the country gentlemen out. Then followed the Nabobs, and after them came the West Indian planters, and, in the time of the war, the Government loan merchants. But I believe that at no period has this country ever been more free in its parliamentary affairs from bribery, than it was in the years that immediately preceded the Reform Bill of Lord Grey. It happened to be a time of tranquillity, when no great changes were occurring, and when no new class was treading upon the heels of those in power, and when the elections of members to this House were purer than usual.—*Speech in House of Commons (Elections Bill), June* 29, 1871.

BROUGHAM (LORD).

It may truly be said of Lord Brougham, that none more completely represented his age, and no one more contributed to the progress of the times in which he lived. He had two qualities, almost in excess, which are rarely combined in the same person—one was energy, and the other versatility. The influence which creative power gave him, combined with strength of character, alone sustained him in a career which for its duration, as well as for its dazzling feats, has rarely been equalled in Europe.—*Speech in House of Commons (the late Lord Brougham), July* 27, 1868.

Brougham is a man who would say anything; and of one thing you may be quite certain, that there is no subject which Lord Brougham knows thoroughly.—(' Mr. Ferrars ') *Endymion,*

BUCKINGHAMSHIRE.

Since our Constitution has been settled, since the accession of the House of Hanover, there have been, I think, not more than thirty Prime Ministers, and four of these have been supplied by the county of Buckingham. I believe there is something in the air favourable to political knowledge and vigour.—*Speech at Buckingham (General Election), February* 10, 1874.

BYRON.

If one thing were more characteristic of Byron's mind than another, it was his strong, shrewd common sense ; his pure, unalloyed sagacity.

The loss of Byron can never be retrieved. He was indeed a real man ; and when I say this, I award him the most splendid character which human nature need aspire to. At least, I, for my part, have no ambition to be considered either a divinity or an angel ; and truly, when I look round upon the creatures alike effeminate in mind and body of which the world is, in general, composed, I fear that even my ambition is too exalted. Byron's mind was, like his own ocean, sublime in its yesty madness, beautiful in its glittering summer brightness, mighty in the lone magnificence of its waste of waters, gazed upon from the magic of its own nature, yet capable of representing, but as in a glass darkly, the natures of all others.'—(' Cleveland ') *Vivian Grey.*

CAB.

A hansom cab—'tis the gondola of London.—*Lothair.*

CABAL.[1]

The motion was brought forward in the House of Commons by a gentleman of unimpeachable reputation (Mr. Cardwell). The Cabal—which has rather a tainted character—chose its instrument with Pharisaical accuracy, and I assure you that when Mr. Cardwell rose to impeach me, I was terrified at my own shortcomings as I listened to a Nisi Prius narrative, ending with a resolution which I think must have been drawn up by a conveyancer. In the other House of Parliament a still greater reputation (Lord Shaftesbury) condescended to appear on the human stage. Gamaliel himself, with the broad phylacteries of faction on his forehead, called God to witness in pious terms of majestic adoration, that he was not like other men, and was never influenced by party motives. Well, gentlemen, what happened under these circumstances? Something I am sure quite unprecedented in the Parliamentary history of England ; and when I hear of faction, when I hear of the acts and manœuvres of parties, when I hear sometimes that party spirit will be the ruin of this country, let us take a calm view of what has occurred during the past fortnight, and I think we shall come to the conclusion that in a country free and enlightened as England, there are limits to party feeling which the most dexterous managers of the passions of mankind cannot overpass, and that in the great bulk of Parliament, as I am sure, whatever may be their opinions, in the great bulk of the people of this country, there is a genuine spirit of patriotism which will always right itself.—*Speech at a Dinner at Slough, May 26, 1858.*

CABINET.

He (Lord Marney) might have found his way into the Cabinet, and like the rest have assisted in registering the decrees of one too powerful individual.—*Tancred.*

[1] Of Opposition on action of Government in condemning Lord Canning's proclamation after rebellion in Oude.

CADURCIS (CAPTAIN)

There was about Captain Cadurcis a natural cheerfulness which animated everyone in his society; a gay simplicity, difficult to define, but very charming, and which, without effort, often produced deeper impressions than more brilliant and subtle qualities. Left alone in the world, and without a single advantage save those that nature had conferred upon him, it had often been remarked, that in whatever circle he moved George Cadurcis always became the favourite and everywhere made friends. His sweet and engaging temper had perhaps as much contributed to his professional success as his distinguished gallantry and skill. Other officers, no doubt, were as brave and able as Captain Cadurcis; but his commanders always signalled him out for favourable notice; and, strange to say, his success, instead of exciting envy and ill-will, pleased even his less fortunate competitors. However hard another might feel his own lot, it was soothed by the reflection that George Cadurcis was at least more fortunate. His popularity, however, was not confined to his profession. His cousin's noble guardian, whom George had never seen until he ventured to call upon his lordship on his return to England, now looked upon him almost as a son, and omitted no opportunity of advancing his interests in the world. Of all the members of the House of Commons he was perhaps the only one that everybody praised, and his success in the world of fashion had been as remarkable as in his profession. These great revolutions in his life and future prospects had, however, not produced the slightest change in his mind and manners; and this was perhaps the secret spell of his prosperity. Though we are most of us the creatures of affectation, simplicity has a great charm, especially when attended, as in the present instance, with many agreeable and some noble qualities.

D

In spite of the rough fortunes of his youth, the breeding of Captain Cadurcis was high ; the recollection of the race to which he belonged had never been forgotten by him. He was proud of his family. He had one of those light hearts, too, which enable their possessors to acquire accomplishments with facility : he had a sweet voice, a quick ear, a rapid eye. He acquired a language as some men learn an air. Then his temper was imperturbable, and although the most obliging and kindest-hearted creature that ever lived, there was a native dignity about him which prevented his goodnature from being abused. No sense of interest either could ever induce him to act contrary to the dictates of his judgment and his heart.—*Venetia.*

CALAMITIES.

What appear to be calamities are often the sources of fortune.—('Mr. Ferrars') *Endymion.*

CALCULATION.

Everything in this world is calculation.—('Lord Marney') *Sybil.*

CANNING.

I never saw Mr. Canning but once, but I can recollect it but as yesterday, when I listened to almost the last accents —I may say the dying words—of that great man. I can recall the lightning flash of that eye, and the tumult of that ethereal brow; still lingers in my ear the melody of that voice. But when shall we see another Canning—a man who ruled this House as a man rules a high-bred steed, as Alexander ruled Bucephalus, of whom it was said that the horse and the rider were equally proud ?—*Speech in House of Commons* (*Protection of Life* [*Ireland*] *Bill*), *June* 15, 1846.

We all deplore his untimely end ; and we all sympathise with him in his fierce struggle with supreme prejudice and sublime mediocrity—with inveterate foes, and with candid friends.—*Speech in House of Commons* (*Opening Letters at Post Office*), *February* 28, 1845.

CAPITAL.

In these days a great capitalist has deeper roots than a sovereign prince, unless he is very legitimate.—*Tancred.*

CARDS.

To a mind like that of Tiresias a pack of cards was full of human nature. A rubber was a microcosm.—*The Infernal Marriage.*

CASUALTIES.

Great things spring from casualties.—(' Gerard') *Sybil.*

CATESBY (MONSIGNORE).

Catesby was a youthful member of an ancient English house, which for many generations had without a murmur, rather in a spirit of triumph, made every worldly sacrifice for the Church and Court of Rome. For that cause they had forfeited their lives, broad estates, and all the honours of a lofty station in their own land. Reginald Catesby, with considerable abilities, trained with consummate skill, inherited their determined will, and the traditionary beauty of their form and countenance. His manners were winning, and he was as well informed in the ways of the world as he was in the works of the great casuists.

Lothair could not have a better adviser on the subject of the influence of architecture on religion than Monsignore Catesby. Monsignore Catesby had been a pupil of Pugin ; his knowledge of ecclesiastical architecture was only equalled by his exquisite taste. To hear him expound the mysteries of symbolical art, and expatiate on the hidden revelations of its beauteous forms, reached even to ecstasy. Lothair hung upon his accents like a neophyte. Conferences with Father Coleman on those points of faith on which they did not differ, followed up by desultory remarks on those points of faith on which they ought not to differ ; critical discussions, with Monsignore Catesby on cathedrals, their forms, their purposes, and the instances in several countries in which those forms were most perfect and those purposes best secured, occupied a good deal of time ; and yet these engaging pursuits were secondary in real emotion to his frequent conversations with Miss Arundel, in whose society every day he took a strange and deeper interest.—*Lothair.*

CAUSE.

It is always when the game is played that we discover the cause of the result.—*Tancred.*

CELIBACY.

Melancholy, which, after a day of action, is the doom of energetic celibacy.—*Sybil.*

CHANCE.

If you mean by chance an absence of accountable cause, I do not believe such a quality as chance exists. Every incident that happens must be a link in a chain.—('Herbert') *Venetia.*

CHANGE.

We all know, especially in free and popular communities, that the few are sensible of the necessity of change before the multitude are convinced of that necessity, and that it is extremely difficult to bring the great body of a community to agree to a change of the necessity of which they are not convinced.—*Speech in House of Commons (Relations with France), February* 18, 1853.

Change, in the abstract, is what is required by a people who are at the same time inquiring and wealthy.—*Tancred.*

Change is inevitable in a progressive country. Change is constant.—*Speech at Conservative Banquet, Edinburgh, October* 29, 1867.

CHAPEL.

At Vauxe.—Although the chapel at Vauxe was, of course, a private chapel, it was open to the surrounding public, who eagerly availed themselves of a permission alike politic and gracious.

Nor was that remarkable. Manifold art had combined to create this exquisite temple, and to guide all its ministrations. But to-night it was not the radiant altar and the splendour of stately priests, the processions and the incense, the divine choir and the celestial harmonies resounding and lingering in arched roofs, that attracted many a neighbour. The altar was desolate, the choir was dumb ; and while the services proceeded in hushed tones of subdued sorrow, and sometimes even of suppressed anguish, gradually, with each psalm and canticle, a light of the altar was extinguished, till at length the Miserere was muttered, and all became darkness. A sound as of a distant and rising wind was heard, and a crash, as it were the fall of trees in a storm. The earth is covered with darkness, and the vail of the temple is rent. But just at this moment of extreme woe, when all human voices are silent, and when it is forbidden even to breathe 'Amen ;' when everything is symbolical of the confusion and despair of the Church at the loss of her expiring Lord, a priest brings forth a concealed light of silvery flame from a corner of the altar. This is the light of the world, and announces the resurrection, and then all rise up and depart in silence.—*Lothair.*

At St. Genevieve.—But what interested them more than the gallery, or the rich saloons, or even the baronial hall, was the chapel, in which art had exhausted all its invention, and wealth offered all its resources. The walls and vaulted roofs entirely painted in encaustic by the first artists of Germany, and representing the principal events of the second Testament, the splendour of the mosaic pavement, the richness of the painted windows, the sumptuousness of the altar, crowned by a masterpiece of Carlo Dolce and surrounded by a silver rail, the tone of rich and solemn light that pervaded all, and blended all the various sources of beauty into one absorbing and harmonious whole : all combined to produce an effect which stilled them into a silence that lasted for some minutes, until the ladies breathed their feelings in an almost inarticulate murmur of reverence and admiration ; while a tear stole to the eye of the enthusiastic Henry Sydney.—*Coningsby.*

CHARACTER.

In all lives there is a crisis in the formation of character. 'It comes from many causes, and from some which on the surface are apparently even trivial. But the result is the same ; a sudden revelation to ourselves of our secret purpose, and a recognition of our perhaps long-shadowed, but now masterful convictions.—*Endymion.*

National Character.—A character is an assemblage of qualities ; the character of England should be an assemblage of great qualities.—(' Sidonia ') *Coningsby.*

CHARITY.

I speak in the capital of an ancient nation, remarkable above all the nations of the world for its rich endowments. Charity in its most gracious, most learned, and most human form has established institutions in this country to soften the asperities of existence.—*Speech in House of Commons (Irish Church Bill), March* 18, 1869.

CHRISTIANITY.

Christians may continue to persecute Jews, and Jews may persist in disbelieving Christianity, but who can deny that Jesus of Nazareth, the incarnate Son of the Most High God, is the eternal glory of the Jewish race ?—*Lie of Lord George Bentinck.*

Christianity is completed Judaism, or it is nothing.—
('Egremont') *Sybil.*

CHURCH.

The Church has no fear of just reasoners.—('Brother
Anthony') *Contarini Fleming.*

The Church is cosmopolitan—the only practical means
by which you can attain to identity of motive and action.—
('Nigel Penruddock') *Endymion.*

The doctrine of evolution affords no instance so striking
as those of sacerdotal development.—*Lothair.*

What the soul is to the man, the Church is to the world.
('Cardinal Grandison') *Lothair.*

The Church is a sacred corporation for the promulgation
and maintenance in Europe of certain Asian principles
which, although local in their birth, are of divine origin and
eternal application.—*Preface to fifth edition of ' Coningsby.'*

The Church comes forward, and without equivocation
offers to establish direct relations between God and man.
Philosophy denies its title, and disputes its power. Why?
Because they are founded on the supernatural. What is
the supernatural? Can there be anything more miraculous
than the existence of man and the world? Anything more
literally supernatural than the origin of things? The
Church explains what no one else pretends to explain, and
which, everyone agrees, it is of first moment should be made
clear.—*Lothair.*

I look upon the existence of parties in the Church as a
necessary and beneficial consequence. They have always
existed, even from apostolic times. They are a natural
development of the religious sentiment in man ; and they
represent fairly the different conclusions at which, upon
subjects that are most precious to him, the mind of man
arrives. Ceremony, enthusiasm, and free speculation are
the characteristics of the three great parties in the Church,
some of which have now modern names, and which the

world is too apt to imagine in their character are original. The truth is, that they have always existed in different forms or under different titles. Whether they are called High Church, or Low Church, or Broad Church, they bear witness, in their legitimate bounds, to the activity of the religious mind of the nation, and in the course of our history this country is deeply indebted to the exertions and the energy of all these parties.—*Speech in House of Commons* (*Public Worship Regulation Bill*), *July* 15, 1874.

There is only one Church and only one religion ; all other forms and phrases are mere phantasms, without root, or substance, or coherency. Look at that unhappy Germany, once so proud of its Reformation. What they call the leading journal tells us to-day, that it is a question there whether four-fifths or three-fourths of the population believe in Christianity. Some portion of it has already gone back, I understand, to Number Nip. Look at this unfortunate land, divided, sub-divided, parcelled out in infinite schism, with new oracles every day, and each more distinguished for the narrowness of his intellect or the loudness of his lungs ; once the land of saints and scholars, and people in pious pilgrimages, and finding always solace and support in the divine offices of an ever-present Church, which were a true though a faint type of the beautiful future that awaited man. Why, only three centuries of this rebellion against the Most High have produced throughout the world, on the subject the most important that man should possess a clear, firm faith, an anarchy of opinion throwing out every monstrous and fantastic form, from a caricature of the Greek philosophy to a revival of Fetishism.—(' Cardinal Grandison ') *Lothair*.

Church of England.—The strength of the Church of England is this : that not being a stipendiary of the State, it was not afraid of being just, and, while professing to be entirely in theory, and actually being very greatly in practice, the Church of the nation, it could still favour the complete development of the principle of religious liberty.—*Speech in House of Commons* (*Prison Ministers Bill*), *May* 7, 1863.

Parliament made the Church of England, and Parliament will unmake the Church of England.—('Cardinal Grandison') *Lothair.*

The Church of England, mainly from its deficiency of oriental knowledge, and from a misconception of the priestly character, which has been the consequence of that want, has fallen of late years into straits.—*Tancred.*

The Church of England is not a mere depositary of doctrine. The Church of England is a part of England—it is a part of our strength and a part of our liberties, a part of our national character. It is a chief security for the local Government, which a Radical Reformer has thought fit to-day to designate as 'an archæological curiosity.' It is a principal barrier against that centralising supremacy, which has been in other countries so fatal to liberty.—*Speech in House of Commons* (*Church Rates Abolition Bill*), *February* 27, 1861.

It is because there is an Established Church that we have achieved religious liberty, and enjoy religious toleration ; and without the union of the Church with the State I do not see what security there would be either for religious liberty or toleration. No error could be greater than to suppose that the advantage of the Church of England is limited to those who are in communion with it. Take the case of the Roman Catholic priest. He will refuse the offices of the Church to anyone not in communion with it. The same with Dissenters. It is just possible—it has happened and might happen frequently—that a Roman Catholic may be excommunicated by his church, or a sectarian may be denounced and expelled by his congregation ; but if that happen in this country, the individual in question is not a forlorn being. There is the Church, of which the Sovereign is the head, which does not acknowledge the principle of Dissent, and which dares not refuse to **that** individual those religious rites which are his privilege and consolation. I therefore hold that the connection between Church and State is really a guarantee for religious liberty and toleration ; that it maintains, as it were, the standard of religious liberty and toleration just as much as we by other means sustain the standard of value. If you wish to break up a state, and destroy and disturb a country, you can never adopt a more effectual method than by destroying at the same time the standards of value and of toleration.—*Irish Church Bill, March* 18, 1869.

Broad Church.—I do perfect justice to the great talent, the great energy, and the considerable information, which the new party command; but I believe that the new party in the Church will fail for two reasons. Having examined all their writings, I believe, without an exception, whether they consist of fascinating eloquence, diversified learning, and picturesque sensibility—I speak seriously what I feel—all these exercised too by one honoured in the great university and whom to know is to admire and regard—or whether I find them in the cruder conclusions of prelates, who appear to me to have commenced their theological studies after they grasped the crozier, and who introduce to society their obsolete discoveries with startling wonder and the frank ingenuousness of their own savages ; or whether I read the lucubrations of nebulous professors, who appear in their style to have revived chaos, and who, if they would only succeed in obtaining a perpetual study of their writings, would go far to realise that eternity of punishment which they object to ; or lastly, whether it be the provincial arrogance and precipitate self-complacency which flash and glare in an essay and review—I find the common characteristic of all their writings, that their learning is always second-hand.—*Speech at Oxford (Meeting of Society for increasing Endowments of Small Livings in the Diocess of Oxford), November* 25, 1864.

Man is a being born to believe, and if no church comes forward with all the title-deeds of truth, and sustained by

the tradition of sacred ages, and the conviction of countless
generations to guide him, he will find altars and idols in his
own heart, and his own imagination. But observe what
must be the relations of a powerful church without distinctive creeds with a being of that nature. Where there is a
great demand, there will be a proportionate supply, and
commencing, as the new school may, by rejecting the principle of inspiration, they may end by every priest being a
prophet ; and beginning as they do by repudiating the
practice of miracles, before long we shall see a flitting scene
of spiritual phantasmagoria. There are no tenets however
extravagant, and no practice however objectionable, we may
not in time develop under such a state of affairs—opinions
the most absurd and ceremonies the most revolting—

> Qualia demens
> Ægyptus portenta colit,—

perhaps to be relieved by the incantations of Canidia and
the Corybantian howl.—*Speech at Oxford (Meeting of Society
for increasing Endowments of Small Livings in the Diocess of
Oxford), November 25, 1864.*

We live in decent times, frigid, latitudinarian, alarmed,
decorous. A priest is scarcely deemed in our days a fit
successor to the authors of the Gospels if he be not the
editor of a Greek play ; and he who follows St. Paul must
now at least have been private tutor of some young nobleman who has taken a good degree ! And then you are all
astonished that the Church is not universal ! Why ! nothing but the indestructibleness of its principles, however
feebly pursued, could have maintained even the disorganised
body that still survives.—(' Mr. Millbank ') *Coningsby.*

Church and State.—As good things as strawberries and
cream, and like them always best together.—(' Dr. Masham ')
Venetia.

The character of a Church is universality. Once the
church in this country was universal in principle and prac-

tice ; when wedded to the State, it continued at least universal in principle, if not in practice. What is it now ? All ties between the State and the Church are abolished, except those which tend to its danger and degradation.

What can be more anomalous than the present connection between State and Church ? Every condition on which it was originally consented to has been cancelled. That original alliance was, in my view, an equal calamity for the nation and the Church ; but, at least, it was an intelligible compact. Parliament, then consisting only of members of the Established Church, was, on ecclesiastical matters, a lay synod, and might, in some points of view, be esteemed a necessary portion of Church government. But you have effaced this exclusive character of Parliament; you have determined that a communion with the Established Church shall no longer be part of the qualification for sitting in the House of Commons. There is no reason, so far as the Constitution avails, why every member of the House of Commons should not be a Dissenter. But the whole power of the country is concentrated in the House of Commons. The House of Lords, even the monarch himself, has openly announced and confessed, within these ten years, that the will of the House of Commons is supreme. A single vote of the House of Commons, in 1832, made the Duke of Wellington declare, in the House of Lords, that he was obliged to abandon his sovereign in 'the most difficult and distressing circumstances.' The House of Commons is absolute. It is the State. 'L'Etat c'est moi.' The House of Commons virtually appoints the bishops. A sectarian assembly appoints the bishops of the Established Church. They may appoint twenty Hoadlys. James II. was expelled the throne because he appointed a Roman Catholic to an Anglican see. A Parliament might do this to-morrow with impunity. And this is the constitution in Church and State which Conservative dinners toast ! The only consequences of the present union of Church and State are, that, on the side of the State, there is perpetual interference in ecclesiastical government, and on the side of the Church a sedulous avoidance of all those principles on which alone Church government can be established, and by the influence of which alone can the Church of England again become universal.—('Mr. Millbank') *Coningsby.*

What I understand by the union of Church and State is an arrangement which renders the State religious by investing authority with the highest sanctions that can influence the sentiments and convictions, and consequently the conduct of the subject ; whilst, on the other hand, that union renders the Church—using that epithet in its noblest and purest sense—political ; that is to say, it blends civil authority with ecclesiastical influence : it defines and defends the rights of the laity, and prevents the Church from subsiding into a sacerdotal corporation. If you divest the State of this connection, it appears to me that you necessarily reduce both the quantity and the quality of its duties. The State will still be the protector of our persons and our property, and no doubt these are most important duties for the State to perform. But these are duties, which in a community rather excite a spirit of criticism than a sentiment of enthusiasm and veneration. All or most of the higher functions of government—take education for example, the formation of the character of the people, and consequently the guidance of their future conduct—depart from the State and become the appanage of religious societies, of the religious organisation of the country—you may call them the various churches if you please—when they are established on what is called independent principles. Now the question which necessarily arises in this altered state of affairs is : are we quite certain that in making this severance between political and religious influence we may not be establishing in a country a power greater than the acknowledged government itself?—*Speech in House of Commons (Irish Church Bill), March* 18, 1869.

Church of Rome.—The Church of Rome is to be respected as the only Hebræo-Christian church extant.—('Mr. St. Lys') *Sybil.*

I look upon our nobility joining the Church of Rome as the greatest national calamity that has ever happened to England. Irrespective of all religious considerations, it is an abnegation of patriotism ; and in this age, where all things are questioned, a love of our country seems to me the one thing to cling to.—('Lady Corisande') *Lothair.*

If Popery were only just the sign of the cross, and music, and censer-pots, though I think them all superstitious, I'd be free to leave them alone if they would leave me. But Popery is a much deeper thing than that, Lothair, and our fathers found it out. They could not stand it, and we should be a craven crew to stand it now. A man should be master in his own house. You will be taking a wife some day ; at least it is to be hoped so ; and how will you like one of these Monsignores to be walking into her bedroom, eh ; and talking to her alone when he pleases, and where he pleases ; and when you want to consult your wife, which a wise man should often do, to find there is another mind between hers and yours?—('Lord Culloden') *Lothair.*

CIRCUIT.

This circuit is a cold and mercantile adventure, and I am disappointed in it. Not so either, for I looked for but little to enjoy. Take one day of my life as a specimen ; the rest are mostly alike. The sheriff's trumpets are playing ; one, some tune of which I know nothing, and the other no tune at all. I am obliged to turn out at eight. It is the first day of the assize, so there is some chance of a brief, being a new place. I push my way into court through files of attorneys, as civil to the rogues as possible, assuring them there is plenty of room, though I am at the very moment gasping for breath wedged in in a lane of well-lined waistcoats. I get into court, take my place in the quietest corner, and there I sit, and pass other men's fees and briefs like a twopenny postman, only without pay. Well ! 'tis six o'clock, dinner-time, at the bottom of the table, carve for all, speak to none, nobody speaks to me, must wait till last to sum up, and pay the bill. Reach home quite devoured by spleen, after having heard everyone abused who happened to be absent.—(' Hargrave Grey ') *Vivian Grey.*

CIRCUMSTANCES.

Man is not the creature of circumstances, circumstances are the creatures of men. We are free agents, and man is more powerful than matter.—(' Beckendorf') *Vivian Grey.*

Circumstances are beyond the control of man ; but his conduct is in his own power.—*Contarini Fleming.*

'Tis circumstance makes conduct ; life's a ship
The sport of every wind.—(' Alarcos ') *Count Alarcos.*

There is nothing in which the power of circumstances is more evident than in politics.—*Life of Lord George Bentinck.*

Circumstance has decided every crisis which I have experienced, and not the primitive facts on which we have consulted.—(' Baroni ') *Tancred.*

Circumstance is the creature of cities, where the action of a multitude, influenced by different motives, produces innumerable and ever-changing combinations.—('Tancred') *Tancred.*

CITY.

A great city, whose image dwells on the memory of man, is the type of some great idea. Rome represents conquest ; faith hovers over Jerusalem ; and Athens embodies the preeminent quality of the antique world-art.—*Coningsby.*

The air of cities
To unaccustomed lungs is very fatal.
('King of Castille ') *Count Alarcos.*

CIVILISATION.

The progressive development of the faculties of man.— (' Lord Henry Vavasour ') *Tancred.*

It is civilisation that makes us awkward, for it gives us an uncertain position ; perplexed we take refuge in pretence, and embarrassed we seek a resource in affectation.—*Sybil.*

I have always felt that the best security for civilisation is the dwelling, and that upon properly appointed and becoming dwellings depends more than anything else the improvement of mankind. Such dwellings are the nursery of all domestic virtues, and without a becoming home the exercise of those virtues is impossible.—*Speech at Opening of the Shaftesbury Park Estate, July* 18, 1874.

Increased means and increased leisure are the two civilisers of man.—*Speech at Manchester, April* 3, 1872.

CLERGYMAN OF THE OLD SCHOOL.

The Doctor was a regular orthodox divine of the eighteenth century ; with a large cauliflower wig, shovel-hat, and huge knee-buckles, barely covered by his top-boots ; learned, jovial, humorous, and somewhat courtly ; truly pious, but not enthusiastic ; not forgetful of his tithes, but generous and charitable when they were once paid ; never neglecting the sick, yet occasionally following a fox ; a fine scholar, an active magistrate, and a good shot ; dreading the Pope, and hating the Presbyterians.—*Venetia.*

CLUB.

This club was Hatton's only relaxation. He had never entered society ; and now his habits were so formed, that the effort would have been a painful one ; though, with a first-rate reputation in his calling, and supposed to be rich, the openings were numerous to a familiar intercourse with those middle-aged nameless gentlemen of easy circumstances who haunt clubs, and dine a great deal at each other's houses and chambers ; men who travel regularly a little, and gossip regularly a great deal ; who lead a sort of facile, slipshod existence, doing nothing, yet mightily interested in what others do ; great critics of little things, profuse in minor luxuries, and inclined to .he respectable practice of a decorous profligacy ; peering through the window of a club-house as if they wefe discovering a planet ; and usually much excited about things with which they have no concern, and personages who never heard of them.—*Sybil.*

COALITION.

Coalitions, although successful, have always this : their triumph has been brief. This I know, that England does not love coalitions.—*Speech in House of Commons (Budget), December* 3, 1852.

When the Coalition Government was formed, I was asked how long it would last, and I ventured to reply, 'Until every member of it is, as a public character, irretrievably injured.'—*Speech in House of Commons (Law of Landlord and Tenant and Leasing [Ireland] Bill), July* 13, 1854.

COBDEN.

What the qualities of Mr. Cobden were in the House all present are aware ; yet, perhaps, I may be permitted to say that as a debater he had few equals. As a logician he was close and complete ; adroit, perhaps even subtle ; yet at the same time he was gifted with such a degree of imagi- nation that he never lost sight of the sympathies of those whom he addressed, and so, generally avoiding to drive his arguments to extremity he became as a speaker both practical and persuasive. I believe that when the verdict of posterity shall be recorded on his life and conduct, it will be said of him that he was, without doubt, the greatest political character the pure middle class of this country has yet produced—an ornament to the House of Commons, and an honour to England.—*Speech in House of Commons (the late Mr. Cobden), April* 3, 1865.

COERCION.

Men are apt to believe that crime and coercion are inevitably associated.—*Life of Lord George Bentinck.*

E

COFFEE.

A good cup of coffee is the most delicious and the rarest beverage in the world.—*Endymion.*

COLONIES.

Colonies do not cease to be colonies because they·are independent.—*Speech in House of Commons (Address to Her Majesty on the Lords Commissioners' Speech), February* 5, 1863.

What is colonial necessarily lacks originality.—(' Lord Roehampton ') *Endymion.*

COMBINATION.

There is a combination for every case.—(' Hatton ') *Sybil.*

COMMERCE.

More pernicious nonsense was never devised by man than treaties of commerce.—(' Job Thornberry ') *Endymion.*

COMMERCIAL DISTRESS.

Commercial distress—its disappearance was always sudden. It was like a long and desperate calm—a breeze suddenly arises, when all are disheartened, and in a moment the character of the sky is changed.—*Speech in House of Commons (Distress of Country), February* 14, 1843.

COMMERCIAL WORLD.

It was impossible to deny that she was interested and amused by the world, which she now witnessed—so energetic, so restless, so various ; so full of urgent and pressing life ; never thinking of the past, and quite heedless of the future, but worshipping an almighty present, that sometimes seemed to roll on like the car of Juggernaut.—*Endymion.*

COMMISSION.

Nowadays public robbery is out of fashion, and takes the milder title of a commission of inquiry.—*Sybil.*

COMMITTEE.

Our statesmen never read, and are only converted by Parliamentary committees.—*Speech in House of Commons* (*Sugar Duties*), *July* 28, 1841.

COMMON SENSE.

There is an extreme Protestant party, who persist in believing that every Roman Catholic is a Jesuit. There is, on the other hand, an extreme Roman Catholic party who, the moment their aggressive indiscretion excites comment, and perhaps a little distrust, immediately raise a howl that their Protestant fellow-countrymen wish to revive all the Roman Catholic disabilities. Fortunately, although noisy and bustling, they are limited in their influence, and the general sentiment of the country controls their violence and extravagance. What may be called the Gulf-Stream of common sense softens and subdues their violence and asperity.—*Speech in House of Commons* (*Roman Catholic Oaths Bill*), *June* 12, 1865.

COMPLAIN.

I make it a point never to complain.—*Speech in House of Commons.*

COMPOSITION.

I have observed that, after writing a book, my mind always makes a great spring. I believe that the act of composition produces the same invigorating effect upon the mind which some exertion does upon the body. Even the writing of 'Manstein' produced a revolution in my nature, which cannot be traced by any metaphysical analysis. In the course of a few days, I was converted from a worldling into a philosopher. I was indeed ignorant, but I had lost the double ignorance of the Platonists; I was no longer ignorant that I was ignorant. No one could be influenced by a greater desire of knowledge, a greater passion for the beautiful, or a deeper regard for his fellow-creatures. And I well remember when, on the evening that I wrote the last sentence of this more intellectual effort, I walked out upon the terrace with that feeling of satisfaction which accompanies the idea of a task completed. So far was I from being excited by the hope of having written a great work, that I even meditated its destruction ; for the moment it was terminated, it seemed to me that I had become suddenly acquainted with the long-concealed principles of my art, which, without doubt, had been slenderly practised in this production. My taste, as it were in an instant, became formed; and I felt convinced I could now produce some lasting creation.

I thought no more of criticism. The breath of man has never influenced me much, for I depend more upon myself than upon others. I want no false fame. It would be no delight to me to be considered a prophet, were I conscious of being an impostor. I ever wish to be undeceived; but if I possess the organisation of a poet, no one can prevent me from exercising my faculty, any more than he can rob the courser of his fleetness, or the nightingale of her song.

The profound thinker always suspects that he is superficial. Patience is a necessary ingredient of genius. Nothing is more fatal than to be seduced into composition by the first flutter of the imagination. This is the cause of so many weak and unequal works, of so many worthy ideas thrown away, and so many good purposes marred. Yet there is a bound to meditation ; there is a moment when further judgment is useless. There is a moment when a heavenly light rises over the dim world you have been so long creating, and bathes it with life and beauty. Accept this omen that your work is good, and revel in the sunshine of composition.—*Contarini Fleming.*

CONCEIT.

Nothing depresses a man's spirits more completely than a self-conviction of self-conceit.—*Popanilla.*

CONCILIATION.

One should always conciliate.—(' Putney Giles ') *Lothair.*
If you are not very clever, you should be conciliatory.— (' The Premier ') *Endymion.*

CONDUCT.

The conduct of men depends upon the temperament, not upon a bunch of musty maxims.—*Henrietta Temple.*

CONFERENCE.

The Conference lasted six weeks. It wasted six weeks. It lasted as long as a carnival, and like a carnival it was an affair of masks and mystification. Our ministers went to it, as men in distressed circumstances go to a place of amusement—to while away the time, with a consciousness of impending failure.—*Speech in House of Commons (Denmark and Germany—Vote of Censure), July* 4, 1864.

CONINGSBY.

His countenance, radiant with health and the lustre of innocence, was at the same time thoughtful and resolute. The expression of his deep blue eye was serious. Without extreme regularity of features, the face was one that would never have passed unobserved. His short upper lip indicated a good breed : and his chestnut curls clustered over his open brow, while his shirt-collar thrown over his shoulders was unrestrained by handkerchief or ribbon. Add to this, a limber and graceful figure, which the jacket of his boyish dress exhibited to great advantage.

There ran through Coningsby's character, as we have before mentioned, a vein of simplicity which was not its least charm. It resulted, no doubt, in a great degree from the earnestness of his nature. There never was a boy so totally devoid of affectation, which was remarkable, for he had a brilliant imagination, a quality that, from its fantasies, and the vague and indefinite desires it engenders, generally makes those whose characters are not formed affected. . . .

As he bowed lowly before the Duchess and her daughter, it would have been difficult to image a youth of a mien more prepossessing and a manner more finished.

A manner that was spontaneous ; nature's pure gift, the reflex of his feeling. No artifice prompted that profound and polished homage. Not one of those influences, the aggregate of whose sway produces, as they tell us, the finished gentleman, had ever exercised its beneficent power on our orphan, and not rarely forlorn, Coningsby. No clever and refined woman, with her quick perception, and nice criticism that never offends our self-love, had ever given him that education that is more precious than Universities. The mild suggestions of a sister, the gentle raillery of some laughing cousin, are also advantages not always appreciated at the time, but which boys, when they have become men, often think over with gratitude, and a little remorse at the ungracious spirit in which they were received. Not even the dancing-master had afforded his mechanical aid to Coningsby, who, like all Eton boys of this generation, viewed that professor of accomplishments with frank repugnance. But even in the boisterous life of school, Coningsby, though his style was free and flowing, was always well-bred. His spirit recoiled from that gross familiarity that is the characteristic of modern manners, and which would destroy all forms and ceremonies merely because they curb and control their own coarse convenience and ill-disguised selfishness. To women, however, Coningsby instinctively bowed, as to beings set apart for reverence and delicate treatment. Little as his experience was of them, his spirit had been fed with chivalrous fancies, and he entertained for them all the ideal devotion of a Surrey or a Sydney. . . .

Our young Coningsby reached Beaumanoir in a state of meditation. He also desired to be great. Not from the restless vanity that sometimes impels youth to momentary exertion, by which they sometimes obtain a distinction as evanescent as their energy. The ambition of our hero was altogether of a different character. It was, indeed, at present not a little vague, indefinite, hesitating, inquiring, sometimes desponding. What were his powers? what should be his aim? were often to him, as to all young aspirants, questions infinitely perplexing and full of pain. But, on the whole, there ran through his character, notwithstanding his many dazzling qualities and accomplishments, and his juvenile celebrity, which has spoiled so much promise, a vein of grave simplicity that was the consequence of an earnest temper, and of an intellect that would be content with nothing short of the profound.

His was a mind that loved to pursue every question to the centre. But it was not a spirit of scepticism that impelled this habit ; on the contrary, it was the spirit of faith. Coningsby found that he was born in an age of infidelity in all things, and his heart assured him that a want of faith was a want of nature. But his vigorous intellect could not take refuge in that maudlin substitute for belief which consists in a patronage of fantastic theories. He needed that deep and enduring conviction that the heart and the intellect, feeling and reason united, can alone supply.—*Coningsby.*

CONSCIENCE.

A pure conscience may defy city gossips.—(' Eva ') *Tancred.*

CONSERVATISM.

The Queen's fancy ball—Peel as Louvois? No, Sir Robert would be content with nothing less than Le Grand

Colbert, Rue Richelieu No. 15, Grand magasin de nou-
veautés très-anciennes : prix fixe, avec quelque rabais.

'A description of Conservatism,' said Coningsby.—*Coningsby*.

CONSERVATISM IN 1834.

Conservatism was an attempt to carry on affairs by substituting the fulfilment of the duties of office for the performance of the functions of government ; and to maintain
this negative system by the mere influence of property,
reputable private conduct, and what are called good connections. Conservatism discards Prescription, shrinks from
Principle, disavows Progress; having rejected all respect
for Antiquity, it offers no redress for the Present, and makes
no preparation for the Future. It is obvious that for a time,
under favourable circumstances, such a confederation might
succeed ; but it is equally clear, that on the arrival of one
of those critical conjunctures that will periodically occur in
all states, and which such an unimpassioned system is even
calculated ultimately to create, all power of resistance will
be wanting : the barren curse of political infidelity will
paralyse all action ; and the Conservative Constitution will
be discovered to be a Caput Mortuum.—*Coningsby*.

'If any fellow were to ask me what the Conservative
Cause is, I am sure I should not know what to say,' said
Backhurst.

'Why, it is the cause of our glorious institutions,' said
Coningsby. 'A Crown robbed of its prerogatives ; a Church
controlled by a commission ; and an Aristocracy that does
not lead.'

'Under whose genial influence the order of the Peasantry, "a country's pride," has vanished from the face of
the land,' said Henry Sydney, 'and is succeeded by a race
of serfs, who are called labourers, and who burn ricks.'

'Under which,' continued Coningsby, 'the Crown has
become a cipher ; the Church a sect ; the Nobility drones ;
and the People drudges.'

'It is the great constitutional cause,' said Lord Vere, 'that refuses everything to opposition ; yields everything to agitation ; conservative in Parliament, destructive out of doors ; that has no objection to any change provided only it be effected by unauthorised means.'

'The first public association of men,' said Coningsby, 'who have worked for an avowed end without enunciating a single principle.'

'And who have established political infidelity throughout the land,' said Lord Henry.—*Coningsby.*

CONSERVATIVE.

Conservative Policy.—I am told sometimes that our policy is not sufficiently startling and melodramatic for the temper of the people of England. I cannot say that I agree with that opinion. I believe that a policy that diminishes the death-rate of a great nation is a feat as considerable as any of those decisive battles of the world that generally decide nothing.—*Speech at Guildhall, November* 9, 1875.

Throughout my public life I have aimed at two chief results. Not insensible to the principle of progress, I have endeavoured to reconcile change with that respect for tradition, which is one of the main elements of our social strength ; and in external affairs I have endeavoured to develop and strengthen our Empire, believing that the combination of achievement and responsibility elevates the character and condition of a people.—*Letter to Electors of Buckinghamshire, August* 22, 1876.

I find that the only charge Lord Hartington makes against the Government is that it makes every class comfortable. I remember—I think I have heard of a time when a Government was accused of harassing every class.— *Speech at Mansion House, November* 9, 1877.

Conservative Principles.—I believe I am right in saying that it is a Conservative principle, which holds that the due influence of property in the exercise of the suffrage is a salutary influence. I think it is a Conservative principle that in any representative scheme the influence of landed property should be sensibly felt. I hold it to be a Conservative principle that we maintain the union between Church and State—that we should not only maintain but expand the ecclesiastical institutions of this country. I hold it to be a Conservative principle that the estate of the Church should be respected, and that the Church itself should not be a stipendiary of the civil power. I hold it to be a Conservative principle that we maintain the Church in Ireland, believing that maintenance perfectly reconcilable with the rights and privileges of all classes of Her Majesty's subjects in that kingdom. I hold it to be a Conservative principle to cherish and protect all traditionary influences, because they are opposed to a crude centralisation, and because they are the source of an authority at once beneficent and economical. I hold it to be a Conservative principle that would respect existing corporations. If I go to another great branch of public life—I mean foreign affairs—I find in the country that there are opinions on all great questions of foreign politics perfectly opposed to each other. I have always considered that there were three great questions upon which it becomes any man who aspires to be a statesman, as well as any Parliamentary party which incurs the responsibility of supporting particular individuals, to have clear and precise ideas. These three subjects are : the Russian Empire, the Austrian Empire, and our relations with the United States of America. For my own part, I have always been of opinion that the dismembering of the Russian Empire is not an object which any statesman ought to propose to himself, and even if the dismemberment took place we should find that the ultimate result would be that the balance of power in Europe would be distributed in a manner prejudicial to our interests. Take, again, the case of the Austrian Empire. I hold that it is the Conservative opinion that the maintenance of the Austrian Empire is necessary to the independence, and, if necessary to the independence, necessary to the civilisation and even to the liberties of Europe. Let us look to our relations with the United States. What is our policy? There are those who view with the utmost jealousy, and regard in a litigious spirit, the progress of the United States of America—who think that any advance in their power, any expansion of their territory is opposed to the commercial interest, and perhaps also to the political influence of England. But I am not of that opinion. I apprehend with respect to these three subjects of foreign policy there are distinctive opinions, and therefore it is idle to pretend that parties have ceased to exist.—*Speech in House of Commons (Review of Session), July* 25, 1856.

A sound Conservative Government, I understand : Tory men and Whig measures.—('Taper') *Coningsby.*

CONSOLS.

The sweet simplicity of the three per cents.—*Endymion.*

There is nothing like a fall in Consols to bring the blood of our good people of England into cool order.—('Cleveland') *Vivian Grey.*

CONSTANCY.

Constancy is human nature.—('Contarini') *Contarini Fleming.*

CONSTANTINOPLE.

No picture can ever convey a just idea of Constantinople. I have seen several that are faithful, as far as they extend ; but the most comprehensive can exhibit only a small portion of this extraordinary city. By land or by water, in every direction, passing up the Golden Horn to the Valley of Fresh Waters, or proceeding, on the other hand, down the famous Bosphorus to Buyukdere and Terapia, to the Euxine, what infinite novelty ! New kiosks, new hills, new

windings, new groves of cypress, and new forests of chestnut, open on all sides.

Conceive the ocean a stream not broader than the
Rhine, with shores presenting all the beauty and variety
of that river, running between gentle slopes covered with
rich woods, gardens, and summer-palaces, cemeteries and
mosques, and villages, and bounded by sublime mountains.
The view of the Euxine from the heights of Terapia, just
seen through the end of the Straits, is like gazing upon
eternity.—*Contarini Fleming.*

CONSTITUENCIES.

You may talk of tampering with the currency, and there
are few things worse ; but that which is worse is tampering
with the constituency of England.   If there is to be a change,
let it be a change called for by clear necessity, and one
which is calculated to give general—I will not say final—
but general and permanent satisfaction.—*Speech in House of
Commons (Elective Franchise), March* 25, 1852.

I have always thought the ideal of the constituent body
in England should be this—it should be numerous enough
to be independent, and select enough to be responsible.—
*Speech in House of Commons (Representation of the People),
February* 28, 1859.

I think it would be well on both sides of the House, if
we were for a moment to consider the tone in which we are
accustomed to speak of the constituencies of this country.
I do not arrogate for those whom I represent, or for the
great body of whom they are a portion, any superiority over
any other body in this country ; but I think the House will
agree with me, that those interested in the cultivation of
land in this country form a class highly respectable for
their private virtues and public spirit.   But if an agricultural
constituency after a sharp contest happen to elect a member
of Parliament—what do we hear ?   They are described as
serfs, they are denounced as the instruments of feudal

tyranny, and the most inventive and skilful cultivators of the soil are described as illiterate boobies. Again, if the conduct of the electors who live in towns and cities is the question, you would suppose from the conversation you hear, that whilst the farmers of England are mere serfs, the dwellers in cities and towns are absolute and arrant traitors, disaffected to all the institutions of the country. I need say nothing about the freemen—they are the pariahs of politics. If this be the true character of the great body of the constituency of England, what must we be who are their choice !—*Speech in House of Commons (Government of India, No. 3 Bill), April 26, 1858.*

CONSTITUTION.

During the last twenty years you have introduced a sentimental instead of a political principle into the conduct of your foreign affairs. You looked upon the English Constitution as a model farm.—*Speech in House of Commons (Expulsion of British Ambassador from Madrid), June 5, 1845.*

We shall never make the Constitution of England a strictly logical one, and I do not think that it is desirable that we should try. But I am not at all ashamed of the principle to which I have often given expression in this House, and which is, I believe, a very sound one, that it is just that a person should vote when his qualification is found.—*Speech in House of Commons (Representation of the People Bill), 1867.*

The Constitution of England is not a paper Constitution. It is an aggregate of institutions, many of them founded merely upon prescription, some of them fortified by muniments, but all of them the fruit and experience of an ancient and illustrious people.—*Speech at Merchant Taylors' Hall, June 17, 1868.*

There is a school of politics who looks at the English Constitution as valetudinarian. They are always looking at its tongue and feeling its pulse, and devising means by which they may give it a tonic.—*Speech at Glasgow* (*Freedom of City*), *November* 20, 1873.

CONVERSATION.

It was a lively dinner ; Lord St. Jerome loved conversation, though he never conversed. 'There must be an audience,' he would say, 'and I am the audience.'—*Lothair.*

It was some time since they had met—not since the end of last season—so there was a great deal to talk about. There had been deaths and births and marriages, which required a flying comment—all important events : deaths, which solved many difficulties, heirs to estates that were not expected, and weddings which surprised everybody.—*Lothair.*

The conversation of lovers is inexhaustible.—*Henrietta Temple.*

Alfred Mountchesney hovered round Lady Joan Fitz-Warene : he uttered inconceivable nothings, and she replied to him in incomprehensible somethings.—*Sybil.*

'He was a great talker,' said Lady Bellair, 'but then he was the tyrant of conversation. Now men were made to listen as well as talk.' 'Without doubt, for Nature has given us two ears, but only one mouth,' said Count Mirabel.—*Henrietta Temple.*

'You must come and dine with me, Count Mirabel, because you talk well across a table. So few can do it without bellowing.'—('Lady Bellair') *Henrietta Temple.*

The art of conversation is to be prompt without being stubborn, to refute without argument, and to clothe great matters in a motley garb.—('Waldershare') *Endymion.*

Lord Roehampton was the soul of the feast, and yet it is difficult to describe his conversation : it was a medley of whim, interspersed now and then with a very short anecdote of a very famous person, or some deeply interesting reminiscence of some critical event.—*Endymion.*

Lady Everingham thoroughly understood the art of conversation, which, indeed, consists of the exercise of two fine qualities. You must originate, and you must sympathise ; you must possess at the same time the habit of communicating and the habit of listening. The union is rather rare, but irresistible.—*Coningsby*.

Compared with their converse, the tattle of our saloons has in it something humiliating. It is not merely that it is deficient in warmth, and depth, and breadth ; that it is always discussing persons instead of principles, and cloaking its want of thought in mimetic dogmas, and its want of feeling in superficial raillery ; it is not merely that it has neither imagination, nor fancy, nor sentiment, nor feeling, nor knowledge to recommend it ; but it appears to me, even as regards manner and expression, inferior in refinement and phraseology ; in short, trivial, uninteresting, stupid, really vulgar.—('Egremont') *Sybil*.

One of the principal causes of our renowned dulness in conversation is our extreme intellectual jealousy. It must be admitted that in this respect authors, but especially poets, bear the palm. They never think they are sufficiently appreciated, and live in tremor lest a brother should distinguish himself.—*Coningsby*.

A great thing is a great book ; but a greater thing than all is the talk of a great man.—*Coningsby*.

Hereupon a conversation took place, principally sustained by the earl and the baronet, which developed all the resources of the great parochial mind. Dietaries, bastardy, gaol regulations, game laws, were amply discussed ; and Lord Marney wound up with a declaration of the means by which the country might be saved, and which seemed principally to consist of high prices and low church.—*Sybil*.

Waldershare talked the whole way. It was a rhapsody of fun, knowledge, anecdote, brilliant badinage and passionate seriousness. Sometimes he recited poetry, and his voice was musical, and then when he had attuned his companions to a sentimental pitch, he would break into mockery and touch with delicate satire every mood of human feeling. *Endymion.*

Do not think, as many young gentlemen are apt to believe, that talking will serve your purpose. That is the quicksand of your young beginners. All can talk in a public assembly : that is to say, all can give us exhortations which do not move, and arguments which do not convince ; but to converse in a private assembly is a different affair, and rare are the characters who can be endured if they exceed a whisper to their neighbours. But though mild and silent, be ever ready with the rapier of repartee, and be ever armed with the breastplate of good temper, for such infallibly gather laurels if you add to these the spear of sarcasm and the shield of nonchalance.

The high style of conversation where eloquence and philosophy emulate each other, where principles are profoundly expounded and felicitously illustrated, all this has ceased. It ceased in this country with Johnson and Burke, and it requires a Johnson and a Burke for its maintenance. There is no mediocrity in such discourse, no intermediate character between the sage and the bore. The second style, where men, not things, are the staple, but where wit, and refinement, and sensibility invest even personal details with intellectual interest, does flourish at present, as it always must in a highly civilised society. S. is, or rather was, a fine specimen of this school, and M. and L. are his worthy rivals. This style is indeed, for the moment, very interesting. Then comes your conversation man, who, we confess, is our aversion. His talk is a thing apart, got up before he enters the company from whose conduct it should grow out. He sits in the middle of a large table, and, with a brazen voice, bawls out his anecdotes about Sir Thomas or Sir Humphry, Lord Blank, or my Lady Blue. He is incessant, yet not interesting ; ever varying, yet always monotonous. Even if we are amused, we are no more grateful for the entertainment than we are to the lamp over the table for the light which it universally sheds, and to yield which it was obtained on purpose. We are more gratified by the slight conversation of one who is often silent, but who speaks from his momentary feelings, than by all this hullaballoo. Yet this machine is generally a favourite piece of furniture with the hostess. You may catch her eye, as he recounts some adventure of the morning, which proves that he not only belongs to every club, but goes to them, light up with approbation ; and then, when the ladies withdraw, and the female senate deliver their criticism upon the late actors, she will observe, with a gratified smile, to her confidante, that the dinner went off well, and that Mr. Bellow was very strong to-day.—*The Young Duke.*

In his mood Lothair found it easier to talk to men than to women. Male conversation is of a coarser grain, and does not require so much play of thought and manner : discourse about the Suez Canal, and Arab horses, and pipes and pachas, can be carried on without much psychological effort, and by degrees banishes all sensibility.—*Lothair.*

There are men whose phrases are oracles ; who condense in a sentence the secrets of a life ; who blurt out an aphorism that forms a character or illustrates an existence. *Coningsby.*

COQUETTE.

A coquette is a being who wishes to please. Amiable being ! If you do not like her, you will have no difficulty in finding a female companion of a different mood. Alas ! coquettes are but too rare. 'Tis a career that requires great abilities, infinite pains, a gay and airy spirit. 'Tis the coquette that provides all amusement ; suggests the riding party, plans the pic-nic, gives and guesses charades, acts them. She is the stirring element amid the heavy congeries of social atoms ; the soul of the house, the salt of the banquet. Let anyone pass a very agreeable week, or it may be ten days, under any roof, and analyse the cause of his

F

satisfaction, and one might safely make a gentle wager that his solution would present him with the frolic phantom of a coquette.—*Coningsby.*

CORISANDE (LADY).

There was one daughter unmarried, and she was to be presented next season. Though the family likeness was still apparent in Lady Corisande, in general expression she differed from her sisters. They were all alike with their delicate aquiline noses, bright complexions, short upper lips, and eyes of sunny light. The beauty of Lady Corisande was even more distinguished and more regular, but whether it were the effect of her dark-brown hair or darker eyes, her countenance had not the lustre of the rest, and its expression was grave and perhaps pensive. . . .

'Her character is not yet formed, and its future is perplexing, at least to me,' murmured her mother. 'She has not the simple nature of her sisters. It is a deeper and more complicated mind, and I watch its development with fond but anxious interest.'—*Lothair.*

CORPORATIONS.

I would now ask permission to state why I am, on the whole, entirely opposed to confiscating the property of corporations ; why I view it alike with dislike and suspicion. The reason is that, in the first place, whatever may have been the origin of corporate property—whether the gift of the nation, which was rarely the case, or the donation of individuals, as was generally its source—one thing is clear, that it is from its use and purpose essentially popular property, the property of the nation, though not of the state. The second reason why I dislike all confiscation of corporate property is that I find no great act of confiscation was ever carried into effect without injurious consequences to the State in which it took place ; either, generally speaking, it has led to civil war, or established, what in the long run is worse, a chronic disaffection for ages amongst the subjects of the Crown. But if there be any corporate property the confiscation of which I most dislike, it is Church property, and for these reasons :—Church property is to a certain degree an intellectual tenure ; in a greater degree, a moral and spiritual tenure. It is the fluctuating patrimony of the great body of the people. It is, I will not say the only, but it is the easiest method by which the sons of the middle, and even of the working classes, can become landed proprietors, and, what is more, can become resident landed proprietors, and fulfil all the elevating duties incident to this position. But there is another reason why I am greatly opposed to the confiscation of Church property, and that is because I invariably observe, that when Church property is confiscated, it is always given to the landed proprietors.— *Speech in House of Commons* (*Irish Church Bill*), *March* 18, 1869.

COUNTRY HOUSES.

A visit to a country-house, as Pinto says, is a series of meals mitigated by the new dresses of the ladies.—*Lothair.*

Armine Place.—In one of the largest parks in England there yet remained a fragment of a vast Elizabethan pile, that in old days bore the name of Armine Place. Long lines of turreted and many-windowed walls, tall towers, and lofty arches, now rose in picturesque confusion on the green ascent where heretofore old Sir Walsingham had raised the fair and convenient dwelling, which he justly deemed might have served the purpose of a long posterity. The hall and chief staircase of the castle and a gallery alone were finished ; and many a day had Sir Ferdinand passed in arranging the pictures, the armour, and choice rarities of these magnificent apartments. The rest of the building was a mere shell ; nor was it in all parts even roofed in. Time, however, that had stained the neglected towers with an antique tint, and had permitted many a generation of summer birds to build their sunny nests on all the coigns of vantage of the unfinished walls, had exercised a mellowing influence even on these rude accessories, and in the course of years they had been so drenched by the rain, and so buffeted by the wind, and had become so covered with moss and ivy, that they rather added to than detracted from the picturesque character of the whole mass.

A few hundred yards from the castle, but situate on the same verdant rising ground, and commanding, although well sheltered, an extensive view over the wide park, was the fragment of the old Place that we have noticed. The rough and undulating rent which marked the severance of the building was now thickly covered with ivy, which in its gamesome luxuriance had contrived also to climb up a remaining stack of tall chimneys, and to spread over the covering of the large oriel window. This fragment contained a set of pleasant chambers, which, having been occupied by the late baronet, were of course furnished with great taste and comfort ; and there was, moreover, accommodation sufficient for a small establishment.

The principal chamber of Armine Place was a large irregular room, with a low but richly-carved oaken roof, studded with achievements. This apartment was lighted by the oriel window we have mentioned, the upper panes of which contained some ancient specimens of painted glass, and, having been fitted up by Sir Ferdinand as a library, contained a collection of valuable books. From the library you entered through an arched door of glass into a small room, of which, it being much out of repair when the family arrived, Lady Armine had seized the opportunity of gratifying her taste in the adornment. She had hung it with some old-fashioned pea-green damask, that exhibited to advantage several copies of Spanish paintings by herself, for she was a skilful artist. The third and remaining chamber was the dining-room, a somewhat gloomy chamber, being shadowed by a neighbouring chestnut. A portrait of Sir Ferdinand, when a youth, in a Venetian dress, was suspended over the old-fashioned fireplace ; and opposite hung a fine hunting-piece by Schneiders.—*Henrietta Temple.*

Beaumanoir.—Beaumanoir was one of those Palladian palaces, vast and ornate, such as the genius of Kent and Campbell delighted in at the beginning of the eighteenth century. Placed on a noble elevation, yet screened from the northern blast, its sumptuous front, connected with its far-spreading wings by Corinthian colonnades, was the boast and pride of the midland counties. The surrounding gardens, equalling in extent the size of ordinary parks, were crowded with temples dedicated to abstract virtues and to departed friends. Occasionally a triumphal arch celebrated a general whom the family still esteemed a hero ; and sometimes a votive column commemorated the great statesman who had advanced the family a step in the peerage. Beyond the limits of this pleasance the hart and hind wandered in a wilderness abounding in ferny coverts and green and stately trees.—*Coningsby.*

Belmont.—There is something very pleasant in a summer suburban ride in the valley of the Thames. London transforms itself into bustling Knightsbridge and airy Brompton brightly and gracefully, lingers cheerfully in the long, miscellaneous, well-watered King's Road, and only says farewell when you come to an abounding river and a picturesque bridge. The boats were bright upon the waters when Lothair crossed it, and his dark chestnut barb, proud of its resplendent form, curvetted with joy when it reached a green common, studded occasionally with a group of pines and well bedecked with gorse. After this he pursued the public road for a couple of miles until he observed on his left hand a gate on which was written 'private road,' and here he stopped. The gate was locked, but when Lothair assured the keeper that he was about to visit Belmont, he was permitted to enter.

He entered a green and winding lane, fringed with tall elms and dim with fragrant shade, and after proceeding about half a mile came to a long low-built lodge with a thatched and shelving roof and surrounded by a rustic colonnade covered with honeysuckle. Passing through the gate at hand, he found himself in a road winding through gently undulating banks of exquisite turf studded with rare shrubs and occasionally rarer trees. Suddenly the confined scene expanded : wide lawns spread out before him, shadowed with the dark forms of many huge cedars and blazing with flower-beds of every hue. The house was also apparent, a stately mansion of hewn stone, with wings and a portico of Corinthian columns, and backed by deep woods.

This was Belmont, built by a favourite Minister of State to whom a grateful and gracious sovereign had granted a slice of a royal park whereon to raise a palace and a garden and find occasionally Tusculan repose.

The inner hall was of noble proportion, and there were ranged in it many Roman busts and some ancient slabs and altars of marble. These had been collected some century ago by the minister ; but what immediately struck the eye of Lothair were two statues by an American artist, and both of fame, the Sibyl and the Cleopatra. He had heard of these, but had never seen them, and could not refrain from lingering a moment to gaze upon their mystical and fascinating beauty.

He proceeded through two spacious and lofty chambers, of which it was evident the furniture was new. It was luxurious and rich and full of taste, but there was no attempt to recall the past in the details : no cabinets and clocks of French kings or tables of French queens, no chairs of Venetian senators, no candelabra that had illumined Doges of Genoa, no ancient porcelain of rare schools and ivory carvings and choice enamels. The walls were hung with masterpieces of modern art, chiefly of the French school, Ingres and Delaroche and Scheffer.

The last saloon led into a room of smaller dimensions opening on the garden, and which Lothair at first thought must be a fernery, it seemed so full of choice and expand- ing specimens of that beautiful and multiform plant ; but when his eye had become a little accustomed to the scene and to the order of the groups, he perceived they were only the refreshing and profuse ornaments of a regularly furnished and inhabited apartment. There was a table covered with writing materials and books and some music. A chair before the table was so placed as if some one had only recently quitted it, a book being open but turned upon its face with an ivory cutter by its side. It would seem that the dweller in the chamber might not be far distant.

The room opened on a terrace adorned with statues and orange trees, and descending gently into a garden in the Italian style, in the centre of which was a marble foun- tain of many figures. The grounds were not extensive, but they were only separated from the royal park by a wire fence, so that the scene seemed alike rich and illimitable. On the boundary was a summer-house in the shape of a classic temple, one of those pavilions of pleasure which nobles loved to raise in the last century.—*Lothair.*

Brentham.—It would be difficult to find a fairer scene than Brentham offered, especially in the lustrous effulgence of a glorious English summer.   It was an Italian palace of free- stone ; vast, ornate, and in scrupulous condition ; its spacious and graceful chambers filled with treasures of art, and rising itself from statued and stately terraces.   At their foot spread a gardened domain of considerable extent, bright with flowers, dim with coverts of rare shrubs, and musical with fountains.   Its limit reached a park, with timber such as the midland counties only can produce.   The fallow deer trooped among its ferny solitudes and gigantic oaks ; but beyond the waters of the broad and winding lake the scene became more savage, and the eye caught the dark form of the red deer on some jutting mount, shrinking with scorn from communion with his gentler brethren.—*Lothair.*

Cadurcis Abbey.—When they emerged from the wood, they found themselves on the brow of the hill, a small down, over which Venetia ran, exulting in the healthy breeze which, at this exposed height, was strong and fresh. As they advanced to the opposite declivity to that which they had ascended, a wide and peculiar landscape opened before them. The extreme distance was formed by an undulating ridge of lofty and savage hills; nearer than these were gentler elevations, partially wooded; and at their base was a rich valley, its green meads fed by a clear and rapid stream, which glittered in the sun as it coursed on, losing itself at length in a wild and sedgy lake that formed the furthest limit of a widely-spreading park. In the centre of this park, and not very remote from the banks of the rivulet, was an ancient gothic building, that had once been an abbey of great repute and wealth, and had not much suffered in its external character by having served for nearly two centuries and a half as the principal dwelling of an old baronial family.

Descending the downy hill, that here and there was studded with fine old trees, enriching by their presence the view from the abbey, Lady Annabel and her party entered the meads, and, skirting the lake, approached the venerable walls without crossing the stream.

It was difficult to conceive a scene more silent and more desolate. There was no sign of life, and not a sound save the occasional cawing of a rook. Advancing towards the abbey, they passed a pile of buildings that, in the summer, might be screened from sight by the foliage of a group of elms, too scanty at present to veil their desolation. Wide gaps in the roof proved that the vast and dreary stables were no longer used; there were empty granaries, whose doors had fallen from their hinges; the gate of the courtyard was prostrate on the ground ; and the silent clock that once adorned the cupola over the noble entrance arch, had long lost its index. Even the litter of the yard appeared dusty and grey with age. You felt sure no human foot could have disturbed it for years. At the back of these buildings were nailed the trophies of the gamekeeper : hundreds of wild cats, dried to blackness, stretched their downward heads and legs from the mouldering wall ; hawks, magpies, and jays hung in tattered remnants ; but all grey, and even green, with age ; and the heads of birds in plenteous rows, nailed beak upward, and so dried and shrivelled by the suns and winds and frosts of many seasons, that their distinctive characters were lost.

The interior of the abbey formed a quadrangle, surrounded by the cloisters, and in this inner court was a curious fountain, carved with exquisite skill by some gothic artist in one of those capricious moods of sportive invention that produced those grotesque medleys for which the feudal sculptor was celebrated. Not a sound was heard except the fall of the fountain and the light echoes that its voice called up.

The staircase led Lady Annabel and her party through several small rooms, scantily garnished with ancient furniture, in some of which were portraits of the family, until they at length entered a noble saloon, once the refectory of the abbey, and not deficient in splendour, though sadly soiled and worm-eaten. It was hung with tapestry representing the Cartoons of Raffael, and their still vivid colours contrasted with the faded hangings and the dingy damask of the chairs and sofas. A mass of Cromwellian armour was huddled together in a corner of a long monkish gallery, with a standard, encrusted with dust, and a couple of old drums, one broken. From one of the windows they had a good view of the old walled garden, which did not tempt them to enter it ; it was a wilderness, the walks no longer distinguishable from the rank vegetation of the once culti-

vated lawns ; the terraces choked up with the unchecked
shrubberies ; and here and there a leaden statue, a goddess
or a satyr, prostrate, and covered with moss and lichen.—
Venetia.

Castle Dacre.—Castle Dacre was the erection of Van-
brugh, an imaginative artist, whose critics we wish no bitterer
fate than not to live in his splendid creations. A spacious
centre, richly ornamented, though broken, perhaps, into rather
too much detail, was joined to wings of a corresponding magnificence by fanciful colonnades. A terrace, extending the
whole front, was covered with orange trees, and many a statue,
and many an obelisk, and many a temple, and many a fountain, were tinted with the warm twilight. The Duke did not
view the forgotten scene of youth without emotion. It was
a palace worthy of the heroine on whom he had been musing.
The carriage gained the lofty portal. Luigi and Spiridion,
who had preceded their master, were ready to receive the
Duke, who was immediately ushered to the rooms prepared
for his reception. He was later than he had intended, and
no time was to be unnecessarily lost in his preparation for
his appearance.— *The Young Duke.*

The Cedars.—The villa of Mr. Vigo was on the banks of
the Thames, and had once belonged to a noble customer.
The Palladian mansion contained a suite of chambers of
majestic dimension—lofty ceilings, rich cornices, and vast
windows of plate glass ; the gardens were rich with the products of conservatories which Mr. Vigo had raised with every
modern improvement, and a growth of stately cedars supported the dignity of the scene and gave to it a name.
Beyond, a winding walk encircled a large field which Mr.
Vigo called the park, and which sparkled with gold and silver
pheasants, and the keeper lived in a newly raised habitation
at the extreme end, which took the form of a Swiss cottage.
Endymion.

Château Desir.—How shall we describe Château Desir,
that place fit for all princes ? In the midst of a park of great

extent, and eminent for scenery, as varied as might please
nature's most capricious lover ; in the midst of green lawns,
and deep winding glens, and cooling streams, and wild forest,
and soft woodland, there was gradually formed an elevation,
on which was situate a mansion of great size, and of that
bastard, but picturesque style of architecture, called the
Italian Gothic. The date of its erection was about the
middle of the sixteenth century. You entered by a noble
gateway, in which the pointed style still predominated, but
in various parts of which the Ionic column, and the prominent keystone, and other creations of Roman architecture,
intermingled with the expiring Gothic, into a large quadrangle, to which the square casement windows, and the
triangular pediments or gable-ends supplying the place of
battlements, gave a varied and Italian feature. In the
centre of the court, from a vast marble basin, the rim of
which was enriched by a splendidly sculptured lotus border,
rose a marble group representing Amphitrite with her
marine attendants, whose sounding shells and coral sceptres
sent forth their subject element in sparkling showers. This
work, the chef d'œuvre of a celebrated artist of Vicenza,
had been purchased by Valerian, first Lord Carabas, who
having spent the greater part of his life as the representative
of his monarch' at the Ducal Court of Venice, at length
returned to his native country ; and in the creation of
Château Desir endeavoured to find some consolation for the
loss of his beautiful villa on the banks of the Adige.

Over the gateway there rose a turreted tower, the small
square window of which, notwithstanding its stout stanchions,
illumined the muniment room of the House of Carabas. In
the spandrils of the gateway and in many other parts of
the building might be seen the arms of the family ; while
the tall twisted stacks of chimneys, which appeared to spring
from all parts of the roof, were carved and built in such
curious and quaint devices that they were rather an ornament than an excrescence. When you entered the quad-

rangle, you found one side solely occupied by the old hall, the huge carved rafters of whose oak roof rested on corbels of the family supporters against the walls. These walls were of stone, but covered half-way from the ground with a panelling of curiously-carved oak ; whence were suspended, in massy frames, the family portraits, painted by Dutch and Italian artists. Near the dais, or upper part of the hall, there projected an oriel window, which as you beheld, you scarcely knew what most to admire, the radiancy of its painted panes or the fantastic richness of Gothic ornament, which was profusely lavished in every part of its masonry. Here too the Gothic pendant and the Gothic fan-work were intermingled with the Italian arabesques, which, at the time of the building of the Château, had been recently introduced into England by Hans Holbein and John of Padua.

How wild and fanciful are those ancient arabesques ! Here at Château Desir, in the panelling of the old hall, might you see fantastic scrolls, separated by bodies ending in termini, and whose heads supported the Ionic volute, while the arch, which appeared to spring from these capitals, had, for a keystone, heads more monstrous than those of the fabled animals of Ctesias ; or so ludicrous, that you forgot the classic griffin in the grotesque conception of the Italian artist. Here was a gibbering monkey, there a grinning pulcinello ; now you viewed a chattering devil, which might have figured in the 'Temptation of St. Anthony ;' and now a mournful, mystic, bearded countenance, which might have flitted in the back scene of a ' Witches' Sabbath.'

A long gallery wound through the upper story of two other sides of the quadrangle, and beneath were the show suite of apartments, with a sight of which the admiring eyes of curious tourists were occasionally delighted.

The grey stone walls of this antique edifice were, in many places, thickly covered with ivy and other parasitical plants, the deep green of whose verdure beautifully contrasted with the scarlet glories of the pyrus japonica, which gracefully clustered round the windows of the lower chambers. The mansion itself was immediately surrounded by numerous ancient forest trees. There was the elm with its rich branches bending down like clustering grapes ; there was the wide-spreading oak with its roots fantastically gnarled ; there was the ash, with its smooth bark and elegant leaf ; and the silver beech, and the gracile birch ; and the dark fir, affording with its rough foliage a contrast to the trunks of its more beautiful companions, or shooting far above their branches, with the spirit of freedom worthy of a rough child of the mountains.—*Vivian Grey.*

Cherbury.—Some ten years before the revolt of our American colonies, there was situate in one of our midland counties, on the borders of an extensive forest, an ancient hall that belonged to the Herberts, but which, though ever well preserved, had not until that period been visited by any member of the family since the exile of the Stuarts. It was an edifice of considerable size, built of grey stone, much covered with ivy, and placed upon the last gentle elevation of a long ridge of hills, in the centre of a crescent of woods, that far overtopped its clusters of tall chimneys and turreted gables. Although the principal chambers were on the first story, you could nevertheless step forth from their windows on a broad terrace, whence you descended into the gardens by a double flight of stone steps, exactly in the middle of its length. These gardens were of some extent, and filled with evergreen shrubberies of remarkable overgrowth, while occasionally turfy vistas, cut in the distant woods, came sloping down to the south, as if they opened to receive the sunbeam that greeted the genial aspect of the mansion. The ground-floor was principally occupied by the hall itself, which was of great dimensions, hung round with many a family portrait and rural picture, furnished with long oaken seats covered with scarlet cushions, and ornamented with a parti-coloured floor of alternate diamonds of black and white marble. From the centre of the roof of the mansion, which was always covered with pigeons, rose the clock-tower of the chapel, surmounted by a vane ; and before the mansion itself was a large plot of grass, with a fountain in the centre, surrounded by a hedge of honeysuckle.

This plot of grass was separated from an extensive park, that opened in front of the hall, by tall iron gates, on each of the pillars of which was a lion rampant supporting the escutcheon of the family. The deer wandered in this en-closed and well-wooded demesne, and about a mile from the mansion, in a direct line with the iron gates, was an old-fashioned lodge, which marked the limit of the park, and from which you emerged into a fine avenue of limes bounded on both sides by fields. At the termination of this avenue was a strong but simple gate, and a woodman's cottage ; and then spread before you a vast landscape of open, wild lands, which seemed on one side interminable, while on the other the eye rested on the dark heights of the neighbour-ing forest.—*Venetia*.

Coningsby Castle.—It was not without emotion that Coningsby beheld for the first time the castle that bore his name. It was visible for several miles before he even entered the park, so proud and prominent was its position, on the richly-wooded steep of a considerable eminence. It was a castellated building, immense and magnificent, in a faulty and incongruous style of architecture, indeed, but compensating in some degree for these deficiencies of external taste and beauty by the splendour and accommodation of its interior, and which a Gothic castle, raised according to the strict rules of art, could scarcely have afforded. The declining sun threw over the pile a rich colour as Coningsby approached it, and lit up with fleeting and fanciful tints the delicate foliage of the rare shrubs and tall thin trees that clothed the acclivity on which it stood.—*Coningsby*.

Ducie Bower.—It was scarcely noon when he reached Ducie Bower. This was a Palladian pavilion, situated in the midst of beautiful gardens, and surrounded by green hills.

The sun shone brightly, the sky was without a cloud; it appeared to him that he had never beheld a more graceful scene.
It was a temple worthy of the divinity it enshrined. A
façade of four Ionic columns fronted an octagon hall,
adorned with statues, which led into a saloon of considerable
size and fine proportion. Ferdinand thought that he had
never in his life entered so brilliant a chamber. The lofty
walls were covered with an Indian paper of vivid fancy, and
adorned with several pictures which his practised eye assured
him were of great merit. The room, without being inconve-
niently crowded, was amply stored with furniture, every
article of which bespoke a refined and luxurious taste : easy
chairs of all descriptions, most inviting couches, cabinets
of choice inlay, and grotesque tables covered with articles
of vertu; all those charming infinite nothings, which a
person of taste might some time back have easily collected
during a long residence on the Continent. A large lamp
of Dresden china was suspended from the painted and
gilded ceiling. The three tall windows opened on the
gardens, and admitted a perfume so rich and various, that
Ferdinand could easily believe the fair mistress, as she
told him, was indeed a lover of flowers. A light bridge in
the distant wood, that bounded the furthest lawn, indicated
that a stream was at hand. What with the beauty of the
chamber, the richness of the exterior scene, and the bright
sun that painted every object with its magical colouring, and
made everything appear even more fair and brilliant, Ferdinand stood for some moments quite entranced. A door
opened, and Mr. Temple came forward and welcomed him
with cordiality.

After they had passed a half-hour in looking at the
pictures and in conversation to which they gave rise, Mr.
Temple, proposing an adjournment to luncheon, conducted
Ferdinand into a dining-room, of which the suitable decora-
tions wonderfully pleased his taste. A subdued tint pervaded
every part of the chamber: the ceiling was painted in grey

tinted frescoes of a classical and festive character, and the side table, which stood in a recess supported by four magnificent columns, was adorned with choice Etruscan vases. The air of repose and stillness which distinguished this apartment was heightened by the vast conservatory into which it led, blazing with light and beauty, groups of exotic trees, plants of radiant tint, the sound of a fountain, and gorgeous forms of tropic birds.—*Henrietta Temple.*

Hainault House.—Hainault House had been raised by a British peer in the days when nobles were fond of building Palladian palaces. It was a chief work of Sir William Chambers, and in its style, its beauty, and almost in its dimensions, was a rival of Stowe or Wanstead. It stood in a deer park, and was surrounded by a royal forest. The family that had raised it wore out in the earlier part of this century. It was supposed that the place must be destroyed and dismantled. It was too vast for a citizen, and the locality was no longer sufficiently refined for a conscript father. In this dilemma Neuchatel stepped in and purchased the whole affair—palace, and park, and deer, and pictures, and halls, and galleries of statue and bust, and furniture, and even wines, and all the farms that remained, and all the seigneurial rights in the royal forest.—*Endymion.*

Hauteville Castle.—The castle, unlike most Yorkshire castles, was a Gothic edifice, ancient, vast, and strong ; but it had received numerous additions in various styles of architecture, which were at the same time great sources of convenience and great violations of taste.—*The Young Duke.*

Hellingsley.—The beautiful light of summer had never shone on a scene and surrounding landscape which recalled happier images of English nature, and better recollections of English manners, than that to which we would now introduce our readers. One of those true old English halls, now unhappily so rare, built in the time of the Tudors, and in its elaborate timber-framing and decorative woodwork indicating, perhaps, the scarcity of brick and stone at the period of its structure, as much as the grotesque genius of its fabricator, rose on a terrace surrounded by ancient and very formal gardens. The hall itself, during many generations, had been vigilantly and tastefully preserved by its proprietors. There was not a point which was not as fresh as if it had been renovated but yesterday. It stood a huge and strange blending of Grecian, Gothic, and Italian architecture, with a wild dash of the fantastic in addition. The lantern watch-towers of a baronial castle were placed in juxtaposition with Doric columns employed for chimneys, while under oriel windows might be observed Italian doorways with Grecian pediments. Beyond the extensive gardens an avenue of Spanish chestnuts at each point of the compass approached the mansion, or led into a small park which was table-land, its limits opening on all sides to beautiful and extensive valleys, sparkling with cultivation, except at one point, where the river Darl formed the boundary of the domain, and then spread in many a winding through the rich country beyond.—*Coningsby.*

Hurstley.—At the foot of the Berkshire downs, and itself on a gentle elevation, there is an old hall with gable-ends and lattice windows, standing in grounds which once were stately, and where there are yet glade-like terraces of yew-trees, which give an air of dignity to a neglected scene. In the front of the hall huge gates of iron, highly wrought, and bearing an ancient date as well as the shield of a noble house, opened on a village green, round which were clustered the cottages of the parish with only one exception, and that was the vicarage. Behind the hall and its enclosure the country was common land, but picturesque. It had once been a beech forest, and though the timber had been greatly cleared, the green land was still occasionally dotted, sometimes with groups and sometimes with single trees, while the juniper, which here abounded and rose to a great height, gave a rich wildness to the scene and sustained its forest character. The house contained an immense hall, which

G

reached the roof, and which would have become a baronial mansion, and a vast staircase in keeping; but the living rooms were moderate, even small in dimensions and not numerous.—*Endymion.*

Marney Abbey.—The building which was still called Marney Abbey, though remote from the site of the ancient monastery, was an extensive structure raised at the latter end of the reign of James I., and in the stately and picturesque style of that age. Placed on a noble elevation in the centre of an extensive and well-wooded park, it presented a front with two projecting wings of equal dimensions with the centre, so that the form of the building was that of a quadrangle, less one of its sides. Its ancient lattices had been removed, and the present windows, though convenient, accorded little with the structure; the old entrance door in the centre of the building, however, still remained, a wondrous specimen of fantastic carving: Ionic columns of black oak, with a profusion of fruits and flowers, and heads of stags, and sylvans. The whole of the building was crowned with a considerable pediment of what seemed at the first glance fanciful open work, but which, examined more nearly, offered in gigantic letters the motto of the house of Marney. The portal opened to a hall, such as is now rarely found; with the dais, the screen, the gallery, and the buttery-hatch all perfect, and all of carved black oak. Modern luxury, and the refined taste of the lady of the late lord, had made Marney Abbey as remarkable for its comfort and pleasantness of accommodation as for its ancient state and splendour. The apartments were in general furnished with all the cheerful ease and brilliancy of the modern mansion of a noble, but the grand gallery of the seventeenth century was still preserved, and was used on great occasions as the chief reception-room. You ascended the principal staircase to reach it through a long corridor. It occupied the whole length of one of the wings; was one hundred feet long, and forty-five feet broad, its walls hung with a collection of choice pictures rich in history; while the Axminster carpets, the cabinets, carved tables, and variety of easy chairs, ingeniously grouped, imparted even to this palatial chamber a lively and habitable air.—*Sybil.*

Marringhurst Rectory.—Marringhurst was only five miles from Cherbury by a cross-road which was scarcely passable for carriages. The rectory house was a substantial, square-built, red brick mansion, shaded by gigantic elms, but .the southern front covered with a famous vine, trained over it with elaborate care, and of which, and his espaliers, the Doctor was very proud. The garden was thickly stocked with choice fruit-trees; there was not the slightest pretence to pleasure grounds; but there was a capital bowling-green, and, above all, a grotto, where the Doctor smoked his evening pipe, and moralised in the midst of his cucumbers and cabbages. On each side extended the meadows of his glebe, where his kine ruminated at will. It was altogether a scene as devoid of the picturesque as any that could well be imagined; flat, but not low, and rich, and green, and still.—*Venetia.*

Montacute Castle.—At the extremity of the town, the ground rises, and on a woody steep, which is in fact the termination of a long range of table-land, may be seen the towers of the outer court of Montacute Castle. The principal building, which is vast and of various ages, from the Plantagenets to the Guelphs, rises on a terrace, from which, on the side opposite to the town, you descend into a well-timbered enclosure, called the Home Park. Further on, the forest again appears; the deer again crouch in their fern, or glance along the vistas; nor does this green domain terminate till it touches the vast and purple moors that divide the kingdoms of Great Britain.—*Tancred.*

Montfort Castle.—Montfort Castle was the stronghold of England against the Scotch invader. It stood on a high and vast table-land, with the town of Montfort on one side at its feet, and on the other a wide-spreading and sylvan domain, herded with deer of various races and terminating in pine forests; beyond them moors and mountains. The donjon-keep, tall and grey, that had arrested the Douglas, still remained intact, and many an ancient battlement; but the long list of the Lords of Montfort had successively added to the great structure according to the genius of the times, so that still with the external appearance generally of a feudal castle, it combined, in its various courts and quadrangles, all the splendour and convenience of a modern palace.—*Endymion.*

Muriel Towers.—Muriel Towers crowned a wooded steep, part of a wild and winding and sylvan valley at the bottom of which rushed a foaming stream. On the other side of the castle the scene, though extensive, was not less striking, and was essentially romantic. A vast park spread in all directions beyond the limit of the eye, and with much variety of character, ornate near the mansion, and choicely timbered; in other parts glens and spreading dells, masses of black pines and savage woods; everywhere, sometimes glittering and sometimes sullen, glimpses of the largest natural lake that inland England boasts, Muriel Mere, and in the extreme distance moors, and the first crest of mountains. The park, too, was full of life, for there were not only herds of red and fallow deer, but, in its more secret haunts, wandered a race of wild cattle, extremely savage, white and dove-coloured, and said to be of the time of the Romans.—*Lothair.*

Pen Bronnock Chase.—It was a pile which the immortal Inigo had raised in sympathy with the taste of a noble employer, who had passed his earliest years in Lombardy. Of stone, and sometimes even of marble, with pediments and balustrades, and ornamental windows, and richly-chased keystones, and flights of steps, and here and there a statue, the structure was quite Palladian, though a little dingy, and, on the whole, very imposing.

There were suites of rooms which had no end, and stair-cases which had no beginning. In this vast pile, nothing was more natural than to lose your way, an agreeable amusement on a rainy morning. There was a collection of pictures, very various, by which phrase we understand not select. Yet they were amusing ; and the Canalettis were unrivalled. There was a regular ball-room, and a theatre ; so resources were at hand. The scenes, though dusty, were numerous ; and the Duke had provided new dresses. The park was not a park ; by which we mean, that it was rather a chase than the highly-finished enclosure which we associate with the first title. In fact, Pen Bronnock Chase was the right name of the settlement ; but some monarch travelling, having been seized with a spasm, recruited his strength under the roof of his loyal subject, then the chief seat of the House of Hauteville, and having in his urgency been obliged to hold a privy council there, the supreme title of palace was assumed by right.

The domain was bounded on one side by the sea ; and here a yacht and some slight craft rode at anchor in a small green bay, and offered an opportunity for the adventurous, and a refuge for the wearied.—*The Young Duke.*

Princedown.—Princedown was situate in a southern county, hardly on a southern coast, for it was ten miles from the sea, though enchanting views of the Channel were frequent and exquisite. It was a palace built in old days upon the downs, but sheltered and screened from every hostile wind. The full warmth of the south fell upon the vast but fantastic pile of the Renaissance style, said to have been built by that gifted but mysterious individual, John of Padua. The gardens were wonderful, terrace upon terrace, and on each terrace a tall fountain. But the most peculiar feature was the park, which was undulating and extensive, but its timber entirely ilex : single trees of an age and size not common in that tree, and groups and clumps of ilex, but always ilex. Beyond the park, and extending far into the horizon, was Princedown forest, the dominion of the red deer.—*Endymion.*

St. Genevieve.—In a valley, not far from the margin of a beautiful river, raised on a lofty and artificial terrace at the base of a range of wooded heights, was a pile of modern building in the finest style of Christian architecture. It was of great extent and richly decorated. Built of a white and glittering stone, it sparkled with its pinnacles in the sunshine as it rose in strong relief against its verdant background. The winding valley, which was studded, but not too closely studded, with clumps of old trees, formed for a great extent on either side of the mansion a grassy demesne, which was called the Lower Park ; but it was a region bearing the name of the Upper Park, that was the peculiar and most picturesque feature of this splendid residence. The wooded heights that formed the valley were not, as they appeared, a range of hills. Their crest was only the abrupt termination of a vast and enclosed table-land, abounding in all the qualities of the ancient chase : turf and trees, a wilderness of under-wood, and a vast spread of gorse and fern. The deer, that abounded, lived here in a world as savage as themselves : trooping down in the evening to the river. Some of them, indeed, were ever in sight of those who were in the valley, and you might often observe various groups clustered on the green heights above the mansion, the effect of which was most inspiriting and graceful. Sometimes in the twilight, a solitary form, magnified by the illusive hour, might be seen standing on the brink of the steep, large and black against the clear sky.—*Coningsby.*

Vauxe.—Vauxe, the seat of the St. Jeromes, was the finest specimen of the old English residence extant. It was the perfection of the style which had gradually arisen after the wars of the Roses had alike destroyed all the castles and the purpose of those stern erections. People said Vauxe looked like a college : the truth is, colleges looked like Vauxe ; for when those fair and civil buildings rose, the wise and liberal spirits who endowed them intended that they should resemble as much as possible the residence of a great noble.

There were two quadrangles at Vauxe of grey stone ;

the outer one of larger dimensions and much covered with ivy; the inner one not so extensive but more ornate, with a lofty tower, a hall, and a chapel. The house was full of galleries, and they were full of portraits. Indeed there was scarcely a chamber in this vast edifice of which the walls were not breathing with English history in this interesting form. Sometimes more ideal art asserted a triumphant claim : transcendental Holy families, seraphic saints, and gorgeous scenes by Tintoret and Paul of Verona.

The furniture of the house seemed never to have been changed. It was very old, somewhat scanty, but very rich ; tapestry and velvet hangings, marvellous cabinets, and crystal girandoles. Here and there a group of ancient plate ; ewers and flagons and tall saltcellars a foot high and richly chiselled ; sometimes a state bed shadowed with a huge pomp of stiff brocade and borne by silver poles.

Vauxe stood in a large park studded with stately trees ; here and there an avenue of Spanish chestnuts or a grove of oaks ; sometimes a gorsy dell and sometimes a great spread of antlered fern, taller than the tallest man.—*Lothair.*

CREDIT.

I see before me the statue of a celebrated minister, who said that confidence was a plant of slow growth. But I believe, however gradual may be the growth of confidence, that of credit requires still more time to arrive at maturity. *Speech at Mansion House, November* 9, 1867.

CREED.

A creed is imagination.—*Contarini Fleming.*

The Athanasian Creed is the most splendid ecclesiastical lyric ever poured forth by the genius of man.—('Nigel Penruddock') *Endymion.*

CRIMEAN WAR.

We may draw at least this conclusion from the war which has broken out. I think what has occurred has shown that the arts of peace, practised by a free people, are not enervating. I think that the deeds which have been referred to, both of the commanders and the common soldiers, have shown that education has not a tendency to diminish, but to refine and raise the standard of the martial character. In these we may proudly recognise the might and prowess of a free and ancient people. These are all circumstances and conditions which are favourable to our confidence in the progress of civilisation and flattering to the consciousness of every Englishman.—*Speech in House of Commons (Vote of Thanks to Allied Armies), December* 15, 1855.

CRITICS.

It is much easier to be critical than to be correct.—*Speech in House of Commons (Address in answer to Her Majesty's Speech), January* 24, 1860.

You know who critics are? The men who have failed in literature and art.—('Mr. Phœbus') *Lothair.*

There are critics, who, abstractedly, do not approve of successful books, particularly if they have failed in the same style.—*Preface to Lothair.*

There is always, both in politics and literature, the race, the Dennises, the Oldmixons, and Curls, who flatter themselves that by systematically libelling some eminent person of their times, they have a chance of descending to posterity.—*Preface to Lothair.*

CYPRUS.

In taking Cyprus—the movement is not Mediterranean; it is Indian. I only hope the House will not misunderstand our motives in occupying Cyprus and in encouraging those intimate relations between ourselves and the government and population of Turkey. They are not movements of war : they are movements of peace and civilisation.—*Speech in House of Commons (Congress Correspondence and Protocols), July* 18, 1878.

There is no doubt that the administration of Cyprus by England will exercise the most beneficial and moral influence upon the contiguous dominions of the Sultan. This was a secondary consideration in inducing us to take the step which we have done. It was as a strong place of arms, for which it is admirably calculated by its geographical position and the variety of its resources, that we fixed on Cyprus, after having examined all the other islands of the Mediterranean.—*Speech at Mansion House, November* 9, 1878.

DACRE (*MAY*).

She was very young ; that is to say, she had, perhaps, added a year or two to sweet seventeen, an addition which, while it does not deprive the sex of the early grace of girlhood, adorns them with that indefinable dignity which is necessary to constitute a perfect woman. She was not tall, but as she moved forward displayed a figure so exquisitely symmetrical that for a moment the Duke forgot to look at her face, and then her head was turned away ; yet he was consoled a moment for his disappointment by watching the movements of a neck so white, and round, and long, and delicate, that it would have become Psyche, and might have inspired Praxiteles. Her face is again turning towards him. It stops too soon ; yet his eye feeds upon the outline of a cheek not too full, yet promising of beauty, like hope of Paradise.

She turns her head, she throws around a glance, and two streams of liquid light pour from her hazel eyes on his. It was a rapid, graceful movement, unstudied as the motion of a fawn, and was in a moment withdrawn, yet was it long enough to stamp upon his memory a memorable countenance. Her face was quite oval, her nose delicately aquiline, and her high pure forehead like a Parian dome. The clear blood coursed under her transparent cheek, and increased the brilliancy of her dazzling eyes. His never left her. There was an expression of decision about her small mouth,

an air of almost mockery in her curling lip, which, though
in themselves wildly fascinating, strangely contrasted with all
the beaming light and beneficent lustre of the upper part of
her countenance.   There was something, too, in the graceful
but rather decided air with which she moved, that seemed
to betoken her self-consciousness of her beauty or her rank ;
perhaps it might be her wit ; for the Duke observed that
while she scarcely smiled, and conversed with lips hardly
parted, her companion, with whom she was evidently intimate, was almost constantly convulsed with laughter, although, as he never spoke, it was clearly not at his own
jokes.—*The Young Duke.*

DANCE.

A waltz of spiriting grace, or a mazy cotillon of jocund
bouquets.—*Endymion.*

DAWN.

Eve has its spell of calmness and consolation, but dawn
brings hope and joy.—*Lothair.*

It was just that single hour of the twenty-four, when
crime ceases, debauchery is exhausted, and even desolation
finds a shelter.—*Sybil.*

DAY.

Twilight makes us pensive : Aurora is the goddess of
activity : despair curses at midnight : hope blesses at noon.
The Young Duke.

DEATH.

The first conviction that there is death in the house is
perhaps the most awful moment of youth.   When we are
young, we think not only ourselves, but that all about us,
are immortal.   Until the arrow has struck a victim round
our own hearth, death is merely an unmeaning word ;
until then, its casual mention has stamped no idea upon our
brain.   There are few, even among those least susceptible
of thought and emotion, in whose hearts and minds the

first death in the family does not act as a powerful revelation of the mysteries of life, and of their own being ; there are few who, after such a catastrophe, do not look upon the world and the world's ways, at least for a time, with changed and tempered feelings. It recalls the past ; it makes us ponder over the future ; and youth, gay and light-hearted youth, is taught, for the first time, to regret and to fear.—
Venetia.

The heavens darken : a new character enters upon the scene.

Ὦ θάνατε, θάνατε, νῦν μ' ἐπισκέψαι μολών.

They say that when great men arise they have a mission to accomplish, and do not disappear until it is fulfilled. Yet this is not always true. After all his deep study and his daring action, Mr. Hampden died on an obscure field, almost before the commencement of that mighty struggle which he seemed born to direct.—*Life of Lord George Bentinck.*

Ah, death ! that is a botherer. What can you make of death ? There are those poor fishermen now ; there will be a white squall some day, and they will go down with those lateen sails of theirs, and be food for the very prey they were going to catch ; and if you continue living here, you may eat one of your neighbours in the shape of a shoal of red mullets, when it is the season. The great secret, we cannot penetrate that with all our philosophy, my dear Herbert. 'All that we know is, nothing can be known.' Barren, barren, barren ! And yet what a grand world it is ! Look at this bay, these blue waters, the mountains, and these chestnuts, devilish fine ! The fact is, truth is veiled, but, like the Shekinah over the tabernacle, the veil is of dazzling light !—('Lord Cadurcis') *Venetia.*

DEBATE.

A dull debate, when the facts are only a refutation of the Blue-books, and the fancy an ingenious appeal to the recrimination of Hansard.—*Sybil.*

Wishy is down, and Washy is up.—('Spencer May')
Sybil.

The debate was opened by a young man with a singularly sunny face and a voice of music. His statement was
clear and calm. Though nothing could be more uncompromising than his opinions, it seemed that nothing could
be fairer than his facts. . . . The debate was concluded
after another hour by Hortensius, and Endymion was struck
by the contrast between his first and second manner. Safe
from reply, and reckless in his security, it is not easy to
describe the audacity of his retorts, or the tumult of his
eloquence. Rapid, sarcastic, humorous, picturesque, impassioned, he seemed to carry everything before him, and to
resemble his former self in nothing but the music of his
voice, which lent melody to scorn and sometimes reached
the depth of pathos.—*Endymion.*

DEBATERS.

The most commanding speaker that I ever listened to is,
I think, Sir Francis Burdett. I never heard him in the
House, but at an election. He was full of music, grace,
and dignity, even amid all the vulgar tumult ; and, unlike
all mob orators, raised the taste of the populace to him,
instead of lowering his own to theirs. His colleague, Mr.
Hobhouse, seemed to me ill qualified for a demagogue,
though he spoke with power. He is rather too elaborate,
and a little heavy, but fluent, and never weak. His thoughtful and highly-cultivated mind maintains him under all circumstances ; and his breeding never deserts him. Sound
sense comes recommended from his lips by the language of
a scholar and the urbanity of a gentleman.

Mr. Brougham, at present, reigns paramount in the
House of Commons. I think the lawyer has spoiled the
statesman. He is said to have great powers of sarcasm.
From what I have observed there, I should think very little
ones would be quite sufficient. Many a sneer withers in

.those walls, which would scarcely, I think, blight a currant-bush out of them ; and I have seen the House convulsed with raillery which, in other society, would infallibly settle the railler to be a bore beyond all tolerance. Even an idiot can raise a smile. They are so good-natured, or find it so dull. Mr. Canning's badinage was the most successful, though I confess I have listened to few things more calcu-lated to make a man gloomy. But the House always ran riot, taking everything for granted, and cracked their universal sides before he opened his mouth. The fault of Mr. Brougham is, that he holds no intellect at present in great dread, and, consequently, allows himself on all occasions to run wild. Few men hazard more unphiloso-phical observations ; but he is safe, because there is no one to notice them. On all great occasions, Mr. Brougham has come up to the mark ; an infallible test of a man of genius.

I hear that Mr. Macaulay is to be returned. If he speaks half as well as he writes, the House will be in fashion again. I fear that he is one of those who, like the individual whom he has most studied, will 'give up to party what was meant for mankind.'

At any rate, he must get rid of his rabidity. He writes now on all subjects as if he certainly intended to be a renegade, and was determined to make the contrast com-plete.

Mr. Peel is the model of a minister, and improves as a speaker ; though, like most of the rest, he is fluent without the least style. He should not get so often in a passion either, or, if he do, should not get out of one so easily. His sweet apologies are cloying. His candour ; he will do well to get rid of that. He can make a present of it to Mr. Huskisson, who is a memorable instance of the value of knowledge, which maintains a man under all circum-stances and all disadvantages, and will.

In the Lords, I admire the Duke. The readiness with

which he has adopted the air of a debater, shows the man
of genius.   There is a gruff, husky sort of a downright
Montaignish naïveté about him, which is quaint, unusual,
and tells.   You plainly perceive that he is determined to
be a civilian ; and he is as offended if you drop a hint that
he occasionally wears a uniform, as a servant on a holiday if
you mention the word *livery*.

Lord Grey speaks with feeling, and is better to hear than
to read, though ever strong and impressive.   Lord Holland's
speeches are like a *rifaccimento* of all the suppressed passages in Clarendon, and the notes in the new edition of
Bishop Burnet's Memoirs : but taste throws a delicate hue
over the curious medley, and the candour of a philosophic
mind shows that in the library at Holland House he can
sometimes cease to be a partisan.

One thing is clear, that a man may speak very well in
the House of Commons, and fail very completely in the
House of Lords.   There are two distinct styles requisite :
I intend, in the course of my career, if I have time, to give
a specimen of both.   In the Lower House 'Don Juan' may
perhaps be our model ; in the Upper House, 'Paradise Lost.'
The Young Duke.

DEBT.

To be harassed about money is one of the most disagreeable incidents of life.   It ruffles the temper, lowers the
spirits, disturbs the rest, and finally breaks up the health.—
('Lord Marney') *Sybil.*

Debt is the prolific mother of folly and crime ; it taints
the course of life in all its dreams.   Hence so many unhappy marriages, so many prostituted pens, and venal poli-
ticians !   It hath a small beginning, but a giant's growth
and strength.   When we make the monster we make our
master, who haunts us at all hours, and shakes his whip of
scorpions for ever in our sight.   The slave hath no overseer
so severe.   Faustus, when he signed the bond with blood,

did not secure a doom more terrific. But when we are young we must enjoy ourselves.—*Henrietta Temple.*

DELICACY.

In my opinion there is no quality in business more dangerous than delicacy. In my limited experience, I can certainly say that whenever delicacy has been admitted in the transaction of business, I have always considerably suffered. Now I do not think a minister ought to be allowed to shrink from the performance of a public duty by telling us he considered it indelicate.—*Speech in House of Commons (Official Salaries), April* 12, 1850.

DEMOCRACY.

Popular privileges are consistent with a state of society in which there is great inequality of position. Democratic rights, on the contrary, demand that there should be equality of condition as the fundamental basis of the society they regulate.—*Speech in House of Commons (Representation of the People Bill), March* 18, 1867.

If you establish a democracy, you must in due time reap the fruits of a democracy. You will in due season have great impatience of the public burdens, combined in due season with great increase of the public expenditure. You will in due season have wars entered into from passion and not from reason ; and you will in due season submit to peace ignominiously sought and ignominiously obtained, which will diminish your authority and perhaps endanger your independence. You will in due season find your property is less valuable, and your freedom less complete.— *Speech in House of Commons (Representation of the People Bill), March* 31, 1859.

There is more true democracy in the Roman Catholic Church than in all the secret societies of Europe.—('Waldershare') *Endymion.*

DEPARTURES.

Departures should be sudden.—('Sidonia') *Coningsby.*

DEPUTATIONS.

And now for these deputations; of all things in the world I dislike a deputation. I do not care how much I labour in the closet or the House; that's real work; the machine is advanced. But receiving a deputation is like sham marching: an immense dust and no progress. To listen to their views! As if I did not know what their views were before they stated them! And to put on a countenance of respectful candour while they are developing their exploded or their impracticable systems! Were it not that, at a practised crisis, I permit them to see conviction slowly stealing over my conscience, I believe the fellows would never stop.—('A Gentleman in Downing Street') *Sybil.*

DERBY (EARL OF).

I do not know that there is anything that excites enthusiasm in him except when he contemplates the surrender of some national policy.—*Speech in House of Lords, March 5, 1881.*

DERBY RACE (THE).

It is the blue ribbon of the turf.—*Life of Lord George Bentinck.*

DESPAIR.

Despair is the conclusion of fools.—('Alroy') *Sybil.*

DESPERATION.

Desperation is sometimes as powerful an inspirer as genius.—*Endymion.*

DESTINY.

Destiny is our will, and our will is our nature.—*Contarini Fleming.*

Destiny bears us to our lot, and destiny is perhaps our own will. — *Contarini Fleming.*

Tastes differ about destinies, as about manners.—(' Lady Montfort ') *Endymion.*

Destiny for its fulfilment ordains action.—(' Prince Florestan ') *Endymion.*

If we cannot shape our destiny, there is no such thing as witchcraft.—(' Lady Montfort ') *Endymion.*

DE TROP.

Endymion felt all that embarrassment mingled with a certain portion of self-contempt, which attends the conviction that we are what is delicately called *de trop.—Endymion.*

DEVELOPMENT.

Development is the discovery of utility.—*Popanilla.*

DIGESTION.

A good eater must be a good man ; for a good eater must have a good digestion, and a good digestion depends upon a good conscience.— *The Young Duke.*

DINNER.

Turtle makes all men equal.—(' Adriana Neuchatel ') *Endymion.*

Tradesmen nowadays console themselves for not getting their bills paid by asking their customers to dinner.— *The Young Duke.*

O London dinners ! Empty artificial nothings ! and that beings can be found, and those too the flower of the land, who, day after day, can act the same part in the same dull, dreamy farce !— *Vivian Grey.*

The glare, and heat, and noise, this congeries of individuals without sympathy, and dishes without flavour ; this is society.—*The Young Duke.*

Two things which are necessary to a perfect dinner are

noiseless attendants and a precision in serving the various dishes of each course.—*Tancred.*

A dinner of wits is proverbially a palace of silence.—*Endymion.*

At Lord St. Jerome's.—It was a lively dinner. Lord St. Jerome loved conversation, though he never conversed. 'There must be an audience,' he would say, 'and I am the audience.' The partner of his life, whom he never ceased admiring, had originally fascinated him by her conversational talents ; and even if nature had not impelled her, Lady St. Jerome was too wise a woman to relinquish the spell. The Monsignore could always, when necessary, sparkle with anecdote or blaze with repartee ; and all the chaplains, who abounded in this house, were men of bright abilities, not merely men of reading but of the world, learned in the world's ways, and trained to govern mankind by the versatility of their sympathies. It was a dinner where there could not be two conversations going on, and where even the silent take their share in the talk by their sympathy.—*Lothair.*

At Mr. Pinto's.—His (St. Aldegonde's) keen though listless glance revealed to him that he was, as he described it to Hugo Bohun, in a social jungle, in which there was a great herd of animals that he particularly disliked, namely what he entitled 'swells.'—*Lothair.*

This was Mr. Brancepeth, celebrated for his dinners and still more for his guests. Mr. Brancepeth was a grave young man. It was supposed that he was always meditating over the arrangement of his menus, or the skilful means by which he could assemble together the right persons to partake of them. Mr. Brancepeth had attained the highest celebrity in his peculiar career. To dine with Mr. Brancepeth was a social incident that was mentioned. Royalty had consecrated his banquets, and a youth of note was scarcely a graduate of society who had not been his guest. There was one person, however, who, in this respect, had not taken his degree, and, as always happens under such circumstances, he was the individual on whom Mr. Brancepeth was most desirous to confer it ; and this was St. Aldegonde. In vain Mr. Brancepeth had approached him with vast cards of invitation to hecatombs, and with insinuating little notes to dinners sans façon ; proposals which the presence of princes might almost construe into a command, or the presence of some one even more attractive than princes must invest with irresistible charm. It was all in vain. 'Not that I dislike Brancepeth,' said St. Aldegonde ; 'I rather like him : I like a man who can do only one thing, but does that well. But then I hate dinners.'— *Lothair.*

Lord Monmouth's dinners at Paris were celebrated. It was generally agreed that they had no rivals ; yet there were others who had as skilful cooks, others who, for such a purpose, were equally profuse in their expenditure. What, then, was the secret spell of his success ? The simplest in the world, though no one seemed aware of it. His Lordship's plates were always hot : whereas at Paris, in the best appointed houses, and at dinners which, for costly materials and admirable art in their preparation, cannot be surpassed, the effect is always considerably lessened, and by a mode the most mortifying : by the mere circumstance that every one at a French dinner is served on a cold plate. The reason of a custom, or rather a necessity, which one would think a nation so celebrated for their gastronomical taste would recoil from, is really, it is believed, that the ordinary French porcelain is so very inferior that it cannot endure the preparatory heat for dinner. The common white pottery, for example, which is in general use, and always found at the cafés, will not bear vicinage to a brisk kitchen fire for half an hour. Now, if we only had that treaty of commerce with France which has been so often on the point of completion, the fabrics of our unrivalled potteries, in exchange for their capital wines, would be found throughout France. The dinners of both nations would be improved :

the English would gain a delightful beverage, and the French, for the first time in their lives, would dine off hot plates.   An unanswerable instance of the advantages of commercial reciprocity !—*Coningsby.*

Dinner at Mr. Vigo's.—The dinner was a banquet,—a choice bouquet before every guest, turtle and venison and piles of whitebait, and pineapples of prodigious size, and bunches of grapes that had gained prizes.   The champagne seemed to flow in fountains, and was only interrupted that the guest might quaff Burgundy or taste Tokay.   But what was more delightful than all was the enjoyment of all present, and especially of the host.   That is a rare sight.   Banquets are not rare, nor choice guests, nor gracious hosts ; but when do we ever see a person enjoy anything ?   But these gay children of art and whim, and successful labour and happy speculation, some of them very rich, and some without a sou, seemed only to think of the festive hour and all its joys. Neither wealth nor poverty brought them cares.   Every face sparkled, every word seemed witty, and every sound seemed sweet.   A band played upon the lawn during the dinner, and were succeeded, when the dessert commenced, by strange choruses from singers of some foreign land, who for the first time aired their picturesque costumes on the banks of the Thames.—*Endymion.*

The banquet of the Neuchatels to the Premier, and some of the principal ambassadors and their wives, and to those of the Premier's colleagues who were fashionable enough to be asked, and to some of the Dukes and Duchesses and other ethereal beings who supported the ministry, was the first event of the season.   The table blazed with rare flowers and rarer porcelain and precious candelabra of sculptured beauty glittering with light ; the gold plate was less remarkable than the delicate ware that had been alike moulded and adorned for a Du Barri or a Marie Antoinette, and which now found a permanent and peaceful home in the proverbial land of purity and order ; and amid

the stars and ribbons not the least remarkable feature of the
whole was Mr. Neuchatel himself, seated at the centre of
his table, alike free from ostentation or over-deference,
talking to the great ladies on each side of him as if he had
nothing to do in life but whisper in gentle ears, and partak-
ing of his own dainties as if he were eating bread and cheese
at a country inn.--*Endymion.*

A little dinner not more than the Muses, with all the
guests clever, and some pretty, offers human life and
human nature under very favourable circumstances.—
Coningsby.

Lady Fitz-pompey determined that the young Duke
should make his début at once, and at her house. Although
it was yet January, she did not despair of collecting a select
band of guests, Brahmins of the highest caste. Some choice
spirits were in office, like her lord, and therefore in town ;
others were only passing through ; but no one caught a
flying-fish with more dexterity than the Countess. The
notice was short, the whole was unstudied. It was a
felicitous impromptu, and twenty guests were assembled,
who were the Corinthian capitals of the Temple of Fashion.

There was the Premier, who was invited, not because he
was a Minister, but because he was a hero. There was
another Duke not less celebrated, whose palace was a
breathing shrine which sent forth the oracles of mode.
True, he had ceased to be a young Duke ; but he might be
consoled for the vanished lustre of youth by the recollection
that he had enjoyed it, and by the present inspiration of an
accomplished manhood. There were the Prince and the
Princess Protocoli : his Highness a first-rate diplomatist,
unrivalled for his management of an opera ; and his consort, with a countenance like Cleopatra and a tiara like a
constellation, famed alike for her shawls and her snuff.
There were Lord and Lady Bloomerly, who were the best
friends on earth : my Lord a sportsman, but soft withal, his
talk the Jockey Club, filtered through White's ; my Lady a

little blue, and very beautiful. Their daughter, Lady Char-
lotte, rose by her mother's side like a tall bud by a full-
blown flower. There were the Viscountess Blaze, a peeress
in her own right, and her daughter, Miss Blaze Dashaway,
who, besides the glory of the future coronet, moved in all
the confidence of independent thousands. There was the
Marquess of Macaroni, who was at the same time a general,
an ambassador, and a dandy ; and who, if he had liked,
could have worn twelve orders ; but this day, being modest,
only wore six. There, too, was the Marchioness, with a
stomacher stiff with brilliants extracted from the snuff-boxes
presented to her husband at a Congress.

There were Lord Sunium, who was not only a peer but a
poet ; and his lady, a Greek, who looked just finished by
Phidias. There, too, was Pococurante, the epicurean and
triple millionnaire, who in a political country dared to despise
politics, in the most aristocratic of kingdoms had refused
nobility, and in a land which showers all its honours upon
its cultivators invested his whole fortune in the funds. He
lived in a retreat like the villa of Hadrian, and maintained
himself in an elevated position chiefly by his wit and a
little by his wealth. There, too, were his noble wife,
thoroughbred to her fingers' tips, and beaming like the
evening star ; and his son, who was an M.P., and thought
his father a fool. In short, our party was no common
party, but a band who formed the very core of civilisation ;
a high court of last appeal, whose word was a fiat, whose
sign was a hint, whose stare was death, and sneer——
damnation !—*The Young Duke.*

The unfortunate, who had no contest, had to dine with
another principal citizen, with real turtle soup and gigantic
turbots, entrees in the shape of volcanic curries, and rigid
venison sent as a compliment by a neighbouring peer.—
Endymion.

The dinner was refined, for Mr. Bertie Tremaine combined the sybarite with the utilitarian sage, and it secretly delighted him to astonish or embarrass an austere brother republican by the splendour of his family plate or the polished appointments of his household.—*Endymion.*

A Sporting Dinner.—It is doubtful whether it ever occurs to anyone present, that there is any other existing combination of atoms than odds and handicaps.—*Endymion.*

A Fish Dinner.—Tancred was going to give them a fish dinner! A what? A sort of banquet which might have served for the marriage feast of Neptune and Amphitrite, and be commemorated by a constellation ; and which ought to have been administered by the Nereids and the Naiads ; terrines of turtle, pools of water souchee, flounders of every hue, and eels in every shape, cutlets of salmon, salmis of carp, ortolans represented by whitebait, and huge roasts carved out of the sturgeon. The appetite is distracted by the variety of objects, and tantalised by the restlessness of perpetual solicitation ; not a moment of repose, no pause for enjoyment ; eventually, a feeling of satiety without satisfaction, and of repletion without sustenance ; till, at night, gradually recovering from the whirl of the anomalous repast, famished yet incapable of flavour, the tortured memory can only recall with an effort, that it has dined off pink champagne and brown bread and butter !—*Tancred.*

A Parliamentary Dinner.—I think a course of Parliamentary dinners would produce a good effect. It gives a tone to a political party. The science of political gastronomy has never been sufficiently studied.—*Vivian Grey.*

A Dinner in Coaching Days.—' The coach stops here half an hour, gentlemen : dinner quite ready ! '

'Tis a delightful sound. And what a dinner ! What a profusion of substantial delicacies ! What mighty and iris-tinted rounds of beef ! What vast and marble-veined ribs ! What gelatinous veal pies ! What colossal hams ! Those are evidently prize cheeses ! And how invigorating is the

perfume of those various and variegated pickles! Then
the bustle emulating the plenty; the ringing of bells, the
clash of thoroughfare, the summoning of ubiquitous waiters,
and the all-pervading feeling of omnipotence, from the
guests, who order what they please, to the landlord, who
can produce and execute everything they can desire. 'Tis
a wondrous sight. Why should a man go and see the
pyramids and cross the desert, when he has not beheld
York Minster or travelled on the Road?—*Henrietta
Temple.*

An Old-fashioned Dinner.—Simple as was the usual diet
at Cherbury, the cook was permitted on Sunday full play
to her art, which, in the eighteenth century, indulged
in the production of dishes more numerous and substantial
than our refined tastes could at present tolerate. The
Doctor appreciated a good dinner, and his countenance
glistened with approbation as he surveyed the ample tureen
of potage royal, with a boned duck swimming in its centre.
Before him still scowled in death the grim countenance of a
huge roast pike, flanked on one side by a leg of mutton
à-la-daube, and on the other by the tempting delicacies of
bombarded veal. To these succeeded that masterpiece of
culinary art, a grand battalia pie, in which the bodies of
chickens, pigeons, and rabbits were embalmed in spices,
cocks' combs, and savoury balls, and well bedewed with one
of those rich sauces of claret, anchovy, and sweet herbs, in
which our great-grandfathers delighted, and which was
technically termed a Lear. But the grand essay of skill was
the cover of this pasty, whereon the curious cook had contrived to represent all the once-living forms that were now
entombed in that gorgeous sepulchre. A Florentine tourte,
or tansy, an old English custard, a more refined blamango,
and a riband jelly of many colours, offered a pleasant relief
after these vaster inventions, and the repast closed with a
dish of oyster loaves and a pompetone of larks.—*Venetia.*

After Dinner.—The entrance of the gentlemen produced

the same effect on the saloon as sunrise on the world, universal animation, a general though gentle stir.—*Coningsby.*

A very great personage in a foreign but not remote country once mentioned to the writer of these pages that he ascribed the superiority of the English in political life, in their conduct of public business, and practical views of affairs to that little half-hour that separates, after dinner, the dark from the fair sex.—*Coningsby.*

DIPLOMACY.

All diplomacy since the Treaty of Utrecht seems to me to be fiddle-faddle, and the country rewarded the great man who made that treaty by an attainder.—('Waldershare') *Endymion.*

Diplomacy is hospitable.—*Endymion.*

DIPLOMATISTS.

I always look upon diplomatists as the Hebrews of politics.—('Sidonia') *Coningsby.*

DISSOLUTION.

Our opponents, indeed, have settled everything. They have exhausted all the arts of unanimous audacity. But I think I have read somewhere that it is the custom of undisciplined hosts on the eve of a battle to anticipate and celebrate their triumph by horrid sounds and hideous yells, the sounding of cymbals, the beating of drums, the shrieks and springs of barbaric hordes. But it is sometimes found that the victory is not to them, but to those who are calm and collected ; the victory is to those who have arms of precision, though they made no noise ; to those who have the breech-loaders, the rocket brigade, and the Armstrong artillery. The fight will soon commence.—*Speech at Mansion House, November* 9, 1868.

DIVINITY.

Human wit ought to be exhausted before we presume to invoke Divine interposition.—('Eva') *Tancred.*

The Divine majesty has never thought fit to communicate except with human beings of the very highest powers.—*Tancred.*

There is but one God—is it Allah or Jehovah? The palm-tree is sometimes called a date-tree, but there is only one tree.—('Amalek') *Tancred.*

DIVORCE.

Lady Gaverslock was pure as snow; but her mother having been divorced, she ever fancied she was paying a kind of homage to her parent by visiting those who might some day be in the same predicament.—*Coningsby.*

DON QUIXOTE.

'There,' said Herbert, as he closed the book. 'In my opinion, Don Quixote was the best man that ever lived.'

'But he did not ever live,' said Lady Annabel, smiling.

'He lives to us,' said Herbert. 'He is the same to this age as if he had absolutely wandered over the plains of Castile and watched in the Sierra Morena. We cannot, indeed, find his tomb; but he has left us his great example. In his hero, Cervantes has given us the picture of a great and benevolent philosopher, and in his Sancho, a complete personification of the world, selfish and cunning, and yet overawed by the genius that he cannot comprehend: alive to all the material interests of existence, yet sighing after the ideal; securing his four young foals of the she-ass, yet indulging in dreams of empire.'

'But what do you think of he assault on the windmills, Marmion?' said Lady Annabel.

'In the outset of his adventures, as in the outset of our lives, he was misled by his enthusiasm,' replied Herbert, 'without which, after all, we can do nothing. But the result is, Don Quixote was a redresser of wrongs, and therefore the world esteemed him mad.'—*Venetia.*

DOWNING STREET.

Happy spot, where they draw up constitutions for Syria and treaties for China with the same self-complacency and the same success.—*Tancred.*

DRESS.

You must dress according to your age, your pursuits, your object in life. You must dress in some cases according to your set. In youth a little fancy is rather expected, but if political life be your object, it should be avoided, at least after one-and-twenty. What all men should avoid is the shabby genteel. No man gets over it. You had better be in rags.—('Vigo') *Endymion.*

The sisters were in demi-toilette, which seemed artless, though in fact it was profoundly devised. Sylvia was the only person who really understood the meaning of 'simplex munditiis,' and this was one of the secrets of her success.—*Endymion.*

DUEL.

A political duel, in which recourse was had to the secure arbitrament of blank cartridges.—*Maiden Speech in House of Commons (Irish Election Petition), December* 7, 1837.

DUKE AND DUCHESS.

The noble proprietor of this demesne had many of the virtues of his class ; a few of their failings. He had that public spirit which became his station. He was not one of those who avoided the exertions and the sacrifices which should be inseparable from high position, by the hollow pretext of a taste for privacy, and a devotion to domestic joys He was munificent, tender, and bounteous to the poor, and loved a flowing hospitality. A keen sportsman, he was not untinctured by letters, and had indeed a cultivated taste for the fine arts. Though an ardent politician, he was tolerant to adverse opinions, and full of amenity to his opponents.

A firm supporter of the corn-laws, he never refused a lease. Notwithstanding there ran through his whole demeanour and the habit of his mind, a vein of native simplicity that was full of charm, his manner was finished. He never offended anyone's self-love. His good breeding, indeed, sprang from the only source of gentle manners, a kind heart. To have pained others would have pained himself. Perhaps, too, this noble sympathy may have been in some degree prompted by the ancient blood in his veins, an accident of lineage rather rare with the English nobility. One could hardly praise him for the strong affections that bound him to his hearth, for fortune had given him the most pleasing family in the world ; but, above all, a peerless wife.

The Duchess was one of those women who are the delight of existence. She was sprung from a house not inferior to that with which she had blended, and was gifted with that rare beauty which time ever spares, so that she seemed now only the elder sister of her own beautiful daughters. She, too, was distinguished by that perfect good breeding which is the result of nature and not of education : for it may be found in a cottage, and may be missed in a palace. 'Tis a genial regard for the feelings of others that springs from an absence of selfishness. The Duchess, indeed, was in every sense a fine lady ; her manners were refined and full of dignity ; but nothing in the world could have induced her to appear bored when another was addressing or attempting to amuse her. She was not one of those vulgar fine ladies who meet you one day with a vacant stare, as if unconscious of your existence, and address you on another in a tone of impertinent familiarity. Her temper, perhaps, was somewhat quick, which made this consideration for the feelings of others still more admirable, for it was the result of a strict moral discipline acting on a good heart. Although the best of wives and mothers, she had some charity for her neighbours. Needing herself no indulgence, she could be indulgent ; and would by no means favour that strait-laced morality that would constrain the innocent play of the social body. She was accomplished, well read, and had a lively fancy. Add to this that sunbeam of a happy home, a gay and cheerful spirit in its mistress, and one might form some faint idea of this gracious personage.

The Duke had a good heart, and not a bad head. If he had not made in his youth so many Latin and English verses, he might have acquired considerable information, for he had a natural love of letters, though his pack were the pride of England, his barrel seldom missed, and his fortune on the turf, where he never betted, was a proverb. He was good, and he wished to do good ; but his views were confused from want of knowledge, and his conduct often inconsistent because a sense of duty made him immediately active ; and he often acquired in the consequent experience a conviction exactly contrary to that which had prompted his activity.—*Coningsby.*

DUKE OF ST. JAMES.

His Grace moved towards them, tall and elegant in figure, and with that air of affable dignity which becomes a noble, and which adorns a court ; none of that affected indifference which seems to imply that nothing can compensate for the exertion of moving, and 'which makes the dandy, while it mars the man.' His large and somewhat sleepy grey eye, his clear complexion, his small mouth, his aquiline nose, his transparent forehead, his rich brown hair, and the delicacy of his extremities, presented, when combined, a very excellent specimen of that style of beauty for which the nobility of England are remarkable. Gentle, for he felt the importance of the tribunal, never loud, ready, yet a little reserved, he neither courted nor shunned examination. His finished manner, his experience of society, his pretensions to taste, the gaiety of his temper, and the liveliness of his imagination, gradually developed themselves with the developing hours.—*The Young Duke.*

DYNASTIES.

Dynasties are unpopular, especially new ones ; the present age is monarchical, but not dynastic.—('Bertie Tremaine') *Endymion.*

EAST.

The East is a career.—('Coningsby') *Tancred.*

EAST INDIA COMPANY.

The East India Company has fallen very much like that great Italian Republic which I have always thought it rivalled and resembled. It has fallen in possession of a gallant army, a powerful fleet, and a considerable territory. It has fallen with all the semblance of authority, and it has met its end in the august fulfilment of its duties. Like Venice, the East India Company has left a legacy of glory to mankind, and in treating of a form of government which has become extinct I hope the House will allow me to express my own feelings and to speak of that Company with that respect which I think every Englishman will extend to its memory.—*Speech in House of Commons (Government of India [No. 2] Bill), March 26, 1858.*

ECONOMY.

Economy does not consist in the reckless reduction of estimates. On the contrary such a course almost necessarily tends to increased expenditure. There can be no economy where there is no efficiency.—*Letter to Constituents, October 3, 1868.*

EDUCATION.

The essence of education is the education of the body. Beauty and health are the chief sources of happiness.—('Mr. Phœbus') *Lothair.*

Those costly ceremonies which, under the name of Eton and Christchurch, in his time fascinated and dazzled mankind.—*Endymion.*

I have found life very gloomy, but I think it arises from our faulty education : we are taught words, not ideas.—*Contarini Fleming.*

Wherever was found what was called a paternal government, was found a State education.   It had been discovered that the best way to insure implicit obedience was to commence tyranny in the nursery.—*Speech in House of Commons (Minister of Education), June* 15, 1874.

Upon the education of the people of this country the fate of this country depends.   There is no period in the history of the world in which I believe it has been more important that the disposition and mind of the people should be considered by the State than it is at present.—*Speech in House of Commons (Minister of Education), June* 15, 1874.

Although it is humiliating to confess, yet I do confess, that cleanliness and order are not matters of instinct ; they are matters of education, and like most great things—mathematics and classics—you must cultivate a taste for them.— *Speech at Aylesbury (Royal and Central Bucks Agricultural Association), September* 21, 1865.

EGYPTIAN ORNAMENT.

There is a charm about Cairo, and it is this, that it is a capital in a desert.   In one moment you are in the stream of existence, and in another in boundless solitude, or, which is still more awful, the silence of tombs.   I speak of the sepulchres of the Mamlouk sultans without the city.   They form what may indeed be styled a City of the Dead, an immense Necropolis, full of exquisite buildings, domes covered with fretwork, and minarets carved and moulded with rich and elegant fancy.   To me they proved much more interesting than the far-famed pyramids, although their cones in a distance are indeed sublime, their grey cones soaring in the light blue sky.

The genius that has raised the tombs of the sultans may also be traced in many of the mosques of the city, splendid specimens of Saracenic architecture.   In gazing upon these brilliant creations, and also upon those of ancient Egypt, I have often been struck by the felicitous system which they display, of ever forming the external ornaments by inscriptions.   How far excelling the Grecian and Gothic method ! Instead of a cornice of flowers, or an entablature of unmeaning fancy, how superior to be reminded of the power of the Creator, or the necessity of government, the deeds of conquerors, or the discoveries of arts !—*Contarini Fleming.*

ELECTION.

We have had a riot, a little riot, just to show that we are freemen.   We have had, as we had in 1832, violent opinions expressed—but in 1832 they were expressed by men of mark.   By whom are they expressed now ?   By the nincompoops of politics—by men more absurd than Hudibras.— *Speech at Conservative Banquet, Edinburgh, October* 29, 1867.

ELOQUENCE.

Knowledge is the foundation of eloquence.—*Endymion.*

EMIGRATION.

When I observe year after year the vast emigration from Ireland, I feel that it is impossible to conceal the fact that we are experiencing a great social and political calamity.   I acknowledge that under some conditions, and even under general conditions, emigration is the safety-valve of a people. But there is a difference between blood-letting and hæmorrhage.—*Election Speech on acceptance of office of Chancellor of Exchequer, July* 13, 1866.

EMPIRE.

It is not on our fleets and armies, however necessary they may be for the maintenance of our imperial strength, that I alone or mainly depend in that enterprise on which this country is about to enter.   It is on what I most highly value—the consciousness that in the Eastern nations there is a confidence in this country, and that while they know we can enforce our policy, at the same time they know that our Empire is an Empire of liberty, of truth, and of justice. *Speech in House of Commons (Congress Correspondence and Protocols), July* 18, 1878.

This Empire was formed by the enterprise and energy of our ancestors, and it is one of remarkable character. I know no example of it either in ancient or modern history. No Cæsar or Charlemagne ever presided over a dominion so peculiar. Its flag floats on many waters : it has provinces in every zone : they are inhabited by persons of different races, with different religions, different laws, manners, customs. Some of them are bound to us by the tie of liberty, fully conscious that without their connection with the metropolis they would have no security for public freedom and self-government. Others united to us by faith and blood are influenced by maternal as well as moral considerations. There are millions who are bound to us by military sway, and they bow to that sway because they know that they are indebted to it for order and justice. But all these communities agree in recognising the commanding spirit of these Islands that has formed and fashioned in such a manner so great a portion of the globe. That Empire is no mean heritage, but it is not a heritage that can only be enjoyed, it must be maintained ; and it can only be maintained by discipline, by patience, by determination, and by a reverence for public law and respect for national rights.— *Speech in House of Commons (Message from the Queen, Army Reserve Forces), April* 8, 1878.

EMS.

The situation of Ems is delightful. The mountains which form the valley are not, as in Switzerland, so elevated that they confine the air or seem to impede the facility of breathing. In their fantastic forms the picturesque is not lost in the monotonous, and in the rich covering of their various woods the admiring eye finds at the same time beauty and repose. Opposite the ancient palace, on the banks of the Lahn, are the gardens. In these, in a pavilion, a band of musicians seldom cease from enchanting the visitors by their execution of the most favourite speci-mens of German and Italian music. Numberless acacia arbours and retired sylvan seats are here to be found, where the student or the contemplative may seek refuge from the noise of his more gay companions, and the tedium of eternal conversation. In these gardens, also, are the billiard-room, and another saloon, in which each night meet not merely those who are interested in the mysteries of rouge-et-noir, and the chances of roulette, but, in general, the whole of the company, male and female, who are fre-quenting the baths. In quitting the gardens for a moment, we must not omit mentioning the interesting booth of our friend the restaurateur, where coffee, clear and hot, and ex-quisite confectionery, are never wanting. Nor should we forget the glittering pennons of the gay boats which glide along the Lahn; nor the handsome donkeys, who, with their white saddles and red bridles, seem not unworthy of the princesses whom they sometimes bear. The gardens, with an alley of limetrees, which aré farther on, near the banks of the river, afford easy promenades to the sick and debili-tated; but the more robust and active need not fear mono-tony in the valley of the Lahn. If they sigh for the cham-paign country, they can climb the wild passes of the encircling mountains, and from their tops enjoy the most magnificent views of the Rhineland. There they may gaze on that mighty river, flowing through the prolific plain which at the same time it nourishes and adorns, bounded on each side by mountains of every form, clothed with wood or crowned with castles. Or, if they fear the fatigues of the ascent, they may wander farther up the valley, and in the wild dells, romantic forests, and grey ruins of Stein and Nassau, conjure up the old times of feudal tyranny when the forest was the only free land, and he who outraged the laws the only one who did not suffer from their authority.

Such is a slight description of Ems, a place almost of unique character; for it is a watering-place with every con-venience, luxury, and accommodation; and yet without shops, streets, or houses.—*Vivian Grey.*

ENDOWMENT.

I have observed that it is a characteristic, a happy characteristic, of the age in which we live, men become their own executors, and I should be delighted to hear of some magnificent endowment, which would place our uni-versity in the position which it deserves.—*Speech at Glasgow (Presentation of Freedom of City), November* 20, 1872.

ENDYMION AND MYRA.

They were twins; children of most singular beauty. They resembled each other, and had the same brilliant com-plexions, rich chestnut hair, delicately arched brows, and dark blue eyes. The expression of their countenances was haughty, disdainful, and supercilious. Their beautiful features seemed quite unimpassioned, and they moved as if they expected everything to yield to them.

ENDYMION.

He was gentle and docile; but he did not acquire knowledge with facility, and was remarkably deficient in that previous information on which his father counted.

Three years later.—Though apparently so uneventful, the period had not been unimportant in the formation, doubtless yet partial, of his character. And all its influences had been beneficial to him. The crust of pride and selfishness with which large prosperity and illimitable indulgence had en-cased a kind, and far from presumptuous, disposition had been removed; the domestic sentiments in their sweetness and purity had been developed ; he had acquired some skill in scholarship and no inconsiderable fund of sound information ; and the routine of religious thought had been superseded in his instance by an amount of knowledge and feeling on matters theological, unusual at his time of life. Though apparently not gifted with any dangerous vivacity, or fatal facility of acquisition, his mind seemed clear and painstaking, and distinguished by common sense. He was brave and accurate. . . Three quarters of a year had elapsed since the twins had parted, and they were at that period of life when such an interval often produces no slight changes in personal appearance. Endymion, always late for his years, had considerably grown ; his air and manner and dress were distinguished.

. . . With all circles Endymion was a favourite. No doubt his good looks, his mien—which was both cheerful and pensive—his graceful and quiet manners, all told in his favour, and gave him a good start, but further acquaintance always sustained the first impression. He was intelligent and well informed without any alarming originality, or too positive convictions. He listened not only with patience, but with interest to all, and ever avoided controversy. Here are some of the elements of a man's popularity : what was his intellectual reach, and what his real character, it was difficult at this time to decide. He was still very young, only on the verge of his twentieth year ; and his character had no doubt been influenced, it might be suppressed, by the crushing misfortunes of his family. The influence of his sister was supreme over him ; she had never omitted an occasion to impress upon him that he had a great mission, and that, aided by her devotion, he would fulfil it. What his own conviction on that subject was may be obscure. Perhaps he was organically of that cheerful and easy nature which is content to enjoy the present and not brood over the past. The future may throw light upon all these points ; at present it may be admitted that the three years of seemingly bitter and mortifying adversity have not been altogether wanting in beneficial elements in the formation of his character and the fashioning of his future life. . . .

Endymion had now one of those rare opportunities which, if men be equal to them, greatly affect their future career. As the session advanced, debates on foreign affairs became frequent and deeply interesting. So far as the Ministry was concerned, the burthen of these fell on the Under-Secretary of State. He was never wanting. The House felt that he had not only the adequate knowledge, but that it was knowledge perfectly digested ; that his remarks and conduct were those of a man who had given constant thought to his duties, and was master of his subject. The power and melody of his voice had been before remarked, and that is a gift which much contributes to success in a popular assembly. He was ready without being too fluent. There was light and shade in his delivery. He repressed his power of sarcasm : but if unjustly and inaccurately attacked, he would be keen. Over his temper he had complete control ; if, indeed, his entire insensibility to violent language on the part of an opponent was not organic. All acknowledged his courtesy, and both sides sympathised with a young man who proved himself equal to no ordinary difficulties. In a word, Endymion was popular, and that popularity was not diminished by the fact of his being the brother of Lady Roehampton, who exercised great influence in society, and was much beloved.

ENERGY.

No conjunction can possibly occur, however fearful, however tremendous, it may appear, from which a man by his own energy may not extricate himself, as a mariner by the rattling of his cannon can dissipate the impending waterspout.—('Beckendorf') *Vivian Grey.*

ENGLAND.

England is a domestic country. Here the home is revered and the hearth sacred. The nation is represented by a family—the Royal family—and if that family is educated with a sense of responsibility and a sentiment of public duty, it is difficult to exaggerate the salutary influence it may exercise over a nation.—*Speech at Manchester, April 3, 1872.*

There is no sovereignty of any first-rate State which costs so little to the people as the sovereignty of England.—*Speech at Manchester, April 3, 1872.*

The people of England are the most enthusiastic in the world. There are others more excitable, but there are none so enthusiastic.—*Speech at Royal and Central Bucks Agricultural Association, September 26, 1876.*

The Continent will not suffer England to be the workshop of the world.—*Speech in House of Commons (Abolition of Corn Laws), March 15, 1838.*

The mind of England is the mind of the rising race.— ('Egremont') *Sybil.*

ENGLISH.

English is an expressive language, but not difficult to master. Its range is limited. It consists, as far as I can observe, of four words, 'nice,' 'jolly,' 'charming,' and 'bore,' and some grammarians add 'fond.'—('Pinto') *Lothair.*

English Climate.—'Oh! the damned climate!'

'On the contrary, it is the only good climate there is. In England you can go out every day, and at all hours; and then, to those who love variety, like myself, you are not sure of seeing the same sky every morning you rise, which, for my part, I think the greatest of all existing sources of ennui.'—('Count Mirabel') *Henrietta Temple.*

English Government.—Insurrections and riots strengthen an English government.—('Lady Montfort') *Endymion.*

English History.—If the history of England be ever written by one who has the knowledge and the courage, and both qualities are equally requisite for the undertaking, the world would be more astonished than when reading the Roman annals by Niebuhr. Generally speaking, all the great events have been distorted, most of the important causes concealed, some of the principal characters never appear, and all who figure are so misunderstood and misrepresented, that the result is a complete mystification, and the perusal of the narrative about as profitable to an Englishman as reading the Republic of Plato or the Utopia of More, the pages of Gaudentio di Lucca or the adventures of Peter Wilkins.

English Nation.—I think there is no mistake so grave on the part of a Minister as to undervalue public peril. The English nation is never so great as in adversity. In prosperity it may be accused, and perhaps justly, of being somewhat ostentatious, and, it may be, even insolent : in middle fortunes it may often prove itself unreasonable, but there never has been a time when a great sense of responsibility has been thrown upon the people of this country, when they have not answered the occasion and shown that matchless energy which has made and will maintain their position as the leading nation of the world.—*Speech in House of Commons* (*Troops for India*), *August* 11, 1857.

What he said was very well said, and it was addressed to a people who, though the shyest in the world, have a passion for public speaking, than which no achievement more tests reserve.—*Lothair.*

ENTERPRISE.

The enterprising are often fortunate.—*Tancrea.*

ENTHUSIASM.

That youthful fervour, which is sometimes called enthusiasm, but which is a heat of imagination subsequently discovered to be inconsistent with the experience of actual life.—*Endymion.*

EQUALITY.

Civil equality prevails in Britain, social equality prevails in France. The essence of civil equality is to abolish privilege ; the essence of social equality is to destroy class. *Speech at Glasgow University, November* 19, 1873.

The equality which is now sought by vast multitudes of men in many countries is physical and material equality. This is the disturbing spirit which is now rising like a moaning wind in Europe, and which, when you enter the world, may possibly be a raging storm. The leading principle of the new school is that there is no happiness which is not material, and that every living being has a right to share in that physical welfare. The first obstacle which they find to this object is found in the rights of property. Therefore they must be abolished. But the social system must be established on some principle ; and therefore for the rights of property they would establish the rights of labour. The great limit to employment, to the rights of labour, and to the physical and material equality of man, is found in the division of the world into States and nations. Thus a civil equality would abolish privilege, social equality would destroy classes ; so material and physical equality strikes at the principle of patriotism and is prepared to abrogate countries. The new philosophy strikes further than at the existence of patriotism. It strikes at the home ; it strikes at the individuality of man. It would reduce civilised society to human flocks and herds.—*Speech at Glasgow University, November* 19, 1873.

The equality of man can only be accomplished by the sovereignty of God.—('The Angel of Arabia') *Tancred.*

ESTATE.

If you want to understand the ups and downs of life, there is nothing like the parchments of an estate.—('Gerard') *Sybil.*

ETERNITY.

The doom of eternity and the fortunes of life cannot be placed in competition.—('Cardinal Grandison') *Lothair.*

ETON.

That delicious plain, studded with every creation of graceful culture ; hamlet, and hall, and grange ; garden, and grove, and park ; that castle-palace, grey with glorious ages ; those antique spires, hoar with faith and wisdom, the chapel and the college ; the river winding through the shady meads ; the sunny glade and the solemn avenue ; the room in the Dame's house where we first order our own breakfast and first feel we are free ; the stirring multitude, the energetic groups, the individual mind that leads, conquers, controls ; the emulation and the affection ; the noble strife and the tender sentiment ; the daring exploit and the dashing scrape ; the passion that pervades our life, and breathes in everything, from the aspiring study to the inspiring sport : oh ! what hereafter can spur the brain and touch the heart like this ; can give us a world so deeply and variously interesting ; a life so full of quick and bright excitement, passed in a scene so fair ?—*Coningsby.*

EVA.

She was young, even for the East ; her stature rather above the ordinary height, and clothed in the rich dress usual among the Syrian ladies. She wore an amber vest of gold-embroidered silk, fitting closely to her shape, and fastening with buttons of precious stones from the bosom to the waist, there opening like a tunic, so that her limbs were free to range in her huge Mamlouk trousers, made of that white Cashmere, a shawl of which can be drawn through a ring. These, fastened round her ankles with clasps of rubies, fell again over her small slippered feet. Over her amber vest she had an embroidered pelisse of violet silk, with long hanging sleeves, which showed occasionally an arm rarer than the costly jewels which embraced it ; a many-coloured Turkish scarf enclosed her waist ; and then, worn loosely over all, was an outer pelisse of amber cashmere, lined with the fur of the white fox. At the back of her head was a cap, quite unlike the Greek and Turkish caps which we are accustomed to see in England, but somewhat resembling the head-dress of a mandarin ; round, not flexible, almost flat ; and so thickly incrusted with pearls, that it was impossible to detect the colour of the velvet which covered it. Beneath it descended two broad braids of dark brown hair, which would have swept the ground had they not been turned half-way up, and there fastened with bunches of precious stones ; these, too, restrained the hair which fell, in rich braids, on each side of her face.

That face presented the perfection of oriental beauty ; such as it existed in Eden, such as it may yet occasionally be found among the favoured races in the favoured climes, and such as it might have been found abundantly and for ever, had not the folly and malignity of man been equal to the wisdom and beneficence of Jehovah. The countenance was oval, yet the head was small. The complexion was neither fair nor dark, yet it possessed the brilliancy of the north without its dryness, and the softness peculiar to the children of the sun without its moisture. A rich subdued and equable tint overspread this visage, though the skin was so transparent that you occasionally caught the streaky splendour of some vein like the dappled shades in the fine peel of beautiful fruit.

But it was in the eye and its overspreading arch that all the Orient spake, and you read at once of the starry vaults of Araby and the splendour of Chaldean skies. Dark, brilliant, with pupil of great size and prominent from its socket, its expression and effect, notwithstanding the long eyelash of the Desert, would have been those of a terrible fascination, had not the depth of the curve in which it reposed softened the spell and modified irresistible power by ineffable tenderness. This supreme organisation is always accompanied, as in the present instance, by a noble forehead, and by an eyebrow of perfect form, spanning its space with undeviating beauty ; very narrow, though its roots are invisible.

The nose was small, slightly elevated, with long oval nostrils fully developed. The small mouth, the short upper lip, the teeth like the neighbouring pearls of Ormuz, the round chin, polished as a statue, were in perfect harmony with the delicate ears, and the hands with nails shaped like almonds.—*Tancred.*

EVENING.

A rosy light hung over the rare shrubs, and tall fantastic trees ; while a rich yet darker tint suffused the distant woods. This euthanasia of the day exercises a strange influence over those who love. Who has not felt it ? Magical emotions that touch the immortal part.—*Coningsby.*

The last beam of the sun flashed across the flaming horizon as they gained the terrace ; the hills, well wooded, or presenting a bare and acute outline to the sky, rose sharply defined in form ; while in another direction some more distant elevations were pervaded with a rich purple tint, touched sometimes with a rosy blaze of soft and flickering light. The whole scene, indeed, from the humble pasture-land that was soon to creep into darkness, to the proud hills whose sparkling crests were yet touched by the living beam, was bathed with lucid beauty and luminous softness, and blended with the glowing canopy of the lustrous sky. But on the terrace, and the groves that rose beyond it, and the glades and vistas into which they opened, fell the full glory of the sunset. Each moment a new shadow, now rosy, now golden, now blending in its shifting tints all the glory of the iris, fell over the rich pleasure-grounds, their groups of rare and noble trees, and their dim or glittering avenues.

The vespers of the birds were faintly dying away, the last low of the returning kine sounded over the lea, the tinkle of the sheep-bell was heard no more, the thin white moon began to gleam, and Hesperus glittered in the fading sky. It was the twilight hour !

That delicious hour that softens the heart of man, what is its magic ? Not merely its beauty ; it is not more beautiful than the sunrise. It is its repose. Our tumultuous passions sink with the sun, there is a fine sympathy between us and our world, and the stillness of Nature is responded to by the serenity of the soul.—*Henrietta Temple.*

It was the twilight hour ; the hour at which in southern climes the peasant kneels before the sunset image of the blessed Hebrew maiden ; when caravans halt in their long course over vast deserts, and the turbaned traveller, bending in the sand, pays his homage to the sacred stone and the sacred city ; the hour, not less holy, that announces the cessation of English toil, and sends forth the miner and the collier to breathe the air of earth, and gaze on the light of heaven.—*Sybil.*

Hesperus rises from the sunset like the fountain of fresh water from the sea. The sky and the ocean have two natures like ourselves.—(' Herbert ') *Venetia.*

EVENTS.

What wonderful things are events ! The least are of greater importance than the most sublime and comprehensive speculations.—*Coningsby.*

Life is not dated merely by years. Events are sometimes the best calendar. There are epochs in our existence which cannot be ascertained by a formal appeal to the registry.—*Venetia.*

If you want to be a leader of the people, you must learn to watch events.—(' Devilsdust ') *Sybil.*

EVERINGHAM (LADY).

Lady Everingham was not a celebrated beauty, but she was something infinitely more delightful, a captivating woman. There were combined in her, qualities not commonly met together, great vivacity of mind with great grace of manner. Her words sparkled and her movements charmed. There was indeed, in all she said and did, that congruity that indicates a complete and harmonious organisation. It was the same just proportion which characterised her form : a shape slight and undulating with grace ; the most beautifully shaped ear ; a small, soft hand ; a foot that would have fitted the glass slipper ; and which, by the bye, she lost no opportunity of displaying ; and she was right, for it was a model.—*Coningsby.*

EXAGGERATION.

There is no greater sin than to be *trop prononcé.*—*The Young Duke.*

EXPEDIENCY.

Expediency is a law of nature. The camel is a wonderful animal, but the desert made the camel.—('Baroni') *Tancred.*

EXPERIENCE.

Experience is a thing that all men praise.—*The Young Duke.*

Great men never want experience.—('Sidonia') *Coningsby.*

The sum of our experience is but a dim dream of the conduct of past generations—generations that lived in a total ignorance of their nature.—*Contarini Fleming.*

Experience, whose result is felt by all, whose nature is described by none.—*Vivian Grey.*

EXPLAIN.

He had lived long enough to know that it is unwise to wish everything explained.—*Coningsby.*

EXTREME.

Extreme views are never just ; something always turns up which disturbs the calculations formed upon their data.— ('Baroni') *Tancred.*

FAITH.

To revive faith is more difficult than to create it.— *Lothair.*

Faith flourishes in solitude.—*Alroy.*

His was a mind that loved to pursue every question to the centre. But it was not a spirit of scepticism that impelled this habit ; on the contrary, it was the spirit of faith. Coningsby found that he was born in an age of infidelity in all things, and his heart assured him that a want of faith was a want of nature. But his vigorous intellect could not take refuge in that maudlin substitute for belief which consists in a patronage of fantastic theories. He needed that deep and enduring conviction that the heart and the intellect, feeling and reason united, can alone supply.— *Coningsby.*

FAME.

Fame has eagle wings, and yet she mounts not so high as man's desires.—*The Young Duke.*

All we poor fellows can do is to wake the Hellenistic raptures of Mayfair ; and that they call fame ; as much like fame as a toadstool is like a truffle.—('Cadurcis') *Venetia.*

To be famous when you are young is the fortune of the gods.—*Tancred.*

FANE (VIOLET).

Her companion was much younger, not so tall, and of slender form. The long tresses of her chestnut hair shaded her oval face. Her small, aquiline nose, bright hazel eyes, delicate mouth, and the deep colour of her lips, were as remarkable as the transparency of her complexion. The flush of her cheek was singular ; it was of a brilliant pink : you may find it in the lip of an Indian shell. The blue veins played beneath her arched forehead, like lightning beneath a rainbow. She was dressed in white, and a damask rose, half hid in her clustering hair, was her only ornament. This lovely creature glided by Vivian Grey almost unnoticed, so fixed was his gaze on her companion. Yet, magnificent as was the style of Lady Madeleine Trevor, there were few who preferred even her commanding graces to the softer beauties of Violet Fane.—*Vivian Grey.*

FAREWELL.

I never like to say farewell even for four-and-twenty hours : one should vanish like a spirit.—(' Theodora ') *Lothair.*

FASHION.

All hurried to pay their devoirs to the King of Fashion ; and each who succeeded in becoming a member of the Court felt as proud as a peer with a new title or a baronet with an old one.—*The Young Duke.*

The Duke of St. James passed the examination with unqualified approval, and having been stamped at the mint of fashion as a sovereign of the brightest die, he was flung forth, like the rest of his golden brethren, to corrupt the society of which he was the brightest ornament.—*The Young Duke.*

The high mode for a real swell is to have a theatre. Brecon has the Frolic ; Kate Simmons is his manager, who calls herself Athalie de Montfort. You ought to have a theatre, Lothair ; and if there is not one to hire, you should build one. It would show that you were alive again and had the spirit of an English noble, and atone for some of your eccentricities.—(' Hugo Bohun ') *Lothair.*

A Man of Fashion.—Dandy has been voted vulgar, and beau is now the word. It may be doubted whether the revival will stand ; and as for the exploded title, though it had its faults at first, the muse of Byron has made it not only English, but classical. Charles Annesley could hardly be called a dandy or a beau. There was nothing in his dress, though some mysterious arrangement in his costume, some rare simplicity, some curious happiness, always made it distinguished ; there was nothing, however, in his dress which could account for the influence which he exercised over the manners of his contemporaries. Charles Annesley was about thirty. He had inherited from his father, a younger brother, a small estate ; and, though heir to a wealthy earldom, he had never abused what the world called ' his prospects.' Yet his establishment, his little house in Mayfair, his horses, his moderate stud at Melton, were all unique, and everything connected with him was unparalleled for its elegance, its invention, and its refinement. But his manner was his magic. His natural and subdued nonchalance, so different from the assumed non-emotion of a mere dandy ; his coldness of heart, which was hereditary, not acquired ; his cautious courage, and his unadulterated self-love, had permitted him to mingle much with mankind without being too deeply involved in the play of their passions ; while his exquisite sense of the ridiculous quickly revealed those weaknesses to him which his delicate satire did not spare, even while it refrained from wounding. All feared, many admired, and none hated him. He was too powerful not to dread, too dexterous not to admire, too superior to hate. Perhaps the great secret of his manner was his exquisite superciliousness, a quality which, of. all, is the most difficult to manage. Even with his intimates he was never confidential, and perpetually assumed his public character with the private coterie which he loved to rule. On the whole, he was unlike any of the leading men of modern days, and rather reminded one of the fine gentlemen of our old brilliant comedy, the Dorimants, the Bellairs, and the Mirabels.—*The Young Duke.*

FATE.

We make our fortunes, and we call them fate.—*Alroy.*

FEEBLENESS.

It may be that words are vain to save us, but feeble deeds are vainer than words.—*Sybil.*

FEELING.

Feeling without sufficient cause is weakness.—('Lady Corisande') *Lothair.*

There is nothing that makes one so thirsty as listening to a song (at a music hall), particularly if it touches the feelings.—('Dandy Dick') *Sybil.*

All feeling which has no object to attain is morbid and maudlin.—('Lady Montfort') *Endymion.*

Never apologise for showing feeling. My friend, remember that when you do so, you apologise for truth.—('Winter') *Contarini Fleming.*

Our feelings affect even scenery.—('Job Thornberry') *Endymion.*

FENIANS.

What the Fenian movement is I do not at this moment understand. I believe it is rather to be accounted for by physical than political causes. I know that in the middle ages there was a dancing mania, and whole nations fell into fits of dancing and passed the borders of contiguous countries till they accomplished a distance of 3,000 leagues. There is no doubt that there is an epileptic feeling which affects nations like individuals, and I can only account for the Fenian movement on the epileptic principle.—*Speech in House of Commons (Ireland, Railways), March* 15, 1867.

FERROL (COUNT OF).

The Count of Ferrol was a young man and yet inclined to be bald. He was chief of a not inconsiderable mission at our Court. Though not to be described as a handsome man, his countenance was striking ; a brow of much intellectual development, and a massive jaw. He was tall,.

K

broad-shouldered, with a slender waist. He greeted Endymion with a penetrating glance, and then with a winning smile.

The Count of Ferrol was the representative of a kingdom which, if not exactly created, had been moulded into a certain form of apparent strength by the Congress of Vienna. He was a noble of considerable estate in a country where possessions were not extensive or fortunes large, though it was ruled by an ancient and haughty and warlike aristocracy. Like his class, the Count had received a military education; but when that education was completed he found but a feeble prospect of his acquirements being called into action. It was believed that the age of great wars had ceased, and that even revolutions were for the future to be controlled by diplomacy. As he was a man of an original, not to say eccentric turn of mind, the Count was not contented with the resources and distraction of his second-rate capital. He was an eminent sportsman, and for some time took refuge and found excitement in the breadth of his dark forests, and in the formation of a stud. But all this time, even in the excitement of the chase, and in the raising of his rare-bred steeds, the Count of Ferrol might be said to have been brooding over the position of what he could hardly call his country, but rather an aggregation of lands baptized by protocols, and christened and consolidated by treaties, which he looked upon as eminently untrustworthy. One day he surprised his sovereign by requesting to be appointed to the legation at London, which was vacant. The appointment was at once made, and the Count of Ferrol had now been two years at the Court of St. James's.

The Count was a favourite in English society, for he possessed every quality which there conduces to success. He was of great family and of distinguished appearance, munificent and singularly frank; was a dead shot, and the boldest of riders, with horses which were the admiration alike of Melton and Newmarket. The ladies also approved of him, for he was a consummate waltzer, and mixed, with a badinage gaily cynical, a tone that could be tender with a bewitching smile.—*Endymion.*

FIGURES.

Figures are not party men. You may cross the House, yet you cannot convert 15,000 tons into 20,000 tons.— *Speech in House of Commons (Sugar Duties), July* 28, 1846.

FINANCE.

The noble Lord (Palmerston) seems to think that posterity is a packhorse, always ready to be loaded.—*Speech in House of Commons (Fortifications and Works), June* 23, 1862.

I have in the course of my life been in communication with some of the most eminent statesmen of various countries, and I have always heard them use this language with regard to the influence of England—that the real cause of the influence of England may be found in this circumstance, that England is the only country which, when it enters into a quarrel that it believes to be just, never ceases its efforts until it has accomplished its aim. Whereas it was always felt in old times that, with scarcely any exception, there was not a State in Europe, not even the proudest and most powerful, that could enter into a third campaign. What then gave us this power of continuing any war on which we entered? It was the financial reserve of England. *Speech in House of Commons (National Expenditure), June* 3, 1862.

William introduced into England the system of Dutch finance. The principle of that system was to mortgage industry in order to protect property. — *Sybil.*

FIRMNESS.

One of the results of my attending the Congress of Berlin has been to prove, what I always suspected before to be an absolute fact—that neither the Crimean war, nor this horrible devastating war, which has just terminated, would have taken place, if England had spoken with the necessary firmness.—*Banquet at Duke of Wellington's Riding School, July* 28, 1878.

It came at last, as everything does if men are firm and calm.—*Sybil.*

FLATTERY.

Mrs. Guy Flouncey was an adroit flatterer, with a temper imperturbable, and gifted with a ceaseless energy of conferring slight obligations. She lent them patterns for new fashions, in all which mysteries she was versant ; and what with some gentle glozing and some gay gossip—sugar for their tongues, and salt for their tails—she contrived pretty well to catch them.—*Coningsby.*

Flattery is the destruction of all good fellowship : it is like a qualmish liqueur in the midst of a bottle of wine.— ('Hunsdrick') *Vivian Grey.*

FLIRTATION.

The soul-subduing sentiment, harshly called flirtation, which is the spell of a country house.—*Coningsby.*

FLORENCE.

I was at length at Florence. The fair city, so much vaunted by poets, at first greatly disappointed me. I could not reconcile myself to those unfinished churches like barns, and those gloomy palaces like prisons. The muddy Arno was not poetical, and the site of the whole place, and the appearance of the surrounding hills, in spite of their white villas, seemed to me confined, monotonous, and dull. Yet there is a charm in Florence, which, although difficult precisely to define, is in its influence great and growing, and I scarcely know a place that I would prefer for a residence. I think it is the character of Art which, both from ancient associations and its present possessions, is forcibly impressed upon this city. It is full of invention. You cannot stroll fifty yards, you cannot enter a church or palace, without being favourably reminded of the power of human thought. It is a famous memorial of the genius of the Italian middle ages, when the mind of man was in one of its spring tides, and in which we mark so frequently what at the present day we too much underrate, the influence of individual character

In Florence the monuments are not only of great men, but of the greatest. You do not gaze upon the tomb of an author who is merely a great master of composition, but of one who formed the language. The illustrious astronomer is not the discoverer of a planet, but the revealer of the whole celestial machinery. The artist and the politician are not merely the first sculptors and statesmen of their time, but the inventors of the very art and the very craft in which they excelled.—*Contarini Fleming.*

FORMALITY

Governments, like individuals, sometimes shrink from formality.—('Prince Florestan') *Endymion.*

FORTUNE.

It is a great thing to make a fortune. There is only one thing greater, and that is to keep it when made.—(' Mr. Bond Sharpe') *Henrietta Temple.*

Good wishes do not always bring good fortunes.—(' Alcesté') *Contarini Fleming.*

FRANKFORT FAIR.

It was Frankfort fair; and all countenances were expressive of that excitement which we always experience at great meetings of our fellow-creatures; whether the assemblies be for slaughter, pleasure, or profit, and whether or not we ourselves join in the banquet, the battle, or the fair. At the top of the hill is an old Roman tower, and from this point the flourishing city of Frankfort, with its picturesque cathedral, its numerous villas, and beautiful gardens in the middle of the fertile valley of the Maine, burst upon Vivian's sight. On crossing the bridge over the river, the crowd became almost impassable, and it was with the greatest difficulty that Vivian steered his way through the old narrow winding streets, full of tall ancient houses, with heavy casements and notched gable-ends. These structures did not, however, at the present moment, greet the traveller with their usual sombre and antique appearance : their outside walls were, in most instances, covered with pieces of broad cloth of the most showy colours, red, blue, and yellow predominating. These standards of trade were not merely used for the purpose of exhibiting the quality of the articles sold in the interior, but also of informing the curious traveller of the name and nation of their adventurous owners. Inscriptions in German, French, Russian, English, Italian, and even Hebrew, appeared in striking characters on each woollen specimen ; and, as if these were not sufficient to attract the attention of the passenger, an active apprentice, or assistant, commented in eloquent terms on the peculiar fairness and honesty of his master. The public squares and other open spaces, and indeed every spot which was secure from the hurrying wheels of the heavy old-fashioned coaches of the Frankfort aristocracy and the spirited pawings of their sleek and long-tailed coach-horses, were covered with large and showy booths, which groaned under the accumulated treasures of all countries. French silks and French clocks rivalled Manchester cottons and Sheffield cutlery, and assisted to attract or entrap the gazer, in company with Venetian chains, Neapolitan coral, and Vienna pipeheads : here was the booth of a great bookseller, who looked to the approaching Leipsic fair for some consolation for his slow sale and the bad taste of the people of Frankfort ; and there was a dealer in Bologna sausages, who felt quite convinced that in some things the taste of the

Frankfort public was by no means to be lightly spoken of. All was bustle, bargaining, and business : there were quarreis and conversation in all languages ; and Vivian Grey, although he had no chance either of winning or losing money, was amused.—*Vivian Grey.*

FRANKNESS.

Candour is a great virtue. There is a charm, a healthy charm, in frankness.—*Venetia.*

There is no wisdom like frankness.—*Sybil.*

Be frank and explicit. That is the right line to take, when you wish to conceal your own mind and to confuse the minds of others.—('The Gentleman in Downing Street.') *Sybil.*

FREEDOM.

Freedom, says the sage, will lead to prosperity, and despotism to destruction.—*Contarini Fleming.*

FREE TRADE.

There was obviously some analogy between civil and commercial freedom. A man was not less free because he was subject to some regulations and taxes. But gentlemen opposite meant by Free-trade an absence from all restriction. A peculiar characteristic of the Free-trade school was their total neglect of circumstances. They never took any circumstances into consideration.—*Speech in House of Commons (Import Duties), April 25, 1843.*

FRENCH.

Coningsby would find some day that there were two educations, one which his position required, and another which was demanded by the world. French is the keystone to this second education.—*Coningsby.*

French Society.—The art of society is, without doubt, perfectly comprehended and completely practised in the bright metropolis of France. An Englishman cannot enter a saloon without instantly feeling he is among a race more social than his compatriots. What, for example, is more consummate than the manner in which a French lady receives her guests? She unites graceful repose and unaffected dignity with the most amiable regard for others. She sees everyone; she speaks to everyone; she sees them at the right moment; she says the right thing; it is utterly impossible to detect any difference in the position of her guests by the spirit in which she welcomes them. There is, indeed, throughout every circle of Parisian society, from the *château* to the *cabaret*, a sincere homage to intellect; and this without any maudlin sentiment. None sooner than the Parisians can draw the line between factitious notoriety and honest fame, or sooner distinguish between the counterfeit celebrity and the standard reputation. In England, we too often alternate between a supercilious neglect of genius and a rhapsodical pursuit of quacks. In England, when a new character appears in our circles, the first question always is, 'Who is he?' In France it is, 'What is he?' In England, How much a year?' In France, 'What has he done?'—*Coningsby*.

'I have already seen many remarkable things,' said Coningsby; 'and met many celebrated persons. Nothing strikes me more in this brilliant city than the tone of its society, so much higher than our own. What an absence of petty personalities! How much conversation, and how little gossip! Yet nowhere is there less pedantry. Here all women are as agreeable as is the remarkable privilege in London of some half-dozen. Men too, and great men, develope their minds. A great man in England, on the contrary, is generally the dullest.—*Coningsby*.

FRIENDSHIP.

Female friendships are of rapid growth.—*The Young Duke*.

Perhaps there is nothing more lovely than the love of two beautiful women, who are not jealous of each other's charms.—*The Young Duke*.

The friendships of the world are wind.—('Lord Cadurcis') *Venetia.*

Sidonia has no friends. No wise man has. What are friends? Traitors.—*Coningsby.*

There have been many instances of friends and friendship. Friendship is the gift of the gods, and the most precious boon to man. It has long occupied the thought and consideration of essayists and philosophers; there has been more analysis of the elements of the different degrees of friendship than of any other quality granted to sustain and solace humanity. There, for instance, is the devoted friend who stands or falls by you. But there is another kind of friend, immortalised by an epithet which should not be mentioned to 'ears polite.' We all know that friend. *Speech in House of Commons (Ministerial Explanation, Resignation of Lord John Russell), July* 16, 1855.

As for modern friendship, it will be found in clubs. It is violent at a house dinner, fervent in a cigar shop, full of devotion at a cricket or a pigeon match, or in the gathering of a steeple-chase. The nineteenth century is not entirely sceptical on the head of friendship, but fears 'tis rare. A man may have friends, but then, are they sincere ones? Do not they abuse you behind your back, and blackball you at societies where they have had the honour to propose you? It might philosophically be suggested, that it is more agreeable to be abused behind one's back than to one's face; and, as for the second catastrophe, it should not be forgotten that, if the sincere friend may occasionally put a successful veto on your election, he is always ready to propose you again. Generally speaking, among sensible persons, it would seem that a rich man deems that friend a sincere one who does not want to borrow his money; while, among the less favoured with fortune's gifts, the sincere friend is generally esteemed to be the individual who is ready to lend it.—*Tancred.*

In short, Vivian and he became what the world calls

friends ; that is to say, they were men who had no objection
to dine in each other's company, provided the dinner were
good ; assist each other in any scrape, provided no particular personal responsibility were incurred by the assistant ;
and live under the same roof, provided each were master of
his own time.—*Vivian Grey.*

I wear my old bonnets at Bath and use my new friends;
but in town I have old friends and new dresses.—(' Lady
Bellair ') *Henrietta Temple.*

It is seldom the lot of husbands, that their confidential
friends gain the regards of their brides.—*Coningsby.*

Schoolboy Friendships.—At school, friendship is a passion.
It entrances the being ; it tears the soul.   All loves of after-
life can never bring its rapture, or its wretchedness ; no bliss
so absorbing, no pangs of jealousy or despair so crushing and
so keen !   What tenderness and what devotion ; what illimitable confidence ; infinite revelations of inmost thoughts ;
what ecstatic present and romantic future ; what bitter
estrangements and what melting reconciliations ; what
scenes of wild recrimination, agitating explanations, passionate correspondence ; what insane sensitiveness, and
what frantic sensibility ; what earthquakes of the heart and
whirlwinds of the soul are confined in that simple phrase,
a schoolboy's friendship !   'Tis some indefinite recollection of these mystic passages of their young emotion
that makes grey-haired men mourn over the memory of their
schoolboy days.   It is a spell that can soften the acerbity
of political warfare, and with its witchery can call forth a
sigh even amid the callous bustle of fashionable saloons.—
Coningsby.

There is a magic in the memory of schoolboy friendships ;
it softens the heart, and even affects the nervous system of
those who have no hearts.—*Endymion.*

FRILL (COUNT).

Count Frill was a different sort of personage. He was all rings and ringlets, ruffles, and a little rouge. Much older than his companion, short in stature, plump in figure, but with a most defined waist, fair, blooming, with a multiplicity of long light curls, and a perpetual smile playing upon his round countenance, he looked like the Cupid of an Opera Olympus.—*The Young Duke.*

FUTURE.

He was famous for discovering the future, when it has taken place.—*Contarini Fleming.*

The past is for wisdom, the present for action, but for joy the future.—*Alroy.*

GAMBLING.

In a brilliantly-illuminated saloon, adorned with Corinthian columns and casts from some of the most famous antique statues, assembled, between nine and ten o'clock in the evening, many of the visitors at Ems. On each side of the room was placed a long narrow table, one of which was covered with green baize, and unattended ; while the variously-coloured leathern surface of the other was closely surrounded by an interested crowd. Behind this table stood two individuals of different appearance. The first was a short, thick man, whose only business was dealing certain portions of playing cards with quick succession one after the other : and as the fate of the table was decided by this process, did his companion, a very tall, thin man, throw various pieces of money upon certain stakes, which were deposited by the bystanders on different parts of the table ; or, which was much oftener the case, with a silver rake with a long ebony handle, sweep into a large enclosure near him the scattered sums. This enclosure was called the Bank, and the mysterious ceremony in

which these persons were assisting was the celebrated
game of *rouge-et-noir*.   A deep silence was strictly preserved by those who immediately surrounded the table ;
no voice was heard save that of the little, short, stout
dealer, when, without an expression of the least interest, .
he seemed mechanically to announce the fate of the different colours.   No other sound was heard, except the
jingle of the dollars and Napoleons, and the ominous rake
of the tall, thin banker.   The countenances of those who
were hazarding their money were grave and gloomy : their
eyes were fixed, their brows contracted, and their lips projected ; and yet there was an evident effort visible to show
that they were both easy and unconcerned.   Each player
held in his hand a small piece of pasteboard, on which,
with a steel pricker, he marked the run of the cards, in
order, from his observations, to regulate his own play.   The
rouge-et-noir player imagines that chance is not capricious.
Those who were not interested in the game promenaded in
two lines within the tables, or, seated in recesses between
the pillars, formed small parties for conversation.—*Vivian
Grey.*

We know that we are broaching a doctrine which many
will start at, and which some will protest against, when we
declare our belief that no person, whatever his apparent
wealth, ever yet gamed except from the prospect of immediate gain.   We hear much of want of excitement, of ennui,
of satiety ; and then the gaming-table is announced as a
sort of substitute for opium, wine, or any other mode of
obtaining a more intense vitality at the cost of reason.
Gaming is too active, too anxious, too complicated, too
troublesome ; in a word, *too sensible* an affair for such spirits,
who fly only to a sort of dreamy and indefinite distraction.
The fact is, gaming is a matter of business.   Its object is
tangible, clear, and evident.   There is nothing high, or
inflammatory, or exciting ; no false magnificence, no visionary
elevation, in the affair at all.   It is the very antipodes to

enthusiasm of any kind. It presupposes in its votary a mind essentially mercantile. All the feelings that are in its train are the most mean, the most commonplace, and the most annoying of daily life, and nothing would tempt the gamester to experience them except the great object which, as a matter of calculation, he is willing to aim at on such terms. No man flies to the gaming-table in a paroxysm. The first visit requires the courage of a forlorn hope. The first stake will make the lightest mind anxious, the firmest hand tremble, and the stoutest heart falter. After the first stake, it is all a matter of calculation and management, even in games of chance. Night after night will men play at *rouge-et-noir*, upon what they call a system, and for hours their attention never ceases, any more than it would if they were in the shop or on the wharf. No manual labour is more fatiguing, and more degrading to the labourer, than gaming. Every gamester feels ashamed. And this vice, this worst vice, from whose embrace, moralists daily inform us, man can never escape, is just the one from which the majority of men most completely, and most often, emancipate themselves. Infinite are the men who have lost thousands in their youth, and never dream of chance again. It is this pursuit which, oftener than any other, leads man to self-knowledge. Appalled by the absolute destruction on the verge of which he finds his early youth just stepping ; aghast at the shadowy crimes which, under the influence of this life, seem, as it were, to rise upon his soul ; often he hurries to emancipate himself from this fatal thraldom, and with a ruined fortune, and marred prospects, yet thanks his Creator that his soul is still white, his conscience clear, and that, once more, he breathes the sweet air of heaven.— *The Young Duke.*

By shutting up gaming-houses, we brought the gaming-table into the streets.—*Endymion.*

GARDEN.

At Armine Place.—Armine Place, before Sir Ferdinand, unfortunately for his descendants, determined in the eighteenth century on building a feudal castle, had been situate in famous pleasure-grounds, which extended at the back of the mansion over a space of some hundred acres. The grounds in the immediate vicinity of the buildings had of course suffered severely, but the far greater portion had only been neglected ; and there were some indeed who deemed, as they wandered through the arbour-walks of this enchanting wilderness, that its beauty had been enhanced even by this very neglect. It seemed like a forest in a beautiful romance ; a green and bowery wilderness where Boccaccio would have loved to woo, and Watteau to paint. So artfully had the walks been planned, that they seemed interminable, nor was there a single point in the whole pleasaunce where the keenest eye could have detected a limit. Sometimes you wandered in those arched and winding walks dear to pensive spirits ; sometimes you emerged on a plot of turf blazing in the sunshine, a small and bright savannah, and gazed with wonder on the group of black and mighty cedars that rose from its centre, with their sharp and spreading foliage. The beautiful and the vast blended together ; and the moment after you had beheld with delight a bed of geraniums or of myrtles, found yourself in an amphitheatre of Italian pines. A strange exotic perfume filled the air ; you trod on the flowers of other lands ; and shrubs and plants, that usually are only trusted from their conservatories, like Sultanas from their jalousies, to sniff the air and recall their bloom, here learning from hardship the philosophy of endurance, had struggled successfully even against northern winters and wantoned now in native and unpruned luxuriance. Sir Ferdinand, when he resided at Armine, was accustomed to fill these pleasure-grounds with macaws and other birds of gorgeous plumage ; but

these had fled away with their master, all but some swans
which still floated on the surface of a lake which marked
the centre of this paradise.—*Henrietta Temple.*

At Brentham.—In the pleasure-grounds of Brentham
were the remains of an ancient garden of the ancient house
that had long ago been pulled down.   When the modern
pleasure-grounds were planned and created, notwithstanding the protests of the artists in landscape, the father of the
present Duke would not allow this ancient garden to be entirely destroyed, and you came upon its quaint appearance in
the dissimilar world in which it was placed, as you might in
some festival of romantic costume upon a person habited in
the courtly dress of the last century.   It was formed upon a
gentle southern slope, with turfen terraces walled in on three
sides, the fourth consisting of arches of golden yew.   The
Duke had given this garden to Lady Corisande, in order
that she might practise her theory, that flower-gardens
should be sweet and luxuriant, and not hard and scentless
imitations of works of art.   Here, in their season, flourished
abundantly all those productions of nature which are now
banished from our once delighted senses : huge bushes of
honeysuckle, and bowers of sweet-pea and sweetbriar and
jessamine clustering over the walls, and gillyflowers scenting
with their sweet breath the ancient bricks from which they
seemed to spring.   There were banks of violets which the
southern breeze always stirred, and mignonette filled every
vacant nook.   As they entered now, it seemed a blaze of
roses and carnations, though one recognised in a moment
the presence of the lily, the heliotrope, and the stock.
Some white peacocks were basking on the southern wall,
and one of them, as their visitors entered, moved and displayed its plumage with scornful pride.   The bees were
busy in the air, but their homes were near, and you might
watch them labouring in their glassy hives.—*Lothair.*

At Château Desir.—The mansion itself was immediately
surrounded by numerous ancient forest trees.   There was

the elm with its rich branches bending down like clustering grapes ; there was the wide-spreading oak with its roots fantastically gnarled ; there was the ash, with its smooth bark and elegant leaf ; and the silver beech, and the gracile birch ; and the dark fir, affording with its rough foliage a contrast to the trunks of its more beautiful companions, or shooting far above their branches, with the spirit of freedom worthy of a rough child of the mountains.

Around the castle were extensive pleasure-grounds, which realised the romance of the ' Gardens of Verulam.' And truly, as you wandered through their enchanting paths, there seemed no end to their various beauties, and no exhaustion to their perpetual novelty. Green retreats succeeded to winding walks ; from the shady berceau you vaulted on the noble terrace ; and if, for an instant, you felt wearied by treading the velvet lawn, you might rest in a mossy cell, while your mind was soothed by the soft music of falling waters. Now your curious eyes were greeted by Oriental animals, basking in a sunny paddock ; and when you turned from the white-footed antelope and the dark-eyed gazelle, you viewed an aviary of such extent, that within its trellised walls the imprisoned songsters could build, in the free branches of a tree, their natural nests.— *Vivian Grey.*

At Ducie Bower.—They went forth ; they stepped into a paradise, where the sweetest flowers seemed grouped in every combination of the choicest forms ; baskets, and vases, and beds of infinite fancy. A thousand bees and butterflies filled the air with their glancing shapes and cheerful music, and the birds from the neighbouring groves joined in the chorus of melody. The wood walks through which they now rambled admitted at intervals glimpses of the ornate landscape, and occasionally the view extended beyond the enclosed limits, and exhibited the clustering and embowered roofs of the neighbouring village, or some woody hill studded with a armhouse, or a distant spire. .

From the conservatory they stepped into the garden. It was a delicious afternoon ; the sun had sunk behind the grove, and the air, which had been throughout the day somewhat oppressive, was now warm, but mild. At Ducie there was a fine old terrace facing the western hills, that bound the valley in which the Bower was situate. These hills, a ridge of moderate elevation, but of picturesque form, parted just opposite the terrace, as if on purpose to admit the setting sun, like inferior existences that had, as it were, made way before the splendour of some mighty lord or conqueror. The lofty and sloping bank which this terrace crowned was covered with rare shrubs, and occasionally a group of tall trees sprang up among them, and broke the view with an interference which was far from ungraceful, while plants spreading forth from large marble vases, had extended over their trunks, and sometimes, in their play, had touched even their topmost branches. Between the terrace and the distant hills extended a tract of pasture land, green and well wooded by its rich hedgerows ; not a roof was visible, though many farms and hamlets were at hand ; and, in the heart of a rich and populous land, here was a region where the shepherd or the herdsman was the only evidence of human existence.—*Henrietta Temple.*

In Germany.—It was a beautiful garden, full of terraces and arched walks of bowery trees. A tall fountain sprang up from a marble basin, and its glittering column broke in its fall into a thousand coloured drops, and woke the gleaming fish that would have slept in the dim water. And I wandered about, and the enchanted garden seemed illimitable, and each turn more magical and more bright. Now a white vase shining in the light, now a dim statue shadowed in a cool grot. I would have lingered a moment at the mossy hermitage, but the distant bridge seemed to invite me to new adventures.— *Contarini Fleming.*

At Muriel Towers.—After luncheon they visited the gardens, which had been formed in a sylvan valley enclosed with

gilded gates. The creator of this paradise had been favoured
by nature, and had availed himself of this opportunity. The
contrast between the parterres blazing with colour and the
sylvan background, the undulating paths over romantic
heights, the fanes and the fountains, the glittering statues, and
the Babylonian terraces, formed a whole much of which was
beautiful, and all of which was striking and singular.

'Perhaps too many temples,' said Lothair, 'but this ancestor of mine had some imagination.'—*Lothair.*

What I admire most in your country are your gravel
walks.—(' Colonel Campion ') *Lothair.*

GARDENER.

The gardener, like all head gardeners, was opinionated.
Lothair.

GAY (*LUCIAN*).

Nature had intended Lucian Gay for a scholar and a
wit ; necessity had made him a scribbler and a buffoon.
He had distinguished himself at the University ; but he had
no patrimony, nor those powers of perseverance which
success in any learned profession requires. He was good-
looking, had great animal spirits, and a keen sense of enjoyment, and could not drudge. Moreover he had a fine
voice, and sang his own songs with considerable taste ;
accomplishments which made his fortune in society and
completed his ruin.—*Coningsby.*

GENIUS.

Nemesis favours genius.—*Sybil.*

He (Sievers) was one of those prudent geniuses who
always leave off with a point.— *Vivian Grey.*

GENTLEMEN.

They say no artist can draw a camel, and I say no
author ever drew a gentleman. How can they, with no
opportunity of ever seeing one?—(' St. Barbe ') *Endymion.*

GEOLOGY.

'Are you fond of geology?'

'I am not in the least acquainted with the science.'

'Naturally so; at your age, if, in fact, we study at all, we are fond of fancying ourselves moral philosophers, and our study is mankind. Trust me, my dear sir, it is a branch of research soon exhausted; and in a few years you will be very glad, for want of something else to do, to meditate upon stones. See now,' said Mr. Sievers, picking up a stone, 'to what associations does this little piece of quartz give rise ! I am already an antediluvian, and instead of a stag bounding by that wood I witness the moving mass of a mammoth. I live in other worlds, which, at the same time, I have the advantage of comparing with the present. Geology is indeed a magnificent study ! What excites more the imagi- nation? What exercises more the reason? Can you con- ceive anything sublimer than the gigantic shadows and the grim wreck of an antediluvian world? Can you devise any plan which will more brace our powers, and develop our mental energies, than the formation of a perfect chain of inductive reasoning to account for these phenomena ? What is the boasted communion which the vain poet holds with nature compared with conversation which the geologist per- petually carries on with the elemental world? Gazing on the strata of the earth, he reads the fate of his species. In the undulations of the mountains is revealed to him the history of the past ; and in the strength of rivers and the powers of the air he discovers the fortunes of the future. To him, indeed, that future, as well as the past and the present, are alike matter for meditation : for the geologist is the most satisfactory of antiquarians, the most interesting of philosophers, and the most inspired of prophets ; demon- strating that which is past by discovery, that which is occurring by observation, and that which is to come by induction.'—*Sybil.*

GERARD (WALTER).

The first was of lofty stature, and, though dressed with simplicity, had nothing sordid in his appearance. His garments gave no clue to his position in life : they might have been worn by a squire or by his gamekeeper ; a dark velveteen dress and leathern gaiters. As Egremont caught his form, he threw his broad-brimmed country hat upon the ground, and showed a frank and manly countenance. His complexion might in youth have been ruddy, but time and time's attendants, thought and passion, had paled it ; his chestnut hair, faded, but not grey, still clustered over a noble brow ; his features were regular and handsome, a well-formed nose, the square mouth and its white teeth, and the clear grey eye, which befitted such an idiosyncrasy. His time of vigorous manhood, for he was nearer forty than fifty years of age, perhaps better suited his athletic form than the more supple and graceful season of youth.—*Sybil.*

GIRL OF THE PERIOD.

She sets up to be natural and is only rude ; mistakes insolence for innocence ; says everything that comes first to her lips, and thinks she is gay when she is only giddy.—*Sybil.*

GLADSTONE.

Although the Prime Minister of England is always writing letters and making speeches, he seems ever to send forth an 'uncertain sound.' If a member of Parliament announces himself a republican, Mr. Gladstone takes the earliest opportunity of describing him as a ' fellow-worker ' in public life. If an inconsiderate multitude calls for the abolition or reform of the House of Lords, Mr. Gladstone says that is no easy task, and that he must think once or twice, or perhaps even thrice, before he can undertake it. If your neighbour, the member for Bradford, Mr. Miall, brings forward a motion in the House of Commons for the severance of Church and State, Mr. Gladstone assures Mr. Miall with the utmost courtesy that he believes the opinion of the House of Commons is against him; but that if Mr. Miall wishes to influence the House of Commons he must address the public out of doors.—*Speech at Manchester, April* 3, 1872.

A sophistical rhetorician, inebriated with the exuberance of his own verbosity, and gifted with an egotistical imagination that can at all times command an interminable and inconsistent series of arguments to malign an opponent and to glorify himself.—*Banquet at Duke of Wellington's Riding School, July* 28, 1878.

GLASTONBURY (ADRIAN).

Adrian Glastonbury was a younger son of an old but decayed English family. He had been educated at a college of Jesuits in France, and had entered at an early period of life the service of the Romish Church, whose communion his family had never quitted. At college young Glastonbury had been alike distinguished for his assiduous talents and for the extreme benevolence of his disposition. His was one of those minds to which refinement is natural, and which learning and experience never deprive of simplicity. Apparently his passions were not violent; perhaps they were restrained by his profound piety. Next to his devotion, Glastonbury was most remarkable for his taste.

If ever there were a man who deserved a serene and happy life, it was Adrian Glastonbury. He had pursued a long career without injuring or offending a human being; his character and conduct were alike spotless; he was void of guile; he had never told a falsehood, never been entangled in the slightest deceit; he was easy in his circumstances; he had no relations to prey upon his purse or his feelings; and, though alone in the world, was blessed with such a sweet and benignant temper, gifted with so many resources, and adorned with so many accomplishments.

that he appeared to be always employed, amused, and contented.—*Henrietta Temple.*

GOVERNMENT.

The greatest of all evils is a weak government. They
cannot carry good measures ; they are forced to carry bad
ones.—*Coningsby.*

The government of the world is carried on by sovereigns
and statesmen, and not by anonymous paragraph writers or
by the hare-brained chatter of irresponsible frivolity.—*Speech
at Mansion House, November* 9, 1878.

I have noticed the sort of anxiety which seems to exist
among the members of the Government, that it would be
generally supposed they had a sort of partnership with
Providence. They seem to entertain a particular desire to
show to the House and the country that they owe a deep
debt of gratitude to them for the good harvest with which
we were blessed.—*Speech in House of Commons (Railway
Bill, Over-speculation), April* 22, 1846.

Our domestic affections are the most salutary basis of all
good government.—*Speech at Salthill (Royal South Buckinghamshire Agricultural Association), October* 5, 1864.

The Government is like a man with a telescope, who by
a flourish of the hand turns it round, so that the glass when
he looks into it, instead of showing him objects greatly magnified, as in the proposition of my noble friend (Lord John
Russell), represents everything under a diminished aspect,
according to the view taken by Her Majesty's Government.
Speech in House of Commons (Cracow), March 16, 1847.

Whatever may have been the faults of the ancient
governments, they were in closer relation to the times, to
the countries and to the governed, than ours. The ancients
invented their governments according to their wants ; the
moderns have adopted foreign policies, and then modelled
their conduct upon this borrowed regulation. This circumstance has occasioned our manners and our customs to be

so confused, and absurd, and unphilosophical. What business had we, for instance, to adopt the Roman law, a law
foreign to our manners, and consequently disadvantageous?
He who profoundly meditates upon the situation of Modern
Europe will also discover how productive of misery has been
the senseless adoption of oriental customs by northern
people. Whence came that divine right of kings, which
has deluged so many countries with blood? that pastoral
and Syrian law of tithes, which may yet shake the foundation of so many ancient institutions?—*Contarini Fleming.*

The divine right of kings may have been a plea for feeble
tyrants, but the divine right of government is the key-stone
of human progress, and without it government sinks into
police, and a nation is degraded into a mob.—*Preface to
'Lothair.'*

GRANDISON (CARDINAL).

The master of the library had risen from his seat when
the chief secretary entered, and was receiving an obeisance.
Above the middle height, his stature seemed magnified by
the attenuation of his form. It seemed that the soul never
had so frail and fragile a tenement. He was dressed in a
dark cassock with a red border, and wore scarlet stockings;
and over his cassock a purple tippet, and on his breast a
small golden cross. His countenance was naturally of an
extreme pallor, though at this moment slightly flushed
with the animation of a deeply interesting conference. His
cheeks were hollow, and his grey eyes seemed sunk into his
clear and noble brow, but they flashed with irresistible pene-
tration. Such was Cardinal Grandison.

The Cardinal was an entire believer in female influence,
and a considerable believer in his influence over females;
and he had good cause for his convictions. The catalogue
of his proselytes was numerous and distinguished. He had
not only converted a duchess and several countesses, but he
had gathered into his fold a real Mary Magdalen. In the

height of her beauty and her fame, the most distinguished member of the demi-monde had suddenly thrown up her golden whip and jingling reins, and cast herself at the feet of the Cardinal. He had a right, therefore, to be confident; and while his exquisite taste and consummate cultivation rendered it impossible that he should not have been deeply gratified by the performance of Theodora, he was really the whole time considering the best means by which such charms and powers could be enlisted in the cause of the Church.— *Lothair.*

GRANTED.

I have learnt again what I have often learnt before, that you should never take anything for granted.—*Speech at Salthill, Royal South Buckinghamshire Agricultural Association, October* 5, 1864.

GRATITUDE.

They (the Neuchatels) deserve their wealth; nobody grudges it them. I declare, when I was eating that trifle, I felt a glow about my heart, which, if it were not indigestion, I think must have been gratitude.—('St. Barbe') *Endymion.*

Bitter thought! that gratitude should cease the moment we become men.—*Vivian Grey.*

GREATNESS.

Greatness no longer depends on rentals, the world is too rich; nor on pedigrees, the world is too knowing.—*Coningsby.*

All the great things have been done by little nations.—*Tancred.*

A great man is one who affects his generation.—*Coningsby.*

The age does not believe in great men, because it does not possess any.—('Sidonia') *Coningsby.*

GRECIAN.

A Grecian sunset !   The sky is like the neck of a dove ; the rocks and waters are bathed with a violet light.   Each moment it changes ; each moment it shifts into more graceful and more gleaming shadows.   And the thin white moon is above all : the thin white moon, followed by a single star, like a lady by a page.—*Contarini Fleming.*

GREECE.

A country of promontories, and gulfs, and islands clustering in an azure sea ; a country of wooded vales and purple mountains, wherein the cities are built on plains covered with olive woods, and at the base of an Acropolis, crowned with a temple or a tower.   And there are quarries of white marble, and vines, and much wild honey.   And wherever you move is some fair and elegant memorial of the poetic past ; a lone pillar on the green and silent plain, once echoing with the triumphant shouts of sacred games, the tomb of a hero, or the fane of a god.   Clear is the sky and fragrant is the air, and at all seasons the magical scenery of this land is coloured with that mellow tint, and invested with that pensive character, which in other countries we conceive to be peculiar to autumn, and which beautifully associate with the recollections of the past.   Enchanting Greece !—*Contarini Fleming.*

GREY (*VIVIAN*).

Although busied with his studies, and professing ' not to visit,' Vivian could not avoid occasionally finding himself in company in which boys should never be seen ; and, what was still worse, from a certain social spirit, an indefinable tact with which Nature had endowed him, this boy of nineteen began to think this society delightful   Most persons of his age would have passed through the ordeal with perfect safety ; they would have entered certain rooms, at certain hours, with stiff cravats, and Nugee coats, and black velvet waistcoats ; and after having annoyed all those who condescended to know of their existence, with their red hands and their white gloves, they would have retired to a corner of the room, and conversationised with any stray four-year-older not yet sent to bed.

But Vivian Grey was a graceful, lively lad, with just enough of dandyism to preserve him from committing gaucheries, and with a devil of a tongue. All men will agree with me that the only rival to be feared by a man of spirit is a clever boy. What makes them so popular with women it is difficult to explain ; however, Lady Julia Knighton, and Mrs. Frank Delmington, and half a score of dames of fashion, were always patronising our hero, who found an evening spent in their society not altogether dull, for there is no fascination so irresistible to a boy as the smile of a married woman. Vivian had passed such a recluse life for the last two years and a half, that he had quite forgotten that he was once considered an agreeable fellow ; and so, determined to discover what right he ever had to such a reputation, he dashed into all these amourettes in beautiful style.

But Vivian Grey was a young and tender plant in a moral hothouse. His character was developing itself too soon. Although his evenings were now generally passed in the manner we have alluded to, this boy was, during the rest of the day, a hard and indefatigable student ; and having now got through an immense series of historical reading, he had stumbled upon a branch of study certainly the most delightful in the world ; but, for a boy, as certainly the most perilous, the study of politics. . . .

It was a rule with Vivian Grey never to advance any opinion as his own. He had been too deep a student of human nature not to be aware that the opinions of a boy of twenty, however sound, and however correct, stand but a poor chance of being adopted by his elder, though feebler, fellow-creatures. In attaining any end, it was therefore his system always to advance his opinion as that of some eminent and considered personage ; and when, under the sanction of this name, the opinion or advice was entertained and listened to, Vivian Grey had no fear that he could prove its correctness and its expediency. He possessed also the singular faculty of being able to improvise quotations, that is, he could unpremeditatedly clothe his conceptions in language characteristic of the style of any particular author ; and Vivian Grey was reputed in the world as having the most astonishing memory that ever existed ; for there was scarcely a subject of discussion in which he did not gain the victory, by the great names he enlisted on his side of the argument.

But it must not be supposed that Vivian was to all the world the fascinating creature that he was to the Marquis of Carabas. Many complained that he was reserved, silent, satirical, and haughty. But the truth was, Vivian Grey often asked himself, 'Who is to be my enemy to-morrow ?' He was too cunning a master of the human mind not to be aware of the quicksands upon which all greenhorns strike ; he knew too well the danger of unnecessary intimacy. A smile for a friend, and a sneer for the world, is the way to govern mankind, and such was the motto of Vivian Grey. *Vivian Grey.*

GRIEF.

What is grief? If it be excited by the fear of some contingency, instead of grieving, a man should exert his energies and prevent its occurrence. If, on the contrary, it be caused by an event, that which has been occasioned by anything human, by the co-operation of human circumstances, can be, and invariably is, removed by the same means. Grief is the agony of an instant; the indulgence of grief the blunder of a life.—(' Beckendorff') *Vivian Grey.*

Want of love, or want of money, lies at the bottom of all our griefs.—*Venetia*.

Those who have known grief seldom seem sad.—('Agrippina') *Endymion*.

GUY FLOUNCEY (MR. AND MRS.).

Lord Monmouth had picked up the Guy Flounceys during a Roman winter. They were people of some position in society. Mr. Guy Flouncey was a man of good estate, a sportsman, proud of his pretty wife. Mrs. Guy Flouncey was even very pretty, dressed in a style of ultra fashion. However, she could sing, dance, act, ride, and talk, and all well ; and was mistress of the art of flirtation. She had amused the Marquis abroad, and had taken care to call at Monmouth House the instant the *Morning Post* apprised her he had arrived in England ; the consequence was an invitation to Coningsby. She came with a wardrobe which, in point of variety, fancy, and fashion, never was surpassed. Morning and evening, every day a new dress equally striking ; and a riding habit that was the talk and wonder of the whole neighbourhood. Mrs. Guy Flouncey created far more sensation in the borough when she rode down the High Street, than what the good people called the real Princesses.

At first the fine ladies never noticed her, or only stared at her over their shoulders ; everywhere sounded, in suppressed whispers, the fatal question, 'Who is she?' After dinner they formed always into polite groups, from which Mrs. Guy Flouncey was invariably excluded ; and if ever the Princess Colonna, impelled partly by goodnature, and partly from having known her on the Continent, did kindly sit by her, Lady St. Julians, or some dame equally benevolent, was sure, by an adroit appeal to Her Highness on some point which could not be decided without moving. to withdraw her from her pretty and persecuted companion.

It was, indeed, rather difficult work the first few days

for Mrs. Guy Flouncey, especially immediately after dinner. It is not soothing to one's self-love to find oneself sitting alone, pretending to look at prints, in a fine drawing-room, full of fine people who don't speak to you. But Mrs. Guy Flouncey, after having taken Coningsby Castle by storm, was not to be driven out of its drawing-room by the tactics even of a Lady St. Julians. Experience convinced her that all that was required was a little patience. Mrs. Guy had confidence in herself, her quickness, her ever ready accomplishments, and her practised powers of attraction. And she was right. She was always sure of an ally the moment the gentlemen appeared. The cavalier who had sat next to her at dinner was only too happy to meet her again. More than once, too, she had caught her noble host, though a whole garrison was ever on the watch to prevent her, and he was greatly amused, and showed that he was greatly amused, by her society. Then she suggested plans to him to divert his guests. In a country-house the suggestive mind is inestimable. Somehow or other, before a week was passed, Mrs. Guy Flouncey seemed the soul of everything, was always surrounded by a cluster of admirers, and with what are called 'the best men' ever ready to ride with her, dance with her, act with her, or fall at her feet. The fine ladies found it absolutely necessary to thaw : they began to ask her questions after dinner. Mrs. Guy Flouncey only wanted an opening. She was an adroit flatterer, with a temper imperturbable, and gifted with a ceaseless energy of conferring slight obligations. She lent them patterns for new fashions, in all which mysteries she was very versant ; and what with some gentle glozing and some gay gossip, sugar for their tongues and salt for their tails, she contrived pretty well to catch them all.—*Coningsby.*

HALF-MEASURES.

D—n all half-measures !—*Ixion.*

HAMPSHIRE (MARQUIS AND MARCHIONESS OF).

It was hardly to be expected that her ladyship would find any relief in the society of the Marquis and Marchioness of Hampshire : for his lordship passed his life in being the President of scientific and literary societies, and was ready for anything, from the Royal, if his turn ever arrived, to opening a Mechanics' Institute in his neighbouring town. Lady Hampshire was an invalid ; but her ailment was one of those mysteries which still remained insoluble, although, in the most liberal manner, she delighted to afford her friends all the information in her power. Never was a votary endowed with a faith at once so lively and so capricious. Each year she believed in some new remedy, and announced herself on the eve of some miraculous cure. But the saint was scarcely canonised before his claims to beatitude were impugned. One year Lady Hampshire never quitted Leamington ; another, she contrived to combine the infinitesimal doses of Hahnemann with the colossal distractions of the metropolis. Now her sole conversation was the water cure. Lady Hampshire was to begin immediately after her visit to Montacute, and she spoke in her sawney voice of factitious enthusiasm, as if she pitied the lot of all those who were not about to sleep in wet sheets.— *Tancred.*

HAND.

It was a beautiful hand that was extended to him ; a beautiful hand is an excellent thing in woman ; it is a charm that never palls, and better than all, it is a means of fascination that never disappears. Women carry a beautiful hand with them to the grave, when a beautiful face has long ago vanished, or ceased to enchant. The expression of the hand, too, is inexhaustible ; and when the eyes we may have worshipped no longer flash or sparkle, the ringlets with which we may have played are covered with a cap, or worse, a turban, and the symmetrical presence which in our sonnets has reminded us so oft of antelopes and wild gazelles, have all, all vanished ; the hand, the immortal hand, defying alike time and care, still vanquishes, and still triumphs ; and small, soft, and fair, by an airy attitude, a gentle pressure, or a new ring, renews with untiring grace the spell that bound our enamoured and adoring youth !—*Henrietta Temple.*

HANSARD.

Why Hansard, instead of being the Delphi of Downing Street, is but the Dunciad of politics.—*Speech in House of Commons (Maynooth College), April* 11, 1845.

HAPPINESS.

The sense of existence is the greatest happiness.—*Contarini Fleming.*

Happiness is only to be found in a recurrence to the principles of human nature, and these will prompt very simple measures.—*Contarini Fleming.*

HEART.

What we call the heart is a nervous sensation, like shyness, which gradually disappears in society. It is fervent in the nursery, strong in the domestic circle, tumultuous at school. The affections are the children of ignorance ; when the horizon of our experience expands, and models multiply, love and admiration imperceptibly vanish.—('Sidonia ') *Coningsby.*

HERBERT (MARMION).

Marmion Herbert, sprung from one of the most illustrious families in England, became at an early age the inheritor of a great estate, to which, however, he did not succeed with the prejudices or opinions usually imbibed or professed by the class to which he belonged. While yet a boy, Marmion Herbert afforded many indications of possessing a mind alike visionary and inquisitive, and both, although not in an equal degree, sceptical and creative. Nature had gifted him with precocious talents ; and with a temperament essentially poetic, he was nevertheless a great student. His early reading, originally by accident and afterwards by an irresistible inclination, had fallen among the works of the English freethinkers : with all their errors, a profound and vigorous race, and much superior to the French philosophers, who were after all only their pupils and their imitators. While his juvenile studies, and in some degree the predisposition of his mind, had thus prepared him to doubt and finally to challenge the propriety of all that was established and received, the poetical and stronger bias of his mind enabled him quickly to supply the place of everything he would remove and destroy ; and, far from being the victim of those frigid- and indifferent feelings which must ever be the portion of the mere doubter, Herbert, on the contrary, looked forward with ardent and sanguine enthusiasm to a glorious and ameliorating future, which should amply compensate and console a misguided and unhappy race for the miserable past and the painful and dreary present. To those, therefore, who could not sympathise with his views, it will be seen that Herbert, in attempting to fulfil them, became not merely passively noxious from his example, but actively mischievous from his exertions. A mere sceptic, he would have been perhaps merely pitied ; a sceptic with a peculiar faith of his own, which he was resolved to promulgate, Herbert became odious. A solitary votary of obnoxious opinions, Herbert would have been looked upon only as a madman ; but the moment he attempted to make proselytes he rose into a conspirator against society.

Young, irresistibly prepossessing in his appearance, with great eloquence, crude but considerable knowledge, an ardent imagination and a subtle mind, and a generous and passionate soul, under any circumstances he must have obtained and exercised influence, even if his Creator had not also bestowed upon him a spirit of indomitable courage ;

but these great gifts of nature being combined with accidents of fortune scarcely less qualified to move mankind, high rank, vast wealth, and a name of traditionary glory, it will not be esteemed surprising that Marmion Herbert, at an early period, should have attracted around him many enthusiastic disciples. . . .

Herbert quitted Oxford in his nineteenth year, yet inferior to few that he left there, even among the most eminent, in classical attainments, and with a mind naturally profound, practised in all the arts of ratiocination. His general knowledge also was considerable, and he was a proficient in those scientific pursuits which were then rare. Notwithstanding his great fortune and position, his departure from the university was not a signal with him for that abandonment to the world, and that unbounded self-enjoyment naturally so tempting to youth. On the contrary, Herbert shut himself up in his magnificent castle, devoted to solitude and study. In his splendid library he consulted the sages of antiquity, and conferred with them on the nature of existence and of the social duties ; while in his laboratory or his dissecting-room he occasionally flattered himself he might discover the great secret which had perplexed generations. The consequence of a year passed in this severe discipline was unfortunately a complete recurrence to those opinions that he had early imbibed, and which now seemed fixed in his conviction beyond the hope or chance of again faltering. In politics a violent republican, and an advocate, certainly a disinterested one, of a complete equality of property and conditions, utterly objecting to the very foundation of our moral system, and especially a strenuous antagonist of marriage, which he taught himself to esteem not only as an unnatural tie, but as eminently unjust towards that softer sex, who had been so long the victims of man ; discarding as a mockery the received revelation of the divine will ; and, if no longer an atheist, substituting merely for such an outrageous dogma a subtle and

M

shadowy Platonism ; doctrines, however, which Herbert at
least had acquired by a profound study of the works of their
great founder ; the pupil of Doctor Masham at length
deemed himself qualified to enter that world which he was
resolved to regenerate ; prepared for persecution, and
steeled even to martyrdom.

But while the doctrines of the philosopher had been
forming, the spirit of the poet had not been inactive.
Loneliness, after all, the best of Muses, had stimulated the
creative faculty of his being. Wandering amid his solitary
woods and glades at all hours and seasons, the wild and
beautiful apparitions of nature had appealed to a sympathetic soul. The stars and winds, the pensive sunset and
the sanguine break of morn, the sweet solemnity of night,
the ancient trees and the light and evanescent flowers, all
signs and sights and sounds of loveliness and power, fell
on a ready eye and a responsive ear. Gazing on the beautiful, he longed to create it. Then it was that the two
passions which seemed to share the being of Herbert appeared simultaneously to assert their sway, and he resolved
to call in his Muse to the assistance of his Philosophy.

Herbert celebrated that fond world of his imagination,
which he wished to teach men to love. In stanzas glittering with refined images, and resonant with subtle symphony,
he called into creation that society of immaculate purity
and unbounded enjoyment which he believed was the natural inheritance of unshackled man. In the hero he pictured a philosopher, young and gifted as himself ; in the
heroine, his idea of a perfect woman. Although all those
peculiar doctrines of Herbert, which, undisguised, must
have excited so much odium, were more or less developed
and inculcated in this work ; nevertheless they were necessarily so veiled by the highly spiritual and metaphorical
language of the poet, that it required some previous acquaintance with the system enforced, to be able to detect
and recognise the esoteric spirit of his Muse. The public

read only the history of an ideal world and of creatures of exquisite beauty, told in language that alike dazzled their fancy and captivated their ear. They were lost in a delicious maze of metaphor and music, and were proud to acknowledge an addition to the glorious catalogue of their poets in a young and interesting member of their aristocracy.— *Venetia.*

HEROES.

The legacy of heroes—the memory of a great name and the inheritance of a great example.—*Speech in House of Commons (Address in answer to the Queen's Speech), February* 1, 1849.

To believe in the heroic makes heroes.—*Coningsby.*

HISTORY.

To study man from the past is to suppose that man is ever the same animal. Those who studied the career of Napoleon had ever a dogs-eared analyst to refer to.—*Contarini Fleming.*

HOLIDAYS.

I have a great confidence in the revelations which holidays bring forth.—*Speech in House of Commons, February* 29, 1864.

HOME.

If kindness make a home,
Believe it such.—*Alroy.*

The inn is a common home.—*Coningsby.*

Home is a barbarous idea ; the method of a rude age : home is isolation, therefore antisocial—what we want is community.—('Stephen Morley') *Sybil.*

HOPE.

Hope and consolation are not the companions of solitude, which are of a darker nature.—('Lady Madeleine Trevor') *Vivian Grey.*

M 2

The iris pencil of Hope.— *Venetia.*

The ministry only expresses 'a confident hope,' which is, at the best, but the language of amiable despair.—*Speech in House of Commons (Address in answer to Queen's Speech), February 4, 1851.*

HORSE EXERCISE.

A canter is the cure for every evil.—*The Young Duke.*

HOUSE OF COMMONS.

All the best speakers in the House of Commons are after-dinner speakers.—*Speech in House of Commons (Budget), April 4, 1851.*

I look upon the House of Commons as a mere vestry. Reform has dished it. There are no men, and naturally, because the constituencies elect themselves, and the constituencies are the most mediocre of the nation.—('Waldershare') *Endymion.*

Nothing is more singular than the various success of men in the House of Commons. Fellows who have been the oracles of coteries from their birth, who have gone through the regular process of gold medals, senior wranglerships, and double firsts, who have nightly sat down amid tumultuous cheering in debating societies, and can harangue with unruffled forehead and unfaltering voice, from one end of a dinner-table to the other, who, on all occasions, have something to say, and can speak with fluency on what they know nothing about, no sooner rise in the House than their spell deserts them. All their effrontery vanishes. Commonplace ideas are rendered even more uninteresting by monotonous delivery ; and keenly alive as even boobies are in those sacred walls to the ridiculous, no one appears more thoroughly aware of his unexpected and astounding deficiencies than the orator himself. He regains his seat hot and hard, sultry and stiff, with a burning cheek and an icy hand, repressing his breath lest it should give evidence of an existence of which he is ashamed, and clenching his fist, that the pressure may secretly convince him that he has not as completely annihilated his stupid body as his false reputation.—*The Young Duke.*

HOUSE OF LORDS.

One thing is clear—a man may speak very well in the House of Commons and fail completely in the House of Lords. There are two distinct styles requisite. In the Lower House, ' Don Juan ' may perhaps be our model ; in the Upper House, ' Paradise Lost.'—*The Young Duke.*

The Lords do not encourage wit, and so are obliged to put up with pertness.—*The Young Duke.*

The Duke of St. James took the oaths and his seat. He heard a debate. We laugh at such a thing, especially in the Upper House ; but on the whole the affair is imposing, particularly if we take part in it.—*The Young Duke.*

Divisions in the House of Lords are nowadays so thinly scattered, that, when one occurs, the peers cackle as if they had laid an egg.—*Tancred.*

Some made a note, some made a bet ; some consulted a book, some their ease ; some yawned, some slept ; yet on the whole there was an air about the assembly which can be witnessed in no other in Europe. Even the most indifferent looked as if he could come forward, should occasion demand him, and the most imbecile as if he could serve his country, if it required him. When a man raises his eye from his bench, and sees his ancestors in the tapestry, he begins to understand the pride of blood.—*The Young Duke.*

I sit now in a House where our opponents never un- sheath their swords, a House where, although the two chief Plenipotentiaries sit, they are met only by innuendo.—*Speech at Banquet at Duke of Wellington's Riding School, July 28, 1878.*

Lord ex-Chamberlain thought the nation going wrong,

and he made a speech full of Currency and Constitution.—
The Young Duke.

I know there are some philosophers who believe that
the best substitute for the House of Lords would be an
assembly formed of ex-governors of colonies. I have not
sufficient experience on the subject to give a decided
opinion upon it. When the Muse of Comedy threw her
frolic grace over society, a retired governor was generally
one of the characters in every comedy.—*Speech at Manchester, April* 3, 1872.

Why should a popular assembly, elected by the flower
of a nation, be precipitate? If precipitate, what senate
could stay an assembly so chosen? No, no, no! the thing
has been tried over and over again ; the idea of restraining
the powerful by the weak is an absurdity ; the question is
settled. If we wanted a fresh illustration, we need only
look to the present state of our own House of Lords. It
originates nothing; it has, in fact, announced itself as a
mere court of registration of the decrees of your House of
Commons ; and if by any chance it ventures to alter some
miserable detail in a clause of a bill that excites public
interest, what a clatter through the country, at Conservative
banquets got up by the rural attorneys, about the power,
authority, and independence of the House of Lords ; nine
times nine, and one cheer more ! No, sir, you may make
aristocracies by laws ; you can only maintain them by
manners. The manners of England preserve it from its
laws. And they have substituted for our formal aristocracy
an essential aristocracy ; the government of those who are
distinguished by their fellow-citizens.— ('Mr. Millbank')
Coningsby.

The House of Commons is a more aristocratic body
than the House of Lords. Nobody wants a second
chamber, except a few disreputable individuals. It is a
valuable institution for any member of it who has no distinction, neither character, talent, nor estate. But a peer

who possesses all these great qualifications would find himself an immensely more important personage in what, by way of jest, they call the Lower House.—('Mr. Millbank') *Coningsby*.

HUME (MR.).

Future Parliaments will do justice to the eminent services of this remarkable man, then the most hard-working member of the House, of which he was the father. His labours on public committees will be often referred to hereafter, and then, perhaps, it will be remembered that, during a career of forty years, and often under circumstances of great provocation, he never once lost his temper.—*Life of Lord George Bentinck*.

IDEA.

One should conquer the world, not to enthrone a man, but an idea, for ideas exist for ever.—*Tancred*.

IGNORANCE.

Ignorance never settles a question.—*Speech in House of Commons (Redistribution of Seats), May* 14, 1866.

IMAGINATION.

You have a great enemy, Contarini, a great enemy in yourself. You have a great enemy in your imagination. I think if you could control your imagination you might be a great man.

It is a fatal gift; for when possessed in its highest quality and strength what has it ever done for its votaries? What were all those great poets of whom we now talk so much, what were they in their lifetime? The most miserable of their species. Depressed, doubtful, obscure, or involved in petty quarrels and petty persecutions; often unappreciated, utterly uninfluential, beggars, flatterers of men unworthy even of their recognition; what a train of disgustful incidents, what a record of degrading circumstances, is the life of a great poet! A man of great energies aspires that they should be felt in his lifetime, that his existence should be rendered more intensely vital by the constant consciousness of his multiplied and multiplying power. Is posthumous fame a substitute for all this? Viewed in every light, and under every feeling, it is alike a mockery. Nay, even try the greatest by this test, and what is the result? Would you rather have been Homer or Julius Cæsar, Shakespeare or Napoleon? No one doubts. Moralists may cloud truth with every possible adumbration of cant, but the nature of our being gives the lie to all their assertions. We are active beings, and our sympathy, above all other sympathies, is with great actions.

Remember, Contarini, that all this time I am taking for granted that you may be a Homer. Let us now recollect that it is perhaps the most improbable incident that can occur. The high poetic talent (as if to prove that a poet is only, at the best, a wild although beautiful error of nature), the high poetic talent is the rarest in creation. What you have felt is what I have felt myself, is what all men have felt : it is the consequence of our native and inviolate susceptibility. As you advance in life and become more callous, more acquainted with man and with yourself, you will find it even daily decrease. Mix in society and I will answer that you lose your poetic feeling ; for in you, as in the great majority, it is not a creative faculty originating in a peculiar organisation, but simply the consequence of a nervous susceptibility that is common to all.—(' Baron Fleming ') *Contarini Fleming.*

The Irish are an imaginative race, and it is said that imagination is too often accompanied by somewhat irregular logic.—*Speech at Guildhall, November* 9, 1879.

IMOGENE.

There was also a sister, a girl not older than Endymion, the very image of Mrs. Rodney, except that she was a brunette—a brilliant brunette. Imogene was only a child when Waldershare first became a lodger. He fell in love with her name, and wrote a series of sonnets, idealising her past, panegyrising her present, and prophetic of her future life. Imogene, who was neither shy nor obtrusive, was calm amid all his vagaries, humoured his fancies, even when she did not understand them, and read his verses as she would a foreign language which she was determined to master. Her culture, according to Waldershare, was to be carried on chiefly by conversation. As Waldershare was eloquent, brilliant, and witty, Imogene listened to him with wondering interest and amusement, even when she found some difficulty in following him ; but her appreciation was so quick and her tact so fine, that her progress, though she was almost unconscious of it, was remarkable. . . .

Lady Beaumaris was different from her sister almost in all respects, except in beauty, though her beauty even was of a higher style than that of Mrs. Rodney. Imogene was quite natural, though refined. She had a fine disposition. All her impulses were good and naturally noble. She had a greater intellectual range than Sylvia and was much more cultivated. This she owed to her friendship with Mr. Waldershare.—*Endymion.*

IMPRUDENCE.

All men have their imprudent days.—(' Prince of Lilliput ') *Vivian Grey.*

IMPUDENCE.

It is better to be impudent than servile.—(' Lady Bellair ') *Henrietta Temple.*

IMPULSE.

It is not the fever of superficial impulse that can remove the deep fixed barriers of centuries of ignorance and crime. (' Egremont ') *Sybil.*

INHERITANCE.

To dream of inheritance is the most enervating of visions.—('Sidonia') *Coningsby.*

INDIA

No difference of opinion can possibly prevail among us as to the unprecedented lustre of the actions of our countrymen generally in India. I do not think there has ever been an instance in which the vigour of personal character has been so remarkably exhibited, and in which individual character has shone with so much splendour. Indeed the story is quite epical. The narrative reads like the Homeric poems. Every scene produces a hero. In these remarkable events there are two incidents, which by their importance immediately attract our attention, and it is curious that in these two instances our countrymen were placed in exactly opposite positions. In one they were besiegers, in the other besieged ; and in both cases they achieved complete success and immortal glory. Between the siege of Delhi and that of Lucknow there was, however, one passage which ought not to be forgotten on this occasion—the connecting link between them—the march of Greathed—worthy, I think, of Cæsar.—*Speech in House of Commons (Indian Mutiny—Vote of Thanks to the Army and Navy in India), February* 8, 1858.

The key of India is not at Candahar. The key of India is in London. The majesty and sovereignty, the spirit and vigour of your Parliament, the inexhaustible resources, the ingenuity and determination of your people, these are the keys of India.—*Speech in House of Lords, March* 5, 1881.

INSIGNIFICANT BEGINNINGS.

It is remarkable how insignificant incidents at the first blush have appeared, which have proved to be pregnant with momentous consequences. A street riot at Boston and at Paris turned out to be the two great revolutions of modern times. I have always thought if mankind could bring themselves to ponder in time on the commencement of those events that greatly affect their fortunes, it is possible that we might bring to the transaction of affairs more prudence and more energy than are generally exercised, and that probably we might prevent many public disasters. *Speech in House of Commons (State of India), July 22, 1857.*

INSTITUTIONS.

Individuals may form communities, but it is institutions alone that can create a nation.—*Speech at Manchester,* 1866.

INTELLECT.

The only human quality that interested Sidonia was Intellect. He cared not whence it came ; where it was to be found : creed, country, class, character, in this respect, were alike indifferent to him. The author, the artist, the man of science, never appealed to him in vain. Often he anticipated their wants and wishes. He encouraged their society ; was as frank in his conversation as he was generous in his contributions ; but the instant they ceased to be authors, artists, or philosophers, and their communications arose from anything but the intellectual quality which had originally interested him, the moment they were rash enough to approach intimacy and appealed to the sympathising man, instead of the congenial intelligence, he saw them no more.—*Coningsby.*

INTRIGUE.

He (Fakredeen) became habituated to the idea that everything could be achieved by dexterity, and that there was no test of conduct except success.—*Tancred.*

Intrigue ! It is life ! It is the only thing ! How do you think Guizot and Aberdeen got to be ministers without intrigue ? Or Riza Pacha himself? How do you think

Mehemet Ali got on ?   Do you believe Sir Canning never intrigues ?   He would be recalled in a week if he did not. Why, I have got one of his spies in my castle at this moment, and I make him write home for the English all that I wish them not to believe.   Intrigue !   Why, England won India by intrigue.   Do you think they are not intriguing in the Punjaub at this moment?   Intrigue has gained half the thrones of Europe : Greece, France, Belgium, Portugal, Spain, Russia.   If you wish to produce a result, you must make combinations : and you call combinations, Eva, intrigue !—(' Fakredeen ') *Tancred.*

I do not believe that anything great is ever effected by management.—*Tancred.*

He was just the animal that Lord Monmouth wanted, for Lord Monmouth always looked upon human nature with the callous eyes of a jockey.   He surveyed Rigby, and he determined to buy him.   He bought him.—*Coningsby.*

INVENTION.

A nation has a fixed quantity of invention, and it will make itself felt.—(' Prince Florestan ') *Endymion.*

IRELAND.

He hoped the time would come, when a party, framed on true principles, would do justice to Ireland, not by satisfying agitators, not by adopting in despair the first quack remedy that was offered from either side of the House, but by really penetrating into the mystery of this great mismanagement.—*Speech in House of Commons (Arms [Ireland] Bill), August* 9, 1843.

There was only one principle for governing such a country, and that was the principle of centralisation.— *Speech in House of Commons (Municipal Corporations [Ireland] Bill), June* 1, 1838.

There is this remarkable characteristic of the agrarian anarchy of Ireland which marks it out from all other similar conditions of other countries : it is a war of the poor against the poor.—*Life of Lord George Bentinck.*

Ireland is in a state of social decomposition.—*Speech in House of Commons (State of the Nation), July* 2, 1849.

The commercial principle does not work in Ireland : all men agree that Ireland has been misgoverned. And who has misgoverned her? The State. It is the conduct of the State, past or present, that prevents the free action of the commercial principle in Ireland.—*Speech in House of Commons (Railways [Ireland]) February* 5, 1847.

IRISH.

Their treason is a fairy tale, and their sedition a child talking in its sleep.—(' Captain Bruges ') *Lothair.*

An Irish business is a thing to be turned over several times.—(' Captain Bruges ') *Lothair.*

I must say that I think that the general expression of feeling on the part of the Irish members appears to be genuine and good-natured—for I cannot believe the opposition which they have shown arises from anything else than a desire to exhibit that power of speech and eloquence which characterises them, and in which I candidly confess they excel both Englishmen and Scotchmen.—*Speech in House of Commons (Budget), April* 19, 1858.

Whatever may be said, and however plausible things may look, in an Irish business there is always a priest at the bottom of it.—(' Captain Bruges ') *Lothair.*

Irish Protestant Clergy.—Men who seldom stepped out of the sphere of their private virtues.—*Maiden Speech in House of Commons (Irish Election Petition), December* 7, 1837.

ISANDULA.

A great nation can endure the loss of a pitched battle with dignity and self-control. They may even find consolation under such circumstances, in the consciousness of a good cause, and in the heroic acts of their countrymen, though defeated. But calamities that commence with treachery, and are consummated by assassination and massacre—when the victims are youth and genius, unrivalled courage, and the highest patriotism—these are the incidents that rend the heart of a nation.—*Speech in Guildhall, November* 9, 1879.

ITALIAN LAKES.

There are few spots more favoured by nature than the Italian lakes and their vicinity, combining, as they do, the most sublime features of mountainous scenery with all the softer beauties and the varied luxuriance of the plain. As the still, bright lake is to the rushing and troubled cataract, is Italy to Switzerland and Savoy. Emerging from the chaotic ravines and the wild gorges of the Alps, the happy land breaks upon us like a beautiful vision. We revel in the sunny light, after the unearthly glare of eternal snow. Our sight seems renovated as we throw our eager glance over those golden plains, clothed with such picturesque trees, sparkling with such graceful villages, watered by such noble rivers, and crowned with such magnificent cities ; and all bathed and beaming in an atmosphere so soft and radiant ! Every isolated object charms us with its beautiful novelty : for the first time we gaze on palaces ; the garden, the terrace, and the statue, recall our dreams beneath a colder sky ; and we turn from these to catch the hallowed form of some cupolaed convent, crowning the gentle elevation of some green hill, and flanked by the cypress or the pine.— *Venetia.*

JACOBIN.

I know nothing more vile than an English Jacobin. It is the feeblest and worst imitation of the most odious of characters.—*Speech at Buckingham (General Election), February* 10, 1874.

JERUSALEM.

The broad moon lingers on the summit of Mount Olivet, but its beam has long left the garden of Gethsemane and the tomb of Absalom, the waters of Kedron, and the dark abyss of Jehoshaphat. Full falls its splendour, however, on the opposite city, vivid and defined in its silver blaze. A lofty wall, with turrets and towers and frequent gates, undulates with the unequal ground which it covers, as it encircles the lost capital of Jehovah. It is a city of hills, far more famous than those of Rome : for all Europe has heard of Sion and of Calvary, while the Arab and the Assyrian, and the tribes and nations beyond, are as ignorant of the Capitolian and Aventine Mounts as they are of the Malvern or the Chiltern Hills.

The broad steep of Sion crowned with the tower of David ; nearer still, Mount Moriah, with the gorgeous temple of the God of Abraham, but built, alas ! by the child of Hagar, and not by Sarah's chosen one ; close to its cedars and its cypresses, its lofty spires and airy arches, the moonlight falls upon Bethesda's pool ; further on, entered by the gate of St. Stephen, the eye, though 'tis the noon of night, traces with ease the Street of Grief, a long winding ascent to a vast cupolaed pile that now covers Calvary, called the Street of Grief, because there the most illustrious of the human, as well as of the Hebrew race, the descendant of King David, and the divine Son of the most favoured of women, twice sank under that burden of suffering and shame which is now throughout all Christendom the emblem of triumph and of honour ; passing over groups and masses of houses built of stone, with terraced roofs, or surmounted with small domes, we reach the hill of Salem, where Melchisedek built his mystic citadel ; and still remains the hill of Scopas, where Titus gazed upon Jerusalem on the eve of his final assault. Titus destroyed the Temple. The religion of Judæa has in turn subverted the fanes which were raised

to his father and to himself in their imperial capital ; and
the God of Abraham, of Isaac, and of Jacob is now worshipped before every altar in Rome.

Jerusalem by moonlight ! 'Tis a fine spectacle, apart
from all its indissoluble associations of awe and beauty.
The mitigating hour softens the austerity of a mountain
landscape magnificent in outline, however harsh and severe
in detail ; and, while it retains all its sublimity, removes
much of the savage sternness of the strange and unrivalled
scene. A fortified city, almost surrounded by ravines, and
rising in the centre of chains of far-spreading hills, occasionally offering, through their rocky glens, the gleams of a
distant and richer land !

What need for nature to be fair in a scene like this,
where not a spot is visible that is not heroic or sacred,
consecrated or memorable ; not a rock that is not the cave
of prophets ; not a valley that is not the valley of heaven-
anointed kings ; not a mountain that is not the mountain of
God !

Before him is a living, a yet breathing and existing city,
which Assyrian monarchs came down to besiege, which the
chariots of Pharaohs encompassed, which Roman emperors
have personally assailed, for which Saladin and Cœur de
Lion, the Desert and Christendom, Asia and Europe, struggled in rival chivalry ; a city which Mahomet sighed to
rule, and over which the Creator alike of Assyrian kings
and Egyptian Pharaohs and Roman Cæsars, the Framer
alike of the Desert and of Christendom, poured forth the
full effusion of his divinely human sorrow.—*Tancred.*

The Christian convents form one of the most remarkable
features of modern Jerusalem. There are three principal
ones : the Latin Convent of Terra Santa, founded, it is
believed, during the last crusade, and richly endowed by
the kings of Christendom ; the Armenian and the Greek
convents, whose revenues are also considerable, but derived
from the numerous pilgrims of their different churches, who

annually visit the Holy Sepulchre, and generally during their sojourn reside within the walls of their respective religious houses. To be competent to supply such accommodation, it will easily be apprehended that they are of considerable size. They are in truth monastic establishments of the first class, as large as citadels, and almost as strong. Lofty stone walls enclose an area of acres, in the centre of which rises an irregular mass of buildings and enclosures ; courts of all shapes, galleries of cells, roofs, terraces, gardens, corridors, churches, houses, and even streets. Sometimes as many as five thousand pilgrims have been lodged, fed, and tended during Easter in one of these convents.—*Tancred.*

The view of Jerusalem is the history of the world ; it is more, it is the history of earth and of heaven.—*Tancred.*

Jerusalem at mid-day in midsummer is a city of stone in a land of iron with a sky of brass.—('Baroni') *Tancred.*

JESUITS.

The Jesuits are wise men, they never lose their temper. *Lothair.*

The influence of the Jesuits is the influence of divine truth. The Jesuits never fell except from conspiracy against them. It is never the public will against them. It is never the public voice that demands their expulsion, or the public effort that accomplishes it.—('Archbishop Penruddock') *Endymion.*

JEWS.

They are not a new people, who have just got into notice, and who, if you do not recognise their claims, may disappear. They are an ancient people, a famous people, an enduring people, and a people who in the end have generally attained their objects. I hope Parliament may endure for ever, and sometimes I think it will ; but I cannot help remembering that the Jews have outlived Assyrian kings, Egyptian

N

Pharaohs, Roman Cæsars, and Arabian Caliphs.—*Speech in House of Commons (Oaths Bill), May 25, 1854.*

'The Jews, Coningsby, are essentially Tories. Toryism, indeed, is but copied from the mighty prototype which has fashioned Europe. And every generation they must become more powerful and more dangerous to the society which is hostile to them. Do you think that the quiet humdrum persecution of a decorous representative of an English university can crush those who have successively baffled the Pharaohs, Nebuchadnezzar, Rome, and the Feudal ages? The fact is, you cannot destroy a pure race of the Caucasian organisation. It is a physiological fact; a simple law of nature, which has baffled Egyptian and Assyrian Kings, Roman Emperors, and Christian Inquisitors. No penal laws, no physical tortures, can effect that a superior race should be absorbed in an inferior, or be destroyed by it. The mixed persecuting races disappear; the pure persecuted race remains. And at this moment, in spite of centuries, of tens of centuries, of degradation, the Jewish mind exercises a vast influence on the affairs of Europe. I speak not of their laws, which you still obey; of their literature, with which your minds are saturated; but of the living Hebrew intellect.

'You never observe a great intellectual movement in Europe in which the Jews do not greatly participate. The first Jesuits were Jews; that mysterious Russian diplomacy which so alarms Western Europe is organised and principally carried on by Jews; that mighty revolution which is at this moment preparing in Germany, and which will be, in fact, a second and greater Reformation, and of which so little is as yet known in England, is entirely developing under the auspices of Jews, who almost monopolise the professorial chairs of Germany. Neander, the founder of Spiritual Christianity, and who is Regius Professor of Divinity in the University of Berlin, is a Jew. Benary, equally famous, and in the same University, is a Jew.

Wehl, the Arabic Professor of Heidelberg, is a Jew. Years ago, when I was in Palestine, I met a German student who was accumulating materials for the History of Christianity, and studying the genius of the place ; a modest and learned man. It was Wehl ; then unknown, since become the first Arabic scholar of the day, and the author of the life of Mahomet. But for the German professors of this race, their name is Legion. I think there are more than ten at Berlin alone.

'I hear of peace and war in newspapers, but I am never alarmed, except when I am informed that the sovereigns want treasure ; then I know that monarchs are serious.

'A few years back we were applied to by Russia. Now, there has been no friendship between the Court of St. Petersburg and my family. It has Dutch connections, which have generally supplied it ; and our representations in favour of the Polish Hebrews, a numerous race, but the most suffering and degraded of all the tribes, have not been very agreeable to the Czar. However, circumstances drew to an approximation between the Romanoffs and the Sidonias. I resolved to go myself to St. Petersburg. I had, on my arrival, an interview with the Russian Minister of Finance, Count Cancrin : I beheld the son of a Lithuanian Jew. The loan was connected with the affairs of Spain ; I resolved on repairing to Spain from Russia. I travelled without intermission. I had an audience immediately on my arrival with the Spanish Minister, Señor Mendizabel : I beheld one like myself, the son of a Nuevo Christiano, a Jew of Arragon. In consequence of what transpired at Madrid, I went straight to Paris to consult the President of the French Council : I beheld the son of a French Jew, a hero, an Imperial marshal, and very properly so, for who should be military heroes if not those who worship the Lord of Hosts ?'

'And is Soult a Hebrew ?'

'Yes, and others of the French marshals, and the most famous—Massena for example ; his real name was Manasseh : but to my anecdote. The consequence of our consultations was, that some Northern power should be applied to in a friendly and mediative capacity. We fixed on Prussia ; and the President of the Council made an application to the Prussian Minister, who attended a few days after our conference. Count Arnim entered the cabinet, and I beheld a Prussian Jew. So you see, my dear Coningsby, that the world is governed by very different personages from what is imagined by those who are not behind the scenes.'

They record our triumphs ; they solace our affliction. Great orators are the creatures of popular assemblies ; we were permitted only by stealth to meet even in our temples. And as for great writers, the catalogue is not blank. What are all the schoolmen, Aquinas himself, to Maimonides ? And as for modern philosophy, all springs from Spinoza.

But the passionate and creative genius, that is the nearest link to Divinity, and which no human tyranny can destroy, though it can divert it ; that should have stirred the hearts of nations by its inspired sympathy, or governed senates by its burning eloquence ; has found a medium for its expression, to which, in spite of your prejudices and your evil passions, you have been obliged to bow. The ear, the voice, the fancy teeming with combinations, the imagination fervent with picture and emotion, that came from Caucasus, and which we have preserved unpolluted, have endowed us with almost the exclusive privilege of Music ; that science of harmonious sounds, which the ancients recognised as most divine, and deified in the person of their most beautiful creation. I speak not of the past ; though, were I to enter into the history of the lords of melody, you would find it the annals of Hebrew genius. But at this moment even, musical Europe is ours. There is not a company of singers, not an orchestra in a single capital, that is not crowded with our children under the feigned names which they adopt to conciliate the dark aversion which your posterity will some day disclaim with shame and disgust. Almost every great composer, skilled musician, almost every voice that ravishes you with its transporting strains, springs from our tribes. The catalogue is too vast to enumerate ; too illustrious to dwell for a moment on secondary names, however eminent. Enough for us that the three great creative minds to whose exquisite inventions all nations at this moment yield, Rossini, Meyerbeer, Mendelssohn, are of Hebrew race ; and little do your men of fashion, your muscadins of Paris, and your dandies of London, as they thrill into raptures at the notes of a Pasta or a Grisi, little do they suspect that they are offering their homage to 'the sweet singers of Israel.'—*Coningsby*.

JOBS.

My own impression is not very strong in that direction, because the experience of a long political life has taught me that nothing is more exaggerated than those mutual imputations which we make against each other to the effect that we take advantage of whatever circumstances may be under our control in our party arrangements.—*Speech in House of Commons* (*Representation of People Bill*), *June* 24, 1867.

JUSTICE.

A great writer has said that 'grace was beauty in action.' I say that Justice is truth in action.—*Speech in House of Commons* (*Agricultural Distress*), *February* 11, 1851.

KITCHEN.

At Montacute.—Everywhere, rich materials and silent artists ; business without bustle ; and the all-pervading magic of method.—*Tancred*.

If artists were sure of being appreciated ; if we were

but understood, a dinner would become a sacrifice to the gods, and a kitchen would be Paradise.—('Leander') *Tancred.*

The tree of knowledge is the tree of death.—('Egremont') *Sybil.*

She is calm, because she is the mistress of her subject ; 'tis the secret of self-possession.—('Sidonia') *Coningsby.*

A man can know nothing of mankind without knowing something of himself. Self-knowledge is the property of that man whose passions have their full play, but who ponders over their results.—*The Young Duke.*

To be conscious that you are ignorant is a great step to knowledge.—*Vivian Grey.*

Eloquence is the child of knowledge. When a mind is full, like a wholesome river, it is also clear. Confusion and obscurity are much oftener the results of ignorance than of inefficiency.—*The Young Duke.*

Knowledge of mankind is a knowledge of their passions. Travel is not, as is imagined, the best school for that sort of science.—*The Young Duke.*

Knowledge must be gained by ourselves. Mankind may supply us with facts ; but the results, even if they agree with previous ones, must be the work of our own minds.—*The Young Duke.*

He would support that system which maintained the preponderance of the landed interest. He believed that preponderance to be essential to the welfare of the country ; he attributed to that preponderance the stability of our institutions. He upheld that preponderance not for the advantage of a class, but for the benefit of the nation.— *Speech in House of Commons (Distress of Country), February 14, 1843.*

The manufacturer aspires to be 'large-acred,' and always

will, so long as we have a territorial constitution ; a better security for the preponderance of the landed interest than any corn-law fixed or fluctuating.—*Sybil.*

LAW.

When men are pure, laws are useless ; when men are corrupt, laws are broken.—(' The Sheikh ') *Contarini Fleming.*

LAWYERS.

All lawyers are loose in their youth ; but an insular country, subject to fogs and with a powerful middle class, requires grave statesmen.—(' Bertie Tremaine ') *Endymion.*

LEARNING.

Learning is better than house and land.—(' Mrs. Carey ') *Sybil.*

LEBANON.

There are regions more lofty than the glaciered crests of Lebanon ; mountain scenery more sublime, perhaps even more beautiful : its peaks are not lost in the clouds like the mysterious Ararat ; its forests are not as vast and strange as the towering Himalaya ; it has not the volcanic splendour of the glowing Andes ; in lake and in cataract it must yield to the European Alps ; but for life, vigorous, varied, and picturesque, there is no highland territory in the globe that can for a moment compare with the great chain of Syria.—*Tancred.*

LEGISLATORS.

The most successful legislators are those who have consulted the genius of the people.—*Contarini Fleming.*

LEMAN, LAKE.

In these moments, rather of humility than despondence, would fly for consolation to the blue waters of that beautiful lake, whose shores have ever been the favourite haunt of genius, the fair and gentle Leman.

Nor is there indeed in nature a sight more lovely than to watch, at decline of day, the last embrace of the sun lingering on the rosy glaciers of the White Mountain. Soon, too soon, the great luminary dies; the warm peaks subside into purple and then die into a ghostly white; but soon, ah! not too soon, the moon springs up from behind a mountain, flings over the lake a stream of light, and the sharp glaciers glitter like silver.

I have often passed the whole night upon these enchanted waters, contemplating their beautiful variety; and, indeed, if anything can console one for the absence of the moon and stars, it would be to watch the lightning, on a dark night, on this superb lake. It is incessant, and sometimes in four or five different places at the same time. In the morning Leman loses its ultramarine tint, and is covered with the shadows of mountains and chateaux.—*Contarini Fleming.*

LETTERS.

Mrs. Neuchatel was a fine penwoman: her feelings were her facts, and her ingenious observations of art and nature were her news.—*Endymion.*

Long Letters.—Perfect Epistolary Boa-constrictors—I have suffered under their voluminous windings.—*Vivian Grey.*

LEWIS (SIR GEORGE C.)

I do not know the man who combined in so eminent a degree as Sir George Lewis, both from acquirement and from nature, power of thought, the faculty upon all public matters of arriving at a sound and thorough opinion. Although he was a man most remarkably free from prejudice and passion, that exemption from sentiments which are supposed in general to be necessary to the possession of active power had not upon him that effect which they generally exercise; and he was a man who, in all the transactions of life, brought a great organising faculty and a great power of sustained perseverance to the transaction of public affairs.—*Speech in House of Commons* (*Death of Sir G. C. Lewis*), *April* 15, 1863.

LIBERALISM.

My objection to Liberalism is this—that it is the introduction into the practical business of life of the highest kind —namely, politics—of philosophical ideas instead of political principles.—*Speech in House of Commons* (*Expulsion of British Ambassador from Madrid*), *June* 5, 1848.

An attempt to govern the country by the assertion of abstract principles, which it was now beginning to be the fashion to call Liberalism.—*Endymion*.

We know what Liberalism means on the Continent. It means the abolition of property and religion.—('Great Personage') *Endymion*.

The tone and tendency of Liberalism cannot be concealed. It is to attack the institutions of the country under the name of Reform and to make war on the manners and customs of the people under the pretext of progress.—*Speech at Crystal Palace* (*Banquet of the National Union of Conservative and Constitutional Associations*), *June* 24, 1872.

I have seen in my time several monopolies terminated, and recently I have seen the termination of the monopoly of Liberalism. Nor are we surprised when we see that ceitain persons who believed that they had an hereditary right whenever it was necessary to renovate the institutions of their country, should be somewhat displeased that any other person should presume to interfere with those changes which I hope, in the spirit of true patriotism, they believed the requirements of the State rendered necessary. But I am sure that when the hubbub has subsided—when the shrieks and screams which were heard some time ago, and which have already subsided into sobs and sighs, shall be thoroughly appeased—nothing more terrible will be discovered to have occurred than that the Tory party has resumed its natural functions in the government of the country. For what is the Tory party unless it represents national feeling?—*Speech at Mansion House, August* 1867.

'The principle of the exclusive constitution of England having been conceded by the Acts of 1827-8-32,' said Coningsby, 'a party has arisen in the State who demand that the principle of political Liberalism shall consequently be carried to its extent; which it appears to them is impossible without getting rid of the fragments of the old constitution that remain. This is the destructive party; a party with distinct and intelligible principles. They seek a specific for the evils of our social system in the general suffrage of the population.—*Coningsby.*

Patriotism was a false idea and entirely repugnant to the principles of the new philosophy.—('Bertie Tremaine') *Endymion.*

The Tory system had degenerated into a policy which formed its basis on the principles of exclusiveness and restriction. A body of public men distinguished by their capacity took advantage of these circumstances. They seized the helm of affairs in a manner, the honour of which I do not for a moment question, but they introduced a new system into our political life. Influenced in a great degree by the philosophy and the politics of the Continent, they endeavoured to substitute cosmopolitan for national principles, and they baptised the new scheme of politics with the plausible name of Liberalism.—*Speech at Crystal Palace (Banquet of the National Union of Conservative and Constitutional Associations), June* 24, 1872.

The noble Lord (Lord John Russell) called every section of the Liberal party to his house in Chesham Place. There was the school of Manchester with its vigilant and justifiable ambition; there were all the administrative reformers in the shell; there were the inexorable assertors.

of pure Radical principles, men of Spartan virtue, who only sought for power to assert a principle, and would never take office except to carry it into successful execution.—*Speech in House of Commons* (*Administrative Reform*), *June* 18, 1855.

What would they say (to their constituencies) when the only result of their nine months' sitting, the ordinary period of gestation, had produced nothing but this abortion, this strangled offspring of the noble Lord (Lord J. Russell)?—*Speech in House of Commons* (*Municipal Corporations* [*Ireland*] *Bill*), *August* 10, 1838.

For my part I consider it a great homage to public opinion to find every scoundrel nowadays professing himself a Liberal.—('Saturn') *Infernal Marriage.*

The Liberals of Darlford were looking for a candidate. But they never could hit on the right man. If principles were right, there was no money ; and if money were ready, money would not take pledges. In fact they wanted a Phœnix—a very rich man who would do exactly as they liked, with very low opinions and with very high connections.—*Coningsby.*

As time advanced it was not difficult to perceive that extravagance was being substituted for energy by the Government. Their paroxysms ended in prostration. Some took refuge in melancholy, and their eminent chief alternated between menace and a sigh.

As I sat opposite the Treasury bench the ministers reminded me of one of those marine landscapes not very unusual on the coasts of South America. You behold a range of exhausted volcanoes—not a flame flickers on a single pallid crest. But the situation is still dangerous. There are occasional earthquakes, and ever and anon the dark rumbling of the sea.—*Speech in Free Trade Hall at Manchester, April* 3, 1872.

For nearly five years the present ministers have harassed every trade, worried every profession, and assailed or menaced every class, institution, and species of property in the country. Occasionally they have varied this state of civil warfare by perpetrating some job which outraged public opinion, or by stumbling into mistakes, which have always been discreditable, and sometimes ruinous. All this they call a policy, and seem quite proud of it ; but the country has, I think, made up its mind to close this career of plundering and blundering.—*Letter to Lord Grev de Wilton before Bath Election, October* 3, 1873.

LIFE.

Life's a tumble-about thing of ups and downs.—('Widow Carey') *Sybil.*

For life in general there is but one decree. Youth is a blunder, manhood a struggle, old age a regret.—('Sidonia') *Coningsby.*

Be like me, live in the present, and when you dream, dream of the future.—('Lady Montfort') *Endymion.*

It is a drear life to do the same thing the same day at the same hour.—*Sybil.*

My life was not monotonous, for my life was only love. *Contarini Fleming.*

Life is adventurous. Events are perpetually occurring, even in the calmness of domestic existence, which change in an instant the whole train and tenor of our thoughts and feelings, and often materially influence our fortunes and our character. It is strange, and sometimes as profitable as it is singular, to recall our state on the eve of some acquaintance which transfigures our being ; with some man whose philosophy revolutionises our mind ; with some woman whose charms metamorphose our career. These retrospective meditations are fruitful of self-knowledge.—*Henrietta Temple.*

Mankind are constantly starting at events which they consider extraordinary. But a philosopher acknowledges only one miracle, and that is life. Political revolutions, changes of empire, wrecks of dynasties and the opinions that support them, these are the marvels of the vulgar, but these are only transient modifications of life. The origin of existence is, therefore, the first object which a true philosopher proposes to himself. Unable to discover it, he accepts certain results from his unbiassed observation of its obvious nature, and on them he establishes certain principles to be our guides in all social relations, whether they take the shape of laws or customs. Nevertheless, until the principle of life be discovered, all theories and all systems of conduct founded on theory must be considered provisional.—('Herbert') *Venetia.*

O Life! what a heart-breaking thing is life! And our affections, our sweet and pure affections, fountains of such joy and solace, that nourish all things, and make the most barren and rigid soil teem with life and beauty, oh! why do we disturb the flow of their sweet waters, and pollute their immaculate and salutary source?—*Henrietta Temple.*

Lord Montfort was a man of deep emotions, and of a very fastidious taste. He was a man of as romantic a temperament as Ferdinand Armine; but with Lord Montfort, life was the romance of reason; with Ferdinand, the romance of imagination. The first was keenly alive to all the imperfections of our nature, but he also gave that nature credit for all its excellencies. He observed finely, he calculated nicely, and his result was generally happiness. Ferdinand, on the contrary, neither observed nor calculated. His imagination created fantasies, and his impetuous passions struggled to realise them.—*Henrietta Temple.*

'Life would be perfect if it would only last.' But it will not last; and what then? He could not reconcile interest in this life with the conviction of another, and an eternal one. It seemed to him that, with such a conviction, man could only have one thought and one occupation, the future, and preparation for it. With such a conviction, what they called reality appeared to him more vain and nebulous than the scenes and sights of sleep. And he

had that conviction ; at least he had it once. Had he it
now? Yes; he had it now, but modified perhaps ; in
detail. He was not so confident as he was a few months
ago, that he could be ushered by a Jesuit from his deathbed
to the society of St. Michael and all the Angels. There
might be long processes of initiation, intermediate states of
higher probation and refinement. There might be a horrible
and apathetic pause. When millions of ages appeared to
be necessary to mature the crust of a rather insignificant
planet, it might be presumption in man to assume that his
soul, though immortal, was to reach its final destination,
regardless of all the influences of space and time.—*Lothair.*

LINEAGE.

What is the use of belonging to an old family unless to
have the authority of an ancestor ready for any prejudice,
religious or political, which your combinations may require ?
(' Fakredeen ') *Tancred.*

How those rooks bore ! I hate staying with ancient
families, you are always cawed to death.—*Vivian Grey.*

'Ancient lineage ! I never heard of a peer with an
ancient lineage. The real old families of this country are
to be found among the peasantry ; the gentry, too, may lay
some claim to old blood. I can point you out Saxon
families in this county who can trace their pedigrees beyond
the Conquest ; I know of some Norman gentlemen whose
fathers undoubtedly came over with the Conqueror. But a
peer with an ancient lineage is to me quite a novelty. No,
no ; the thirty years of the wars of the Roses freed us from
those gentlemen. I take it, after the battle of Tewkesbury,
a Norman baron was almost as rare a being in England as a
wolf is now.'

'I have always understood,' said Coningsby, 'that our
peerage was the finest in Europe.'

'From themselves,' said Millbank, 'and the heralds they
pay to paint their carriages. But I go to facts. When

Henry VII. called his first Parliament, there were only twenty-nine temporal peers to be found, and even some of them took their seats illegally, for they had been attainted. Of those twenty-nine not five remain, and they, as the Howards for instance, are not Norman nobility. We owe the English peerage to three sources : the spoliation of the Church ; the open and flagrant sale of its honours by the elder Stuarts ; and the boroughmongering of our own times. Those are the three main sources of the existing peerage of England, and in my opinion disgraceful ones. But I must apologise for my frankness in thus speaking to an aristocrat.'

' Oh, by no means, sir; I like discussion.'

' And where will you find your natural aristocracy ? ' asked Coningsby.

' Among those men whom a nation recognises as the most eminent for virtue, talents, and property, and, if you please, birth and standing in the land. They guide opinion ; and, therefore, they govern. I am no leveller ; I look upon an artificial equality as equally pernicious with a factitious aristocracy ; both depressing the energies, and checking the enterprise of a nation. I like man to be free, really free : free in his industry as well as his body. What is the use of Habeas Corpus, if a man may not use his hands when he is out of prison ? '—*Coningsby.*

LITERATURE.

I may say of our literature that it has one characteristic which distinguishes it from almost all the other literatures of modern Europe, and that is its exuberant reproductiveness.— *Speech at Royal Literary Fund Dinner, May* 6, 1868.

LOCAL.

The local sentiment in man is the strongest passion in his nature. This local sentiment is the parent of most of our virtues.—*Speech at Royal South Buckinghamshire Agricultural Association Dinner at Salthill, November 5, 1864.*

LOCALITIES.

One should generally mention localities, because very often they indicate character.—*Tancred.*

LONDON.

What I miss here are the cafés.   Now in Paris you can dine every day exactly as it suits your means and mood : you may dine for a couple of francs in a quiet unknown street, and very well, or you may dine for a couple of Napoleons in a flaming saloon with windows opening on a crowded boulevard.   London is deficient in dining capabilities.—('St. Barbe') *Endymion.*

A city of cities, an aggregation of humanity, that probably has never been equalled in any period of the history of the world, ancient or modern.—*Speech in House of Commons (Direct and Indirect Taxation), May 1, 1873.*

There never was such a great city with such small houses.—('Lady Montfort') *Endymion.*

London is a roost for every bird.—('Felix Drolin') *Lothair.*

Mr. Glastonbury hailed a coach, into which, having safely deposited their portmanteaus, he and Ferdinand Armine entered ; but our young friend was so entirely overcome by his feelings and the genius of the place, that he was quite unable to make an observation.   Each minute the streets seemed to grow more spacious and more brilliant, and the multitude more dense and more excited.   Beautiful buildings, too, rose before him, palaces, and churches, and streets, and squares of imposing architecture ; to his inexperienced eye and unsophisticated spirit their route appeared a never-ending triumph.   To the hackney-coachman, however, who had no imagination, and who was quite satiated with metropolitan experience, it only appeared that he had

had an exceeding good fare, and that he was jogging up from Bishopsgate Street to Charing Cross.—*Henrietta Temple.*

What is most striking in London is its vastness. It is the illimitable feeling that gives it a special character. London is not grand. It possesses only one of the qualifications of a great city, size ; but it wants the equally important one, beauty. It is the union of these two qualities that produced the grand cities, the Romes, the Babylons, the hundred portals of the Pharaohs ; multitudes and magnificence ; the millions influenced by art. Grand cities are unknown since the beautiful has ceased to be the principle of invention. Paris, of modern capitals, has aspired to this character ; but if Paris be a beautiful city, it certainly is not a grand one ; its population is too limited, and, from the nature of their dwellings, they cover a comparatively small space. Constantinople is picturesque ; nature has furnished a sublime site, but it has little architectural splendour, and you reach the environs with a fatal facility. London overpowers us with its vastness. Though London is vast, it is very monotonous. All those new districts that have sprung up within the last half-century, the creatures of our commercial and colonial wealth, it is impossible to conceive anything more tame, more insipid, more uniform Pancras is like Marylebone, Marylebone is like Paddington ; all the streets resemble each other, you must read the names of the squares before you venture to knock at a door. This amount of building capital ought to have produced a great city. What an opportunity for Architecture suddenly summoned to furnish habitations for a population equal to that of the city of Bruxelles, and a population, too, of great wealth ! Marylebone alone ought to have produced a revolution in our domestic architecture. It did nothing. It was built by Act of Parliament. Parliament prescribed even a façade. It is Parliament to whom we are indebted for your Gloucester Places, and Baker Streets, and Harley Streets, and Wimpole Streets.

and all those flat, dull, spiritless streets, resembling each other like a large family of plain children, with Portman Place and Portman Square for their respectable parents. The influence of our Parliamentary government upon the fine arts is a subject worth pursuing. The power that produced Baker Street as a model for street architecture in its celebrated Building Act, is the power that prevented Whitehall from being completed, and which sold to foreigners all the pictures which the King of England had collected to civilise his people.—*Tancred.*

Social London.—That is to say, a park or so, two or three squares, and a dozen streets, where society lives, where it dines and dances and blackballs and bets and spouts.—*Endymion.*

Belgrave Square.—In our own days we have witnessed the rapid creation of a new metropolitan quarter, built solely for the aristocracy by an aristocrat. The Belgrave district is as monotonous as Marylebone, and is so contrived as to be at the same time both insipid and tawdry.—*Tancred.*

The only quarter which Lady Bardolf thought worthy of her new coronet, and Mrs. Guy Florence of her new visiting list.—*Tancred.*

Bond Street.—There is no street in the world that can furnish such a collection, filled with so many objects of beauty, curiosity, and interest.—*Lothair.*

Charing Cross.—Where London becomes more interesting is Charing Cross. Looking to Northumberland House, and turning your back upon Trafalgar Square, the Strand is perhaps the finest street in Europe, blending the architecture of many periods ; and its river ways are a peculiar feature and rich with associations. Fleet Street with its Temple is not unworthy of being contiguous to the Strand. The fire of London has deprived us of the delight of a real old quarter of the city ; but some bits remain, and everywhere there is a stirring multitude, and a great crush and crash of carts and wains. The Inns of Court, and the quarters in the vicinity of the port, Thames Street, Tower Hill, Billingsgate, Wapping, Rotherhithe, are the best parts of London ; they are full of character : the buildings bear a nearer relation to what the people are doing than in the more polished quarters.— *Tancred.*

The City.—The old merchants of the times of the first Georges were a fine race. They knew their position, and built up to it. While the territorial aristocracy, pulling down their family hotels, were raising vulgar streets and squares upon their site, and occupying themselves one of the new tenements, the old merchants filled the straggling lanes which connected the Royal Exchange with the Port of London with mansions which, if not exactly equal to the palaces of stately Venice, might at least vie with many of the hotels of old Paris. Some of these, though the great majority have been broken up into chambers and counting-houses, still remain intact.—*Tancred.*

Hyde Park.—Hyde Park has still about it something of Arcadia. There are woods and waters, and the occasional illusion of an illimitable distance of sylvan joyance.—*Tancred.*

Kensington Gardens.—So Ferdinand entered Kensington Gardens, and walked in those rich glades and stately avenues. It seems to the writer of this history that the inhabitants of London are scarcely sufficiently sensible of the beauty of its environs. On every side the most charming retreats open to them, nor is there a metropolis in the world surrounded by so many rural villages, picturesque parks, and elegant casinos. With the exception of Constantinople, there is no city in the world that can for a moment enter into competition with it. For himself, though in his time something of a rambler, he is not ashamed in this respect to confess to a legitimate Cockney taste ; and for his part he does not know where life can flow on more pleasantly than in sight of Kensington Gardens, viewing the silver Thames winding by the bowers of Rosebank, or inhaling from its terraces the refined air of graceful Richmond.

In exactly ten minutes it is in the power of every man to free himself from all the tumult of the world ; the pangs of love, the throbs of ambition, the wear and tear of play, the recriminating boudoir, the conspiring club, the rattling hell ; and find himself in a sublime sylvan solitude superior to the cedars of Lebanon, and inferior only in extent to the chestnut forests of Anatolia.   It is Kensington Gardens that is almost the only place that has realised his idea of the forests of Spenser and Ariosto.   What a pity, that instead of a princess in distress we meet only a nursery-maid !   But here is the fitting and convenient locality to brood over our thoughts ; to project the great and to achieve the happy. It is here that we should get our speeches by heart, invent our impromptus ; muse over the caprices of our mistresses, destroy a cabinet, and save a nation.—*Henrietta Temple.*

Regent's Park.—The Duke of St. James took his way to the Regent's Park, a wild sequestered spot, whither he invariably repaired when he did not wish to be noticed ; for the inhabitants of this pretty suburb are a distinct race, and although their eyes are not unobserving, from their inability to speak the language of London they are unable to communicate their observations.

The spring sun was setting, and flung a crimson flush over the blue waters and the white houses.—*The Young Duke.*

St. James's Park.—It was a real summer day ; large, round, glossy, fleecy clouds, as white and shining as glaciers, studded with their immense and immovable forms the deep blue sky.   There was not even a summer breeze, though the air was mellow, balmy, and exhilarating.   There was a bloom upon the trees, the waters glittered, the prismatic wild-fowl dived, breathed again, and again disappeared. Beautiful children, fresh and sweet as the new-born rose, glanced about with the gestures and sometimes the voices of Paradise. And in the distance rose the sacred towers of the great Western Minster.

How fair is a garden amid the toils and passions of existence ! A curse upon those who vulgarise and desecrate these holy haunts ; breaking the hearts of nursery-maids, and smoking tobacco in the palace of the rose !—*Sybil*.

St. James's Place.—St. James's Place, that is always my idea of solitude.—('Ferrars') *Endymion*.

St. James's Street.—That celebrated eminence the top of St. James's Street.—*Endymion*.

Westminster Abbey.—The Abbey of Westminster rises amid the strife of factions. Around its consecrated precinct some of the boldest and some of the worst deeds have been achieved or perpetrated ; sacrilege, rapine, murder, and treason. Here robbery has been practised on the greatest scale known in modern ages ; here ten thousand manors belonging to the order of the Templars, without any proof, scarcely with a pretext, were forfeited in one day and divided among the monarch and his chief nobles ; here the great estate of the Church, which, whatever its articles of faith, belonged and still belongs to the people, was seized at various times under various pretences, by an assembly that continually changed the religion of their country and their own by a parliamentary majority, but which never refunded the booty. Here too was brought forth that monstrous conception which even patrician Rome in its most ruthless period never equalled, the mortgaging of the industry of the country to enrich and to protect property ; an act which is now bringing its retributive consequences in a degraded and alienated population. Here too have the innocent been impeachéd and hunted to death ; and a virtuous and able monarch martyred, because, among other benefits projected for his people, he was of opinion that it was more for their advantage that the economic service of the state should be supplied by direct taxation levied by an individual known to all, than by indirect taxation, raised by an irresponsible and fluctuating assembly. But, thanks to parliamentary patriotism, the people of England were saved from ship money, which money the wealthy paid, and only got in its stead the customs and excise, which the poor mainly supply. Rightly was King Charles surnamed the Martyr ; for he was the holocaust of direct taxation. Never yet did man lay down his life for so great a eause : the cause of the Church and the cause of the Poor.—*Sybil.*

Suburbs.—London transforms itself into bustling Knights-bridge and airy Brompton brightly and gracefully, lingers cheerfully in the long, miscellaneous, well-watered King's Road, and only says farewell when you come to an abounding river and a picturesque bridge.—*Lothair.*

LONG-SIGHT.

I look upon a long-sighted man as a brute, who, not being able to see with his mind, is obliged to see with his body.—*The Young Duke.*

LORD MAYOR.

The associations of mysterious power and magnificence connected with the title and character of Lord Mayor.—*Endymion.*

LORD MAYOR'S DAY.

There is an air of enjoyment that pervades the whole City of London, in which all parties sympathise, and in which particularly the two parties in the State can meet together in the spirit of good-fellowship—opposed to each other like the two giant forms before me, but still meeting under the same roof.—*Speech at Mansion House, November 9, 1868.*

LOUIS XIV.

Louis XIV., though a king, was one of the greatest ministers that ever lived ; for he personally conducted the most important correspondence and transacted the most important affairs for a longer period than any minister who ever ruled.—*Speech in House of Commons* (*Cracow*), *March* 16, 1847.

LOVE.

Love is the May-day of the heart.—*Henrietta Temple.*

A simple story, and yet there are so many ways of telling it.—*Henrietta Temple.*

The principle of every motion—that is of life—is desire or love.—*Venetia.*

There is no usury for love.—('Herbert') *Venetia.*

Those feelings which still echo in the heights of Meillerie, and compared with which all the glittering accidents of fortune sink into insignificance.—*Endymion.*

The magic of first love is the ignorance that it can ever end.—*Henrietta Temple.*

To a man who is in love the thought of another woman is uninteresting if not repulsive.—*Contarini Fleming.*

The affections of the heart are property, and the sympathy of the right person is often worth a good estate.—*Endymion.*

Instead of love being the occasion of all the misery of this world, as is sung by fantastic bards, I believe that the misery of this world is occasioned by there not being love enough.—*Contarini Fleming.*

Experience is the best security for enduring love.—*Tancred.*

What a mystery is Love! All the necessities and habits of our life sink before it. Food and sleep, that seem to divide our being as day and night divide Time, lose all their influence over the lover. He is a spiritualised being, fit only to live upon ambrosia, and slumber in an imaginary paradise. The cares of the world do not touch him; its most stirring events are to him but the dusty incidents of bygone annals. All the fortune of the world without his mistress is misery; and with her all its mischances a transient dream. Revolutions, earthquakes, the change of governments, the fall of empires, are to him but childish games, distasteful to a manly spirit. Men love in the plague, and forget the pest, though it rages about them. They bear a charmed life, and think not of destruction until it touches their idol, and then they die without a pang, like zealots for their persecuted creed. A man in love wanders in the world as a somnambulist, with eyes that seem open to those that watch him, yet in fact view nothing but their own inward fancies.—*Henrietta Temple*.

Love at first sight is often a genial and genuine sentiment, but first love at first sight is ever eventually branded as spurious.—*Tancred*.

There is no love but love at first sight. This is the transcendent and surpassing offspring of sheer and unpolluted sympathy. All other is the illegitimate result of observation, of reflection, of compromise, of comparison, of expediency. The passions that endure flash like the lightning : they scorch the soul, but it is warmed for ever. Miserable man whose love rises by degrees upon the frigid morning of his mind ! Some hours indeed of warmth and lustre may perchance fall to his lot ; some moments of meridian splendour, in which he basks in what he deems eternal sunshine. But then how often overcast by the clouds of care, how often dusked by the blight of misery and misfortune ! And certain as the gradual rise of such affection is its gradual decline, and melancholy set. Then, in the chill dim twilight of his soul, he execrates custom ; because he has madly expected that feelings could be habitual that were not homogeneous, and because he has been guided by the observation of sense, and not by the inspiration of sympathy.

Amid the gloom and travail of existence suddenly to behold a beautiful being, and as instantaneously to feel an overwhelming conviction that with that fair form for ever our destiny must be entwined ; that there is no more joy but in her joy, no sorrow but when she grieves ; that in her sigh of love, in her smile of fondness, hereafter is all bliss ; to feel our flaunty ambition fade away like a shrivelled gourd before her vision ; to feel fame a juggle and posterity a lie ; and to be prepared at once, for this great object, to forfeit and fling away all former hopes, ties, schemes, views ; to violate in her favour every duty of society ; this is a lover, and this is love ! Magnificent, sublime, divine sentiment ! An immortal flame burns in the breast of that man who adores and is adored. He is an ethereal being. The accidents of earth touch him not. Revolutions of empire, changes of creed, mutations of opinion, are to him but the clouds and meteors of a stormy sky. The schemes and struggles of mankind are, in his thinking, but the anxieties of pigmies and the fantastical achievements of apes. Nothing can subdue him. He laughs alike at loss of fortune, loss of friends, loss of character. The deeds and thoughts of men are to him equally indifferent. He does not mingle in their paths of callous bustle, or hold himself responsible to the airy impostures before which they bow down. He is a mariner, who, in the sea of life, keeps his gaze fixedly on a single star ; and if that do not shine, he lets go the rudder, and glories when his barque descends into the bottomless gulf.—*Henrietta Temple.*

When a man is really in love, he is disposed to believe that, like himself, everyone is thinking of the person who engrosses his brain and heart.—*Endymion.*

The enamoured are always delighted with what is fanciful.—*The Young Duke.*

Restless are the dreams of the lover that is young.—*Henrietta Temple.*

I see no use of speaking to a man about love or religion : they are both stronger than friendship.—('Bertram') *Lothair.*

The lot the most precious to man, and which a beneficent Providence has made not the least common : to find in another heart a perfect and profound sympathy ; to unite his existence with one who would share all his joys, soften all his sorrows, aid him in all his projects, respond to all his fancies, counsel him in his cares, and support him in his perils ; make life charming by her charms, interesting by her intelligence, and sweet by the vigilant variety of her tenderness ; to find your life blessed by such an influence, and to feel that your influence can bless such a life : this lot, the most divine of divine gifts, that power and even fame can never rival in its delights, all this Nature had denied to Sidonia.—*Coningsby.*

Where we do not respect, we soon cease to love ; where we cease to love, virtue weeps and flies.—*The Young Duke.*

If it be agonising to be deserted, there is at least consolation in being cherished.—*Henrietta Temple.*

He had not yet learned the bitter lesson that unless we despise a woman when we cease to love her, we are still a slave, without the consolation of intoxication.—*The Young Duke.*

Lady Aphrodite still trembled when she recalled the early anguish of her broken sleep of love, and had not courage to hope that she might dream again. Like the old Hebrews she had been so chastened for her wild idolatry that she dared not raise an image to animate the wilderness of her existence.—*The Young Duke.*

Sweet is the voice of a sister in the season of sorrow, and wise is the counsel of those who love us.—*Alroy.*

A Father's Love.—Beautiful Venetia ! so fair, and yet so dutiful ; with a bosom teeming with such exquisite sensibilities, and a mind bright with such acute and elevated intelligence ! An abstract conception of the sentiments that might subsist between a father and a daughter, heightened by all the devices of a glowing imagination, had haunted indeed occasionally the solitary musing of Marmion Herbert ; but what was this creation of his poetic brain compared with the reality that now had touched his human heart? Vainly had he believed that repose was the only solace that remained for his exhausted spirit. He found that a new passion now swayed his soul ; a passion, too, that he had never proved ; of a nature most peculiar ; pure, gentle, refined, yet ravishing and irresistible, compared with which all former transports, no matter how violent, tumultuous, and exciting, seemed evanescent and superficial: they were indeed the wind, the fire, and the tempest that had gone before, but this was the still small voice that followed, excelled, and survived their might and majesty, unearthly and eternal!

His heart melted to his daughter, nor did he care to live without her love and presence. His philosophical theories all vanished. He felt how dependent we are in this world on our natural ties, and how limited, with all his arrogance, is the sphere of man. Dreaming of philanthropy, he had broken his wife's heart, and bruised, perhaps irreparably, the spirit of his child ; he had rendered those miserable who depended on his love, and for whose affection his heart now yearned to that degree, that he could not contemplate existence without their active sympathy.— *Venetia.*

A Mother's Love.—It was the inspiration of this sacred love that hovered like a guardian angel over the life of Venetia. It roused her from her morning slumbers with an embrace, it sanctified her evening pillow with a blessing ; it anticipated the difficulty of the student's page, and guided the faltering hand of the hesitating artist ; it refreshed her memory, it modulated her voice ; it accompanied her in the cottage, and knelt by her at the altar. Marvellous and beautiful is a mother's love. And when Venetia, with her strong feelings and enthusiastic spirit, would look around and mark that a graceful form and a bright eye were for ever watching over her wants and wishes, instructing with sweetness, and soft even with advice, her whole soul rose to her mother, all thoughts and feelings were concentrated in that sole existence, and she desired no happier destiny than to pass through life living in the light of her mother's smiles, and clinging with passionate trust to that beneficent and guardian form.— *Venetia.*

LOWE, ROBERT (LORD SHERBROOKE).

He has no sympathy with the past, no respect for tradition ; he has confidence in his own individual infallibility. But from the first moment that he entered public life—and I would prophesy that it will be to the last—he has offended the English nation, who can have no sympathy with a man who is proud of having no heart.—*General Election Speech at Newport Pagnell, February* 5, 1874.

The right honourable member for Calne is a very remarkable man. He is a very learned man, though he despises history. He can chop logic like Dean Aldrich ; but what is more remarkable than his learning and his logic is that power of spontaneous aversion which particularly characterises him. There is nothing that he likes, and almost everything that he hates. He hates the working classes of England. He hates the Roman Catholics of Ireland. He hates the Protestants of Ireland. He hates Her Majesty's Ministers ; and until the right honourable member for South Lancashire placed his hand upon the ark, he seemed almost to hate that right honourable gentleman. But now all is changed. Now we have the hour and the man. But I believe the clock goes wrong, and the man is mistaken.—*Speech in House of Commons (Established Church [Ireland]), April* 3, 1868.

LUCK.

Mrs. Darlington Vere was a most successful woman, lucky in everything—lucky even in her husband ; for he died.—*The Young Duke.*

It was what is called a lucky family ; that is to say, a family with a charm, that always attracted and absorbed heiresses.—*Lothair.*

Lucky is he who has neither creditors nor offspring, and who owes neither money, nor affection—after all the mos* difficult to pay of the two.—('Cadurcis') *Venetia.*

LYLE (EUSTACE).

'By the bye,' said Coningsby, 'what sort of fellow is Eustace Lyle? I rather like his look.'

'Oh! I will tell you all about him,' said Lord Henry. 'He is a great ally of mine, and I think you will like him very much. It is a Roman Catholic family, about the oldest we have in the county, and the wealthiest. You see, Lyle's father was the most violent ultra Whig, and so were all Eustace's guardians; but the moment he came of age, he announced that he should not mix himself up with either of the parties in the county, and that his tenantry might act exactly as they thought fit. My father thinks, of course, that Lyle is a Conservative, and that he only waits the occasion to come forward; but he is quite wrong. I know Lyle well, and he speaks to me without disguise. You see 'tis an old Cavalier family, and Lyle has all the opinions and feelings of his race. He will not ally himself with anti-monarchists, and democrats, and infidels, and sectarians; at the same time, why should he support a party who pretend to oppose these, but who never lose an opportunity of insulting his religion, and would deprive him, if possible, of the advantages of the very institutions which his family assisted in establishing?'

'Why, indeed? I am glad to have made his acquaintance,' said Coningsby. 'Is he clever?'

'I think so,' said Lord Henry. 'He is the most shy fellow, especially among women, that I ever knew, but he is very popular in the county. He does an amazing deal of good, and is one of the best riders we have. My father says, the very best; bold, but so very certain.'—*Coningsby.*

MACHINE.

A machine is a slave that neither brings nor bears degradation.—*Coningsby.*

The mystery of mysteries is to view machinery making machinery.—*Coningsby.*

MAJORITY.

A majority is always better than the best repartee.— ('Coningsby') *Tancred.*

The resolution has been carried by a very small majority —as it is in its 'teens,' it can hardly be called a majority at all.—*Speech in House of Commons (Ways and Means), May 3, 1861.*

MAN.

When a man is not speaking, or writing, from his own mind, he is as insipid company as a looking-glass.—*The Young Duke.*

The man who anticipates his century is always persecuted when living, and is always pilfered when dead.—(' Sievers ') *Vivian Grey.*

No affections and a great brain—these are the men to command the world. No affections and a little brain—such is the stuff of which they make petty villains.—('Baroni') *Tancred.*

It is not at all impossible that a man, always studying one subject, will view the general affairs of the world through the coloured prism of his own atmosphere.—*Speech in House of Commons (Railways [Ireland]), Feb. 15, 1847.*

To rule men we must be men ; to prove that we are strong we must be weak; to prove that we are giants we must be dwarfs—our wisdom must be concealed under folly, and our constancy under caprice.—*Vivian Grey.*

You cannot judge of a man by only knowing what his debts are ; you must be acquainted with his resources. (' Fakredeen ') *Tancred.*

Men do not like to be baulked when they think they are doing a very kind and generous and magnanimous thing. *Tancred.*

Man is an animal, and his nature must be studied as that of all other animals. The Almighty Creator has breathed his spirit into us ; and we testify our gratitude for this choice boon by never deigning to consider what may be the nature of our intelligence. The philosopher, however, amid this darkness, will not despair. He will look forward to an age of rational laws and beneficent education. He will remember that all the truth he has attained has been by one process. He will also endeavour to become acquainted with himself by demonstration, and not by dogma. *Contarini Fleming.*

Man is born to observe, but if he falls into psychology he observes nothing.—(' Mr. Phœbus ') *Lothair.*

A smile for a friend, and a sneer for the world, is the way to govern mankind.—*Vivian Grey.*

Man is mimetic : we repeat without thought the opinions of some third person, who has adopted them without inquiry.—*Tancred.*

Man is only great when he acts from the passions ; never irresistible, but when he appeals to the imagination. Even Mormon counts more votaries than Bentham.— (' Sidonia ') *Coningsby.*

Man is made to adore and obey ; but if you do not command him, if you give him nothing to worship, he will fashion his own divinities and find a chieftain in his own passions.—(' Sidonia ') *Coningsby.*

When a man at the same time believes in and sneers at his destiny, we may be sure that he considers his condition past redemption.—*Vivian Grey.*

Men never congregate together for any beneficial purpose. (' Violet Fane ') *Vivian Grey.*

Man is made to create, from the poet to the potter.--- (' Winter ') *Contarini Fleming.*

MANNERS.

Nowadays manners are easy and life is hard. —*Sybil.*

Manners change with time and circumstances ; customs may be observed everywhere.—*Alroy.*

His spirit recoiled from that gross familiarity that is the characteristic of modern manners, and which would destroy all forms and ceremonies, merely because they curb and control their own coarse convenience and ill-disguised selfishness.—*Coningsby.*

Lady Armine's manners were graceful, for she had visited courts and mixed in polished circles, but she had fortunately not learnt to affect insensibility as a system, or to believe that the essence of good-breeding consists in showing your fellow-creatures that you despise them.—*Henrietta Temple.*

A manner that was spontaneous ; nature's pure gift, the reflex of her feelings.—*Coningsby.*

The haughty suavity of that sunny glance, which was not familiar enough for a smile or foolish enough for a simper. *Tancred.*

MANUFACTURER.

The factory was about a mile distant from their cottage, which belonged indeed to Mr. Trafford, and had been built by him. He was the younger son of a family that had for centuries been planted in the land, but who, not satisfied with the factitious consideration with which society compensates the junior members of a territorial house for their entailed poverty, had availed himself of some opportunities that offered themselves, and had devoted his energies to those new sources of wealth that were unknown to his ancestors. His operations at first had been extremely limited, like his fortunes; but with a small capital, though his profits were not considerable, he at least gained experience. With gentle blood in his veins, and old English feelings, he imbibed, at an early period of his career, a correct conception of the relations which should subsist between the employer and the employed. He felt that between them there should be other ties than the payment and the receipt of wages.

A distant and childless relative, who made him a visit, pleased with his energy and enterprise, and touched by the development of his social views, left him a considerable sum, at a moment, too, when a great opening was offered to manufacturing capital and skill. Trafford, schooled in rigid fortunes, and formed by struggle, if not by adversity, was ripe for the occasion, and equal to it. He became very opulent, and he lost no time in carrying into life and being the plans which he had brooded over in the years when his good thoughts were limited to dreams. On the banks of his native Mowe he had built a factory, which was now one of the marvels of the district ; one might almost say, of the country : a single room, spreading over nearly two acres, and holding more than two thousand workpeople. The roof of groined arches, lighted by ventilating domes at the height of eighteen feet, was supported by hollow cast-iron columns, through which the drainage of the roof was effected. The height of the ordinary rooms in which the workpeople in manufactories are engaged, is not more than from nine to eleven feet ; and these are built in stories, the heat and effluvia of the lower rooms communicated to those above, and the difficulty of ventilation insurmountable. At Mr. Trafford's, by an ingenious process, not unlike that which is practised in the House of Commons, the ventilation was also carried on from below, so that the whole building was kept at a steady temperature, and little susceptible to atmospheric influence. The physical advantages of thus carrying on the whole work in one chamber are great : in the improved health of the people, the security against dangerous accidents to women and youth, and the reduced fatigue resulting from not having to ascend and descend, and carry materials to the higher rooms. But the moral

P

advantages resulting from superior inspection and general observation are not less important : the child works under the eye of the parent, the parent under that of the superior workman ; the inspector or employer at a glance can behold all.

When the workpeople of Mr. Trafford left his factory they were not forgotten. Deeply had he pondered on the influence of the employer on the health and content of his workpeople. He knew well that the domestic virtues are dependent on the existence of a home, and one of his first efforts had been to build a village where every family might be well lodged. Though he was the principal. proprietor, and proud of that character, he nevertheless encouraged his workmen to purchase the fee : there were some who had saved sufficient money to effect this ; proud of their house and their little garden, and of the horticultural society, where its produce permitted them to be annual competitors. In every street there was a well : behind the factory were the public baths ; the schools were under the direction of the perpetual curate of the church, which Mr. Trafford, though a Roman Catholic, had raised and endowed. In the midst of this village, surrounded by beautiful gardens, which gave an impulse to the horticulture of the community, was the house of Trafford himself, who comprehended his position too well to withdraw himself with vulgar exclusiveness from his real dependents, but recognise the baronial principle, reviving in a new form, and adapted to the softer manners and more ingenious circumstances of the times.

And what was the influence of such an employer and such a system of employment on the morals and manners of the employed ? Great ; infinitely beneficial. The connection of a labourer with his place of work, whether agricultural or manufacturing, is itself a vast advantage. Proximity to the employer brings cleanliness and order, because it brings observation and encouragement. In the settlement of Trafford crime was positively unknown, and offences were slight. There was not a single person in the village of a reprobate character. The men were well clad ; the women had a blooming cheek ; drunkenness was unknown ; while the moral condition of the softer sex was proportionately elevated.—*Sybil.*

MARRIAGE.

Some experience of society before we settle is most desirable, and is one of the conditions, I cannot but believe, of that felicity which we seek.—('The Duchess')—*Lothair.*

I respect the institution—I have always thought that every woman should marry, and no man.—('Hugo Bohun') *Lothair.*

The day before marriage and the hour before death is when a man thinks least of his purse and most of his neighbour.—*Vivian Grey.*

It is very immoral and very unfair, that any man should marry for tin, who does not want it.—('Lord Milford') *Tancred.*

It destroys one's nerves to be amiable every day to the same human being.—*The Young Duke.*

The character of a woman rapidly develops after marriage, and sometimes seems to change, when in fact it is only complete.—*Tancred.*

The married life of a woman of the working class in the present condition of our country is a lease of woe.— ('Gerard') *Sybil.*

Early Marriages.—For myself, I believe that permanent unions of the sexes should be early encouraged ; nor do I conceive that general happiness can ever flourish but in societies where it is the custom for all males to marry at eighteen. This custom, I am informed, is not unusual in the United States of America, and its consequence is a simplicity of manners and a purity of conduct which Europeans cannot comprehend, but to which they must ulti-

mately have recourse.   Primeval barbarism and extreme
civilisation must arrive at the same results.   Men, under
these circumstances, are actuated by their structure ; in
the first instance, instinctively ; in the second, philosophically.   At present, we are all in the various gradations of
the intermediate state of corruption.—*Contarini Fleming*.

Early marriages are to be deprecated, especially for men,
because they are too frequently imprudent.—('Lady Roehampton') *Endymion*.

MEASURES.

Their leader had on more than one occasion given what
he might call a pedigree of patriotism, proud of the great
measures which in the last two hundred years his party had
introduced and carried.—*Speech in House of Commons
(Arms [Ireland] Bill), August 9*, 1843.

The noble Lord called it an extraordinary measure, but
I object to it, that it is not an extraordinary measure.   It is
an ordinary measure, a vulgar measure.   The noble Lord
said, that when a man's house is on fire, you must have recourse to extraordinary measures to meet the calamity.   Sir,
I deny it.   You don't have recourse to extraordinary measures when your house is on fire ; you adopt ordinary
measures—you send for the parish engine.—*Speech in House
of Commons (Relief of Distress [Ireland]), November* 16, 1849.

MEDITERRANEAN.

'Say what they like,' said Herbert, 'there is a spell in
the shores of the Mediterranean Sea which no others can
rival.   Never was such a union of natural loveliness and
magical associations !   On these shores have risen all that
interests us in the past : Egypt and Palestine, Greece, Rome,
and Carthage, Moorish Spain, and feodal Italy.   These
shores have yielded us our religion, our arts, our literature,
and our laws.   If all that we have gained from the shores of

the Mediterranean was erased from the memory of man, we should be savages.—*Venetia.*

MELBOURNE (LORD)

A mild, middle-aged, lounging man—gifted with no ordinary abilities, cultivated with no ordinary care, but the victim of sauntering—his sultana queen.—*Runnymede Letters,* 1836.

MEMORY.

Reverie in the flush of our warm youth generally indulges in the future. When we advance a little on our limited journey, and an act or two of the comedy, the gayest in all probability, are over, the wizard memory dethrones the wild imagination, and 'tis the past on which the mind feeds in its musings.—*The Young Duke.*

We sometimes find that memory is as rare a quality as prediction.—*Tancred.*

What was most remarkable in him (Mr. Rodney) was the convenient and complete want of memory.—*Endymion.*

METAPHYSICS.

Yes, yes ! we have plenty of metaphysicians, if you mean them. Watch that lively-looking gentleman, who is stuffing kalte schale so voraciously in the corner. The leader of the Idealists, a pupil of the celebrated Fichte ! To gain an idea of his character, know that he out-Herods his master ; and Fichte is to Kant what Kant is to the un-enlightened vulgar. You can now form a slight conception of the spiritual nature of our friend who is stuffing kalte schale. The first principle of his school is to reject all expressions which incline in the slightest degree to substantiality. Existence is, in his opinion, a word too absolute. Being, principle, essence, are terms scarcely sufficiently ethereal even to indicate the subtle shadowings of his opinions. Some say that he dreads the contact of all real things, and that he makes it the study of his life to avoid them. Matter is his great enemy. When you converse with him you lose all consciousness of this world. My dear sir, observe how exquisitely nature revenges herself upon those capricious and fantastic children. Believe me, nature is the most brilliant of wits ; and that no repartees that ever were inspired by hate, or wine, or beauty, ever equalled the calm effects of her indomitable power upon those who are rejecting her authority. You understand me ? Methinks that the best answer to the idealism of M. Fichte is to see his pupil devouring kalte schale.—('Sievers') *Vivian Grey.*

MILLBANK (MR.).

At length there was a general stir, and they all did come forth, Mr. Millbank among them, a well-proportioned, comely man, with a fair face inclining to ruddiness, a quick glancing, hazel eye, the whitest teeth, and short, curly, chestnut hair, here and there slightly tinged with grey. It was a visage of energy and decision.—*Coningsby.*

MILLBANK (OSWALD).

Millbank was the son of one of the wealthiest manufacturers in Lancashire. His father, whose opinions were of a very democratic bent, sent his son to Eton, though he disapproved of the system of education pursued there, to show that he had as much right to do so as any duke in the land. He had, however, brought up his only boy with a due prejudice against every sentiment or institution of an aristocratic character, and had especially impressed upon him, in his school career, to avoid the slightest semblance of courting the affections or society of any member of the falsely held superior class.

The character of the son, as much as the influence of the father, tended to the fulfilment of these injunctions. Oswald Millbank was of a proud and independent nature ; reserved, a little stern. The early and constantly reiterated dogma of his father, that he belonged to a class debarred from its just position in the social system, had aggravated the grave and somewhat discontented humour of his blood. His talents were considerable, though invested with no dazzling quality. He had not that quick and brilliant apprehension, which, combined with a memory of rare retentiveness, had already advanced Coningsby far beyond his age, and made him already looked to as the future hero of the school. But Millbank possessed one of those strong industrious volitions whose perseverance amounts almost to genius, and nearly attains its results. Though Coningsby was by a year his junior, they were rivals. This circumstance had no tendency to remove the prejudice which Coningsby entertained against him, but its bias on the part of Millbank had a contrary effect.

The influence of the individual is nowhere so sensible as at school. There the personal qualities strike without any intervening and counteracting causes. A gracious presence, noble sentiments, or a happy talent, make their way there at once, without preliminary inquiries as to what set they are in, or what family they are of, how much they have a year, or where they live. Now, on no spirit had the influence of Coningsby, already the favourite, and soon probably to become the idol, of the school, fallen more effectually than on that of Millbank, though it was an influence that no one could suspect except its votary or its victim. . . .

The secret of Millbank's life was a passionate admiration and affection for Coningsby. Pride, his natural reserve, and his father's injunctions, had, however, hitherto successfully combined to restrain the slightest demonstration of these sentiments. Indeed, Coningsby and himself were never companions, except in school, or in some public game. The demeanour of Coningsby gave no encouragement to intimacy to one, who, under any circumstances, would have required considerable invitation to open himself. So Millbank fed in silence on a cherished idea. It was his happiness to be in the same form, to join in the

same sport, with Coningsby ; occasionally to be thrown in
unusual contact with him, to exchange slight and not un-
kind words.   In their division they were rivals ; Millbank
sometimes triumphed, but to be vanquished by Coningsby
was for him not without a degree of wild satisfaction.   Not
a gesture, not a phrase from Coningsby, that he did not
watch and ponder over and treasure up.   Coningsby was
his model, alike in studies, in manners, or in pastimes ; the
aptest scholar, the gayest wit, the most graceful associate,
the most accomplished playmate : his standard of the excellent.   Yet Millbank was the very last boy in the school
who would have had credit given him by his companions
for profound and ardent feeling.   He was not indeed
unpopular.   The favourite of the school like Coningsby, he
could, under no circumstances, ever have become ; nor was
he qualified to obtain that general graciousness among
the multitude, which the sweet disposition of Henry
Sydney, or the gay profusion of Buckhurst, acquired without an effort.   Millbank was not blessed with the charm
of manner.   He seemed close and cold ; but he was
courageous, just, and inflexible ; never bullied, and to his
utmost would prevent tyranny.   The little boys looked up
to him as a stern protector ; and his word, too, throughout
the school was a proverb : and truth ranks a great quality
among boys.   In a word, Millbank was respected by those
among whom he lived ; and schoolboys scan character
more nicely than men suppose. —*Coningsby.*

MILLBANK (EDITH).

This daughter of his host was of tender years ; apparently
she could scarcely have counted sixteen summers.   She was
delicate and fragile, but as she raised her still blushing
visage to her father's guest, Coningsby felt that he had never
beheld a countenance of such striking and such peculiar
beauty.

'My only daughter, Mr. Coningsby, Edith ; a Saxon name, for she is the daughter of a Saxon.'

But the beauty of the countenance was not the beauty of the Saxons. It was a radiant face, one of those that seem to have been touched in their cradle by a sunbeam, and to have retained all their brilliancy and suffused and mantling lustre. One marks sometimes such faces, diaphanous with delicate splendour, in the southern regions of France. Her eye, too, was the rare eye of Aquitaine ; soft and long, with lashes drooping over the cheek, dark as her clustering ringlets.

MINISTER.

The minister of a free people, he (Baron Fleming) was the personal as well as the political pupil of Metternich. Yet he respected the institutions of his country, because they existed, and because experience proved that under their influence the natives had become more powerful machines.

His practice of politics was compressed in two words, subtlety and force. The minister of an emperor, he would have maintained his system by armies ; in the cabinet of a small kingdom, he compensated for his deficiency by intrigue.

His perfection of human nature was a practical man. He looked upon a theorist either with alarm or with contempt. Proud in his own energies, and conscious that he owed everything to his own dexterity, he believed all to depend upon the influence of individual character. He required men not to think but to act, not to examine but to obey ; and, animating their brute force with his own intelligence, he found the success, which he believed could never be attained by the rational conduct of an enlightened people.

Out of the cabinet the change of his manner might perplex the superficial. The moment that he entered society his thoughtful face would break into a fascinating smile,

and he listened with interest to the tales of levity, and
joined with readiness in each frivolous pursuit. He was
sumptuous in his habits, and was said to be even voluptuous.
Perhaps he affected gallantry, because he was deeply impressed with the influence of women both upon public and
upon private opinion.   With them he was a universal
favourite ; and as you beheld him assenting with conviction to their gay or serious nonsense, and gracefully waving
his handkerchief in his delicate and jewelled hand, you
might have supposed him 'for a moment a consummate lord
chamberlain ; but only for a moment, for had you caught
his eye, you would have withdrawn your gaze with precipitation, and perhaps with awe.   For the rest, he spoke all
languages, never lost his self-possession, and never, in my
recollection, had displayed a spark of strong feeling.—*Contarini Fleming.*

Who may be the ministers of the Queen are the accidents
of history—what will remain on that enduring page is the
policy pursued, and its consequence on her realm.—*Conservative Manifesto, May* 20, 1865.

Gentlemen, you have given me credit individually for
possession and exercise of some happy arts in the carrying
these measures (Reform).   If I have shown patience, it
becomes my position ; if I have listened to the opinions of
my opponents with deference, I only fulfilled the duty of a
British Minister ; but, believe me, I am not entitled to those
compliments.   I will explain to you all to-night all the arts
by which I contrived to achieve this great success : all the
black devices which I applied were simply these—upon
every question I took my own party into confidence, and
when I had to appeal to an independent opposition, I remembered at all times they were men of sense and gentleness.—*Speech in Music Hall, Edinburgh, Working Men's
Address, October* 30, 1867.

No minister ever yet fell but from his own inefficiency.
If his downfall be occasioned, as it generally is, by the

intrigues of one of his own creatures, his downfall is merited for having been the dupe of a tool, which in all probability he should never have employed.—('Beckendorf') *Vivian Grey.*

A prudent minister certainly would not enter recklessly into any responsibility ; but a minister who is afraid to enter into responsibility is in my mind not a prudent minister. We do not wish to enter into any unnecessary responsibility ; but there is one responsibility from which we certainly shrink—we shrink from the responsibility of handing to our successors a diminished or a weakened empire.—*Speech in House of Commons (Congress, Correspondence and Protocols),* *July* 18, 1878.

There is a difference in the demeanour of the same individual, as leader of the Opposition and as Minister of the Crown—you must not contrast too strongly the hours of courtship with the years of possession.—*Speech in House of Commons (Agricultural Interest), March* 17, 1845.

MINISTRY.

One of the greatest of Romans, when asked what were his politics, replied : ' Imperium et libertas.' That would not make a bad programme for a British ministry.—*Speech in Guildhall, November* 9, 1879.

MISSION.

A special mission was at all times a delicate measure, and in general it was safest to make a special mission with some purpose really different from that which it was sent to fulfil.—*Speech in House of Commons (Distress of the Country), September* 14, 1843.

MONASTICS.

' A drone is one who does not labour ; whether he wear a cowl or a coronet, 'tis the same to me. Somebody, I suppose, must own the land ; though I have heard say that this individual tenure is not a necessity ; but, however this may be, I am not one who would object to the lord, provided he were a gentle one. All agree that the Monastics were easy landlords ; their rents were low ; they granted leases in those days. Their tenants, too, might renew their term before their tenure ran out : so they were men of spirit and property. There were yeomen then, sir : the country was not divided into two classes, masters and slaves ; there was some resting-place between luxury and misery. Comfort was an English habit then, not merely an English word.'

'And do you really think they were easier landlords than our present ones ?' said Egremont, inquiringly.

'Human nature would tell us that, even if history did not confess it. The Monastics could possess no private property ; they could save no money ; they could bequeath nothing. They lived, received, and expended in common. The monastery, too, was a proprietor that never died and never wasted. The farmer had a deathless landlord then ; not a harsh guardian, or a grinding mortgagee, or a dilatory master in chancery : all was certain ; the manor had not to dread a change of lords, or the oaks to tremble at the axe of the squandering heir. How proud we are still in England of an old family, though, God knows, 'tis rare to see one now. Yet the people like to say, We held under him, and his father and his grandfather before him : they know that such a tenure is a benefit. The abbot was ever the same. The monks were, in short, in every district a port of refuge for all who needed succour, counsel, and protection ; a body of individuals having no cares of their own, with wisdom to guide the inexperienced, with wealth to relieve the suffering, and often with power to protect the oppressed.'—('Gerard') *Sybil.*

MONEY.

Money is power, and rare are the heads that can withstand the possession of great power.—('Bond Sharpe') *Henrietta Temple.*

As men advance in life, all passions resolve themselves into money. Love, ambition, even poetry, end in this.— *Henrietta Temple.*

MONMOUTH (LORD).

The lord of the house slowly rose, for he was suffering slightly from the gout, his left hand resting on an ivory stick.

Lord Monmouth was in height above the middle size, but somewhat portly and corpulent. His countenance was strongly marked; sagacity on the brow, sensuality in the mouth and jaw. His head was bald, but there were remains of the rich brown locks on which he once prided himself. His large deep blue eye, madid and yet piercing, showed that the secretions of his brain were apportioned, half to voluptuousness, half to common sense. But his general mien was truly grand; full of a natural nobility, of which no one was more sensible than himself.

MONTFORT (LORD).

Simon, Earl of Montfort, may be said to have been a minor in his cradle. Under ordinary circumstances his inheritance would have been one of the most considerable in England. His castle in the north was one of the glories of the land, and becomingly crowned his vast domain. Under the old parliamentary system he had the greatest number of nomination boroughs possessed by any Whig noble. The character and conduct of an individual so qualified were naturally much speculated on and finely scanned. Nothing very decided transpired about them in his boyhood, but certainly nothing adverse. He was good-looking and athletic, and was said to be generous and good-natured, and when he went to Harrow he became popular. In his eighteenth year, while he was in correspondence with his guardians about going to Christchurch, he suddenly left his country without giving notice of his intentions, and entered into, and fulfilled, a vast scheme of adventure. He visited countries then rarely reached, and some of which were almost unknown. When he was of age, he returned, and communicated with his guardians, as if nothing remarkable had happened in his life. His hunters and his cooks were both first-rate. Although he affected to take little interest in politics, the events of the time forced him to consider them and to act. Lord Grey wanted to carry his Reform Bill, and the sacrifice of Lord Montfort's numerous boroughs was a necessary ingredient in the spell. He was appealed to as the head of one of the greatest Whig houses, and he was offered a dukedom. He relinquished his boroughs without hesitation, but he preferred to remain with one of the oldest earldoms of England for his chief title. All honours, however, clustered about him, though he never sought them, and in the same year he tumbled into the lord lieutenancy of his county, unexpectedly vacant, and became the youngest knight of the Garter. Society was looking forward with the keenest interest to the impending season, when Lord Montfort would formally enter its spell-bound ranks, and multiform were the speculations on his destiny. He attended an early levée in order that he might be presented, and then again quitted his country, and for years. He was heard of in every capital except his own. Wonderful exploits at St. Petersburg, and Paris, and Madrid, deeds of mark at Vienna, and eccentric adventures at Rome. At last it would appear that the restless Lord Montfort had found his place, and that place was Paris. There he dwelt for years in Sybarite seclusion. He built himself a palace, which he called a villa, and which was the most fanciful of structures, and full of every beautiful object which rare taste and boundless wealth could procure, from undoubted

Raffaelles to jewelled toys. It was said that Lord Montfort saw no one ; he certainly did not court or receive his own countrymen ; and this perhaps gave rise to, or at least caused to be exaggerated, the tales that were rife of his profusion, and even his profligacy.

Lord Montfort was the only living Englishman who gave one an idea of the nobleman of the eighteenth century. He was totally devoid of the sense of responsibility, and he looked what he resembled. His manner, though simple and natural, was finished and refined, and, free from forbidding reserve, was yet characterised by an air of serious grace.

There was no subject, divine or human, in which he took the slightest interest. He entertained for human nature generally, and without any exception, the most cynical appreciation. He had a sincere and profound conviction, that no man or woman ever acted except from selfish and interested motives. Society was intolerable to him ; that of his own sex and station wearied him beyond expression. As for female society, if they were ladies, it was expected that, in some form or other, he should make love to them, and he had no sentiment. If he took refuge in the demi-monde, he encountered vulgarity, and that to Lord Montfort was insufferable. He had tried them in every capital, and vulgarity was the badge of the whole tribe.

No one could say Lord Montfort was a bad-hearted man, for he had no heart. He was good-natured, provided it brought him no inconvenience ; and as for temper, his was never disturbed, but this not from sweetness of disposition, rather from a contemptuous fine taste, which assured him that a gentleman should never be deprived of tranquillity in a world where nothing was of the slightest consequence.—*Endymion.*

MONTFORT (LADY).

She was then in her second season, but still unparagoned, for she was a fastidious, not to say disdainful lady. The highest had been at her feet, and sued in vain. She was a stirring spirit, with great ambition and a daring will ; never content except in society, and influencing it, for which she was qualified by her grace and lively fancy, her ready though capricious sympathy, and her passion for admiration ; and Lady Berengaria was a first-rate horsewoman, and really in the saddle looked irresistible.

There was one lady who much attracted the attention of Myra, interested in all she observed. This lady was evidently a person of importance, for she sat between an ambassador and a knight of the Garter, and they vied in homage to her. They watched her every word, and seemed delighted with all she said. Without being strictly beautiful, there was an expression of sweet animation in her physiognomy which was highly attractive ; her eye was full of summer lightning, and there was an arch dimple in her smile which seemed to irradiate her whole countenance. She was quite a young woman, hardly older than Myra. What most distinguished her was the harmony of her whole person ; her graceful figure, her fair and finely moulded shoulders, her pretty teeth and her small extremities, seemed to blend with and become the soft vivacity of her winning glance.—*Endymion.*

Moon.

O thou bright moon ! thou object of my first love ! thou shalt not escape an invocation, although perchance at this very moment some varlet sonnetteer is prating of 'the boy Endymion' and 'thy silver bow.' Here to thee, Queen of the Night ! in whatever name thou most delightest ! Or Bendis, as they hailed thee in rugged Thrace ; or Bubastis, as they howled to thee in mysterious Egypt ; or Dian, as they sacrificed to thee in gorgeous Rome ; or Artemis, as they sighed to thee on the bright plains of ever glorious Greece ! Why is it that all men gaze on thee? Why is it that all men love thee ? Why is it that all men worship thee ?

Shine on, shine on, sultana of the soul ! the Passions are thy eunuch slaves. Ambition gazes on thee, and his burning brow is cooled, and his fitful pulse is calm. Grief wanders in her moonlit walk and sheds no tear ; and when thy crescent smiles the lustre of Joy's revelling eye is dusked. Quick Anger, in thy light, forgets revenge ; and even dove-eyed Hope feeds on no future joys when gazing on the miracle of thy beauty.

Shine on, shine on ! although a pure Virgin, thou art the mighty mother of all abstraction ! The eye of the weary peasant returning from his daily toil, and the rapt gaze of the inspired poet, are alike fixed on thee ; thou stillest the roar of marching armies, and who can doubt thy influence o'er the waves who has witnessed the wide Atlantic sleeping under thy silver beam?

Shine on, shine on ! they say thou art Earth's satellite ; yet when I gaze on thee my thoughts are not of thy suzerain. They teach us that thy power is a fable, and that thy divinity is a dream. Oh, thou bright Queen ! I will be no traitor to thy sweet authority ; and verily, I will not believe that thy influence o'er our hearts is, at this moment, less potent than when we worshipped in thy glittering fane of Ephesus, or trembled at the dark horrors of thine Arician rites. Then, hail to thee, Queen of the Night !—*Vivian Grey.*

It is impossible to conceive anything more brilliant than an Andalusian summer moon. You lose nothing of the landscape, which is only softened, not obscured ; and absolutely the beams are warm.—*Contarini Fleming*

MORALITY.

Lady St. Julians knew no crime except a woman not living with her husband ; that was past pardon. So long as his presence sanctioned her conduct, however shameless, it did not signify ; but if the husband were a brute, neglected his wife first and then deserted her ; then if a breath but sullies her name, she must be crushed ; unless, indeed, her own family were very powerful, which makes a difference, and sometimes softens immorality into indiscretion.— *Coningsby*.

MORLEY (*STEPHEN*).

It was a still voice that uttered these words, yet one of a peculiar character ; one of those voices that instantly arrest attention : gentle and yet solemn, earnest yet unimpassioned. With a step as whispering as his tone, the man who had been kneeling by the tomb had unobserved joined his associate and Egremont. He hardly reached the middle height ; his form slender, but well proportioned ; his pale countenance, slightly marked with the small-pox, was redeemed from absolute ugliness by a highly intellectual brow, and large dark eyes that indicated deep sensibility and great quickness of apprehension. Though young, he was already a little bald ; he was dressed entirely in black ; the fairness of his linen, the neatness of his beard, his gloves much worn, yet carefully mended, intimated that his faded garments were the result of necessity rather than of negligence.— *Sybil*.

MORNING.

Morning is not romantic. Romance is the twilight spell ; but morn is bright and joyous, prompt with action and full of sanguine hope.—*Endymion*.

A bloom was spread over the morning sky. A soft golden light bathed with its fresh beam the bosom of the valley, except where a delicate haze, rather than a mist, still partially lingered over the river, which yet occasionally gleamed and sparkled in the sunshine. A sort of shadowy lustre suffused the landscape, which, though distinct, was mitigated in all its features : the distant woods, the clumps of tall trees that rose about the old grey bridge, the cottage chimneys that sent their smoke into the blue still air, amid their clustering orchards and gardens of flowers and herbs.

Ah! what is there so fresh and joyous as a summer morn! that springtime of the day, when the brain is bright, and the heart is brave; the season of daring and of hope; the renovating hour!—*Sybil.*

There is something especially in the hour which precedes a Syrian dawn, which invigorates the frame and elevates the spirits. One cannot help fancying that angels may have been resting on the mountain tops during the night, the air is so sweet, the earth so still.—*Tancred.*

MOUNTAIN AIR.

There is something magical in the mountain air. There my heart is light, my spirits cheerful, everything is exhilarating; there I am in every respect a different being from what I am in lowlands. I cannot even speak; I dissolve into a delicious reverie, in which everything occurs to me without effort. Whatever passes before me gives birth in my mind to a new character, a new image, a new train of fancies. I sing, I shout, I compose aloud, but without premeditation, without any attempt to guide my imagination by my reason. How often, after journeying along the wild muletrack, how often, on a sunny day, have I suddenly thrown myself upon the turf, revelled in my existence, and then as hastily jumped up and raised the wild birds with a wilder scream! I think that these involuntary bursts must have been occasioned by the unconscious influence of extreme health. As for myself, when I succeed in faintly recalling the rapture which I have experienced in these solitary rambles, and muse over the flood of fancy which then seemed to pour itself over my whole being, and gush out of every feeling and every object, I contrast, with mortification, those warm and pregnant hours with this cold record of my maturer age.—*Contarini Fleming.*

MOUNTAIN VALLEYS.

In mountain valleys it is beautiful to watch the effect of the rising and setting of the sun. The high peaks are first illumined, the soft yellow light then tips the lower elevations, and the bright golden showers soon bathe the whole valley, excepting a dark streak at the bottom, which is not often visited by sunlight. The effect of sunset is perhaps still more lovely. The highest peaks are those which the sun loves most. One by one the mountains, according to their elevation, steal into darkness, and the rosy tint is often suffused over the peaks and glaciers of Mont Blanc, while the whole world below is enveloped in the darkest twilight. *Contarini Fleming.*

MUSIC.

The greatest advantage that a writer can derive from music is, that it teaches most exquisitely the art of development.—*Contarini Fleming.*

O Music ! miraculous art, that makes the poet's skill a jest, revealing to the soul inexpressible feelings by the aid of inexplicable sounds ! A blast of thy trumpet, and millions rush forward to die ; a peal of thy organ, and uncounted nations sink down to pray. Mighty is thy three-fold power !

First, thou canst call up all elemental sounds, and scenes, and subjects, with the definiteness of reality. Strike the lyre ! Lo ! the voice of the winds, the flash of the lightning, the swell of the wave, the solitude of the valley !

Then thou canst speak to the secrets of a man's heart as if by inspiration. Strike the lyre ! Lo ! our early love, our treasured hate, our withered joy, our flattering hope !

And, lastly, by thy mysterious melodies thou canst recall man from all thought of this world and of himself, bringing back to his soul's memory dark but delightful recollections of the glorious heritage which he has lost, but which he may win again. Strike the lyre ! Lo ! Paradise, with its palaces of inconceivable splendour and its gates of unimaginable glory !—*Contarini Fleming.*

MYRA.

The young lady was now thirteen, and though her parents were careful to say nothing in her presence which would materially reveal their situation, the scrutinising powers with which nature had prodigally invested their daughter were not easily baffled. She asked no questions, but nothing seemed to escape the penetrative glance of that dark blue eye, calm amid all the mystery, and tolerating rather than sharing the frequent embrace of her parents. . . . She learned with a glance, and remembered with extraordinary tenacity everything she had acquired. But she was neither tender nor deferential, and to induce her to study you could not depend on the affections, but only on her intelligence. So she was often fitful, capricious, or provoking, and her mother was often annoyed and irritated. Then there were scenes, or rather ebullitions on one side, for Myra was always unmoved and enraging from her total want of sensibility.—(Five years later) her beauty was not less striking, but it was now the beauty of a woman. Her mien was radiant but commanding, and her brow, always remarkable, was singularly impressive. 'She has more common sense than any woman I ever knew, and more,' Mr. Neuchatel would add, 'than most men. If she were not so handsome, people would find it out ; but they cannot understand that so beautiful a woman can have a headpiece that, I really believe, could manage the affairs in Bishopsgate Street !'—*Endymion.*

MYSTERY.

Mystery too often presupposes the idea of guilt.— *Venetia.*

All is mystery ; but he is a slave who will not struggle to penetrate the dark veil.—*Contarini Fleming.*

NATION.

The fate of a nation will ultimately depend upon the strength and health of the population.—(' Mr. Phœbus ') *Lothair*.

NATIONAL PETITION.

The prayer of the national petition involved the fallacy of supposing that social evils would be cured by political rights.—*Speech in House of Commons* (*National Petition*), *July* 12, 1839.

NATIONALITY.

There is a great difference between nationality and race. Nationality is the miracle of political independence. Race is the principle of physical analogy.—*Speech in House of Commons* (*Navy Estimates*), *August* 9, 1848.

NATURE.

Nature is stronger than education.—*Contarini Fleming*.

Nature has her laws, and this is one,—a fair day's wage for a fair day's work.—(' Nixon ') *Sybil*.

NECESSITY.

The necessities of things are sterner stuff than the hopes of men.—(' Theodora ') *Lothair*.

NEUCHATEL (ADRIAN, LORD HAINAULT).

Adrian had inherited something more, and something more precious, than his father's treasure—a not inferior capacity, united, in his case, with much culture, and with a worldly ambition to which his father was a stranger. So long as his father lived, Adrian had been extremely circumspect. He seemed only devoted to business, and to model his conduct on that of his eminent sire. . . . He was passionately fond of horses, and even in his father's lifetime had run some at Newmarket in another name. . . . Adrian

Neuchatel was, what very few people are—master in his own house. With a rich varnish of graciousness and favour, he never swerved from his purpose ; and though willing to effect all things by smiles and sweet temper, he had none of that morbid sensibility which allows some men to fret over a phrase, to be tortured by a sigh, or to be subdued by a tear.—*Endymion.*

NEUCHATEL, MRS. (LADY HAINAULT).

She was the daughter of an eminent banker, and had herself, though that was of slight importance, a large portion. She was a woman of abilities, highly cultivated. Nothing had ever been spared that she should possess every possible accomplishment, and acquire every information and grace that it was desirable to attain. She was a linguist, a fine musician, no mean artist, and she threw out, if she willed it, the treasures of her well-stored and not unimaginative mind with ease and sometimes eloquence. Her person, without being absolutely beautiful, was interesting. There was even a degree of fascination in her brown velvet eyes. And yet Mrs. Neuchatel was not a contented spirit ; and though she appreciated the great qualities of her husband and viewed him even with reverence as well as affection, she scarcely contributed to his happiness as much as became her. And for this reason. Whether it were the result of physical organisation, or whether it were the satiety which was the consequence of having been born, and bred, and lived for ever, in a society in which wealth was the prime object of existence, and practically the test of excellence, Mrs. Neu-chatel had imbibed not merely a contempt for money, but absolutely a hatred for it. The prosperity of her house depressed her.—*Endymion.*

NEUCHATEL (ADRIANA).

She was now about seventeen ; and had she not been endowed with the finest disposition and the sweetest temper in the world, she must have been spoiled, for both her parents idolised her. All that was rare and beautiful in the world was at her command. There was no limit to the gratification of her wishes. But, alas ! this favoured maiden wished for nothing. Her books interested her, and a beautiful nature ; but she liked to be alone, or with her mother. She was impressed with the horrible and humiliating conviction, that she was courted and admired only for her wealth.—*Endymion.*

NEUTRALITY.

If neutrality depends on holding that the interests of the country are not to be maintained and vindicated, then I am no longer in favour of neutrality, but in favour of the interests of the army and the honour of the Sovereign.— *Speech in House of Commons (Eastern Question), Jan.* 29, 1878.

We declared at the same time that neutrality must cease if British interests were assailed or menaced. Cosmopolitan critics, men who are the friends of every country save their own, have condemned this policy as a selfish policy. My Lord Mayor, it is as selfish as patriotism.—*Speech at Mansion House, November* 9, 1877.

NEWS.

News has been described by the initial letters of the four points of the compass. It is the initial letters of the four points of the compass that make the word N E W S, and it is to be understood that news is that which comes from the North, East, West, and South, and if it comes from only one point of the compass, then it is a class publication and not news.—*Speech in House of Commons (Newspaper Stamp Duties Bill), March* 26, 1855.

NIGHT.

Night brings rest ; night brings solace ; rest to the weary, solace to the sad ; and to the desperate night brings despair.—*Alroy.*

The summer twilight had faded into sweet night; the young and star-attended moon glittered like a sickle in the deep purple sky; of all the luminous host Hesperus alone was visible; and a breeze, that bore the last embrace of the flowers by the sun, moved languidly and fitfully over the still and odorous earth.

The moonbeam fell upon the roof and garden of Gerard. It suffused the cottage with its brilliant light, except where the dark depth of the embowered porch defied its entry. All around the beds of flowers and herbs spread sparkling and defined. You could trace the minutest walk; almost distinguish every leaf. Now and then there came a breath, and the sweet-peas murmured in their sleep; or the roses rustled, as if they were afraid they were about to be roused from their lightsome dreams. Farther on the fruit trees caught the splendour of the night; and looked like a troop of sultanas taking their garden air, when the eye of man could not profane them, and laden with jewels. There were apples that rivalled rubies; pears of topaz tint; a whole paraphernalia of plums, some purple as the amethyst, others blue and brilliant as the sapphire; an emerald here, and now a golden-drop that gleamed like the yellow diamond of Gengis Khan.—*Sybil.*

NON-INTERVENTION.

I am far from wishing to enforce a pedantic adherence to that passive policy which in the barbarous dialect of the day is called 'non-intervention.' On the contrary, I am persuaded that, in the settlement of the great affairs of Europe, the presence of England is the best guarantee of peace. But it should be the presence of England with the law of nations and with the stipulations of treaties.—*Speech in House of Commons (Address in answer to the Queen's Speech), February* 1, 1849.

The ineffable blessing of peace cannot be obtained by the passive principle of non-intervention. Peace rests on the presence, not to say ascendency of England in the counsels of Europe.—*Dissolution of Parliament (Letter to Lord Lieutenant of Ireland), March* 8, 1880.

NONSENSE.

Nonsense when earnest is impressive and sometimes takes you in. If you are in a hurry, you occasionally mistake it for sense.—*Contarini Fleming.*

NOVEL (RECEIPT FOR WRITING A).

Take a pair of pistols and a pack of cards, a cookery-book and a set of new quadrilles; mix them up with half an intrigue and a whole marriage, and divide them into three equal portions.—*The Young Duke.*

NOVELTY.

Novelty is an essential attribute of the beautiful.—*Vivian Grey.*

OBLIVION.

It is the lot of man to suffer, it is also his fortune to forget. Oblivion and sorrow share our being, as darkness and light divide the course of time.—*Vivian Grey.*

OBSCURE.

The obscure is a principal ingredient of the sublime.—*Contarini Fleming.*

OFFER.

A good offer should never be refused, unless we have a better one at the same time.—('Essker') *Vivian Grey.*

OLD GENTLEMAN.

There is no affectation of juvenility about him ('the Duke of Burlington'). He involuntarily reminds you of youth, as an empty orchestra does of music.—*The Young Duke.*

OPPORTUNITY.

Opportunity is more powerful even than conquerors and prophets.— *Tancred.*

Great men should think of opportunity and not of time. Time is the excuse of feeble and puzzled spirits.—('Lady Roehampton') *Endymion.*

OPPOSITION.

In opposition numbers often embarrass.—('Bertie Tremaine') *Endymion.*

Believe me, Opposition has its charms; indeed I sometimes think the principal reason why I have enjoyed our ministerial life so much is that it has been from the first a perpetual struggle for existence.—('Lady Montfort') *Endymion.*

It is evident that the suicidal career of what was then styled the Liberal party had been occasioned and stimulated by its unnatural excess of strength. The apoplectic plethora of 1834 was not less fatal than the paralytic tenuity of 1841. It was not feasible to gratify so many ambitions or to satisfy so many expectations. Every man had his double; the heels of every placeman were dogged by friendly rivals ready to trip them up. There were even two cabinets : the one that met in council, and the one that met in cabal. The consequence of destroying the legitimate Opposition of the country was, that a moiety of the supporters of Government had to discharge the duties of Opposition.

Herein, then, we detect the real cause of all that irregular and unsettled carriage of public men which so perplexed the nation after the passing of the Reform Act. No government can be long secure without a formidable Opposition. It reduces their supporters to that tractable number which can be managed by the joint influences of fruition and of hope. It offers vengeance to the discontented, and distinction to the ambitious ; and employs the energies of aspiring spirits, who otherwise may prove traitors in a division or assassins in a debate.—*Coningsby*.

ORATOR (JOB THORNBERRY).

Endymion listened with interest, soon with delight, soon with a feeling of exciting and not unpleasing perplexity, to the orator; for he was an orator, though then unrecognised, and known only in his district. He was a pale and slender man, with a fine brow and an eye that occasionally flashed with the fire of a creative mind. His voice certainly was not like Hollaballoo's. It was rather thin, but singularly clear. There was nothing clearer except his meaning. Endymion never heard a case stated with such pellucid art; facts marshalled with such vivid simplicity, and inferences so natural and spontaneous and irresistible, that they seemed, as it were, borrowed from his audience, though none of that audience had arrived at them before. The meeting was hushed, was rapt in intellectual delight, for they did not give the speaker the enthusiasm of their sympathy. That was not shared perhaps by the moiety of those who listened to him. When his case was fairly before them, the speaker dealt with his opponents—some in the press, some in Parliament—with much power of sarcasm, but this power was evidently rather repressed than allowed to run riot. What impressed Endymion as the chief quality of this remarkable speaker was his persuasiveness, and he had the air of being too prudent to offend even an opponent unnecessarily. His language, though natural and easy, was choice and refined. He was evidently a man who had read, and not a little; and there was no taint of vulgarity, scarcely a provincialism, in his pronunciation.—*Endymion*.

ORATORY.

His (Ferrars') Corinthian style, in which the Mœnad of Mr. Burke was habited in the last mode of Almack's.—*Endymion*.

ORIGINALITY.

The originality of a subject is in its treatment.—(' Mr. Phœbus ') *Lothair.*

ORTOLANS.

A pink *carte* succeeded to the satin play-bill. Vitellius might have been pleased with the banquet. Ah, how shall we describe those soups, which surely must have been the magical elixir ! How paint those ortolans dressed by the inimitable artist, à la St. James, for the occasion, and which look so beautiful in death that they must surely have preferred such an euthanasia even to flying in the perfumed air of an Ausonian heaven !

Sweet bird ! though thou hast lost thy plumage, thou shalt fly to my mistress ! Is it not better to be nibbled by her than mumbled by a cardinal? I, too, will feed on thy delicate beauty. Sweet bird ! thy companion has fled to my mistress ; and now thou shalt thrill the nerves of her master ! Oh ! doff, then, thy waistcoat of wine-leaves, pretty rover ! and show me that bosom more delicious even than woman's. What gushes of rapture ! What a flavour ! How peculiar ! Even how sacred ! Heaven at once sends both manna and quails. Another little wanderer ! Pray follow my example ! Allow me. All Paradise opens ! Let me die eating ortolans to the sound of soft music !

Even the supper was brief, though brilliant.—*The Young Duke.*

OXFORD.

It is a most interesting seat of learning. Whether we consider its antiquity, its learning, the influence it has exercised upon the history of the country, its magnificent endowments, its splendid buildings, its great colleges, libraries, and museums, or that it is one of the principal head-quarters of all the hope of England, our youth, it is not too much to affirm that there is scarcely a spot on the face of the globe of equal interest and importance.—('Dr. Masham') *Venetia.*

OXFORD (*A PROFESSOR AT*).

The Oxford Professor, who was the guest of the American Colonel, was quite a young man, of advanced opinions on all subjects, religious, social, and political. He was clever, extremely well-informed, so far as books can make a man knowing, but unable to profit even by that limited experience of life from a restless vanity and overflowing conceit, which prevented him from ever observing or thinking of anything but himself. He was gifted with a great command of words, which took the form of endless exposition, varied by sarcasm and passages of ornate jargon. He was the last person one would have expected to recognise in an Oxford professor; but we live in times of transition.

A Parisian man of science, who had passed his life in alternately fighting at barricades and discovering planets, had given Colonel Campian, who had lived much in the French capital, a letter of introduction to the Professor, whose invectives against the principles of English society were hailed by foreigners as representative of the sentiments of venerable Oxford. The Professor, who was not satisfied with his home career, and, like many men of his order of mind, had dreams of wild vanity which the New World, they think, can alone realise, was very glad to make the Colonel's acquaintance, which might facilitate his future movements. So he had lionised the distinguished visitors during the last few days over the University, and had availed himself of plenteous opportunities for exhibiting to them his celebrated powers of exposition, his talent for sarcasm, which he deemed peerless, and several highly finished picturesque passages, which were introduced with extemporary art.—*Lothair.*

PALMERSTON (LORD).

The noble lord (Palmerston) cannot bear coalitions. The noble lord has acted only with those amongst whom he was born and bred in politics ! That infant Hercules was taken out of a Whig cradle ! and how consistent has been his private life ! Looking back upon the past half-century, during which he has professed almost every principle, and connected himself with almost every party, the noble lord has raised a warning voice to-night against coalitions, because he fears that a majority of the House of Commons, ranking in its numbers some of the most eminent members of this House, may not approve a policy with respect to China, which has begun in outrage, and which, if pursued, will end in ruin. Let the noble lord not only complain to the country—let him appeal to the country. I should like to see the programme of the proud leader of the Liberal party. 'No reform ! new taxes ! Canton blazing ! Persia invaded !' That would be the programme of the statesman who appeals to a great nation as the worthy leader of the cause of progress and civilisation.—*Speech in House of Commons (China War), February* 29, 1857.

He is the Tory chief of a Radical cabinet. With no domestic policy, he is obliged to divert the attention of the people from the consideration of their own affairs to the distraction of foreign politics. His external system is turbulent and aggressive, that his rule at home may be tranquil and unassailed. Hence arise excessive expenditure, heavy taxation, and the stoppage of all social improvement. His scheme of conduct is so devoid of all political principle, that when forced to appeal to the people, his only claim to their confidence is his name.—*Address to Electors of Buckinghamshire, March* 17, 1857.

A great Apollo of aspiring understrappers, he has the smartness of an attorney's clerk, and the intrigues of a Greek of the Lower Empire.

, A crimping lordship with a career as insignificant as his intellect.

He reminds one of a favourite footman on easy terms with his mistress.

He is the Sporus of politics, cajoling France with an airy compliment, and menacing Russia with a perfumed cane.—*Runnymede Letters*, 1836.

PARENTS.

All was forgotten of his parent, except the intimate and natural tie, and her warm and genuine affection. He was now alone in the world ; for reflection impressed upon him at this moment what the course of existence too generally teaches to us all, that mournful truth, that, after all, we have no friends that we can depend upon in this life but our parents. All other intimacies, however ardent, are liable to cool ; all other confidence, however unlimited, to be violated. In the phantasmagoria of life, the friend with whom we have cultivated mutual trust for years is often suddenly or gradually estranged from us, or becomes, from painful, yet irresistible circumstances, even our deadliest foe. As for women, as for the mistresses of our hearts, who has not learnt that the links of passion are fragile as they are glittering ; and that the bosom on which we have reposed with idolatry all our secret sorrows and sanguine hopes, eventually becomes the very heart that exults in our misery and baffles our welfare ? Where is the enamoured face that smiled upon our early love, and was to shed tears over our grave ? Where are the choice companions of our youth, with whom we were to breast the difficulties and share the triumphs of existence? Even in this inconstant world, what changes like the heart ? Love is a dream, and friendship a delusion. No wonder we grow callous ; for how few have the opportunity of returning to the hearth which they quitted in levity or thoughtless weariness, yet which alone is faithful to them ; whose sweet affections require not the stimulus of prosperity or fame, the lure of accomplishments, or the tribute of flattery; but which are constant to us in distress, and console us even in disgrace! *Venetia.*

PARIS.

Paris was the university of the world, where everybody should graduate. Paris and London ought to be the great objects of all travellers, the rest was mere landscape.— ('Lord Monmouth') *Coningsby.*

PARLIAMENT.

I look upon Parliamentary Government as the noblest government in the world, and certainly one most suited to England. But without the discipline of political connection animated by the principle of private honour, I feel certain that a popular assembly would sink before the power or the corruption of a minister.—*Speech at Manchester, April* 3, 1872.

Parliament was never so great as when they debated with closed doors.—('Tancred') *Tancred.*

A parliamentary career, that old superstition of the eighteenth century, was important when there was no other source of power and fame.—*Tancred.*

I go to a land that has never been blessed by that fatal drollery called a representative government, though omniscience once deigned to trace out the polity which should rule it.—*Tancred.*

Parliamentary speaking, like playing on the fiddle, requires practice.—*Speech in House of Commons (Elections Bill), July* 13, 1871.

PARTY.

Party is organised opinion.—*Speech at Meeting of Society for increasing Endowments of small Livings in Diocese of Oxford, November* 25, 1864.

I have had to prepare the mind of the country, and to

R

educate—if it be not arrogant to use such a phrase—to educate our party. It is a large party, and requires its attention to be called to questions of this kind (Reform) with some pressure.—*Speech at Banquet at Edinburgh, October* 1867.

The favour of courts and the applause of senates may have their moments of excitement and delight, but the incident of deepest and most enduring gratification in public life is to possess the cordial confidence of a high-spirited party, for it touches the heart, and combines all the softer feelings of private life with the ennobling consciousness of public duty.—*Life of Lord George Bentinck.*

I do not depreciate party connection. I believe that so long as we have a Parliamentary Constitution, party connection is absolutely necessary, and without it a Parliamentary Constitution would degenerate into a corrupt despotism. I want to see the action of two great parties in this House.— *Speech in House of Commons* (*Official Salaries*), *April* 11, 1850.

When a nation is thoroughly perplexed and dispirited, it soon ceases to make distinctions between political parties. The country is out of sorts, and the government is held responsible for the disorder.—*Endymion.*

The Whigs are worn out, Conservatism is a sham, and Radicalism a pollution.—('Lord Vere') *Coningsby.*

Whigs like Tories are dependent on quarter sessions : on the judgment of a lord lieutenant and the statistics of a bench of magistrates.—('Sidney Wilton') *Endymion.*

Disputes of parties in Parliament are very much like some of those traditionary misunderstandings between man and wife. They treat each other often with a freedom of recrimination, which probably has no great foundation : but however liberal may be their epithets under these circumstances, both parties much question the right of anybody interfering between them, and adopting their opinions.— *Speech at Mansion House Banquet, July* 30, 1868.

PARVENUS.

There is little doubt that parvenus as often owe their advancement in society to their perseverance as to their pelf. *The Young Duke.*

PAST.

There is so much to lament in the world in which we live that I can spare no pang for the past.—('Stephen Morley') *Sybil.*

PATIENCE.

I think if one is patient and watches, all will come of which one is capable ; but no one can be patient who is not independent.—*Endymion.*

Patience is a necessary ingredient of genius.—*Contarini Fleming.*

Everything comes if a man will only wait.—(' Fakredeen ') *Tancred.*

They waited with that patience, which insulted beings can alone endure.—*Vivian Grey.*

Greece has a future ; and I would say, if I might be permitted, to Greece, what I would say to an individual who has a future—' Learn to be patient.'—*Speech in House of Commons (Congress: Correspondence and Protocols), July* 18, 1878.

PATRIOTISM.

Patriotism depends as much on mutual suffering as on mutual success, and it is by that experience of all fortunes and all feelings that a great national character is created.—*Speech in House of Commons (International Maritime Law), March* 18, 1862.

PEACE.

I believe there is no country in the world that benefits more by peace than England, though, materially speaking, peace is more necessary to every other country in Europe than to England.—*Speech in House of Commons (Financial Policy of late Government), July 21, 1854.*

Lord Salisbury and myself have brought you back peace —but a peace I hope with honour, which may satisfy our Sovereign and tend to the welfare of the country.—*Speech on Return from Congress, July 16, 1878.*

The outcome has been a peace, which I believe will be enduring. And why do I believe that peace will be enduring? Because I see that every one of the Powers is benefited by that peace, and no one is humiliated.—*Banquet at Mansion House (Freedom of City), October 8, 1878.*

PEARLS.

Pearls are like girls, they require quite as much attention. ('Mr. Ruby') *Lothair.*

PEEL (SIR ROBERT).

If, instead of having recourse to obloquy, he would only stick to quotation, he may rely upon it it would be a safer weapon.

I look upon him as a man who has tamed the shrew of Liberalism by her own tactics. He is the political Petruchio who has outbid you all.—*Opening Letters at Post Office, February 28, 1845.*

I find that for between thirty and forty years that right honourable gentleman has traded on the ideas and intelligence of others. His life has been one great appropriation clause. He is a burglar of others' intellect. There is no statesman who has committed political petty larceny on so great a scale.—*Speech in House of Commons (Corn Importation Bill), May 15, 1846.*

I care not what may be the position of a man who never originates an idea—a watcher of the atmosphere—a man, who, as he says, takes observations and when he finds the wind in a certain quarter, turns to suit it. Such a person may be a powerful minister, but he is no more a great statesman than the man who gets up behind a carriage is a good whip. Both are disciples of progress—both may get a good place. But how far the original momentum is indebted to their power, and how far their guiding prudence regulates the lash or rein, it is not necessary for me to notice.—*Speech in House of Commons (Address in answer to Queen's Speech), January* 22, 1846.

Sir Robert Peel was a very good-looking man. He was tall, and though of later years he had become portly, had to the last a comely presence. Thirty years ago, when he was young and lithe, with curling brown hair, he had a radiant expression of countenance. His brow was distinguished, not so much for its intellectual development, although that was of a high order, as for its remarkably frank expression, so different from his character in life. The expression of the brow might even be said to amount to beauty. The rest of the features did not however sustain this expression. The eye was not good ; it was sly, and he had an awkward habit of looking askance. He had the fatal defect also, of a long upper lip, and his mouth was compressed.—*Life of Lord George Bentinck.*

Sir Robert Peel had a peculiarity which is perhaps natural with men of great talents who have not the creative faculty : he had a dangerous sympathy with the creations of others.—*Life of Lord George Bentinck.*

Sir Robert Peel had a bad manner of which he was sensible : he was by nature very shy, but forced early in life into eminent positions, he had formed an artificial manner, haughtily stiff, or exuberantly bland, of which generally he could not divest himself.—*Life of Lord George Bentinck.*

As an Orator.—As an orator, Sir Robert Peel had perhaps the most available talent that has ever been brought to bear in the House of Commons. We have mentioned that in exposition and in reply he was equally eminent. His statements were perspicuous, complete, and dignified ; when he combated the objections or criticised the propositions of an opponent, he was adroit and acute ; no speaker ever sustained a process of argumentation in a public assembly more lucidly, and none as debaters have united in so conspicuous a degree prudence with promptness.   In the higher efforts of oratory he was not successful.   His vocabulary was ample, and never mean ; but it was neither rich nor rare. His speeches will afford no sentiment of surpassing grandeur or beauty that will linger in the ears of coming generations. He embalmed no great political truth in immortal words. His flights were ponderous : he soared with the wing of a vulture rather than the plume of the eagle ; and his perorations when most elaborate were most unwieldy.   In pathos he was quite deficient : when he attempted to touch the tender passions, it was painful.   His face became distorted, like that of a woman who wants to cry but cannot succeed. *Life of Lord George Bentinck.*

As a Statesman.—One cannot say of Sir Robert Peel, notwithstanding his unrivalled powers of despatching affairs, that he was the greatest minister that this country ever produced ; because, twice placed at the helm, and on the second occasion with the Court and the Parliament equally devoted to him, he never could maintain himself in power. Nor, notwithstanding his consummate parliamentary tactics, can he be described as the greatest party leader that ever flourished amongst us, for he contrived to destroy the most compact, powerful, and devoted party that ever followed a British statesman.   Certainly, notwithstanding his great sway in debate, we cannot recognise him as our greatest orator, for in many of the supreme requisites of oratory he was singularly deficient.   But what he really was, and what posterity will acknowledge him to have been, is the greatest member of Parliament that ever lived.

Peace to his ashes !   His name will be often appealed to in that scene which he loved so well, and never without homage of his opponents.—*Life of Lord George Bentinck.*

PEERAGE. ·

We owe the English peerage to three sources : the spoliation of the Church ; the open and flagrant sale of its honours by the elder Stuarts; and the boroughmongering of our own times.—('Mr. Millbank ') *Coningsby.*

PEOPLE.

Who should sympathise with the poor but the poor? When the people support the people, the divine blessing will not be wanting.—*Sybil.*

My sympathies and feelings have always been with the people, from whom I sprang ; and when obliged to join a party, I joined that party with which I believed the people sympathised.—*Speech in House of Commons (Corn Importation Bill), May 8, 1846.*

The people do not want employment ; it is the greatest mistake in the world—all this employment is a stimulus to population.—('Lord Marney') *Sybil.*

We still remember in this country the tender and happy consequences of being governed by 'the people.' We have not forgotten that 'the people' established courts more infamous than the Star Chamber in every county in England with the power of fining, sequestrating, imprisoning, and corporally punishing all who opposed or even murmured against their decrees ; that under the plea of malignancy, 'the people' avenged their private hatreds and seized for their private gain and gratification any estates or property to which they took a fancy ; that 'the people' consigned to bastilles and perpetual imprisonment all those who refused to answer their illegal inquiries, and bored red-hot irons through the tongues of the contumacious ; that not an appearance of law or liberty remained in the land ; that 'the people' enlarged the laws of high treason so that they comprehended verbal offences and even intentions ; that 'the people' practised decimation ; that 'the people'

voted trial by jury a breach of Parliamentary privilege ; that
' the people ' deprived of authority all persons of family and
distinction who had originally adhered to their party because
men of blood and breeding would not submit to be their
disgraceful and ignoble tools, and filled every office under
them with the scum of the nation ; that the very individuals
who had suffered and struggled under the Star Chamber
were visited by ' the people ' with punishments and imprison-
ments infinitely more bloody and more grievous ; that ' the
people' sequestrated nearly one half of the goods and
chattels of the nation, and at least one half of its rents and
revenues ; that in seven years ' the people' raised the taxation of the country from eight hundred thousand pounds
per annum to seven millions per annum ; that ' the people '
invented the excise, and applied that odious impost even to
provisions and the common necessaries of life ; that ' the
people' became so barefaced in their vile extortions that one
morning they openly divided three hundred thousand pounds
amongst themselves, and settled an annuity of four pounds
a day upon each of their number ; that ' the people' committed all these enormities in the teeth of outraged England
by the aid of an anti-national compact with the Scottish
Covenanters; and that finally the nation, the insulted and
exhausted nation, sought refuge from the government of
' the people' in the arms of a military despot.— *Vindication
of the Constitution* (*Pamphlet*, 1835), *in a Letter to a noble
and learned Lord* (*Lyndhurst*).

There is no merit in my conduct, for there is no sacrifice.   When I remember what this English people once
was ; the truest, the freest, and the bravest, the best-natured
and the best-looking, the happiest and most religious race
upon the surface of this globe ; and think of them now,
with all their crimes and all their slavish sufferings, their
soured spirits and their stunted forms ; their lives without
enjoyment, and their deaths without hope ; I may well feel

for them, even if I were not the daughter of their blood.—
Sybil.

A year ago, I presumed to offer to the public some
volumes that aimed at calling their attention to the state of
our political parties ; their origin, their history, their present
position.   In an age of political infidelity, of mean passions,
and petty thoughts, I would have impressed upon the rising
race not to despair, but to seek in a right understanding of
the history of their country and in the energies of heroic
youth, the elements of national welfare.   The present work
advances another step in the same emprise.   From the state
of Parties it now would draw public thought to the state of
the People whom those parties for two centuries have
governed.   The comprehension and the cure of this greater
theme depend upon the same agencies as the first : it is the
past alone that can explain the present, and it is youth that
alone can mould the remedial future.   The written history
of our country for the last ten reigns has been a mere
phantasma ; giving to the origin and consequence of public
transactions a character and colour in every respect
dissimilar to their natural form and hue.   In this mighty
mystery all thoughts and things have assumed an aspect and
title contrary to their real quality and style : Oligarchy has
been called Liberty ; an exclusive Priesthood has been
christened a National Church ; Sovereignty has been the
title of something that has had no dominion, while absolute
power has been wielded by those who profess themselves
the servants of the People.   In the selfish strife of factions,
two great existences have been blotted out of the history of
England, the Monarch and the Multitude ; as the power
of the Crown has diminished, the privileges of the People
have disappeared ; till at length the sceptre has become a
pageant, and its subject has degenerated again into a serf.

It is nearly fourteen years ago, in the popular frenzy of
a mean and selfish revolution which emancipated neither

the Crown nor the People, that I first took the occasion to intimate, and then to develop, to the first assembly of my countrymen that I ever had the honour to address, these convictions. They have been misunderstood, as is ever for a season the fate of Truth, and they have obtained for their promulgator much misrepresentation, as must ever be the lot of those who will not follow the beaten track of a fallacious custom. But Time, that brings all things, has brought also to the mind of England some suspicion that the idols they have so long worshipped, and the oracles that have so long deluded them, are not the true ones. There is a whisper rising in this country that Loyalty is not a phrase, Faith not a delusion, and Popular Liberty something more diffusive and substantial than the profane exercise of the sacred rights of sovereignty by political classes.

That we may live to see England once more possess a free Monarchy, and a privileged and prosperous People, is my prayer ; that these great consequences can only be brought about by the energy and devotion of our Youth is my persuasion. We live in an age when to be young and to be indifferent can be no longer synonymous. We must prepare for the coming hour. The claims of the Future are represented by suffering millions ; and the Youth of a Nation are the trustees of Posterity.—*Sybil*.

PERSEVERANCE.

The determined and persevering need never despair of gaining their object in this world.—*Lothair*.

PERSONAL.

Nothing is great but the personal.—*Coningsby*.

It is the personal that interests mankind, that frees their imagination, and wins their hearts. A cause is a great abstraction and fit only for students ; embodied in a party it stirs men to action ; but place at the head of a party a leader who can inspire enthusiasm, he commands the world. *Coningsby*.

PERSONALITY OF CREATOR.

Is it more unphilosophical to believe in a personal God, omnipotent and omniscient, than in natural forces unconscious and irresistible? Is it unphilosophical to combine power with intelligence? Goethe, a Spinozist who did not believe in Spinoza, said that he could bring his mind to the conception that in the centre of space we might meet with a monad of pure intelligence. What may be the centre of space I leave to the dædal imagination of the author of 'Faust;' but a monad of pure intelligence, is that more philosophical than the truth, first revealed to man amid these everlasting hills, that God made man in his own image? ('Paraclete') *Lothair*.

PERSONALITY OF DEVIL.

It is not good taste to believe in the Devil—give me a single argument against his personality which is not applicable to the personality of the Deity. Will you give that up? If so, where are you?—('Nigel Penruddock?') *Endymion*.

PETRARCH.

There is not perhaps in all the Italian region, fertile as it is in interesting associations and picturesque beauty, a spot that tradition and nature have so completely combined to hallow, as the last residence of Petrarch, Arqua. It seems, indeed, to have been formed for the retirement of a pensive and poetic spirit. It recedes from the world by a succession of delicate acclivities clothed with vineyards and orchards, until, winding within these hills, the mountain hamlet is at length discovered, enclosed by two ridges that slope towards each other, and seem to shut out all the passions of a troubled race. The houses are scattered at intervals on the steep sides of these summits, and on a little knoll is the mansion of the poet, built by himself, and commanding a rich and extensive view, that ends only with the shores of the Adriatic sea. His tomb, a sarcophagus of red marble, supported by pillars, doubtless familiar to the reader, is at hand ; and, placed on an elevated site, gives a solemn impression to a scene, of which the character would otherwise be serenely cheerful.—*Venetia.*

PHILOSOPHY.

We hear in these days a great deal of philosophy. Now it is my happiness to be acquainted with eminent philosophers. They all agree in one thing. They will all tell you that, however brilliant may be the discoveries of physical science, however marvellous those demonstrations which attempt to penetrate the mysteries of the human mind, greatly as they have contributed to the comfort and con-venience of man, or confirmed his consciousness of the nobility of nature, yet all these great philosophers agree in one thing—that in these investigations there is an inevitable term where they meet the insoluble, where all the most transcendent powers of intellect dissipate and disappear. Here commences the religious principle. It is universal, and it will assert its universal influence in the government of man.—*Speech in House of Commons (Irish Church Bill), March* 18, 1869.

'A philosopher,' said Mr. Sievers, 'as most of us call ourselves here ; that is to say, his profession is to observe the course of Nature; and if by chance he can discover any slight deviation of the good dame from the path which our ignorance has marked out as her only track, he claps his hands, cries εὕρηκα ! and is dubbed " illustrious " on the spot. Such is the world's reward for a great discovery, which generally, in a twelvemonth's time, is found out to be a blunder of the philosopher, and not an eccentricity of Nature. I am not underrating those great men who, by deep study, or rather by some mysterious inspiration, have produced combinations and effected results which have materially assisted the progress of civilisation and the security of our happiness. No, no ! to them be due adoration. Would that the reverence of posterity could be some consolation to these great spirits for neglect and persecution when they lived ! I have invariably observed of great natural philosophers, that if they lived in former ages they were persecuted as magicians, and in periods which profess to be more enlightened they have always been ridiculed as quacks. The succeeding century the real quack arises. He adopts and develops the suppressed, and despised, and forgotten discovery of his unfortunate predecessor ; and Fame trumpets this resurrection-man of science with as loud a blast of rapture as if, instead of being merely the accidental animator of the corpse, he were the cunning artist himself who had devised and executed the miraculous machinery which the other had only wound up.'— *Vivian Grey.*

New School of Philosophy.—The philosophers and distinguished men of science with whom of late he had frequently enjoyed the opportunity of becoming acquainted, what were their views ? They differed among themselves : did any of them agree with him ? How they accounted for everything except the only point on which man requires revelation ! Chance, necessity, atomic theories, nebular hypotheses, development, evolution, the origin of worlds, human ancestry —here were high topics on none of which was there lack of argument ; and, in a certain sense, of evidence ; and what then ? There must be design. The reasoning and the research of all philosophy could not be valid against that conviction. If there were no design, why, it would all be nonsense ; and he could not believe in nonsense. And if there were design, there must be intelligence ; and if intelligence, pure intelligence ; and pure intelligence was inconsistent with any disposition but perfect good. But between the all-wise and the all-benevolent and man, according to the new philosophers, no relations were to be any longer acknowledged. They renounce in despair the possibility of bringing man into connection with that First Cause which they can neither explain nor deny. But man requires that there shall be direct relations between the created and the Creator ; and that in those relations he should find a solution of the perplexities of existence. The brain that teems with illimitable thought will never recognise as his creator any power of nature, however irresistible, that is not gifted with consciousness. Atheism may be consistent with fine taste, and fine taste under certain conditions may for a time regulate a polished society ; but ethics with atheism are impossible ; and without ethics no human order can be strong or permanent.—*Lothair.*

There is no bigotry so terrible as the bigotry of a country that flatters itself that it is philosophical.—*Contarini Fleming.*

PHŒBUS (MR.).

This person was a young man, though more than ten years older than Lothair. His appearance was striking. Above the middle height, his form, athletic though lithe and symmetrical, was crowned by a countenance aquiline but delicate, and from many circumstances of a remarkable radiancy. The lustre of his complexion, the fire of his eye, and his chestnut hair in profuse curls, contributed much to this dazzling effect. A thick but small moustache did not conceal his curved lip or the scornful pride of his distended nostril, and his beard, close but not long, did not veil the singular beauty of his mouth. It was an arrogant face, daring and vivacious, yet weighted with an expression of deep and haughty thought.

The costume of this gentleman was rich and picturesque. Such extravagance of form and colour is sometimes encountered in the adventurous toilette of a country house, but rarely experienced in what might still be looked upon as a morning visit in the metropolis.

Mr. Phœbus was the most successful, not to say the most eminent, painter of the age. He was the descendant of a noble family of Gascony that had emigrated to England from France in the reign of Louis XIV. Unquestionably they had mixed their blood frequently during the interval and the vicissitudes of their various life ; but in Gaston Phœbus nature, as is sometimes her wont, had chosen to reproduce exactly the original type. He was the Gascon noble of the sixteenth century, with all his brilliancy, bravery, and boastfulness, equally vain, arrogant, and eccentric, accomplished in all the daring or the graceful pursuits of man, yet nursed in the philosophy of our times.--- *Lothair.*

PHŒBUS (*MADAME*).

Colonel Campian was attending a lady to the piano where a celebrity presided, a gentleman with cropped head and a long black beard. · The lady was of extraordinary beauty ; one of those faces one encounters in Asia Minor, rich, glowing, with dark fringed eyes of tremulous lustre ; a figure scarcely less striking, of voluptuous symmetry. Her toilette was exquisite, perhaps a little too splendid for the occasion, but abstractedly of fine taste, and she held, as she sang, a vast bouquet entirely of white stove flowers. The voice was as sweet as the stephanotis, and the execution faultless. It seemed the perfection of chamber-singing : no shrieks and no screams, none of those agonising experiments which result from the fatal competition of rival prima donnas.—*Lothair.*

PHYSICIAN.

What a wise physician was Æsculapius ! Physic was his abhorrence. He never was known ever to have prescribed a drug. When he visited Proserpine, he neither examined her tongue nor felt her pulse, but gave her an account of a fancy ball, which he had attended the last evening he passed on terra firma.—*The Infernal Marriage.*

PIETY.

One should never think of death, one should think of life. That is real piety.—('Waldershare') *Endymion.*

For the pious, Paradise exists everywhere.—('Lady Annabel') *Venetia.*

PIGEON-SHOOTING.

A tournament of doves.—('Lady Corisande') *Lothair.*

PINTO (MR.).

Mr. Pinto was one of the marvels of English society ; the most sought after of all its members, though no one could tell you exactly why. He was a little oily Portuguese, middle-aged, corpulent, and somewhat bald, with dark eyes of sympathy, not unmixed with humour. No one knew who he was, and in a country the most scrutinising as to personal details, no one inquired or cared to know. A quarter of a century ago an English noble had caught him in his travels, and brought him young to England, where he had always remained. From the favourite of an individual he had become the oracle of a circle, and then the idol of society. All this time his manner remained unchanged. He was never at any time either humble or pretentious. Instead of being a parasite, everybody flattered him ; and instead of being a hanger-on of society, society hung on Pinto.

It must have been the combination of many pleasing qualities rather than the possession of any commanding one, that created his influence. He certainly was not a wit, yet he was always gay, and always said things that made other people merry. His conversation was sparkling, interesting and fluent, yet it was observed he never gave an opinion on any subject and never told an anecdote. Indeed he would sometimes remark, when a man fell into his anecdotage it was a sign for him to retire from the.

world. And yet Pinto rarely opened his mouth without everybody being stricken with mirth. He had the art of viewing common things in a fanciful light, and the rare gift of raillery which flattered the self-love of those whom it seemed sportively not to spare. Sometimes those who had passed a fascinating evening with Pinto would try to remember on the morrow what he had said, and could recall nothing. He was not an intellectual Crœsus, but his pockets were full of sixpences.—*Lothair.*

PITT.

The Chatterton of politics to understand Mr. Pitt one must understand one of the suppressed characters of English history, and that is Lord Shelburne.—*Sybil.*

PLATO.

His spirit alternately bowed in trembling and in admiration, as he seemed to be listening to the secrets of the universe revealed in the glorious melodies of an immortal voice (Plato's).—*Vivian Grey.*

I look upon Plato as the wisest and the profoundest of men, and upon Epicurus as the most humane and gentle.— ('Herbert') *Venetia.*

'Plato believed, and I believe with him, in the existence of a spiritual antitype of the soul, so that when we are born, there is something within us which, from the instant we live and move, thirsts after its likeness. This propensity develops itself with the development of our nature. The gratification of the senses soon becomes a very small part of that profound and complicated sentiment, which we call love. Love, on the contrary, is a universal thirst for a communion, not merely of the senses, but of our whole nature, intellectual, imaginative, and sensitive. He who finds his antitype, enjoys a love perfect and enduring; time cannot change it, distance cannot remove it; the sympathy is complete. He who loves an object that approaches his

S

antitype is proportionately happy, the sympathy is feeble or strong, as it may be. If men were properly educated, and their faculties fully developed,' continued Herbert, ' the discovery of the antitype would be easy ; and, when the day arrives that it is a matter of course, the perfection of civilisation will be attained.'—*Venetia.*

PLEASURE.

His (Duke of St. James) life was an ocean of enjoyment, and each hour, like each wave, threw up its pearl.—*The Young Duke.*

Pleasure should follow business.—('Wilton') *Endymion.*

POET.

Poets are the unacknowledged legislators of the world.—('Marmion Herbert') *Venetia.*

Is not a poet an artist, and is not writing an art equally with painting ?—words are but chalk and colour.—('Winter') *Contarini Fleming.*

But while the doctrines of the philosopher had been forming, the spirit of the poet had not been inactive. Loneliness, after all, the best of Muses, had stimulated the creative faculty of his being. Wandering amid his solitary woods and glades at all hours and seasons, the wild and beautiful apparitions of nature had appealed to a sympathetic soul. The stars and winds, the pensive sunset and the sanguine break of morn, the sweet solemnity of night, the ancient trees and the light and evanescent flowers, all signs and sights and sounds of loveliness and power, fell on a ready eye and a responsive ear. Gazing on the beautiful, he longed to create it. Then it was that the two passions which seemed to share the being of Herbert appeared simultaneously to assert their sway, and he resolved to call in his Muse to the assistance of his Philosophy.

Herbert celebrated that fond world of his imagination, which he wished to teach men to love. In stanzas glittering with refined images, and resonant with subtle symphony, he called into creation that society of immaculate purity and unbounded enjoyment which he believed was the natural inheritance of unshackled man. In the hero he pictured a philosopher, young and gifted as himself ; in the heroine, his idea of a perfect woman. Although all those peculiar doctrines of Herbert, which, undisguised, must have excited so much odium, were more or less developed and inculcated in this work, nevertheless they were necessarily so veiled by the highly spiritual and metaphorical language of the poet, that it required some previous acquaintance with the system enforced, to be able to detect and recognise the esoteric spirit of his Muse. The public read only the history of an ideal world and of creatures of exquisite beauty, told in language that alike dazzled their fancy and captivated their ear. They were lost in a delicious maze of metaphor and music, and were proud to acknowledge an addition to the glorious catalogue of their poets in a young and interesting member of their aristocracy.—*Venetia.*

POETRY.

TO A BEAUTIFUL MUTE (THE ELDEST CHILD OF MR. FAIRLIE).

Tell me the star from which she fell,
 Oh ! name the flower
From out whose wild and perfumed bell
 At witching hour,
Sprang forth this fair and fairy maiden
Like a bee with honey laden.

They say that those sweet lips of thine
 Breathe not to speak :
Thy very ears that seem so fine
 No sound can seek,
And yet thy face beams with emotion,
Restless as the waves of ocean.

'Tis well.   Thy face and form agree,
     And both are fair.
I would not that this child should be
     As others are :
I love to mark her indecision,
Smiling with seraphic vision

At our poor gifts of vulgar sense
     That cannot stain
Nor mar her mystic innocence,
     Nor cloud her brain
With all the dreams of worldly folly,
And its creature melancholy.

To thee I dedicate these lines,
     Yet read them not,
Cursed be the art that e'er refines
     Thy natural lot :
Read the bright stars and read the flowers,
And hold converse with the bowers.
Life of Countess of Blessington.

Dreams come from Jove, the poet says ;
     But as I watch the smile
That on thy lips now softly plays,
     I can but deem the while,
Venus may also send a shade
To whisper to a slumbering maid.

What dark-eyed youth now culls the flower
     That radiant brow to grace,
Or whispers in the starry hour
     Words fairer than thy face ?
Or singles thee from out the throng
To thee to breathe his minstrel song ?

The ardent vow that ne'er can fail,
    The sigh that is not sad,
The glance that tells a secret tale,
    The spirit hushed yet glad :
These weave the dreams that maidens prove
The fluttering dream of virgin love.

Sleep on, sweet maid, nor sigh to break
    The spell that binds thy brain,
Nor struggle from thy trance to wake
    To life's impending pain.
Who wakes to love awake but knows
Love is a dream without repose.

                        Book of Beauty, 1837.

ON THE PORTRAIT OF LADY MAHON.

Fair lady ! this the pencil of Vandyke
    Might well have painted : thine the English air,
    Graceful yet earnest, that his portraits bear,
In that far troubled time, when sword and pike
    Gleamed round the ancient halls and castles fair
That shrouded Albion's beauty : though, when need,
    They too, though soft withal, would boldly dare,
Defend the leaguered breach, or charging steed,
    Mount in their trampled parks.   Far different scene
The bowers present before thee ; yet serene
Though nowadays, if coming time impart
Our ancient troubles, well I ween thy life
Would not reproach thy lot and what thou art,—
A warrior's daughter and a statesman's wife.

                        Book of Beauty, 1839.

Not only that thy puissant arm could bind
    The Tyrant of a world and, conquering fate,
    Enfranchise Europe, so I deem thee great :

But that in all thy actions I do find
Exact propriety : no gusts of mind
  Fitful and wild, but that continuous state
  Of ordered impulse mariners await,
In some benignant and enriching wind,
  The break ordained of nature.　Thy calm mie
Recalls old Rome as much as thy high deed ;
  Duty thy only idol, and serene
When all are troubled ; in the utmost need
  Prescient thy country's servant ever seen,
Yet sovereign of thyself whate'er may speed.

Upon a Statuette in silver of the Duke of
Wellington, at Stowe.

I.

Within a cloistered pile, whose Gothic towers
Rose by the margin of a sedgy lake,
Embosomed in a valley of green bowers,
And girt by many a grove and ferny brake
Loved by the antlered deer, a tender youth,
Whom Time to childhood's gentle sway of love
'Still spared ; yet innocent as is the dove,
Nor wounded yet by Care's relentless tooth,
Stood musing, of that fair antique domain
The orphan lord !　And yet, no childish thought
With wayward purpose holds its transient reign
In his young mind, with deeper feelings fraught ;
Then mystery all to him, and yet a dream
That Time has touched with its revealing beam.

II.

There came a maiden to that lonely boy,
And like to him as is the morn to night ;
Her sunny face a very type of joy,
And with her soul's unclouded lustre bright.

Still scantier summers had her brow illumed
Than that on which she threw a witching smile,
Unconscious of the spell that could beguile
His being of the burthen it was doomed
By his ancestral blood to bear : a spirit,
Rife with desponding thoughts and fancies drear,
A moody soul that men sometimes inherit,
And worse than all the woes the world may bear.
But when he met that maiden's dazzling eye,
He bade each gloomy image baffled fly.

III.

Amid the shady woods and sunny lawns
The maiden and the youth now wander, gay
As the bright birds, and happy as the fawns,
Their sportive rivals, that around them play ;
Their light hands linked in love, the golden hours
Unconscious fly, while thus they graceful roam,
And careless ever till the voice of home
Recalled them from their sunshine and their flowers;
For then they parted : to his lonely pile
The orphan-chief, for though his woe to lull,
The maiden called him brother, her fond smile
Gladdened another hearth, while his was dull.
Yet as they parted, she reproved his sadness,
And for his sake she gaily whispered gladness.

IV.

She was the daughter of a noble race,
That beauteous girl, and yet she owed her name
To one who needs no herald's skill to trace
His blazoned lineage, for his lofty fame
Lives in the mouth of men, and distant climes
Re-echo his wide glory ; where the brave
Are honoured, where 'tis noble deemed to save
A prostrate nation, and for future times

Work with a high devotion, that no taunt,
Or ribald lie, or zealot's eager curse,
Or the short-sighted world's neglect can daunt,
That name is worshipped ! His immortal verse
Blends with his god-like deeds, a double spell
To bind the coming age he loved too well !

v.

For, from his ancient home, a scatterling,
They drove him forth, unconscious of their prize,
And branded as a vile unhallowed thing,
The man who struggled only to be wise.
And even his hearth rebelled, the duteous wife,
Whose bosom well might soothe in that dark hour,
Swelled with her gentle force the world's harsh power,
And aimed her dart at his devoted life.
That struck ; the rest his mighty soul might scorn,
But when his household gods averted stood,
'Twas the last pang that cannot well be borne
When tortured e'en to torpor : his heart's blood
Flowed to the unseen blow : then forth he went,
And gloried in his ruthless banishment.

vi.

A new-born pledge of love within his home,
His alien home, the exiled father left ;
And when, like Cain, he wandered forth to roam,
A Cain without his solace, all bereft,
Stole down his pallid cheek the scalding tear,
To think a stranger to his tender love
His child must grow, untroubled where might rove
His restless life, or taught perchance to fear
Her father's name, and bred in sullen hate,
Shrink from his image. Thus the gentle maid,
Who with her smiles had soothed an orphan's fate,
Had felt an orphan's pang ; yet undismayed,

Though taught to deem her sire the child of shame,
She clung with instinct to that reverent name !

VII.

Time flew ; the boy became a man ; no more
His shadow falls upon his cloistered hall,
But to a stirring world he learn'd to pour
The passion of his being, skilled to call
From the deep caverns of his musing thought
Shadows to which they bowed, and on their mind
To stamp the image of his own ; the wind,
Though all unseen, with force or odour fraught,
Can sway mankind, and thus a poet's voice,
Now touched with sweetness, now inflamed with rage,
Though breath, can make us grieve and then rejoice :
Such is the spell of his creative page,
That blends with all our moods ; and thoughts can yield
That all have felt, and yet till then were sealed.

VIII.

The lute is sounding in a chamber bright
With a high festival ; on every side,
Soft in the gleamy blaze of mellowed light,
Fair women smile, and dancers graceful glide ;
And words still sweeter than a serenade
Are breathed with guarded voice and speaking eyes,
By joyous hearts in spite of all their sighs ;
But bygone fantasies that ne'er can fade
Retain the pensive spirit of the youth ;
Reclined against a column he surveys
His laughing compeers with a glance, in sooth,
Careless of all their mirth : for other days
Enchain him with their vision, the bright hours
Passed with the maiden in their sunny bowers.

IX.

, Why turns his brow so pale, why starts to life
That languid eye?   What form before unseen,
With all the spells of hallowed memory rife,
Now rises on his vision ?   As the Queen
Of Beauty from her bed of sparkling foam
Sprang to the azure light, and felt the air,
Soft as her cheek, the wavy dancers bear
To his rapt sight a mien that calls his home,
His cloistered home, before him, with his dreams
Prophetic strangely blending.   The bright muse
Of his dark childhood still divinely beams
Upon his being ; glowing with the hues
That painters love, when raptured pencils soar
To trace a form that nations may adore !

X.

One word alone, within her thrilling ear,
Breathed with hushed voice the brother of her heart,
And that for aye is hidden.   With a tear
Smiling she strove to conquer, see her start,
The bright blood rising to her quivering cheek,
And meet the glance she hastened once to greet,
When not a thought had he, save in her sweet
And solacing society ; to seek
Her smiles his only life !   Ah ! happy prime
Of cloudless purity, no stormy fame
His unknown sprite then stirred, a golden time
Worth all the restless splendour of a name ;
And one soft accent from those gentle lips
Might all the plaudits of a world eclipse.

XI.

My tale is done ; and if some deem it strange
My fancy thus should droop, deign then to learn
My tale is truth : imagination's range
Its bounds exact may touch not : to discern

Far stranger things than poets ever feign,
In life's perplexing annals, is the fate
Of those who act; and musing, penetrate
The mystery of Fortune : to whose reign
The haughtiest brow must bend ; 'twas passing strange
The youth of these fond children ; strange the flush
Of his high fortunes and his spirit's change ;
Strange was the maiden's tear, the maiden's blush ;
Strange were his musing thoughts and trembling heart,
'Tis strange they met, and stranger if they part !

Venetia.

ON THE NIGHT OUR DAUGHTER WAS BORN.

I.

Within our heaven of love, the new-born star
We long devoutly watched, like shepherd kings,
Steals into light, and, floating from afar,
Methinks some bright transcendent seraph sings,
Waving with flashing light her radiant wings,
Immortal welcome to the stranger fair :
To us a child is born. With transport clings
The mother to the babe she sighed to bear ;
Of all our treasured loves the long-expected heir !

II.

My daughter ! can it be a daughter now
Shall greet my being with her infant smile ?
And shall I press that fair and taintless brow
With my fond lips, and tempt, with many awhile
Of playful love, those features to beguile
A parent with their mirth ? In the wild sea
Of this dark life, behold a little isle
Rises amid the waters, bright and free,
A haven for my hopes of fond security !

IIL

And thou shalt bear a name my line has loved,
And their fair daughters owned for many an age,
Since first our fiery blood a wanderer roved,
And made in sunnier lands his pilgrimage,
Where proud defiance with the waters wage
The sea-born city's walls ; the graceful towers
Loved by the bard and honoured by the sage !
My own VENETIA now shall gild her bowers,
And with her spell enchain our life's enchanted hours !

IV.

Oh ! if the blessing of a father's heart
Hath aught of sacred in its deep-breath'd prayer,
Skilled to thy gentle being to impart,
As thy bright form itself, a fate as fair ;
On thee I breathe that blessing !   Let me share,
O God ! her joys ; and if the dark behest
Of woe resistless, and avoidless care,
Hath not gone forth, oh ! spare this gentle guest,
And wreak thy needful wrath on my resigned breast !

Venetia.

CAPTAIN ARMINE'S SONG.

I.

My heart is like a silent lute
  Some faithless hand has thrown aside ;
Those chords are dumb, those tones are mute,
  That once sent forth a voice of pride !
Yet even o'er the lute neglected
  The wind of heaven will sometimes fly,
And even thus the heart dejected
  Will sometimes answer to a sigh !

II.

And yet to feel another's power
  May grasp the prize for which I pine,
And others now may pluck the flower
  I cherished for this heart of mine !
No more, no more ! The hand forsaking,
  The lute must fall, and shivered lie
In silence : and my heart thus breaking,
  Responds not even to a sigh.

                                    Henrietta Temple.

I.

Spring in the Apennine now holds her court
Within an amphitheatre of hills
Clothed with the blooming chestnut ; musical
With murmuring pines, waving their light green cones
Like youthful Bacchants ; while the dewy grass,
The myrtle and the mountain violet,
Blend their rich odours with the fragrant trees,
And sweeten the soft air. Above us spreads
The purple sky, bright with the unseen sun
The hills yet screen, although the golden beam
Touches the topmost boughs, and tints with light
The grey and sparkling crags. The breath of morn
Still lingers in the valley ; but the bee
With restless passion hovers on the wing,
Waiting the opening flower, of whose embrace
The sun shall be the signal Poised in air,
The winged minstrel of the liquid dawn,
The lark, pours forth his lyric, and responds
To the fresh chorus of the sylvan doves,
The stir of branches and the fall of streams,
The harmonies of nature !

II.

            Gentle Spring !
Once more, oh, yes ! once more I feel thy breath,

And charm of renovation ! To the sky
Thou bringest light, and to the glowing earth
A garb of grace : but sweeter than the sky
That hath no cloud, and sweeter than the earth
With all its pageantry, the peerless boon
Thou bearest to me, a temper like thine own ;
A springlike spirit, beautiful and glad !
Long years, long years of suffering, and of thought
Deeper than woe, had dimmed the eager eye
Once quick to catch thy brightness, and the ear
That lingered on thy music, the harsh world
Had jarred. The freshness of my life was gone,
And hope no more an omen in thy bloom
Found of a fertile future ! There are minds
Like lands, but with one season, and that drear :
Mine was eternal winter !

III.

A dark dream
Of hearts estranged, and of an Eden lost
Entranced my being ; one absorbing thought,
Which, if not torture, was a dull despair
That agony were light to. But while sad
Within the desert of my life I roamed,
And no sweet springs of love gushed for to greet
My wearied heart, behold two spirits came
Floating in light, seraphic ministers,
The semblance of whose splendour on me fell
As on some dusky stream the matin ray,
Touching the gloomy waters with its life.
And both were fond, and one was merciful !
And to my home long forfeited they bore
My vagrant spirit, and the gentle hearth,
I reckless fled, received me with its shade
And pleasant refuge. And our softened hearts
Were like the twilight, when our very bliss

Calls tears to soothe our rapture ; as the stars
Steal forth, then shining smiles their trembling ray
Mixed with our tenderness ; and love was there
In all his manifold forms ; the sweet embrace,
And thrilling pressure of the gentle hand,
And silence speaking with the melting eye !

IV.

And now again I feel thy breath, O spring !
And now the seal hath fallen from my gaze,
And thy wild music in my ready ear
Finds a quick echo ! The discordant world
Mars not thy melodies ; thy blossoms now
Are the emblems of my heart ; and through my veins
The flow of youthful feeling, long pent up,
Glides like thy sunny streams ! In this fair scene,
On forms still fairer I my blessing pour ;
On her the beautiful, the wise, the good,
Who learnt the sweetest lesson to forgive ;
And on the bright-eyed daughter of our love,
Who soothed a mother, and a father saved !

Venetia.

It appears to me that the age of versification has passed.
The mode of composition must ever be greatly determined
by the manner in which the composition can be made public. In ancient days the voice was the medium by which
we became acquainted with the inventions of a poet. In
such a method, where those who listened had no time to
pause, and no opportunity to think, it was necessary that
everything should be obvious. The audience who were
perplexed would soon become wearied. The spirit of
ancient poetry, therefore, is rather material than metaphysical, superficial, not internal. There is much simplicity
and much nature, but little passion, and less philosophy.
To obviate the baldness, which is the consequence of a

style where the subject and the sentiments are rather intimated than developed, the poem was enriched by music and enforced by action. Occasionally were added the enchantment of scenery and the fascination of the dance. But the poet did not depend merely upon these brilliant accessories. He resolved that his thoughts should be expressed in a manner different from other modes of communicating ideas. He caught a suggestion from his sister art, and invented metre. And in this modulation he introduced a new system of phraseology, which marked him out from the crowd, and which has obtained the title of ' poetic diction.'

His object in this system of words was to heighten his meaning by strange phrases and unusual constructions. Inversion was invented to clothe a commonplace with an air of novelty ; vague epithets were introduced to prop up a monotonous, modulation. Were his meaning to be enforced, he shrank from wearisome ratiocination and the agony of precise conceptions, and sought refuge in a bold personification or a beautiful similitude. The art of poetry was, to express natural feelings in unnatural language.

Institutions ever survive their purpose, and customs govern us when their cause is extinct. And this mode of communicating poetic invention still remained, when the advanced civilisation of man, in multiplying manuscripts, might have made many suspect that the time had arrived when the poet was to cease to sing, and to learn to write. Had the splendid refinement of Imperial Rome not been doomed to such rapid decay, and such mortifying and degrading vicissitudes, I believe that versification would have worn out. Unquestionably that empire, in its multifarious population, scenery, creeds, and customs, offered the richest materials for emancipated fiction ; materials, however, far too vast and various for the limited capacity of metrical celebration.

That beneficent Omnipotence, before which we must

bow down, has so ordered it, that imitation should be the mental feature of modern Europe; and has ordained that we should adopt a Syrian religion, a Grecian literature, and a Roman law. At the revival of letters, we beheld the portentous spectacle of national poets communicating their inventions in an exotic form. Conscious of the confined nature of their method, yet unable to extricate themselves from its fatal ties, they sought variety in increased artifice of diction, and substituted the barbaric clash of rhyme for the melody of the lyre.

A revolution took place in the mode of communicating thought. Now, at least, it was full time that we should have emancipated ourselves for ever from sterile metre. One would have supposed that the poet who could not only write, but even print his inventions, would have felt that it was both useless and unfit that they should be communicated by a process invented when his only medium was simple recitation. One would have supposed that the poet would have rushed with desire to the new world before him, that he would have seized the new means which permitted him to revel in a universe of boundless invention; to combine the highest ideal creation with the infinite delineation of teeming Nature; to unravel all the dark mysteries of our bosoms and all the bright purposes of our being; to become the great instructor and champion of his species; and not only delight their fancy, and charm their senses, and command their will, but demonstrate their rights, illustrate their necessities, and expound the object of their existence; and all this too in a style charming and changing with its universal theme, now tender, now sportive; now earnest, now profound; now sublime, now pathetic; and substituting for the dull monotony of metre the most various, and exquisite, and inexhaustible melody.

When I remember the trammels to which the poet has been doomed, and the splendour with which consummate genius has invested him, and when, for a moment, I con-

T

ceive him bursting asunder his bonds, I fancy that I behold
the sacred bird snapping the golden chain that binds him
to Olympus, and soaring even above Jove !—*Contarini
Fleming.*

A delicious maze of metaphor and music.—*Venetia.*

What is poetry but a lie, and what are poets but liars ?—
('Cadurcis ') *Venetia.*

'It is in poetry, and poetry alone, that modern nations
have maintained the majesty of genius. Do we equal the
Greeks ? Do we even excel them ?'

'Let us prove the equality first,' said Cadurcis. 'The
Greeks excelled in every species of poetry. In some we do
not even attempt to rival them. We have not a single
modern ode, or a single modern pastoral. We have no one
to place by Pindar, or the exquisite Theocritus. As for the
epic, I confess myself a heretic as to Homer ; I look upon
the Iliad as a remnant of national songs ; the wise ones
agree that the Odyssey is the work of a later age. My
instinct agrees with the result of their researches. I credit
their conclusion. The Paradise Lost is, doubtless, a great
production, but the subject is monkish. Dante is national,
but he has all the faults of a barbarous age. In general the
modern epic is framed upon the assumption that the Iliad is
an orderly composition. They are indebted for this fallacy
to Virgil, who called order out of chaos ; but the Æneid, all
the same, appears to me an insipid creation. And now for
the drama. You will adduce Shakespeare ?'

'There are passages in Dante,' said Herbert, 'not inferior, in my opinion, to any existing literary composition ;
but, as a whole, I will not make my stand on him ; I am
not so clear that, as a lyric poet, Petrarch may not rival the
Greeks. Shakespeare I esteem of ineffable merit.'

'And who is Shakespeare ?' said Cadurcis. 'We know
of him as much as we do of Homer. Did he write half the
plays attributed to him? Did he ever write a single whole
play ? I doubt it. He appears to me to have been an

inspired adapter for the theatres, which were then not as good as barns. I take him to have been a botcher-up of old plays. His popularity is of modern date, and it may not last ; it would have surprised him marvellously. Heaven knows, at present, all that bears his name is alike admired ; and a regular Shakespearian falls into ecstasies with trash which deserves a niche in the Dunciad. For my part, I abhor your irregular geniuses, and I love to listen to the little nightingale of Twickenham.'

' I have often observed,' said Herbert, ' that writers of an unbridled imagination themselves, admire those whom the world, erroneously, in my opinion, and from a confusion of ideas, esteems correct. I am myself an admirer of Pope, though I certainly should not ever think of classing him among the great creative spirits. And you, you are the last poet in the world, Cadurcis, whom one would have fancied his votary.'

' I have written like a boy,' said Cadurcis. ' I found the public bite, and so I baited on with tainted meat. I have never written for fame, only for notoriety ; but I am satiated ; I am going to turn over a new leaf.'

' For myself,' said Herbert, ' if I ever had the power to impress my creations on my fellow-men, the inclination is gone, and perhaps the faculty is extinct. My career is over ; perhaps a solitary echo from my lyre may yet, at times, linger about the world like a breeze that has lost its way. But there is a radical fault in my poetic mind, and I am conscious of it. I am not altogether void of the creative faculty, but mine is a fragmentary mind ; I produce no whole. Unless you do this, you cannot last ; at least, you cannot materially affect your species. But what I admire in you, Cadurcis, is that, with all the faults of youth, of which you will free yourself, your creative power is vigorous, prolific, and complete ; your creations rise fast and fair, like perfect worlds.'— *Venetia.*

T 2

POLICY.

He knew that it was said this remarkable policy, this paralysis of policy, which was now fashionable, was in fact occasioned by a dissension in the Cabinet.—*Speech in House of Commons (Arms [Ireland] Bill), August* 9, 1843.

POLITICS.

Real politics are the possession and distribution of power.—('Lady Montfort') *Endymion.*

Finality is not the language of politics.—*Speech in House of Commons (Representation of People Bill), February* 28, 1859.

In politics unreasonable circumstances are elements of the problem to be solved.—*Endymion.*

In politics nothing is contemptible.—('Sievers') *Vivian Grey.*

There is no gambling like politics.—('Lord Roenampton') *Endymion.*

The practice of politics in the East may be defined by one word—dissimulation.—*Contarini Fleming.*

A very famous monarch, King Louis Philippe, once said to me that he attributed the great success of the British nation in political life to their talking politics after dinner.—*Banquet to Lord Rector, Glasgow, November* 19, 1873.

It is not impossible that the political movements of our time, which seem on the surface to have a democratic tendency, may have in reality a monarchical bias.—*Coningsby.*

I will keep each faction in awe by the bugbear of the other's supremacy. Trust me, I am a profound politician.—('Pluto') *Infernal Marriage.*

You must show that democracy is aristocracy in disguise, and that aristocracy is democracy in disguise. It will carry you through everything.—('Bertie Tremaine') *Endymion.*

England should think more of the community and less of the Government.—('Sidonia') *Coningsby.*

The power of the future is ministerial capacity.—('Bertie Tremaine') *Endymion.*

Muddlebrains is a political humbug, the greatest of all humbugs ; a man who swaggers about London clubs and consults solemnly about his influence, and in the country is a nonentity.—*Sybil.*

In estimating the accuracy of political opinion one should take into consideration the standing of the opinionist.— *Sybil.*

POLITICAL ECONOMY.

The right honourable gentleman has uttered three or four commonplaces—the prostitutes of political economy whom gentlemen on each side in turn embrace—to show that you may fight hostile tariffs with free imports.—*Speech in House of Commons (Corn Importation Bill), May 4, 1846.*

POPULAR GRATITUDE.

When the British nation is at once grateful and enthusiastic, they always call you 'My Lord.'—*Lothair.*

POPULATION.

The population returns of this country are very instructive reading.—('Gerard') *Sybil.*

POST OFFICE.

A member of Parliament is a sort of political confessor, and even if a constituent were to consult him about a conspiracy, it is better that he should be dissuaded by his representative than have his letters opened by a Secretary of State.—*Speech in House of Commons (Opening Letters at Post-office), February 20, 1845.*

POWER.

In this country the depository of power is always unpopular ; all combine against it ; it always falls.—*Coningsby.*

Next to the assumption of power was the responsibility of relinquishing it.—*Speech in House of Commons (Want of Confidence), May 27, 1841.*

The very exercise of power only teaches me that it may be wielded for a greater purpose.—*Contarini Fleming.*

Everyone loves power, even if they do not know what to do with it.—*Endymion.*

The most powerful men are not public men : a public man is responsible, and a responsible man is a slave. It is private life that governs the world.—(' Baron Sergius ') *Endymion.*

The more you are talked about, the less powerful you are.—(' Baron Sergius ') *Endymion.*

PRACTICAL.

Everything is practical which we believe.—(' Nigel Penruddock ') *Endymion.*

PRAYER.

Innocence has prayed for fresh support, and young devotion told her beads. She (May Dacre) rises with an eye of mellowed light, and her soft cheek is tinted with the flush that comes from prayer.—*The Young Duke.*

The tears trickled down the pale cheek of Glastonbury as he revolved in his mind these mournful thoughts ; and almost unconsciously he wrung his hands as he felt his utter want of power to remedy these sad and piteous circumstances. Yet he was not absolutely hopeless. There was ever open to the pious Glastonbury one perennial source of trust and consolation. This was a fountain that was ever fresh and sweet, and he took refuge from the world's harsh courses and exhausting cares in its salutary flow and its refreshing shade, when, kneeling before his crucifix, he commended the unhappy Ferdinand and his family to the superintending care of a merciful Omnipotence.—*Henrietta Temple.*

PRECEDENT.

A precedent embalms a principle.—*Speech in House of Commons (Expenditure of Country), February* 22, 1848.

The right honourable gentleman (Sir R. Peel) tells us to go back to precedents : with him a great measure is always founded on a small precedent. He traces the steam-engine always back to the tea-kettle.—*Speech in House of Commons* (*Maynooth*), *April* 11, 1845.

PRESS.

As for the press, I am myself a gentleman of the press, and bear no other scutcheon.—*Speech in House of Commons* (*Relations with France*), *February* 18, 1853.

Public opinion has a more direct, a more comprehensive, a more efficient organ for its utterance, than a body of men sectionally chosen. The Printing-press is a political element unknown to classic or feudal times. It absorbs in a great degree the duties of the Sovereign, the Priest, the Parliament ; it controls, it educates, it discusses. That public opinion, when it acts, would appear in the form of one who has no class interests. In an enlightened age the monarch on the throne, free from the vulgar prejudices and the corrupt interests of the subject, becomes again divine ! *Coningsby.*

PRETENDERS.

Ministers do not love pretenders.—*Endymion.*

PRIDE OF ANCESTRY.

There is no pride like the pride of ancestry, for it is a blending of all emotions. How immeasurably superior to the herd is the man whose father only is famous ! Imagine then the feelings of one who can trace his line through a thousand years of heroes and of princes.—*The Young Duke.*

PRINCESS ALICE.

The subject to which I have to refer is one on which there will be unanimity ; but alas ! it is the unanimity of sorrow. A Princess, who loved us though she left us, and who always revisited her Fatherland with delight—one of those women the brightness of whose being adorns society and inspires the circle in which she lives—has been removed from this world, to the anguish of her family, her friends, and her subjects. The Princess Alice—for I will venture to call her by that name, though she wore a crown—afforded one of the most striking instances that I can remember of rich ness of culture and rare intelligence combined with the most pure and refined domestic sentiments. You, my Lords, who knew her life well, can recall those agonising hours when she attended the dying bed of her illustrious father, who had directed her studies and formed her tastes. You can recall, too, the moment at which she attended her royal brother at a time when the hopes of England seemed to depend on his life ; and now can you remember too well how, when the whole of her own family were stricken by a malignant disease, she had been to them the angel in the house ; but at last, her own vital power perhaps exhausted, she has herself fallen. My Lords, there is something wonderfully piteous in the immediate cause of her death. The physicians who permitted her to watch over the suffer-ing family enjoined her under no circumstances whatever to be tempted into an embrace. Her admirable self-con-straint guarded her through the crises of this terrible com-plaint in safety. She remembered and observed the injunc-tions of her physicians. But it became her lot to break to her son—quite a youth—the death of his youngest sister, to whom he was devotedly attached. The boy was so over-come with misery that the agitated mother to console him clasped him in her arms—and thus received the kiss of death. My Lords, I hardly know an incident more pa-thetic. It is one by which poets might be inspired, and which the artist in every class, whether in picture, in statue, or in gem, might find a fitting subject of commemoration. My Lords, we will not dwell at this moment on the suffer-ings of the husband whom she has left behind, and of the children who were so devoted to her ; but our immediate duty is to offer our condolence to one whose happiness and whose sorrow always excite and command the loyalty and affectionate respect of this House. Upon her Majesty a great grief has fallen which none but the Queen can so completely and acutely feel. Seventeen years ago her Majesty experienced the crushing sorrow of her life, and then she was particularly sustained by the daughter whom she has now lost, who assisted her by her labours, and aided her by her presence and counsel. Her Majesty now feels that the cup of sorrow was not then exhausted. No language can express the consolation we wish to extend to our Sovereign in her sorrow—such suffering is too fresh to allow of solace ; but, however exalted, there are none but must be sustained by the consciousness that they possess the sympathy of a nation.—*Speech in House of Lords, December* 17, 1878.

PRINCE CONSORT.

The loss was so sudden, so unexpected, that the natural emotions of the community were all directed to the personal character of him who had passed away. The peerless husband, perfect father, the master whose yoke was gentleness, the wise and faithful counsellor of the Sovereign who was his consort—these were the traits in the character of the Prince that attached and appealed to all hearts ; and whilst there was a general desire, by public contributions, to show a sense of those qualities, every community felt that it was equally a judge of those virtues with the metropolis ; and there was an immense amount of local subscriptions dedicated to the ornament or utility of the district in which the subscriptions were raised. This is the reason why the public contributions were not directed to one centre. But as time drew on, something of the influence of posterity was exercised upon the opinion of the country, and it became conscious that it had lost not merely a man of virtuous and benignant character, who had exercised the fine qualities he

possessed for the advantage of the community of which he
was a prominent member, but it felt that it had lost a man
of very original and peculiar character, who had exercised
a great influence upon the age, and which it felt as time
advanced would have been still more sensibly experienced.
The character of Prince Albert was peculiar in this respect,
that he combined two great qualities which are generally
considered to be incompatible, and combined those qualities
in a high degree. He united the faculty of contemplation
with the talent of action, and was equally remarkable for profundity of thought and promptitude of organisation. Add
to these qualities all the virtues of the heart, and the House
will see that the character thus composed was a very remarkable one. He brought this peculiar temperament to
act upon the public mind for purposes of great moment,
but of great difficulty. The task which the Prince proposed to himself was to extend the knowledge, refine the
tastes, and enlarge the sympathies of a proud and ancient
people. Had he not been gifted with deep thought and a
singular facility and happiness of applying and mastering
details, he could not have succeeded so fully as he did in
those efforts, the results of which we shall find so much the
greater as time goes on. Such being now the impression
of the country—that we have lost not simply an accomplished and benignant Prince, but one of those minds
which influence their age and mould the character of a
people—a strong feeling prevails that a memorial should be
raised in the metropolis of the empire. A public memorial
such as the country requires should be of a universal and
complete description. It should apply to the general sentiments of the country, and should represent, as far as Art
can represent, the full career of the man, so that future
generations may behold a monument which may serve for
their instruction and encouragement. It should, as it were,
represent the character of the Prince himself : in the harmony of its proportions, in the beauty of its ornament, and

in its enduring nature. It should be something direct, significant, and choice : so that those who come after us may say, this is the type and testimony of a sublime life and a transcendent career, and thus they were recognised by a grateful and admiring people !—*Speech in House of Commons, April* 23, 1863.

PRINCES.

Princes go for nothing, without a loan.—('Fakredeen') *Tancred.*

The Crown Prince of all countries is only a puppet in the hands of the people to be played against his own father. ('Sievers') *Vivian Grey.*

PRIVATE SECRETARIES.

The relations between a minister and his secretary are, or at least should be,· among the finest that can subsist between two individuals. Except the married state, there is none in which so great a confidence ·is involved, in which more forbearance ought to be exercised, or more sympathy ought to exist. There is usually in the relations an identity of interest, and that of the highest kind ; and the perpetual difficulties, the alternations of triumph and defeat, develop devotion.—*Endymion.*

The right honourable gentleman drew a most interesting picture of himself overwhelmed with the cares of state, and supported on each side by a private secretary, one of whom received 300*l.* and the other 150*l.* a year. Are the private secretaries of a Prime Minister in such a position that they are only to be rewarded by their salaries? He is to be rewarded· by the confidence which is reposed in him, and by the prospects which are opened to him, and any reference to the salary of the receiver is a mere *ad captandum* argument.—*Speech in House of Commons (Salaries and Wages [Public Service] Bill).*

PROCESSIONS.

Every procession must end. It is a pity, for there is nothing so popular with mankind.—*Endymion.*

PROFOUND.

A profound thinker always suspects that he is superficial.— *Contarini Fleming.*

PROPERTY.

One of the elements of territorial property is that it is representative.—*Speech at Manchester, April* 3, 1872.

What is the first quality which is required in a second chamber? Without doubt independence. What is the best foundation for independence? Without doubt property.— *Speech at Manchester, April* 3, 1872.

PROPHECY (*A*).

I have begun several times many things, and I have often succeeded at last. I will sit down, but the time will come when you will hear me.—*Maiden Speech in House of Commons (Irish Election Petition), December* 7, 1837.

PROPHET.

Many a prophet is little honoured till the future proves his inspiration.—*Alroy.*

PROTECTION.

To tax the community for the advantage of a class is not protection : it is plunder, and I disclaim it : but I ask you to protect the rights and interests of labour generally, in the first place by allowing no free imports from countries which meet you with countervailing duties, and in the second place, with respect to agricultural produce, to compensate the soil for the burdens from which other classes are free by an equivalent duty. This is my view of what is called 'protection.'—*Speech in House of Commons (Foreign Corn), May* 14, 1850.

PROVERBS.

We cannot eat the fruit whilst the tree is in blossom.— *Alroy.*

One grape will not make a bunch, even though it be a great one.—*Tancred.*

When the infant begins to walk, it thinks it lives in strange times.—*Sybil.*

A frying egg will not wait for the King of Cordova.— *Count Alarcos.*

Who drinks, first chinks.

In a long journey and a small inn, one knows one's company.

An ass covered with gold has more respect than a horse with a pack saddle.

Courage is fire, and bullying is smoke.

The sheep should have his belly full who quarrels with his mate.

Who asks in God's name, asks for two.

There's no fishing for trout in dry breeches.

The fool wonders, the wise man asks.

An obedient wife commands her husband.

Business with a stranger is title enough.

The oldest pig must look for the knife.—*Count Alarcos.*

PRUDENCE.

We live in an age of prudence. The leaders of the people now generally follow.—*Coningsby.*

PUBLIC.

God made man in his own image; but the public is made by newspapers, members of Parliament, excise officers, and poor-law guardians.—('Sidonia') *Coningsby.*

Besides a free press, you must have a servile public.—
Tancred.

Change in the abstract is what is wanted by a people
who are at the same time inquiring and wealthy.   Instead
of statesmen they desire shufflers ; and compromise in
conduct and ambiguity in speech are, though no one will confess it, the public qualities now most in vogue.—*Tancred.*

Public Building.—Nothing more completely represents
a nation than a public building.—*Tancred.*

Public Credit.—India with all its myriads of population
and crowds of kings, with its 'mountains of light ' and pil-
lared palanquins of precious metal, showered like tribute at
the feet of our Queen, with all the science and security of
British administration, cannot produce from its broad and
exuberant bosom a sum equal to that afforded by the cur-
tailed custom-houses of England.   What is the magic spell
—what is the cause of all this?   That this island should produce a revenue greater than all those vast dominions ?   It
is that in this country we associated our material interests
with the inspiration of a great moral principle, and that we
have built up public wealth on the foundation of public
credit.—*Speech in House of Commons (Inhabited House Duty
Bill), June* 30, 1851.

Public Opinion.—Who will define public opinion ?   Any
human conclusion that is arrived at with adequate knowledge
and with sufficient thought is entitled to respect, and the
public opinion of a great nation under such conditions is
irresistible, and ought to be so.   But what we call public
opinion is generally public sentiment.—*Speech in House
of Commons (Compensation for Disturbance Bill), August* 3,
1880.

The opinion of the reflecting majority.—(' Lord Henry
Vavasour ') *Tancred.*

Public opinion on the Continent has turned out to be
the voice of secret societies ; and public opinion in England is the clamour of organised clubs.—*Speech in House*

of Commons (*Address in answer to Speech*), *February* 1, 1849.
The public passion, which is called opinion.—*Endymion.*
His lordship found time to lead by the nose a most meek and milkwhite jackass that immediately followed him, and which, in spite of the remarkable length of its ears, seemed the object of great veneration. Among other characteristics, it was said at different seasons to be distinguished by different titles ; for sometimes it was styled 'the public,' at others 'opinion,' and occasionally was saluted as the king's conscience.—*The Infernal Marriage.*

PUBLICITY.

Without publicity there can be no public spirit, and without public spirit every nation must decay.—*August* 8, 1871.
We have year after year been struggling to make political life more public. Publicity is now the soul of our political life. We owe to the principle of publicity our chief blessings. We have introduced publicity in the affairs of Parliament, into the judicial bench, into the press. Now we are called upon to act contrary to this course, which we have so long pursued.—*Speech in House of Commons* (*Parliamentary and Municipal Elections Bill*), *June* 28, 1872.

PURPOSE.

The secret of success is constancy to purpose.—*Speech at Crystal Palace* (*Banquet of National Union of Conservative and Constitutional Associations*) *June* 24, 1872.
Duty scorns prudence, and criticism has few terrors for a man with a great purpose.—*Life of Lord George Bentinck.*
I have brought myself by long meditation to the conviction that a human being with a settled purpose must accomplish it, and that nothing can resist a will that will stake even existence for its fulfilment.—('Myra') *Endymion.*
He (Bertie Tremaine) had a purpose, and they say

that a man with a purpose generally sees it realised.— *Endymion.*

He really owed his social advancement to his indomitable will. That quality governs all things, and though the will of Seymour Hicks was directed to what many may deem a petty or contracted purpose, life is always interesting when you have a purpose and live in its fulfilment.— *Endymion.*

QUEEN.

He who serves queens may expect backsheesh.— ('Darkush') *Tancred.*

QUESTION.

Questions are always easy.—('Morley') *Sybil.*

RACE.

The truth is, progress and reaction are but words to mystify the millions. They mean nothing, they are nothing, they are phrases and not facts. In the structure, the decay, and the development of the various families of man, the vicissitudes of history find their main solution—all is race.— *Life of Lord George Bentinck.*

No one will treat with indifference the principle of race. It is the key of history.—('Baron Sergius') *Endymion.*

Language and religion do not make a race. There is only one thing which makes a race, and that is blood.— ('Baron Sergius') *Endymion.*

The Semites are unquestionably a great race, for among the few things in this world which appear to be certain, nothing is more sure than that they invented the alphabet.— ('Baron Sergius') *Endymion.*

The decay of a race is an inevitable necessity unless it lives in deserts and never mixes its blood.—('Sidonia') *Tancred.*

Saxon industry and Norman manners never will agree.— ('Mr. Millbank') *Coningsby.*

An unmixed race of a first-rate organisation are the aristocracy of nature.—*Coningsby.*

The difference of race is unfortunately one of the reasons why I fear war may always exist ; because race implies difference, difference implies superiority, and superiority leads to predominance.—*Speech in House of Commons* (*Address in answer to Queen's Speech*), *February* 1, 1849.

RADICAL.

There is no doubt that there is a party in England—I don't believe a very numerous party, but a very busy one— who always view with hostility the agricultural interest. They do so because they are opposed to the free and aristocratic government. You may get rid of that government, but if you do, you will have either a despotism that ends in democracy, or a democracy that ends in despotism.—*Speech at Aylesbury, Royal and Central Bucks Agricultural Association, September* 18, 1879.

He was a pretentious, underbred, half-educated man, fluent with all the commonplaces of middle-class ambition, which are humorously called democratic opinions, but at heart a sycophant of the aristocracy.—*Endymion.*

Pretending that the people can be better off than they are, is Radicalism and nothing else.—('Warwickshire Peer') *Sybil.*

Hump Chippendale had none of those gentle failings ; he was a democratic leg who loved to fleece a noble, and thought all men were born equal ; a consoling creed that was a hedge for his hump.—*Sybil.*

RAGLAN (*LORD*).

After half a century of public service all that which was noble and sometimes illustrious ought not to be permitted to pass away without the record and recognition of a nation's gratitude. The career of Lord Raglan was remarkable. Forty years ago he sealed with his blood the brilliant close

U

of a great struggle against the danger of universal empire, and after that long interval he has given to his country his life in order to guard it against the menaces of a new and overwhelming enemy. The qualities of Lord Raglan were remarkable, and it may be doubted whether they will be supplied by a successor, however able. That which perhaps most distinguished him was an elevation and serenity of mind that invested him, as it were, with an heroic and classical repose, that permitted him to bring to the management of men and the transaction of great affairs the magic influence of character, and that often in his case accomplished results otherwise produced by the inspiration of genius. Perhaps there is no instance on record in which valour of so high a character was so happily and so singularly allied to so disciplined a discretion. Never were courage and caution united in so great a degree of either quality. Sir, over the tomb of the great departed criticism must be silent ; but even then it must be permitted to all of us to remember that the course of events has sanctioned the judgments of that commander with respect to those difficulties with which it was his hard fate to cope, but which his country must recollect he did not choose to create. May those who succeed him encounter a happier fortune ; they will not need a more glorious end, for there is nothing more admirable than self-sacrifice to public duty. That was the principle which regulated the life of Somerset ; it was the principle which he carried with him to the grave. *Speech in House of Commons (The Queen's Message, the late Lord Raglan), July 3, 1855.*

RAILWAY MANIA.

Political connection, political consistency, political principle, all vanished before the fascination of premiums.— *Endymion.*

RANK.

You think, as property has its duties as well as its rights, rank has its bores as well as its pleasures.—('Lady Marney') *Sybil.*

REACTION.

Reaction is the law of life, and it is the characteristic of the House of Commons.—*Speech in House of Commons (Address on Queen's Speech), February* 6, 1867.

Reaction is the law of life.—('Zenobia') *Endymion.*

Reaction is the ebb and flow of opinion incident to fallible beings ; the consequence of hope deferred, of false representations, of expectations baulked. Reaction is the consequence of a nation waking from its illusions.—*Speech in House of Commons (Sugar Duties), February* 3, 1848.

RECESS.

It would seem that this paragraph (in the Queen's speech) must have been drawn up by some individual who has digested with the greatest interest all that vagrant rhetoric that distinguishes the Recess. After Parliament is prorogued we have several months not idle in respect of rhetoric. It is about that time that we have schemes brought forward by which the country is promised that every man shall be a landed proprietor without paying for it ; schemes to settle the great question of local taxation, which generally end in the novelty of the expense being defrayed in Downing Street ; schemes for relieving the House of Lords of its judicial functions, retaining however their political ones, but upon these conditions—that they do not exercise them ; schemes for the Government taking all the railways, and, I suppose, if it be necessary, all the collieries. I look upon the Recess as a safety-valve. In a free country with the right of petition and the right of holding public meetings, with even a halfpenny press, and other blessings of that kind, when every town has a debating club, and every village has its agitator, I cannot conceive how it is possible to prevent a certain degree of nonsense from being uttered during the Recess.   But I have always considered these projects very much as I would the autumnal foliage, and believed that as the year advanced, and Parliament met, and we came to real business; and entered into a more vigorous and healthy atmosphere, we should give our attention to subjects which had at least the recommendation of the necessities of the country, and which might be brought about by sober and prudent legislation. But when I read this paragraph in which so many and such varied subjects are specifically mentioned, and so many more indirectly alluded to, I confess that I do not look forward to the result of the present session with the sanguine spirit that I did twenty-four hours ago.   I think there is a prospect of a terrible July.—*Speech in House of Commons (Address in answer to Queen's Speech), February 6, 1872.*

RECIPROCITY.

The principle of reciprocity appears to rest on scientific grounds, and it is probable that experience may teach us that it has recklessly been disregarded by our legislators. *Life of Lord George Bentinck.*

REFORM.

D——n the Reform Bill ! If the Duke had not quarrelled with Lord Grey on a coal committee, we should never have had the Reform Bill.—('Lord Monmouth') *Coningsby.*

The Reform Act has not placed the administration of our affairs in abler hands than conducted them previously to the passing of the measure, for the most efficient members of the present cabinet, with some few exceptions, and those attended by peculiar circumstances, were ministers before the Reform Act was contemplated. Nor has that memorable statute created a Parliament of a higher reputation for public qualities, such as politic ability, and popular eloquence, and national consideration, than was furnished by the old scheme. On the contrary, one House of Parliament has been irremediably degraded into the decaying position of a mere court of registry, possessing great privileges, on condition that it never exercises them ; while the other chamber, that, at the first blush, and to the superficial, exhibits symptoms of almost unnatural vitality, engrossing in its orbit all the business of the country, assumes on a more studious inspection somewhat of the character of a select vestry, fulfilling municipal rather than imperial offices, and beleaguered by critical and clamorous millions, who cannot comprehend why a privileged and exclusive senate is requisite to perform functions which immediately concern all, which most personally comprehend, and which many in their civic spheres believe they could accomplish in a manner not less satisfactory, though certainly less ostentatious.

But if it have not furnished us with abler administrators or a more illustrious senate, the Reform Act may have exercised on the country at large a beneficial influence. Has it ? Has it elevated the tone of the public mind ? Has it cultured the popular sensibilities to 'noble and ennobling ends ? Has it proposed to the people of England a higher test of national respect and confidence than the debasing qualification universally prevalent in this country since the fatal introduction of the system of Dutch finance ? Who will pretend it ? If a spirit of rapacious covetousness, desecrating all the humanities of life, has been the besetting sin of England for the last century and a half, since the passing of the Reform Act the altar of Mammon has blazed with triple worship. To acquire, to accumulate, to plunder each other by virtue of philosophic phrases, to propose a Utopia to consist only of wealth and toil, this has been the breathless business of enfranchised England for the last twelve years, until we are startled from our voracious strife by the wail of intolerable serfage.

Are we then to conclude, that the only effect of the

Reform Act has been to create in this country another of those class interests which we now so loudly accuse as the obstacles to general amelioration? Not exactly that. The indirect influence of the Reform Act has been not inconsiderable, and may eventually lead to vast consequences. It set men a-thinking; it enlarged the horizon of political experience; it led the public mind to ponder somewhat on the circumstances of our national history; to pry into the beginnings of some social anomalies, which, they found, were not so ancient as they had been led to believe, and which had their origin in causes very different from what they had been educated to credit; and insensibly it created and prepared a popular intelligence to which one can appeal, no longer hopelessly, in an attempt to dispel the mysteries with which for nearly three centuries it has been the labour of party writers to involve a national history, and without the dispersion of which no political position can be understood and no social evil remedied.—*Sybil.*

With property and pluck, Parliamentary Reform is not such a very bad thing.—('Lord Monmouth') *Coningsby.*

The (Reform) Bill is founded on three great principles. The first principle is that the constituent body of the country shall be increased by the introduction to it of a large number of persons, and a vast variety of population, who shall in future possess the suffrage. The second principle on which the Bill is founded is that those large communities whose wealth and population and distinctive characters have been developed since the Act of 1832, shall be summoned to direct representation in the House. The third principle is that this Bill maintains generally the present borough system of representation in the country on the ground that no efficient substitute has yet been offered for it; and on the ground also that it is the only means by which you can obtain an adequate representation of the various interests and classes of the country; and that all other changes would only lead to the predominance of a numerical majority of the people.—*Speech in House of Commons* (*Representation of the People Bill*), *March* 31, 1859.

RELIGION.

Religion should be the rule of life, not a casual incident of it.—('Cardinal Grandison') *Lothair.*

What you call forms and ceremonies represent the devotional instincts of our nature.—('Mr. St. Lys') *Sybil.*

'What is your religion?' asked Lothair.

'The true religion, I think. I worship in a church where I believe God dwells, and dwells for my guidance and my good : my conscience.'—('Theodora') *Lothair.*

All things that are good and beautiful make us more religious. They tend to the development of the religious principle in us, which is our divine nature.—('Cardinal Grandison') *Lothair.*

I would wish Church men, and especially the clergy, always to remember that in our Father's home there are many mansions, and I believe that comprehensive spirit is perfectly consistent with the maintenance of formularies and the belief in dogmas, without which, I hold, no practical religion can exist.—*Speech at Manchester, April* 2, 1872.

Religion is civilisation, the highest ; it is a reclamation of man from savageness by the Almighty.—('Cardinal Grandison') *Lothair.*

There is a Pharos in the world, and its light will never be extinguished, however black the clouds and wild the waves. Man is on his trial now, not the Church, but in the Church his highest energies may be developed and his noblest qualities moved.—('Monsignore Catesby') *Lothair.*

The soul requires a sanctuary.—('Cardinal Grandison') *Lothair.*

I was a Parliamentary Christian, till despondency and study, and ceaseless thought and prayer, and the divine will brought me to light and rest.—('Cardinal Grandison') *Lothair.*

The spiritual nature of man is stronger than codes or constitutions. No government can endure which does not recognise that for its foundation, and no legislation last which does not flow from this fountain. As time is divided into day and night, so religion rests upon the providence of God and the responsibility of man. One is manifest, the other mysterious ; but both are divine.—*Speech at Glasgow University, November* 19, 1872.

A fine writer of antiquity, perhaps the finest, has recorded in a passage his belief in Divine providence, and in the necessity of universal toleration :

> 'Εγὼ μὲν κλαὼν ταῦτα καὶ τὰ πάντ' ἀεὶ
> Φάσκοιμ' ἂν ἀνθρώποισι μηχανᾶν θεούς·
> "Οτῳ δὲ μὴ τάδ' ἐστὶν ἐν γνώμῃ φίλα,
> Κεῖνός τ' ἐκεῖνα στεργέτω, κἀγὼ τάδε.

These lines were written more than two thousand years ago, by the most Attic of Athenian poets. In the perplexities of life I have sometimes found them a solace and a satisfaction; and I now deliver them to you, to guide your consciences and to guard your lives.—*Speech at Glasgow University, November* 19, 1872.

REMORSE.

There is anguish in the recollection that we have not adequately appreciated the affection of those whom we have loved and lost.—*Endymion.*

REPUBLICAN.

Notwithstanding the apathy which had been engendered by premature experience, St. Aldegonde held extreme opinions, especially on political affairs, being a republican of the reddest dye. He was opposed to all privilege, indeed to all orders of men, except Dukes, who were a necessity. He was also strongly in favour of the equal division of all property, except land. Liberty depended on land, and the greater the landowners, the greater the liberty of a country *Lothair.*

RESOLUTION.

The honourable and gallant gentleman (Captain Vivian) seems to me not to have understood the position in which by a fortunate accident he found himself (in carrying a re-solution opposed by the Government). It is not the first time I have seen men who really deserve success and have laboured to attain it, embarrassed by unexpected good fortune. It is said that a bird never makes so much noise as when she lays her first egg ; and I can easily conceive that in carrying his first resolution the honourable and gallant gentleman was overpowered with excitement. But, after all, laying the first egg is only a very natural operation. So carrying a resolution is really in the due course of Parliamentary nature.—*Speech in House of Commons (Military Organisation), June* 28, 1858.

RETIREMENT.

He (Ferrars senior) retired with the solace of a sinecure, a pension, and a privy councillorship.—*Endymion.*

RETRENCHMENT.

If you make your establishments efficient, you will find, almost as a natural consequence, that you will save money ; and therefore I take it to be efficiency, and not retrench-ment, which is the parent of economy. There is nothing easier in opposition than to call for retrenchment ; there is nothing more difficult in administration than to comply with the demand.—*Speech in House of Commons (Budget), December* 3, 1852.

RETROGRESSION.

I have observed in our history that it is the characteristic of this country that it always retraces its steps. I believe the prosperity of England may be attributed to this cause, not that it has committed less blunders than other countries;

but that the people are a people more sensible of their errors.—*Speech in House of Commons (Sugar Duties), July 25,* 1846.

REVOLUTION.

Since the settlement of the Constitution, now nearly two centuries ago, England has never experienced a revolution, though there is no country in which there has been so continuous and such considerable change. How is this? Because the wisdom of our forefathers placed the prize of supreme power without the sphere of human passions.—*Speech in Free Trade Hall, Manchester, April* 3, 1872.

Great revolutions, whatever may be their causes, are not lightly commenced, and are not concluded with precipitation.—*Speech in House of Commons (Address on Speech), February* 5, 1863.

RIDICULE.

A fear of becoming ridiculous is the best guide in life, and will save a man from all sorts of scrapes.—('Lord Monmouth') *Coningsby.*

RIGBY (MR.).

He who uttered these words was a man of middle size and age, originally in all probability of a spare habit, but now a little inclined to corpulency. Baldness, perhaps, contributed to the spiritual expression of a brow which was, however, essentially intellectual, and gave some character of openness to a countenance which, though not ill-favoured, was unhappily stamped by a sinister cast that was not to be mistaken. His manner was easy, but rather audacious than well-bred. Indeed, while a visage which might otherwise be described as handsome was spoilt by a dishonest glance, so a demeanour that was by no means deficient in self-possession and facility, was tainted by an innate vulgarity, which in the long run, though seldom, yet surely developed itself.—*Coningsby.*

RITUALISM.

What I do object to is the mass in masquerade.—*Speech in House of Commons* (*Public Worship Regulation Bill*), *May* 15, 1874.

I mean by ritualism the practice by a certain portion of the clergy of the Church of England of ceremonies which they themselves confess are symbolical of doctrine which they are pledged by every solemn compact which can bind men to their sovereign and their country to denounce and repudiate.—*Speech in House of Commons.* (*Public Worship Regulation Bill*), *August* 5, 1874.

RIVERS.

Thou rapid Aar! thy waves are swollen by the snows of a thousand hills; but for whom are thy leaping waters fed? Is it for the Rhine?

Calmly, O placid Neckar! does thy blue stream glide through thy vine-clad vales; but calmer seems thy course when it touches the rushing Rhine!

How fragrant are the banks which are cooled by thy dark-green waters, thou tranquil Maine! but is not the perfume sweeter of the gardens of the Rhine?

Thou impetuous Nah! I lingered by thine islands of nightingales, and I asked thy rushing waters why they disturbed the music of thy groves? They told me they were hastening to the Rhine!

Red Moselle! fierce is the swell of thy spreading course; but why do thy broad waters blush when they meet the Rhine?

Thou delicate Meuse! how clear is the current of thy limpid wave; as the wife yields to the husband do thy pure waters yield to the Rhine!

And thou, triumphant and imperial River, flushed with the tribute of these vassal streams! thou art thyself a tributary, and hastenest even in the pride of conquest to

confess thine own vassalage !   But no superior stream
exults in the homage of thy servile waters : the Ocean, the
eternal Ocean, alone comes forward to receive thy kiss !
not as a conqueror, but as a parent, he welcomes with
proud joy his gifted child, the offspring of his honour ; thy
duty, his delight ; thy tribute, thine own glory !

Once more upon thy banks, most beauteous Rhine ! In
the spring-time of my youth I gazed on thee, and deemed
thee matchless.   Thy vine-enamoured mountains, thy
spreading waters, thy traditionary crags, thy shining cities,
the sparkling villages of thy winding shores, thy antique
convents, thy grey and silent castles, the purple glories of
thy radiant grape, the vivid tints of thy teeming flowers,
the fragrance of thy sky, the melody of thy birds, whose
carols tell the pleasures of their sunny woods ; are they
less lovely now, less beautiful, less sweet ?—*Vivian Grey.*

RODNEY (MRS.).

Her figure was slight and undulating, and she was
always exquisitely dressed.   A brilliant complexion set off
to advantage her delicate features, which, though serene,
were not devoid of a certain expression of archness.   Her
white hands were delicate, her light eyes inclined to merriment, and her nose quite a gem though a little turned up.

Sylvia was really peerless.   She was by birth half a
Frenchwoman, and she compensated for her deficiency in
the other moiety by a series of exquisite costumes, in which
she mingled with the spell-born fashion of France her own
singular genius in dress.   She spoke not much, but looked
prettier than ever ; a little haughty, and now and then
faintly smiling.   What was most remarkable about her was
her convenient and complete want of memory.   Sylvia had
no past.   She could not have found her way to Warwick
Street to save her life   She conversed with Endymion with
ease and not without gratification ; but from all she said you
might have supposed that they had been born in the same

sphere and always lived in the same sphere, that sphere being one peopled by duchesses and countesses and gentlemen of fashion and ministers of state.

RODNEY (MR.).

Mr. Rodney was a remarkably good-looking person, by nature really a little resembling his principal, and completing the resemblance by consummate art. If there were anything confidential to be accomplished in their domestic life, everything might be trusted to his discretion and entire devotion. Mr. Rodney was the most official personage in the ministerial circle. He considered human nature only with reference to office. No one was so intimately acquainted with all the details of the lesser patronage as himself, and his hours of study were passed in the pages of the 'Peerage' and in penetrating the mysteries of the 'Royal Calendar.'—*Endymion.*

ROEHAMPTON (LORD).

He was somewhat advanced in middle life, tall and of a stately presence, with a voice more musical even than the tones, which had recently enchanted everyone. His countenance was impressive, a truly Olympian brow, but the lower part of the face indicated not feebleness but flexibility, and his mouth was somewhat sensuous ; natural, and singularly unaffected, and seemed to sympathise entirely with those whom he addressed.

The Earl of Roehampton was the strongest member of the government, except, of course, the premier himself. He was the man from whose combined force and flexibility of character the country had confidence that in all their councils there would be no lack of courage, yet tempered with discretion. Lord Roehampton, though an Englishman, was an Irish peer, and was resolved to remain so, for he fully appreciated the position, which united social distinction and the power of a seat in the House of Commons. He was a very ambitious, and, as it was thought, worldly man, deemed even by many to be unscrupulous, and yet he was romantic. A great favourite in society and especially with the softer sex, somewhat late in life he had married suddenly a beautiful woman, who was without fortune, and not a member of the enchanted circle in which he flourished. He had been a widower for two years, and in addition to his many recommendations he had now the inestimable reputation, which no one had ever contemplated for him, of having been a good husband.—*Endymion.*

ROME.

I speak of that country which first impressed upon the world a general and enduring form of masculine virtue ; the land of liberty and law, and eloquence and military genius, now garrisoned by monks and governed by a doting priest.— (' Theodora ') *Lothair.*

The Roman Empire was the empire of great cities. Man was then essentially municipal.—(' Coningsby ') *Tancred.*

I leant against a column of the Temple of Castor. On one side was the Palace of the Cæsars ; on the other, the colossal amphitheatre of Vespasian. Arches of triumph, the pillars of Pagan temples, and the domes of Christian churches rose around me. In the distance was the wide Campagna, the Claudian Aqueduct, and the Alban Mount.

Solitude and silence reigned on that sacred road once echoing with the shouts and chariots of three hundred triumphs ; solitude and silence, meet companions of imperial desolation ! Where are the spoils of Egypt and of Carthage ? Where the golden tribute of Iberia ? Where the long Gallic trophies ? Where are the rich armour and massy cups of Macedon ? Where are the pictures and statues of Corinth ? Where the libraries of Athens ? Where is the broken bow of Parthia ? Where the elephants of Pontus, and the gorgeous diadems of the Asian Kings ?

And where is Rome ? All nations rose and flourished

only to swell her splendour, and now I stand amid her ruins.

In such a scene what are our private griefs and petty sorrows ? And what is man ? I felt my nothingness. Life seemed flat, and dull, and trifling. I could not conceive that I could again become interested in its base pursuits. I believed that I could no longer be influenced by joy or by sorrow. Indifference alone remained.—*Contarini Fleming.*

ROUTINE.

It seems to me that the world is withering under routine. 'Tis the inevitable lot of humanty ; but in old days it was a routine of great thoughts, and now it is a routine of little ones.—('Sidonia') *Coningsby.*

ROYALTY.

England is a domestic country ; there the home is revered, the hearth sacred. The nation is represented by a family—the Royal Family—and if that family is educated into a sense of responsibility and a sentiment of public duty, it is difficult to exaggerate the salutary influence it may exercise over a nation.—*Speech at Manchester, April* 3, 1872.

Nothing, in my opinion, has been more remarkable or more interesting in the late unanimous feeling with regard to the Royal marriage on the part of this country than the strong domestic principle which has pervaded the whole of this great and powerful nation. That general homage was offered, I am sure, on this occasion principally because there has been a conviction on the part of the country that this alliance has been brought about not so much by political considerations as from the impulses of nature and affection. That domestic feeling has been strongly exhibited from the wishes that have been felt by the nation to express their attachment and respect for the royal parents of our Princess, because they felt that under the illustrious roof under which she has dwelt, there is as much respect felt for the happiness of the hearth as for the splendour of the throne.—*Speech in House of Commons (Princess Royal's Marriage), February* 5, 1858.

RUMOUR.

A common rumour—and therefore probably a common falsehood.—('Waldershare') *Endymion.*

RUSSELL (LORD JOHN).

Lord John Russell has that degree of imagination, which, though evinced rather in sentiment than expression, still enables him to generalise from the details of his reading and experience ; and to take those comprehensive views, which, however easily depreciated by ordinary men in an age of routine, are indispensable to a statesman in the conjunctures in which we live. He understands, therefore, his position ; and he has the moral intrepidity which prompts him ever to dare that which his intellect assures him is politic. He is consequently, at the same time, sagacious and bold in council. As an administrator he is prompt and indefatigable. He is not a natural orator, and labours under physical deficiencies which even a Demosthenic impulse could scarcely overcome. But he is experienced in debate, quick in reply, fertile in resource, takes large views, and frequently compensates for a dry and hesitating manner by the expression of those noble truths that flash across the fancy, and rise spontaneously to the lip, of men of poetic temperament when addressing popular assemblies. If we add to this a private life of dignified repute, the accidents of his birth and rank, which never can be severed from the man, the scion of a great historic family, and born, as it were, to the hereditary service of the State, it is difficult to ascertain at what period, or under what circumstances, the Whig party have ever possessed, or could obtain, a more efficient leader.— *Coningsby.*

Lord John Russell was a man of letters, and it is a common opinion that a man cannot be successful both in meditation and action. But in life it is best to judge men individually, and not to decide upon them by general rules. *Life of Lord George Bentinck.*

Lord John Russell was born with a feeble intellect and a strong ambition. He was busied with the battle of valets. A feeble Cataline, he had a propensity to degrade everything to his own mean level, and to measure everything by his own malignant standard.—*Runnymede Letters,* 1836.

All great catastrophes which have occurred in our external affairs of late years had arisen from slight circumstances. The noble Lord could not find time to prevent the siege of a town, and so he invaded a country. So it was in all his policy. There was an alternation from fatal inertness to still more terrible energy. With him it was ever one step from collapse to convulsion. We commence by neglecting our duties, we terminate by violating their rights.—*Speech in House of Commons (War in Afghanistan), June* 23, 1842.

RUSSIA.

It was the geographical position of the Russian Empire which rendered it necessary. Look at the map. Those two spots would be seen, the Dardanelles and the Sound, which if possessed by the same power must give that power universal empire.—*Speech in House of Commons (War with Afghanistan), June* 23, 1842.

RUSSIAN.

A Russian does not care much for rosaries unless they are made of diamonds.—('Pasqualigo') *Tancred.*

SACERDOTAL.

The idea of a sacerdotal despotism, in the times in which we live, is not that the Inquisition will appear, in this country, or that Archbishop Laud, in the form of the mild and benignant Metropolitan of Lambeth, may summon us again to a High Commission Court. But my idea of sacerdotal despotism is this : that a minister of the Church of England, who is appointed to expound doctrine, should deem that he has a right to invent doctrine. That, sir, is the sacerdotal despotism that I fear.—*Speech in House of Commons (Uniformity Act), June* 9, 1863.

SANITAS.

A very great scholar observes that in his opinion the declaration of the wisest of mankind, ' Vanity of vanities, all is vanity,' was not a misprint, but a mistake of the copyist, and that he believed the words were not 'Vanitas vanitatum, omnia vanitas,' but 'Sanitas sanitatum, omnia sanitas.' Now I quite agree that it must have been a misquotation of the words of the wise king of Israel, and, if so, that they would have constituted one of his best claims to be considered the wisest of mankind.—*Speech at Aylesbury, Royal and Central Bucks Agricultural Association, September* 21, 1864.

SATIETY.

I have always thought that the feeling of satiety, almost inseparable from large possessions, is a surer cause of misery than ungratified desires.—('Theodora') *Lothair.*

SCEPTICISM.

With the characteristic caprice and impetuosity of youth, Cadurcis rapidly and ardently imbibed all these doctrines, captivated alike by their boldness and their novelty. Hitherto the child of prejudice, he flattered himself that he was now the creature of reason, and, determined to take nothing for granted, he soon learned to question everything that was received.—*Venetia.*

Doubt as you like, credulity will come, and in good season.—*Count Alarcos.*

SCHOOL.

The hour came, and I was placed in the heart of a little and busy world. For the first time in my life I was surrounded by struggling and excited beings. Joy, hope, sorrow, ambition, craft, courage, wit, dulness, cowardice, beneficence, awkwardness, grace, avarice, generosity, wealth, poverty, beauty, hideousness, tyranny, suffering, hypocrisy, truth, love, hatred, energy, inertness ; they were all there, and all sounded, and moved, and acted, about me. Light laughs, and bitter cries, and deep imprecations, and the deeds of the friendly, the prodigal, and the tyrant, and the exploits of the brave, the graceful, and the gay, and the flying words of native wit, and the pompous sentences of acquired knowledge ; how new, how exciting, how wonderful !

Did I tremble ? Did I sink into my innermost self? Did I fly ? Never. As I gazed upon them, a new principle rose up in my breast, and I perceived only beings whom I was determined to control. They came up to me with a curious glance of half-suppressed glee, breathless and mocking. They asked me questions of gay nonsense with a serious voice and solemn look. I answered in their kind. On a sudden I seemed endowed with new powers, and blessed with the gift of tongues. I spoke to them with a levity which was quite strange to me, a most unnatural ease. I even, in my turn, presented to them questions, to which they found it difficult to respond. Some ran away to communicate their impression to their comrades, some stayed behind, but these became more serious and more natural. When they found that I was endowed with a pregnant and decided character, their eyes silently pronounced me a good fellow ; they vied with each other in kindness, and the most important led me away to initiate me in their mysteries.

Weeks flew away, and I was intoxicated with my new life and my new reputation. I was in a state of ceaseless excitement. It seemed that my tongue never paused : yet each word brought forth a new laugh, each sentence of gay nonsense fresh plaudits. All was rattle, frolic, and wild mirth. My companions caught my unusual manner, they adopted my new phrases, they repeated my extraordinary apophthegms. Everything was viewed and done according to the new tone which I had introduced. It was decided that I was the wittiest, the most original, the most diverting of their society. A coterie of the congenial insensibly formed around me, and my example gradually ruled the choice spirits of our world. I even mingled in their games although I disliked the exertion, and in those in which the emulation was very strong I even excelled. My ambition conquered my nature. It seemed that I was the soul of the school. Wherever I went my name sounded, whatever was done my opinion was quoted. I was caressed, adored, idolised. In a word, I was popular.—*Contarini Fleming.*

There is no place in the world where greater homage is paid to talent than an English school.—*Vivian Grey.*

A Select School.—The Rev. Dr. Coronel was so extremely exclusive in his system, that it was reported that he had once refused the son of an Irish Peer.—*The Young Duke.*

SCHOOLBOY.

Character.—We are too apt to believe that the character of a boy is easily read. 'Tis a mystery the most profound. Mark what blunders parents constantly make as to the nature of their own offspring, bred, too, under their eyes, and displaying every hour their characteristics. How often in the nursery does the genius count as a dunce because he is pensive ; while a rattling urchin is invested with almost supernatural qualities because his animal spirits make him impudent and flippant ! The schoolboy, above all others, is not the simple being the world imagines. In that young bosom are often stirring passions as strong as our own, desires not less violent, a volition not less supreme. In that young bosom what burning love, what intense ambition, what avarice, what lust of power ; envy that fiends might emulate, hate that man might fear !—*Coningsby.*

SCIENCE.

I hold that the highest function of science is the interpretation of nature, and the interpretation of the highest nature is the highest science. But I say that when I compare the most fashionable and modern school of modern science with the older teachings with which we are familiar, I am not prepared to say that the lecture-room is more scientific than the church. What is the case now placed before society with a glib assurance which is to me most astonishing? The question is this—is a man an ape or an angel? *I am on the side of the angels.* I repudiate with indignation and abhorrence these new-fangled theories. *Oxford Diocesan Society for Increasing Small Benefices.*

What art was to the ancient world, science is to the modern.—*Coningsby.*

The pursuit of science leads only to the insoluble.— ('Cardinal Grandison') *Lothair.*

Scientific, like spiritual truth, has ever from the beginning been descending from heaven to man.—*Preface to Lothair.*

Modern Scientific Book ('Revelation of Chaos').—It is treated scientifically ; everything is explained by geology and astronomy, and in that way. It shows you exactly how a star is formed ; nothing can be so pretty ! A cluster of vapour, the cream of the milky way, a sort of celestial cheese, churned into light.

Read the book. It is impossible to contradict anything in it. You understand, it is all science ; it is not like those books in which one says one thing and another the contrary, and both may be wrong. Everything is proved : by geology, you know. You see exactly how everything is made ; how many worlds there have been ; how long they

lasted ; what went before, what comes next. We are a
link in the chain, as inferior animals were that preceded us :
we in turn shall be inferior ; all that will remain of us will
be some relics in a new red sandstone. This is development. We had fins ; we may have wings.—('Lady Constance') *Tancred*.

Modern science has vindicated the natural equality of
man.—('Delegate from National Convention') *Sybil*.

SCOTCH.

It has been my lot to have found myself in many
distant lands. I have never been in one without finding a
Scotchman, and I never found a Scotchman who was not at
the head of the poll—he was prosperous ; he was thriving ;
often the confidential adviser of persons of the highest position, even of rulers of States ; and although I myself am
inclined to attribute much to organisation and race, I am
bound to say I never met a Scotchman, even if he were the
confidential adviser of a Pasha, who did not tell me he owed
his rise to his parish school.—*Speech at Glasgow, November*
19, 1873.

SCROPE (SIR FRAUNCEYS).

One of the most interesting members of the House of
Commons was Sir Fraunceys Scrope. He was the father of
the House of Commons, though it was difficult to believe
that from his appearance. He was tall, and had kept his
distinguished figure ; a handsome face with a musical voice
and a countenance now benignant, though very bright and
once haughty. He still retained the same fashion of
costume in which he had ridden up to Westminster more
than half a century ago, from his seat in Derbyshire, to
support his dear friend Charles Fox ; real top-boots, and a
blue coat and buff waistcoat. He was a great friend of
Lord Roehampton, had a large estate in the same county,
and had refused an earldom.—*Endymion*.

SEA.

It was a grand idea of our kings making themselves sovereigns of the sea. The greater part of this planet is water ; so we at once became a first-rate power.—(' Waldershare ') *Endymion.*

Well, they may talk of a sea-life, but for my part, I never saw the use of the sea. Many a sad heart it has caused, and many a sick stomach has it occasioned ! The boldest sailor climbs on board with a heavy soul, and leaps on land with a light spirit. O ! thou indifferent ape of Earth ! thy houses are of wood and thy horses of canvas ; thy roads have no landmarks and thy highways no inns ; thy hills are green without grass and wet without showers ! and as for food, what art thou, O, bully Ocean ! but the stable of horse-fishes, the stall of cow-fishes, the sty of hog-fishes, and the kennel of dog-fishes ! Commend me to a fresh-water dish for meagre days ! Sea-weeds stewed with chalk may be savoury stuff for a merman ; but, for my part, give me red cabbage and cream : and as for drink, a man may live in the midst of thee his whole life and die for thirst at the end of it ! Besides, thou blasphemous salt lake, where is thy religion ? Where are thy churches, thou heretic ?—(' Essper ') *Vivian Grey.*

SEASON.

Town was beginning to blaze. Broughams whirled and bright barouches glanced, troops of social cavalry cantered and caracoled in morning rides, and the bells of prancing ponies, lashed by delicate hands, jingled in the laughing air. There were stoppages in Bond Street, which seems to cap the climax of civilisation, after crowded clubs and swarming parks.—*Lothair.*

The season then was brilliant and sustained, but it was not flurried. People did not go to various parties on the same night. They remained where they were, and, not being in a hurry, were more agreeable than they are at the present day. Conversation was more cultivated, manners, though unconstrained, were more stately ; and the world, being limited, knew itself much better.—*Endymion.*

If one could contrive our lives, so as to go into the country for the first note of the nightingale, and return to town for the first note of the muffin-bell, existence, it is humbly presumed, might be more enjoyable.—*Lothair.*

The end of the season is a pang to society.—*Endymion.*

One by one the great houses shut ; shoal by shoal the little people sail away. The park is not yet empty, and perhaps is even more fascinating ; like a beauty in a consumption, who each day gets thinner and more fair. —*The Young Duke.*

The social critics cease to be observant towards the end of July. All the world then are thinking of themselves, and have no time to speculate on the fate and fortunes of their neighbours. The campaign is too near its close ; the balance of the season must soon be struck, the great book of society made. In a few weeks, even in a few days, what long and subtle plans shattered or triumphant ! what prizes gained or missed ! what baffled hopes and what broken hearts ! The baffled hopes must go to Cowes, and the broken hearts to Baden.—*Lothair.*

SEDITION.

Unquestionably there was more or less a leaven of sedition mixing itself with all popular commotions.—*Speech in House of Commons (National Petition), July* 12, 1839.

SELF-COMPLACENCY.

He (the Duke) smiled with the calm, amiable complacency of a man who feels the world is quite right.— *The Young Duke.*

SELF-RESPECT.

Self-respect is a superstition of past centuries, an affair of the Crusaders.—('Fakredeen') *Tancred*.

All must respect those who respect themselves.— *Coningsby*.

SENSIBLE.

I think the best thing is always to put a good face upon a disagreeable state of affairs, and take that sensible view which may be taken even of the most distressing and adverse occurrences, if you have a command over your temper and your head.—*Speech in House of Commons* (*National Expenditure*), *June* 5, 1862.

SENTIMENTAL.

If to feel is to be sentimental, I cannot help it.— *Endymion*.

SERGIUS (BARON).

A man of middle age. His countenance was singularly intelligent, tempered with an expression mild and winning. He had attended the Congress of Vienna to represent a fallen party, a difficult and ungracious task; but he had shown such high qualities in the fulfilment of his painful duties—so much knowledge, so much self-control, and so much wise and unaffected conciliation, that he had won universal respect, and especially with the English plenipotentiaries, so that when he visited England, which he did frequently, the houses of both parties were open to him, and he was as intimate with the Whigs as he was with the great Duke, by whom he was highly esteemed.—*Endymion*.

SERVICES.

The services in war time are fit only for desperadoes, but in peace are fit only for fools.—*Vivian Grey*.

SERVILITY.

How singular it is that those who love servility are always the victims of impertinence !—*The Young Duke.*

SEVILLE.

There is not a more beautiful and solemn temple in the world than the great Cathedral of Seville. When you enter from the glare of a Spanish sky, so deep is the staining of the glass, and so small and few the windows, that, for a moment, you feel in darkness. Gradually, the vast design of the Gothic artist unfolds itself to your vision ; gradually, rises up before you the profuse sumptuousness of the high altar, with its tall images, and velvet and gold hangings, its gigantic railings of brass and massy candlesticks of silver, all revealed by the dim and perpetual light of the sacred and costly lamps.

You steal with a subdued spirit over the marble pavement. All is still, save the hushed muttering of the gliding priests. Around you are groups of kneeling worshippers, some prostrate on the ground, some gazing upwards, with their arms crossed, in mute devotion, some beating their breasts, and counting their consoling beads. Lo ! the tinkling of a bell. The mighty organ bursts forth. Involuntarily you fall upon your knees, and listen to the rising chanting of the solemn choir. A procession moves from an adjoining chapel. A band of crimson acolytes advance waving censers, and the melody of their distant voices responds to the deep-toned invocations of the nearer canons. There are a vast number of chapels in this cathedral on each side of the principal nave. Most of them are adorned with masterpieces of the Spanish school. Let us approach one. The light is good, and let us gaze through this iron railing upon the picture it encloses.

I see a saint falling upon his knees, and extending his enraptured arm to receive an infant God. What mingled love, enthusiasm, devotion, reverence, blend in the countenance of the holy man ! But, oh ! that glowing group of seraphim, sailing and smiling in the sunny splendour of that radiant sky, who has before gazed upon such grace, such ineffable and charming beauty ! And in the background is an altar, whereon is a vase holding some lilies, that seem as if they were just gathered. There is but one artist who could have designed this picture ; there is but one man who could have thus combined ideal grace with natural simplicity; there is but one man who could have painted that diaphanous heaven, and those fresh lilies. Inimitable Murillo !— *Contarini Fleming*.

SHOWER.

Nature, like man, sometimes weeps for gladness.— *Coningsby*.

SIDNEY (LORD HENRY).

Sidonia welcomed Tancred, and introduced him to a guest who had preceded them, Lord Henry Sidney.

It was a name that touched Tancred, as it has all the youth of England, significant of a career that would rescue public life from that strange union of lax principles and contracted sympathies which now form the special and degrading features of British politics. It was borne by one whose boyhood we have painted amid the fields and schools of Eton, and the springtime of whose earliest youth we traced by the sedgy waters of the Cam. We left him on the threshold of public life ; and, in four years, Lord Henry had created that reputation which now made him a source of hope and solace to millions of his countrymen. But they were four years of labour which outweighed the usual exertions of public men in double that space. His regular attendance in the House of Commons alone had given him as much Parliamentary experience as fell to the lot of many of those who had been first returned in 1837, and had been, therefore, twice as long in the House. He was not only a vigilant member of public and private committees, but had succeeded in appointing and conducting several on topics which he esteemed of high importance. Add to this, that he took an habitual part in debate, and was a frequent and effective public writer ; and we are furnished with an additional testimony, if that indeed were wanting, that there is no incentive to exertion like the passion for a noble renown. Nor should it be forgotten that, in all he accomplished, he had but one final purpose, and that the highest. The debate, the committee, the article in the Journal or the Review, the public meeting, the private research, these were all means to advance that which he had proposed as the object of his public life, namely, to elevate the condition of the people.

Although there was no public man whose powers had more rapidly ripened, still it was interesting to observe that their maturity had been faithful to the healthy sympathies of his earlier years. The boy, whom we have traced intent upon the revival of the pastimes of the people, had expanded into the statesman, who, in a profound and comprehensive investigation of the elements of public wealth, had shown that a jaded population is not a source of national prosperity. What had been a picturesque emotion had now become a statistical argument. The material system that proposes the supply of constant toil to a people as the perfection of polity, had received a staggering blow from the exertions of a young patrician, who announced his belief that labour had its rights as well as its duties. What was excellent about Lord Henry was, that he was not a mere philanthropist, satisfied to rouse public attention to a great social evil, or instantly to suggest for it some crude remedy.

A scholar and a man of the world, learned in history and not inexperienced in human nature, he was sensible that we must look to the constituent principles of society for the causes and the cures of great national disorders.

He therefore went deeply into the question, nor shrank
from investigating how far those disorders were produced
by the operation or the desuetude of ancient institutions,
and how far it might be necessary to call new influences
into political existence for their remedy.   Richly informed,
still studious, fond of labour and indefatigable, of a gentle
disposition though of an ardent mind, calm yet energetic,
very open to conviction, but possessing an inflexibility
amounting even to obstinacy when his course was once
taken, a ready and improving speaker, an apt and attractive writer, affable and sincere, and with the undesigning
faculty of making friends, Lord Henry seemed to possess
all the qualities of a popular leader, if we add to them the
golden ones, high lineage, an engaging appearance, youth,
and a temperament in which the reason had not been
developed to the prejudice of the heart.—*Tancred.*

SIDONIA.

As he stood at the window of his little apartment,
watching the large drops that were the heralds of a coming
hurricane, and waiting for his repast, a flash of lightning
illumined the whole country, and a horseman at full speed,
followed by his groom, galloped up to the door. . . .

He was above the middle height and of a distinguished
air and figure ; pale, with an impressive brow, and dark eyes
of great intelligence. . . .

Sidonia had exhausted all the sources of human knowledge ; he was master of the learning of every nation, of all
tongues dead or living, of every literature, Western and
Oriental.   He had pursued the speculations of science to
their last term, and had himself illustrated them by observation and experiment.   He had lived in all orders of
society, had viewed every combination of Nature and of
Art, and had observed man under every phasis of civilisation.   He had even studied him in the wilderness.   The
influence of creeds and laws, manners, customs, traditions,

in all their diversities, had been subjected to his personal scrutiny.

He brought to the study of this vast aggregate of knowledge a penetrative intellect that, matured by long meditation, and assisted by that absolute freedom from prejudice, which was the compensatory possession of a man without a country, permitted Sidonia to fathom, as it were by intuition, the depth of questions apparently the most difficult and profound. He possessed the rare faculty of communicating with precision ideas the most abstruse, and in general a power of expression which arrests and satisfies attention.

With all this knowledge, which no one knew more to prize, with boundless wealth, and with an athletic frame, which sickness had never tried, and which had avoided excess, Sidonia nevertheless looked upon life with a glance rather of curiosity than content. His religion walled him out from the pursuits of a citizen ; his riches deprived him of the stimulating anxieties of a man. He perceived himself a lone being, alike without cares and without duties.

To a man in his position there might yet seem one unfailing source of felicity and joy ; independent of creed, independent of country, independent even of character. He might have discovered that perpetual spring of happiness in the sensibility of the heart. But this was a sealed fountain to Sidonia. In his organisation there was a peculiarity, perhaps a great deficiency. He was a man without affections. It would be harsh to say he had no heart, for he was susceptible of deep emotions, but not for individuals. He was capable of rebuilding a town that was burned down ; of restoring a colony that had been destroyed by some awful visitation of Nature ; of redeeming to liberty a horde of captives ; and of doing these great acts in secret ; for, void of all self-love, public approbation was worthless to him ; but the individual never touched him. Woman was to him a toy, man a machine. . .

The only human quality that interested Sidonia was Intellect. He cared not whence it came ; where it was to be found : creed, country, class, character, in this respect, were alike indifferent to him. The author, the artist, the man of science, never appealed to him in vain, Often he anticipated their wants and wishes. He encouraged their society ; was as frank in his conversation as he was generous in his contributions ; but the instant they ceased to be authors, artists, or philosophers, and their communications arose from anything but the intellectual quality which had originally interested him, the moment they were rash enough to approach intimacy and appealed to the sympathising man, instead of the congenial intelligence, he saw them no more. It was not, however, intellect merely in these unquestionable shapes that commanded his notice. There was not an adventurer in Europe with whom he was not familiar. No Minister of State had such communication with secret agents and political spies as Sidonia. He held relations with all the clever outcasts of the world. The catalogue of his acquaintance in the shape of Greeks, Armenians, Moors, secret Jews, Tartars, Gipsies, wandering Poles and Carbonari, would throw a curious light on those subterranean agencies of which the world in general knows so little, but which exercise so great an influence on public events. His extensive travels, his knowledge of languages, his daring and adventurous disposition, and his unlimited means, had given him opportunities of becoming acquainted with these characters, in general so difficult to trace, and of gaining their devotion. To these sources he owed that knowledge of strange and hidden things which often startled those who listened to him. Nor was it easy, scarcely possible, to deceive him, Information reached him from so many and such contrary quarters, that, with his discrimination and experience, he could almost instantly distinguish the truth. The secret history of the world was his pastime.

His great pleasure was to contrast the hidden motive, with the public pretext, of transactions. . . .

The somewhat hard and literal character of English life suited one who shrank from sensibility, and often took refuge in sarcasm. Its masculine vigour and active intelligence occupied and interested his mind. Sidonia, indeed, was exactly the character who would be welcomed in our circles. His immense wealth, his unrivalled social knowledge, his clear vigorous intellect, the severe simplicity of his manners, frank, but neither claiming nor brooking familiarity, and his devotion to field-sports, which was the safety-valve of his energy, were all circumstances and qualities which the English appreciate and admire ; and it may be fairly said of Sidonia that few men were more popular, and none less understood.—*Coningsby.*

SILENCE.

Silence often expresses more powerfully than speech the verdict and judgment of society.—*Speech in House of Commons (Administration of Viscount Palmerston), August 1, 1862.*

SLEEP.

Slavery's only service money, sweet sleep.—(' Mrs. Lorraine ') *Vivian Grey.*

No one but an adventurous traveller can know the luxury of sleep. There is not a greater fallacy in the world than the common creed that sweet sleep is labour's guerdon. Mere regular, corporeal labour may certainly procure us a good, sound, refreshing slumber, disturbed often by the consciousness of the monotonous duties of the morrow ; but how sleep the other great labourers of this laborious world? Where is the sweet sleep of the politician ? After hours of fatigue in his office and hours of exhaustion in the House, he gains his pillow ; and a brief, feverish night, disturbed by the triumph of a cheer and the horrors of a reply. Where is the sweet sleep of the poet ? We all know how harassing are the common dreams which are made up of incoherent images of our daily life, in which the actors are individuals that we know, and whose conduct generally appears to be regulated by principles which we can comprehend. How much more enervating and destroying must be the slumber of that man who dreams of an imaginary world ! waking, with a heated and excited spirit, to mourn over some impressive incident of the night, which is nevertheless forgotten, or to collect some inexplicable plot which has been revealed in sleep, and has fled from the memory as the eyelids have opened. Where is the sweet sleep of the artist ? of the lawyer ? Where, indeed, of any human being to whom to-morrow brings its necessary duties ? Sleep is the enemy of Care, and Care is the constant companion of regular labour, mental or bodily.—*Vivian Grey*.

SMILE.

There are few faces that can afford to smile : a smile is sometimes bewitching, in general vapid, often a contortion. *Tancred*.

SOCIAL.

The darkest hour precedes the dawn, and a period of unusual stillness often, perhaps usually, heralds the social convulsion.—*Endymion*.

To throw over a host is the most heinous of social crimes.—*Lothair*.

He was an excellent host, which no one can be who does not combine a good heart with high breeding.—*Lothair*.

To be king of your company is a poor ambition ; yet homage is homage, and smoke is smoke whether it comes out of the chimney of a palace or of a workhouse.—*The Young Duke*.

To be his uninvited guest proved at once that you had entered the highest circle of the social paradise.—*Endymion*.

Y

My idea of an agreeable person is a person who agrees with me.—('Hugo Bohun') *Lothair.*

There is not less treasure in the world because we use paper currency ; and there is not less passion than of old, though it is thought *bon ton* to be tranquil.—('Sidonia') *Coningsby.*

However vast may appear the world in which we move, we all of us live in a limited circle.—*Endymion.*

Society and politics have much to do with each other, but they are not identical.—('Lady Roehampton') *Endymion.*

Teach us that wealth is not elegance ; that profusion is not magnificence ; and that splendour is not beauty. Teach us that taste is a talisman which can do greater wonders than the millions of the loanmonger. Teach us that to vie is not to rival, and to imitate not to invent. Teach us that pretension is a bore. Teach us that wit is excessively good-natured, and, like champagne, not only sparkles, but is sweet. Teach us the vulgarity of malignity. Teach us that envy spoils our complexions, and that anxiety destroys our figure. Catch the fleeting colours of that shy chameleon, Cant, and show what excessive trouble we are ever taking to make ourselves miserable and silly. Teach us all this, and Aglaia shall stop a crow in its course and present you with a pen, Thalia hold the golden fluid in a Sevres vase, and Euphrosyne support the violet-coloured scroll.—*The Young Duke.*

SOCIETY.

There is no doubt that that great pumice-stone, society, smooths down the edges of your thoughts and manners.— *The Young Duke.*

Sidonia obtained at an early age that experience of refined and luxurious society which is a necessary part of a finished education. It gives the last polish to the manners ;

it teaches us something of the power of the passions, early developed in the hot-bed of self-indulgence ; it instils into us that indefinable tact seldom obtained in later life, which prevents us from saying the wrong thing, and often inspires us to do the right.—*Coningsby.*

Some people have great knowledge of society, and little of mankind.— *Vivian Grey.*

Christianity teaches us to love our neighbour as ourself ; modern society acknowledges no neighbour.—('Stephen Morley.') *Sybil.*

The manœuvres and tactics of society are infinitely more numerous and infinitely finer than those of strategy. *The Young Duke.*

When we first enter society, we are everywhere ; yet there are few, I imagine, who after a season do not subside into a coterie.—*The Infernal Marriage.*

It is a community of purpose that constitutes society. Without that men may be drawn into contiguity, but they still continue virtually isolated.—('Stephen Morley') *Sybil.*

What necessity can there be in your troubling yourself to amuse people you meet every day of your life, and who, from the vulgar perversity of society, value you in exact proportion as you neglect them ?—*Venetia.*

One cannot ask any person to meet another in one's own house, without going through a sum of moral arithmetic.—('Neuchatel') *Endymion.*

There are no fits of caprice so hasty and so violent as those of society. Society indeed is all passion and no heart.— *Venetia.*

How I hate a 'small and early'—shown into a room where you meet a silent few who have been asked to dinner, and who are chewing the cud like a herd of kine, and you are expected to tumble before them to assist their digestion.—('St. Barbe') *Endymion.*

Talk of Catholic emancipation ! O ! thou Imperial Parliament, emancipate the forlorn wretches who have got into a bad set ! Even thy omnipotence must fail.—*The Young Duke.*

Nonchalance is the *métier* of your modern hostess ; and so long as the house is not on fire, or the furniture not kicked, you may be even ignorant who is the priestess of the hospitable fane in which you worship.—*The Young Duke.*

Although it was yet January, she (Lady Fitz-Pompey) did not despair of collecting a select band of guests, Brahmins of the highest caste.—*The Young Duke.*

Lady St. Jerome received Lothair, as Pinto said, with extreme unction.—*Lothair.*

It often happens that worthless people are merely people who are worth knowing.—*Coningsby.*

What is crime amongst the multitude, is only vice among the few.—*Tancred.*

[After the ladies had retired for the night], the gentlemen lingered and looked at each other, as if they were an assembly of poachers, gathering for an expedition, and then Lord St. Aldegonde said to Lothair, 'Do you smoke?'—*Lothair.*

Introduction is a formality and a bore, and is never resorted to by your well-bred host, save in a casual way. When proper people meet at proper houses, they give each other credit for propriety, and slip into an acquaintance by degrees.—*The Young Duke.*

SORROW.

I am one of those who would rather cherish affection than indulge grief, but everyone must follow his mood.— ('Adrian Neuchatel') *Endymion.*

His heart was so crushed, that hope could not find even one desolate chamber to smile in.—*The Young Duke.*

SOUTHEY.

The most philosophical of bigots and the most poetical of prose-writers.—('Cleveland') *Vivian Grey.*

SOVEREIGNTY.

There is no sovereignty of any first-rate state which costs so little to the people as the sovereignty of England.—*Speech at Manchester, April* 3, 1872.

SPANIARDS.

Certainly the Spaniards are a noble race. They are kind and faithful, courageous and honest, with a profound mind, that will nevertheless break into rich humour, and a dignity which, like their passion, is perhaps the legacy of their oriental sires.—*Contarini Fleming.*

SPANISH BULL-FIGHT.

A Spanish bull-fight taught me fully to comprehend the rapturous exclamation of ' Panem et Circenses! ' The amusement apart, there is something magnificent in the assembled thousands of an amphitheatre. It is the trait in modern manners which most effectually recalls the nobility of antique pastimes.

The poetry of a bull-fight is much destroyed by the appearance of the cavaliers. Instead of gay, gallant knights bounding on caracoling steeds, three or four shapeless, unwieldy beings cased in armour of stuffed leather, and looking more like Dutch burgomasters than Spanish chivalry, enter the lists on limping rips. The bull is, in fact, the executioner for the dogs ; and an approaching bull-fight is a respite for any doomed steed throughout all Seville.

The tauridors, in their varying, fanciful, costly, and splendid dresses, compensate in a great measure for your disappointment. It is difficult to conceive a more brilliant band. These are ten or a dozen footmen, who engage the bull unarmed, distract him as he rushes at one of the cavaliers by unfolding and dashing before his eyes a glittering scarf, and saving themselves from an occasional chase by practised agility, which elicits great applause. The performance of these tauridors is, without doubt, the most graceful, the most exciting, and the most surprising portion of the entertainment.

The ample theatre is nearly full. Be careful to sit on the shady side. There is the suspense experienced at all public entertainments, only here upon a great scale. Men are gliding about selling fans and refreshments ; the governor and his suite enter their box ; a trumpet sounds ! all is silent.

The knights advance, poising their spears, and for a moment trying to look graceful. The tauridors walk behind them, two by two. They proceed around and across the lists ; they bow to the viceregal party, and commend themselves to the Virgin, whose portrait is suspended above.

Another trumpet ! A second and a third blast ! The governor throws the signal ; the den opens, and the bull bounds in. That first spring is very fine. The animal stands for a moment still, staring, stupefied. Gradually his hoof moves ; he paws the ground ; he dashes about the sand. The knights face him with their extended lances at due distance. The tauridors are still. One flies across him, and waves his scarf. The enraged bull makes at the nearest horseman ; he is frustrated in his attack. Again he plants himself, lashes his tail, and rolls his eye. He makes another charge, and this time the glance of the spear does not drive him back. He gores the horse ; rips up its body : the steed staggers and falls. The bull rushes at the rider, and his armour will not now preserve him ; but, just as his awful horn is about to avenge his future fate, a skilful tauridor skims before him, and flaps his nostrils with his scarf. He flies after his new assailant, and immediately finds another. Now you are delighted by all the evolutions of this consummate band ; occasionally they can save themselves only by leaping the barrier. The knight, in the meantime, rises, escapes, and mounts another steed.

The bull now makes a rush at another horseman ; the

horse dexterously veers aside. The bull rushes on, but the knight wounds him severely in the flank with his lance. The tauridors now appear, armed with darts. They rush with extraordinary swiftness and dexterity at the infuriated animal, plant their galling weapons in different parts of his body, and scud away. To some of their darts are affixed fireworks, which ignite by the pressure of the stab. The animal is then as bewildered as infuriate; the amphitheatre echoes to his roaring, and witnesses the greatest efforts of his rage. He flies at all, staggering and streaming with blood; at length, breathless and exhausted, he stands at bay, his black, swollen tongue hanging out, and his mouth covered with foam.

'Tis horrible! Throughout, a stranger's feelings are for the bull, although this even the fairest Spaniard cannot comprehend. As it is now evident that the noble victim can only amuse them by his death, there is a universal cry for the matador; and the matador, gaily dressed, appears amid a loud cheer. The matador is a great artist. Strong nerves must combine with great quickness and great experience to form an accomplished matador. It is a rare character, highly prized; their fame exists after their death, and different cities pride themselves on producing or possessing the eminent.

The matador plants himself before the bull, and shakes a red cloak suspended over a drawn sword. This last insult excites the lingering energy of the dying hero. He makes a violent charge: the mantle falls over his face, the sword enters his spine, and he falls amid thundering shouts. The death is instantaneous, without a struggle and without a groan. A car, decorated with flowers and ribbons, and drawn by oxen, now appears, and bears off the body in triumph.

I have seen eighteen horses killed in a bull-fight, and eight bulls; but the sport is not always in proportion to the slaughter. Sometimes the bull is a craven, and then, if, after recourse has been had to every mode of excitement, he will not charge, he is kicked out of the arena amid the jeers and hisses of the audience. Every act of skill on the part of the tauridors elicits applause ; nor do the spectators hesitate, if necessary, to mark their temper by a contrary method.· On the whole, it is a magnificent but barbarous spectacle ; and, however disgusting the principal object, the accessories of the entertainment are so brilliant and inte-resting that, whatever may be their abstract disapprobation, those who have witnessed a Spanish bull-fight will not be surprised at the passionate ‚attachment of the Spanish people to their national pastime.—*Contarini Fleming.*

SPANISH FAN.

All is now life and animation. Such bowing, such kissing, such fluttering of fans, such gentle criticisms of gentle friends ! But the fan is the most wonderful part of the whole scene. A Spanish lady, with her fan, might shame the tactics of a troop of horse. Now she unfurls it with the slow pomp and conscious elegance of the bird of Juno ; now she flutters it with all the languor of a listless beauty, now with all the liveliness of a vivacious one. Now, in the midst of a very tornado, she closes it with a whirr, which makes you start. In the midst of your confusion Dolores taps you on your elbow ; you turn round to listen, and Catalina pokes you in your side. Magical instrument ! In this land it speaks a particular language, and gallantry requires no other mode to express its most subtle conceits or its most unreasonable· demands than this delicate ma-chine. Yet we should remember that here, as in the north, it is not confined to the delightful sex. The cavalier also has his fan ; and, that the habit may not be considered an indication of effeminacy, learn that in this scorching clime the soldier will not mount guard without this solace.—*Contarini Fleming.*

SPECIAL CORRESPONDENT.

Fancy sending a man who has never used his pen except upon those dismal statistics, and what he calls first principles! I hate his style, so neat and frigid—no colour, sir! I hate his short sentences, like a dog barking—we want a word-painter, sir.—('St. Barbe') *Endymion.*

SPEECH.

Then there was a maiden speech, so inaudible that it was doubted whether, after all, the young orator really did lose his virginity.—*The Young Duke.*

A First Speech.—He (Endymion) has since admitted, though he has been through many trying scenes, that it was the most nervous moment of his life. 'After Calais,' as a wise wit said, 'nothing surprises;' and the first time a man speaks in public, even if only at a debating society, is also the unequalled incident in its way.—*Endymion.*

SPEED.

Notwithstanding Solomon, in a race speed must win.—('Sidonia') *Coningsby.*

SPIRITS.

Fancy a man ever being in low spirits. Life is too short for such *bêtises.* The most unfortunate wretch alive calculates unconsciously that it is better to live than to die. Well, then, he has something in his favour. Existence is a pleasure, and the greatest. The world cannot rob us of that; and if it is better to live than to die, it is better to live in a good humour than a bad one. If a man be convinced that existence is the greatest pleasure, his happiness may be increased by good fortune, but it will be essentially independent of it. He who feels that the greatest source of pleasure always remains to him ought never to be miserable. The sun shines on all: every man can go to sleep: if you cannot ride a fine horse, it is something to look upon one;

if you have not a fine dinner, there is some amusement in a crust of bread and Gruyere. Feel slightly, think little, never plan, never brood. Everything depends upon the circulation ; take care of it. Take the world as you find it ; enjoy everything. Vive la bagatelle !—(' Count Mirabel ') *Henrietta Temple.*

SPRING.

It was a bright and soft spring morning : the dewy vistas of Cherbury sparkled in the sun, the cooing of the pigeons sounded around, the peacocks strutted about the terrace and spread their tails with infinite enjoyment and conscious pride, and Lady Annabel came forth with her little daughter, to breathe the renovating odours of the season. The air was scented with the violet, tufts of daffodils were scattered all about, and though the snowdrop had vanished, and the primroses were fast disappearing, their wild and shaggy leaves still looked picturesque and glad.— *Venetia.*

Restless and disquieted, she knew not why, Venetia went forth again into the garden. All nature smiled around her ; the flitting birds were throwing their soft shadows over the sunny lawns, and rustling amid the blossoms of the variegated groves. The golden wreaths of the laburnum and the silver knots of the chestnut streamed and glittered around ; the bees were as busy as the birds, and the whole scene was suffused and penetrated with brilliancy and odour. It still was spring, and yet the gorgeous approach of summer, like the advancing procession of some triumphant king, might almost be detected amid the lingering freshness of the year ; a lively and yet magnificent period, blending, as it were, Attic grace with Roman splendour ; a time when hope and fruition for once meet, when existence is most full of delight, alike delicate and voluptuous, and when the human frame is most sensible to the gaiety and grandeur of nature.— *Venetia.*

ST. ALDEGONDE (LORD).

Tall, fair, and languid, St. Aldegonde was the heir apparent of the wealthiest, if not the most ancient, dukedom in the United Kingdom. He was spoiled, but he knew it. Had he been an ordinary being, he would have merely subsided into selfishness and caprice, but having good abilities and a good disposition, he was eccentric, adventurous, and sentimental. Notwithstanding the apathy which had been engendered by premature experience, St. Aldegonde held extreme opinions, especially on political affairs, being a republican of the reddest dye. He was opposed to all privilege, and indeed to all orders of men, except dukes, who were a necessity. He was also strongly in favour of the equal division of all property, except land. Liberty depended on land, and the greater the landowners, the greater the liberty of a country. He would hold forth on this topic even with energy, amazed at anyone differing from him ; 'as if a fellow could have too much land,' he would urge with a voice and glance which defied contradiction. St. Aldegonde had married for love, and he loved his wife, but he was strongly in favour of woman's rights and their extremest consequences. It was thought that he had originally adopted these latter views with the amiable intention of piquing Lady St. Aldegonde ; but if so, he had not succeeded. Beaming with brightness, with the voice and airiness of a bird, and a cloudless temper, Albertha St. Aldegonde had, from the first hour of her marriage, concentrated her intelligence, which was not mean, on one object ; and that was never to cross her husband on any conceivable topic. They had been married several years, and she treated him as a darling spoiled child. When he cried for the moon, it was promised him immediately ; however irrational his proposition, she always assented to it, though generally by tact and vigilance she guided him in the right direction. Nevertheless, St. Aldegonde was sometimes in scrapes ; but then he always went and told his best friend, whose greatest delight was to extricate him from his perplexities and embarrassments.

Lord St. Aldegonde loved to preside over the mysteries of the smoking-room. There, enveloped in his Egyptian robe, occasionally blurting out some careless or headstrong paradox to provoke discussion among others, which would amuse himself, rioting in a Rabelaisian anecdote, and listening with critical delight to endless memoirs of horses and prima donnas, St. Aldegonde was never bored. Sometimes too, when he could get hold of an eminent traveller, or some individual distinguished for special knowledge, St. Aldegonde would draw him out with skill, himself displaying an acquaintance with the particular topic which often surprised his companions, for St. Aldegonde professed never to read ; but he had no ordinary abilities and an original turn of mind and habit of life, which threw him in the way of unusual persons of all classes, from whom he imbibed or extracted a vast variety of queer, always amusing, and not altogether useless information.—*Lothair.*

STATESMANSHIP.

You will find it of the first importance in public life to know personally those who are carrying on the business of the world ; so much depends on the character of an individual, his habits of thought, his prejudices, his superstitions, his social weaknesses, his health. Conducting affairs without this advantage is, in effect, an affair of stationery : it is pens and paper who are in communication, not human beings.— ('Count Ferroll') *Endymion.*

He (Ferrars) had read very little more than some Latin writers, some Greek plays, and some treatises of Aristotle. These, with a due course of Bampton Lectures, and some dipping into the 'Quarterly Review,' qualified a man in those days not only for being a member of Parliament, but becoming a candidate for the responsibility of statesman-ship.—*Endymion.*

STATESMEN.

All lawyers are loose in their youth ; but an insular country subject to fogs, and with a powerful middle class, requires grave statesmen.—*Endymion.*

STATION.

Great duties could alone confer great station.—*Speech in House of Commons (National Petition), July* 12, 1839.

ST. JEROME (LADY).

Lady St. Jerome was still the young wife of a nobleman not old. She was the daughter of a Protestant house, but, during a residence at Rome after her marriage, she had reverted to the ancient faith, which she professed with the enthusiastic convictions of a convert. Her whole life was dedicated to the triumph of the Catholic cause ; and being a woman of considerable intelligence and of an ardent mind, she had become a recognised power in the great confederacy which has so much influenced the human race, and which has yet to play perhaps a mighty part in the fortunes of the world. She was a woman to inspire crusaders. Not that she ever condescended to vindicate her own particular faith, or spoke as if she were conscious that Lothair did not possess it.—*Lothair.*

STOCK EXCHANGE.

She was diverted by the gentlemen of the Stock Ex-change, so acute, so audacious, and differing so much from the merchants in the style even of their dress, and in the ease, perhaps too great facility, of their bearing. They called each other by their Christian names, and there were allusions to practical jokes, which intimated a life something between a public school and a garrison.—*Endymion.*

STRENGTH.

Human strength always seems to me the natural process of settling affairs.—('Delegate to National Convention') *Sybil.*

SUBLIMITY.

We have long been induced to suspect that the seeds of true sublimity lurk in a life which, like this book, is half fashion and half passion.—*The Young Duke.*

SUCCESS.

Success is the child of audacity.—*Iskander.*

As a general rule the most successful man in life is the man who has the best information.—('Baron Sergius') *Endymion.*

The impromptu is always successful in life.—('Pinto') *Lothair.*

For my success in life, it may be principally ascribed to the observance of a simple rule—I never trust either God or man.—('Tiresias') *Infernal Marriage.*

SUMMER EVENING.

The clouds of a summer eve were glowing in the creative and flickering blaze of the vanished sun, that had passed like a monarch from the admiring sight, yet left his pomp behind. The golden and umber vapours fell into forms that to the eye of the musing Lothair depicted the objects of his frequent meditation. There seemed to rise in the horizon the dome and campaniles and lofty aisles of some celestial fane, such as he had often more than dreamed of raising to the revealed author of life and death. Altars arose and sacred shrines, and delicate chantries and fretted spires ; now the flashing phantom of heavenly choirs, and then the dim response of cowled and earthly cenobites :

These are black Vesper's pageants !

Lothair.

SUN.

The sun is not the light for study.—('Sievers') *Vivian Grey.*

SUNDAY.

There is always a danger of the day becoming a course of heavy meals and stupid walks.—*Lothair.*

The gentlemen habited themselves, both as regards form and character, in a style indicative of the subdued gravity of their feelings.—*Lothair.*

SUNRISE.

It is the hour before the labouring bee has left his golden hive ; not yet the blooming day buds in the blushing East ;: not yet has the victorious Lucifer chased from the early sky the fainting splendour of the stars of night. All is silent,. save the light breath of morn waking the slumbering leaves. Even now a golden streak breaks over the grey mountains. Hark to shrill chanticleer ! As the cock crows the owl ceases. Hark to shrill chanticleer's feathered rival ! The mountain lark springs from the sullen earth, and welcomes with his hymn the coming day. The golden streak has expanded into a crimson crescent, and rays of living fire flame over the rose-enamelled East. Man rises sooner than the sun, and already sound the whistle of the ploughman, the song of the mower, and the forge of the smith ; and hark to the bugle of the hunter, and the baying of his deep-mouthed hound. The sun is up, the generating sun ! and temple, and tower, and tree, the massy wood, and the broad field, and the distant hill, burst into sudden light ; quickly upcurled is the dusky mist from the shining river ; quickly is the cold dew drunk from the raised heads of the drooping flowers !—*Vivian Grey.*

SUPERANNUATION.

The history of superannuation in this country is the history of spoliation. It is a very short history, for it may be condensed in one sentence, 'You promised a fund and you exacted a tax.'—*Speech in House of Commons (Civil Service Superannuation Bill), February* 15, 1856.

SUPERIOR PERSONS.

He (Mr. Horsman) denounces the Government, he derides the Opposition, he detests the peace party, he attacks the whole House of Commons, because we did not move in the matter.   But why did not the right honourable gentleman move in it ?   He had for three months on the paper a motion, which was without exception the most unconstitutional that was ever placed on the table of this House. Why did he not move that preposterous proposition ?   Why, because he knew that if he had moved that revolutionary rigmarole, he would have been left without a teller, had he gone to a division.   And this is the gentleman who lectures Parliament in a body, and every individual in particular, with a recklessness of assertion unequalled.   We know that in private life there is always in every circle some person, male or female, who is regarded as a ' superior person.' They decide on everything, they lecture everybody : all acknowledge their transcendent qualities ; but everyone gets out of their way.   The right honourable member for Stroud is the ' superior person ' of the House of Commons.—*Speech in House of Commons (Denmark and Germany, Vote of Censure), July* 8, 1864.

SUSPENSE.

Decision destroys suspense, and suspense is the charm of existence.—(' Mrs. Coningsby ') *Tancred.*

SWITZERLAND.

I had thought of Switzerland only as of a rude barrier between me and the far object of my desires. The impression that this extraordinary country made upon me was perhaps increased by my previous thoughts having so little brooded over the idea of it. It was in Switzerland that I first felt how the constant contemplation of sublime creation develops the poetic power. It was here that I first began to study nature. Those forests of black gigantic pines, rising out of the deep snows ; those tall white cataracts, leaping like headstrong youth into the world, and dashing from their precipices, as if allured by the beautiful delusion of their own rainbow mist ; those mighty clouds sailing beneath my feet, or clinging to the bosoms of the dark green mountains, or boiling up like a spell from the invisible and unfathomable depths ; the fell avalanche, fleet as a spirit of evil, terrific when its sound suddenly breaks upon the almighty silence, scarcely less terrible when we gaze upon its crumbling and pallid frame, varied only by the presence of one or two blasted firs ; the head of a mountain loosening from its brother peak, rooting up, in the roar of its rapid rush, a whole forest of pines, and covering the earth for miles with elephantine masses ; the supernatural extent of landscape that opens to us new worlds ; the strong eagles, and the strange wild birds that suddenly cross you in your path, and stare, and shrieking fly ; and all the soft sights of joy and loveliness that mingle with these sublime and savage spectacles, the rich pastures, and the numerous flocks, and the golden bees, and the wild flowers, and the carved and painted cottages, and the simple manners and the primeval grace, wherever I moved I was in turn appalled or enchanted.—*Contarini Fleming.*

SYBIL.

The divine melody ceased ; the elder stranger rose ; the words were on the lips of Egremont, that would have asked some explanation of this sweet and holy mystery, when, in the vacant and star-lit arch on which his glance was fixed, he beheld a female form. She was apparently in the habit of a Religious, yet scarcely could be a nun, for her veil, if indeed it were a veil, had fallen on her shoulders, and revealed her thick tresses of long fair hair. The blush of deep emotion lingered on a countenance which, though extremely young, was impressed with a character of almost divine majesty ; while her dark eyes and long dark lashes, contrasting with the brightness of her complexion and the luxuriance of her radiant locks, combined to produce a beauty as rare as it is choice ; and so strange, that Egremont might for a moment have been pardoned for believing her a seraph, who had lighted on this sphere, or the fair phantom of some saint haunting the sacred ruins of her desecrated fane.—*Sybil.*

Afterwards Lady Marney.—Although received by society with open arms, especially by the high nobility, who affected to look upon Sybil quite as one of themselves, Lady Marney, notwithstanding the homage that everywhere awaited her, had already shown a disposition to retire as much as possible within the precinct of a chosen circle.

This was her second season, and Sybil ventured to think that she had made, in the general gaieties of her first, a sufficient oblation to the genius of fashion, and the immediate requirements of her social position. Her life was faithful to its first impulse. Devoted to the improvement of the condition of the people, she was the moving spring of the charitable development of this great city. Her house, without any pedantic effort, had become the focus of a refined society, who, though obliged to show themselves for the moment in the great carnival, wear their masks, blow their trumpets, and pelt the multitude with sugar-plums, were glad to find a place where they could at all times divest themselves of their mummery, and return to their accustomed garb of propriety and good taste.

Sybil, too, felt alone in the world. Without a relation, without an acquaintance of early and other days, she clung to her husband with a devotion which was peculiar as well as profound. Egremont was to her more than a husband and a lover ; he was her only friend ; it seemed to Sybil that he could be her only friend. The disposition of Lord

Marney was not opposed to the habits of his wife. Men, when they are married, often shrink from the glare and bustle of those social multitudes which are entered by bachelors with the excitement of knights-errant in a fairy wilderness, because they are supposed to be rife with adventures, and, perhaps, fruitful of a heroine. The adventure sometimes turns out to be a catastrophe, and the heroine a copy instead of an original ; but let that pass.—*Tancred.*

SYMPATHY.

Sympathy is the solace of the poor ; but for the rich there is compensation.—('Simmons') *Sybil.*

There is a strange sympathy which whispers convictions that no evidence can authorise, and no arguments dispel.— *Venetia.*

Sympathy and antipathy share our being, as day and darkness share our lives.—*Lothair.*

The sympathy of Sidonia, so complete, and as instructive as it was animating, was a sustaining power which we often need when we are meditating great deeds. How often, when all seems dark, and hopeless, and spiritless, and tame, when slight obstacles figure in the cloudy landscape as Alps, and the rushing cataracts of our invention have subsided into drizzle, a single phrase of a great man instantaneously flings sunshine on the intellectual landscape, and the habitual features of power and beauty, over which we have so long mused in secret confidence and love, resume all their energy and lustre.—*Tancred.*

We exist because we sympathise. If we did not sympathise with the air, we should die. But, if we only sympathised with the air, we should be in the lowest order of brutes, baser than the sloth. Mount from the sloth to the poet. It is sympathy that makes you a poet. It is your desire that the airy children of your brain should be born anew within another's, that makes you create ; therefore, a

z 2

misanthropical poet is a contradiction in terms.—('Herbert') *Venetia.*

Man is neither vile, nor the excellent being which he sometimes imagines himself to be. He does not so much act by system as by sympathy. If the creature cannot always feel for others, he is doomed to feel for himself; and the vicious are, at least, blessed with the curse of remorse.— ('Horace Grey') *Vivian Grey.*

SYSTEM.

A series of systems have mystified existence.—*Contarini Fleming.*

TACT.

Without tact you can learn nothing. Tact teaches you when to be silent. Inquirers who are always inquiring never learn anything.—('Wilton') *Endymion.*

A want of tact is worse than a want of virtue. Some women, it is said, work on pretty well without the last : I never knew one who did not sink, who ever dared to sail without the other.—*The Young Duke.*

Perseverance and tact are the two great qualities most valuable for all men who would mount, but especially for those who have to step out of the crowd.—('Sidney Wilton') *Endymion.*

Tact does not remove difficulties, but difficulties melt away under tact.—*Tancred.*

Lothair had a greater degree of tact than usually falls to the lot of the ingenuous.—*Lothair.*

TANCRED (LORD MONTACUTE).

The duke bowed to the corporation, with the duchess on his left hand; and on his right there stood a youth, above the middle height and of a frame completely and gracefully formed. His dark brown hair, in those hyacinthine curls which Grecian poets have celebrated, and which Grecian sculptors have immortalised, clustered over his brow, which, however, they only partially concealed. It was pale, as was his whole countenance, but the liquid richness of the dark brown eye, and the colour of the lip, denoted anything but a languid circulation. The features were regular, and inclined rather to a refinement which might have imparted to the countenance a character of too much delicacy, had it not been for the deep meditation of the brow, and for the lower part of the visage, which intimated indomitable will and an iron resolution.

Placed for the first time in his life in a public position and under circumstances which might have occasioned some degree of embarrassment even to those initiated in the world, nothing was more remarkable in the demeanour of Lord Montacute than his self-possession ; nor was there in his carriage anything studied, or which had the character of being preconceived. Every movement or gesture was distinguished by what may be called a graceful gravity. With a total absence of that excitement which seemed so natural to his age and situation, there was nothing in his manner which approached to nonchalance or indifference. It would appear that he duly estimated the importance of the event they were commemorating, yet was not of a habit of mind that over-estimated anything.—*Tancred.*

TASTE.

There is no accounting for tastes. My grandmother loved a brindled cat.—(' Essper ') *Vivian Grey.*

TAXATION.

Confiscation is a blunder that destroys public credit ; taxation, on the contrary, improves it ; and both come to the same thing.—*Tancred.*

TEMPER.

A man's fate is his own temper ; and according to that will be his opinion as to the particular manner in which the course of events is regulated. A consistent man believes in destiny, a capricious man in chance.—(' Beckendorf') *Vivian Grey.*

TEMPLE (HENRIETTA).

To his surprise, as he was about to emerge from a berceau on to a plot of turf, in the centre of which grew a large cedar, he beheld a lady in a riding-habit standing before the tree, and evidently admiring its beautiful proportions.

Her countenance was raised and motionless. It seemed to him that it was more radiant than the sunshine. He gazed with rapture on the dazzling brilliancy of her complexion, the delicate regularity of her features, and the large violet-tinted eyes, fringed with the longest and the darkest lashes that he had ever beheld. From her position her hat had fallen back, revealing her lofty and pellucid brow, and the dark and lustrous locks that were braided over her temples. The whole countenance combined that brilliant health and that classic beauty which we associate with the idea of some nymph tripping over the dew-bespangled meads of Ida, or glancing amid the hallowed groves of Greece. Although the lady could scarcely have seen eighteen summers, her stature was above the common height ; but language cannot describe the startling symmetry of her superb figure.—*Henrietta Temple.*

TESTIMONIAL.

The moral which this case, as well as the whole experience of my life, teaches me is to beware of testimonials. Nobody ever acted on a testimonial who had not afterwards cause to regret it.—*Speech in House of Commons (Pension to Irish Poet, Mr. Young), March* 22, 1867.

THAMES.

The being who would be content with nothing less than communing with celestial powers in sacred climes, standing at a tavern window, gazing on the moonlit mud-banks of the barbarous Thames, a river which neither angel nor prophet had ever visited ! Before him was the Isle of Dogs ! It should at least have been Cyprus !—*Tancred.*

THEODORA (MRS. CAMPIAN).

It was the face of a matron, apparently of not many summers, for her shapely figure was still slender, though her mien was stately. But it was the countenance that had commanded the attention of Lothair : pale, but perfectly Attic in outline, with the short upper lip and the round chin, and a profusion of dark chestnut hair bound by a Grecian fillet, and on her brow a star.

He had read of such countenances in Grecian dreams : in Corinthian temples, in fanes of Ephesus, in the radiant shadow of divine groves.

'She is called Theodora, though married, I believe, to an Englishman, a friend of Garibaldi. Her birth unknown ; some say an Italian, some a Pole ; all sorts of stories. But she speaks every language, is ultracosmopolitan, and has invented a new religion.—*Lothair.*

THEOLOGY.

Theology requires an apprenticeship of some thousand years at least ; to say nothing of clime or race. You cannot get on with theology as you do with chemistry and mechanics. Trust me, there is something deeper in it.— *Tancred.*

THUG.

A Thug is a person of very gentlemanlike, even fascinating manners : he courts your acquaintance, he dines with you, he drinks with you, he smokes with you ; he not only shares your pleasures, but even your pursuits ; whatever you wish done, he is always ready to perform it ; he is the companion of your life and probably a member of the same joint-stock company ; but at that very moment when you are, as it were, reposing on the bosom of his friendship, the mission of the Thug is fulfilled, and you cease to exist. I confess I shall be curious to see who are the Thugs. [The Court of Directors of the East India Company were to select fifteen out of their number to become directors under the Government of India Bill.]—*Speech in House of Commons, June* 30, 1857.

TIME.

He who gains time gains everything.—('Baroni') *Tancred.*

Time moves with equal slowness whether we experience many impressions or none. In a new circle every character is a study and every incident an adventure : and the multitude of images and emotions restrains the hours.— *Lothair.*

'TIMES' (THE).

I read this morning an awful, though monotonous, manifesto in the great organ of public opinion, which always makes me tremble: Olympian bolts ; and yet I could not help fancying amid their rumbling terrors I heard the plaintive treble of the Treasury Bench.—*Speech in House of Commons (Agricultural Distress), February* 13, 1851.

TOBACCO.

Others who never went to balls, looked forward with refined satisfaction to a night of unbroken tobacco.— *Lothair.*

TOIL.

Toil without glory is a menial's lot.—*Alroy.*
When toil ceases the people suffer.—*Sybil.*

TONGUE.

The tongue is a less deceptive organ than the heart.— ('Lord Cadurcis') *Venetia.*

TORY.

It has been our habit, in counselling the Tory party, to recur gradually, but most sincerely, to the original elements

of that great political connection; to build up a community, not upon liberal opinions, which any man may
fashion to his fancy, but upon popular principles, which
assert equal rights, civil and religious; to uphold the institutions of the country, because they are the embodiment of
the wants and wishes of the nation, and protect us alike
from individual tyranny and popular outrage; especially to
resist democracy and oligarchy, and favour that principle
of free aristocracy which is the only basis and security for
constitutional government; to be vigilant to guard and
prompt to vindicate the honour of the country, but to hold
aloof from that turbulent diplomacy which only distracts the
mind of a people from internal improvement; to lighten
taxation; frugally, but wisely, to administer the public
treasure; to favour popular education, because it is the best
guarantee for public order; to defend local government and
to be as jealous of the rights of the working man as of the
prerogatives of the crown and the privileges of the senate.
These were once the principles which regulated Tory statesmen, and I, for one, have no wish that the Tory party should
ever be in power unless they practise them.—*Speech in
House of Commons (Administration of Viscount Palmerston),
August 1, 1862.*

But we forget, Sir Robert Peel is not the leader of the
Tory party; the party that resisted the ruinous mystification
that metamorphosed direct taxation by the Crown into
indirect taxation by the Commons; that denounced the
system which mortgaged industry to protect property; the
party that ruled Ireland by a scheme which reconciled both
churches, and by a series of parliaments which counted
among them lords and commons of both religions; that has
maintained at all times the territorial constitution of England
as the only basis and security for local government, and
which nevertheless once laid on the table of the House of
Commons a commercial tariff negotiated at Utrecht, which
is the most rational that was ever devised by statesmen; a

party that has prevented the Church from being the salaried agent of the State, and has supported through many struggles the parochial polity of the country which secures to every labourer a home.

In a parliamentary sense, that great party has ceased to exist ; but I will believe that it still lives in the thought and sentiment and consecrated memory of the English nation. It has its origin in great principles and in noble instincts ; it sympathises with the lowly, it looks up to the Most High ; it can count its heroes and its martyrs ; they have met in its behalf plunder, proscription, and death. Nor, when it finally yielded to the iron progress of oligarchical supremacy, was its catastrophe inglorious. Its genius was vindicated in golden sentences and with fervent arguments of impassioned logic by St. John ; and breathed in the intrepid eloquence and patriot soul of William Wyndham. Even now it is not dead, but sleepeth ; and, in an age of political materialism, of confused purposes and perplexed intelligence, that aspires only to wealth because it has faith in no other accomplishment, as men rifle cargoes on the verge of shipwreck, Toryism will yet rise from the tomb over which Bolingbroke shed his last tear, to bring back strength to the Crown, liberty to the Subject, and to announce that power has only one duty : to secure the social welfare of the People.—*Sybil.*

Is not the Tory party a succession of heroic spirits, ' beautiful and swift,' ever in the van and foremost of the age—Hobbes and Bolingbroke, Hume and Adam Smith, Wyndham and Cobham, Pitt and Grenville, Canning and Huskisson ? Are not the principles of Toryism those popular rights which men like Shippen and Hynde Cotton flung in the face of an alien monarch and his mushroom aristocracy ? Place Bills, triennial Bills, opposition to standing armies, to Peerage Bills ? Are not the traditions of the Tory party the noblest pedigree in the world ? are not its illustrations that glorious martyrology that opens with the name of Falkland and closes with that of Canning?— (' Waldershare ') *Endymion.*

TOWN HOUSES.

Bellair House.—Bellair House was the prettiest mansion in Mayfair. It was a long building, in the Italian style, situate in the midst of gardens, which, though not very extensive, were laid out with so much art and taste, that it was very difficult to believe that you were in a great city. The house was furnished and adorned with all that taste for which Lady Bellair was distinguished. All the reception rooms were on the ground floor, and were all connected. Ferdinand, who remembered Lady Bellair's injunctions not to leave cards, attracted by the spot, and not knowing what to do with himself, determined to pay her ladyship a visit, and was ushered into an octagon library, lined with well-laden dwarf cases of brilliant volumes, crowned with no lack of marble busts, bronzes, and Etruscan vases. On each side opened a magnificent saloon, furnished in that classic style which the late accomplished and ingenious Mr. Hope first rendered popular in this country. The wings, projecting far into the gardens, comprised respectively a dining-room and a conservatory of considerable dimensions. Isolated in the midst of the gardens was a long building, called the summer-room, lined with Indian matting, and screened on one side from the air, merely by Venetian blinds. The walls of this chamber were almost entirely covered with caricatures and prints of the country seats of Lady Bellair's friends, all of which she took care to visit. Here also were her parrots, and some birds of a sweeter voice, a monkey, and the famous squirrel.—*Henrietta Temple.*

Hexham House.—One of the least known squares in London is Hexham Square, though it is one of the oldest. Not that it is very remote from the throng of existence, but it is

isolated in a dingy district of silent and decaying streets
Once it was a favoured residence of opulence and power, and
its architecture still indicates its former and prouder destiny.
But its noble mansions are now divided and broken up into
separate dwellings, or have been converted into chambers
and offices. Lawyers, and architects, and agents dwell in
apartments where the richly-sculptured chimney-pieces, the
carved and gilded pediments over the doors, and sometimes
even the painted ceilings, tell a tale of vanished stateliness
and splendour.

A considerable portion of the north side of the square is
occupied by one house standing in a courtyard, with iron
gates to the thoroughfare. This is Hexham House, and
where Lord Hexham lived in the days of the first Georges.
It is reduced in size since his time, two considerable wings
having been pulled down about sixty years ago, and their
materials employed in building some residences of less
pretension. But the body of the dwelling-house remains,
and the courtyard, though reduced in size, has been retained.

Hexham House has an old oak entrance hall panelled
with delicacy, and which has escaped the rifling arts of
speculators in furniture; and out of it rises a staircase of
the same material, of a noble character, adorned occasionally with figures; armorial animals holding shields, and
sometimes a grotesque form rising from fruits and flowers,
all doubtless the work of some famous carver.—*Lothair.*

Crecy House.—The Duke was one of the few gentlemen
in London who lived in a palace. One of the half-dozen of
those stately structures that our capital boasts had fallen to
his lot.

An heir apparent to the throne, in the earlier days of the
present dynasty, had resolved to be lodged as became a
prince, and had raised, amid gardens which he had diverted
from one of the royal parks, an edifice not unworthy of
Vicenza in its best days, though on a far more extensive scale

than any pile that favoured city boasts. Before the palace was finished the prince died, and irretrievably in debt. His executors were glad to sell to the trustees of the ancestors of the chief of the house of Brentham the incomplete palace, which ought never to have been commenced. The ancestor of the Duke was by no means so strong a man as the Duke himself, and prudent people rather murmured at the exploit. But it was what is called a lucky family; that is to say, a family with a charm that always attracted and absorbed heiresses; and perhaps the splendour of Crecy House, for it always retained its original title, might have in some degree contributed to fascinate the taste or imagination of the beautiful women who, generation after generation, brought their bright castles and their broad manors to swell the state and rent-rolls of the family who were so kind to Lothair.

The centre of Crecy House consisted of a hall of vast proportion, and reaching to the roof. Its walls commemorated, in paintings by the most celebrated artists of the age, the exploits of the Black Prince; and its coved ceiling, in panels resplendent with Venetian gold, was bright with the forms and portraits of English heroes. A corridor round this hall contained the most celebrated private collection of pictures in England, and opened into a series of sumptuous saloons.—*Lothair.*

Lord St. Jerome's House.—The mansion of Lord St. Jerome was a real family mansion, built by his ancestors a century and a half ago, when they believed that from its central position, its happy contiguity to the Court, the Senate, and the seats of Government, they at last in St. James's Square had discovered a site which could defy the vicissitudes of fashion, and not share the fate of their river palaces, which they had been obliged in turn to relinquish. And in a considerable degree they were right in their anticipation; for although they have somewhat unwisely permitted the clubs to invade too successfully their territory, St. James's Square may be looked upon as our Faubourg St. Germain, and a great patrician residing there dwells in the heart of that free and noble life of which he ought to be a part.

A marble hall and a marble staircase, lofty chambers with silk or tapestried hangings, gilded cornices, and painted ceilings, gave a glimpse of almost Venetian splendour rare in our metropolitan houses of this age ; but the first dwellers in St. James's Square had tender recollections of the Adrian, had frolicked in St. Mark's, and glided in adventurous gondolas.—*Lothair.*

Monmouth House.—The gates were opened by a gigantic Swiss, and the carriage rolled into a huge courtyard. At its end Coningsby beheld a Palladian palace, with wings and colonnades encircling the court.

A double flight of steps led into a circular aud marble hall, adorned with colossal busts of the Cæsars ; the staircase, in fresco by Sir James Thornhill, breathed with the loves and wars of gods and heroes. It led into a vestibule, painted in arabesque, hung with Venetian girandoles, and looking into gardens. Opening a door in this chamber, and proceeding some little way down a corridor, Mr. Rigby and his companion arrived at the base of a private staircase. Ascending a few steps, they reached a landing-place hung with tapestry. Drawing this aside, Mr. Rigby opened a door, and ushered Coningsby through an antechamber into a small saloon, of beautiful proportions, and furnished in a brilliant and delicate taste.

The walls of the saloon, which were covered with light blue satin, held, in silver panels, portraits of beautiful women, painted by Boucher. Couches and easy chairs of every shape invited in every quarter to luxurious repose ; while amusement was afforded by tables covered with caricatures, French novels, and endless miniatures of foreign dancers, princesses, and sovereigns.

'Come,' said Mr. Rigby, when Coningsby was somewhat composed, ' come with me, and we will see the house.'

So they descended once more the private staircase, and again entered the vestibule.

'If you had seen these gardens when they were illuminated for a fête to George IV.,' said Rigby, as crossing the chamber he ushered his charge into the state apartments. The splendour and variety of the surrounding objects soon distracted the attention of the boy, for the first time in the palace of his fathers. He traversed saloon after saloon hung with rare tapestry and the gorgeous products of foreign looms; filled with choice pictures and creations of curious art; cabinets that sovereigns might envy, and colossal vases of malachite presented by emperors. Coningsby alternately gazed up to ceilings glowing with colour and with gold, and down upon carpets bright with the fancies and vivid with the tints of Aubusson and of Axminster.—*Coningsby.*

Muriel House.—Muriel House was a family mansion in the Green Park. It was built of hewn stone during the last century; a Palladian edifice, for a time much neglected, but now restored and duly prepared for the reception of its lord and master by the same combined energy and taste which had proved so successful at Muriel Towers.—*Lothair.*

Sidonia's House in Paris.—Sidonia lived in the Faubourg St. Germain, in a large hotel that, in old days, had belonged to the Crillons; but it had received at his hands such extensive alterations, that nothing of the original decoration, and little of its arrangement, remained.

A flight of marble steps, ascending from a vast court, led into a hall of great dimensions, which was at the same time an orangery and a gallery of sculpture. It was illumined by a distinct, yet soft and subdued light, which harmonised with the beautiful repose of the surrounding forms, and with the exotic perfume that was wafted about. A gallery led from this hall to an inner hall of quite a different character; fantastic, glittering, variegated; full of strange shapes and dazzling objects.

The roof was carved and gilt in that honeycomb style prevalent in the Saracenic buildings ; the walls were hung with leather stamped in rich and vivid patterns ; the floor was a flood of mosaic ; about were statues of negroes of human size with faces of wild expression, and holding in their outstretched hands silver torches that blazed with an almost painful brilliancy.

From this inner hall a double staircase of white marble led to the grand suite of apartments.

These saloons, lofty, spacious, and numerous, had been decorated principally in encaustic by the most celebrated artists of Munich. The three principal rooms were only separated from each other by columns, covered with rich hangings, on this night drawn aside. The decoration of each chamber was appropriate to its purpose. On the walls of the ball-room nymphs and heroes moved in measure in Sicilian landscapes, or on the azure shores of Ægean waters. From the ceiling beautiful divinities threw garlands on the guests, who seemed surprised that the roses, unwilling to quit Olympus, would not descend on earth. The general effect of this fair chamber was heightened, too, by that regulation of the house which did not permit any benches in the ball-room. That dignified assemblage who are always found ranged in precise discipline against the wall, did not here mar the flowing grace of the festivity. The chaperons had no cause to complain. A large saloon abounded in ottomans and easy chairs at their service, where their delicate charges might rest when weary, or find distraction when not engaged.—*Coningsby.*

TRADE.

Trade always comes back, and finance never ruined a country, or an individual either, if he had pluck.—('Lady Montfort') *Endymion*

TRAVEL.

Our first scrape generally leads to our first travel.—
Contarini Fleming.

Every moment is travel, if understood.—('Sidonia')
Coningsby.

Travel is the great source of true wisdom ; but to travel
with profit you must have such a thing as previous knowledge.
(' Winter') *Contarini Fleming.*

Travel teaches toleration.—*Contarini Fleming.*

In my time travelling was undertaken on a very different
system to what it is now. The English youth then travelled
to frequent, what Lord Bacon says are 'especially to be seen
and observed, the Courts of Princes.' You all travel now, it
appears, to look at mountains, and catch cold in spouting
trash on lakes by moonlight.—('St. George') *Vivian Grey.*

But, my dear sir ! although I grant you that the
principal advantages of travel must be the opportunity
which it affords us of becoming acquainted with human
nature—knowledge, of course, chiefly gained where human
beings most congregate, great cities, and, as you say, the
Courts of Princes ; still, one of its great benefits is, that
it enlarges a man's experience, not only of his fellow-
creatures in particular, but of nature in general. Many men
pass through life without seeing a sunrise : a traveller cannot. If human experience be gained by seeing men in
their undress, not only when they are conscious of the presence of others, natural experience is only to be acquired by
studying nature at all periods, not merely when man is busy
and the beasts asleep.—('Baron de Konigstein') *Vivian
Grey.*

TREMAINE (MR. BERTIE).

Mr. Bertie Tremaine was always playing at politics, and,
being two-and-twenty, was discontented he was not chancellor of the exchequer like Mr. Pitt.

Mr. Bertie Tremaine, who had early succeeded to the family estate, lived in Grosvenor Street, and in becoming style. His house was furnished with luxury and some taste. The host received his guests in a library well stored with political history and political science, and adorned with busts of celebrated statesmen and of profound political sages. Bentham was the philosopher then affected by young gentlemen of ambition, and who wished to have credit for profundity and hard heads. Mr. Bertie Tremaine had been the proprietor of a close borough, which for several generations had returned his family to Parliament, the faithful supporters of Pitt, and Perceval, and Liverpool, and he had contemplated following the same line, though with larger and higher objects than his ancestors. Being a man of considerable and versatile ability, and ample fortune, with the hereditary opportunity which he possessed he had a right to aspire, and, as his vanity more than equalled his talents, his estimate of his own career was not mean. Unfortunately, before he left Harrow, he was deprived of his borough, and this catastrophe eventually occasioned a considerable change in the views and conduct of Mr. Bertie Tremaine. In the confusion of parties and political thought which followed the Reform Act of Lord Grey, an attempt to govern the country by the assertion of abstract principles, and which it was now beginning to be the fashion to call Liberalism, seemed the only opening to public life ; and Mr. Bertie Tremaine, who piqued himself on recognising the spirit of the age, adopted Liberal opinions with that youthful fervour, which is sometimes called enthusiasm, but which is a heat of imagination subsequently discovered to be inconsistent with the experience of actual life. At Cambridge Mr. Bertie Tremaine was at first the solitary pupil of Bentham, whose principles he was prepared to carry to their extreme consequences, but being a man of energy and in possession of a good estate, he soon found followers, for the sympathies of youth are quick, and even with an original bias, it is essentially mimetic. When he left the university he found in the miscellaneous element of the London Union many of his former companions of school and college, and from them and the new world to which he was introduced it delighted him to form parties and construct imaginary cabinets.—*Endymion.*

TRUTH.

When little is done, little is said. Silence is the mother of truth.—('Sheikh Hassan') *Tancred.*

Truth is not truth to the false.—('Brother Anthony') *Contarini Fleming.*

Sidonia was a great philosopher, who took comprehensive views of human affairs, and surveyed every fact in its relative position to other facts, the only mode of obtaining truth.—*Coningsby.*

'After all, what is truth? It changes as you change your clime or your country; it changes with the century. The truth of a hundred years ago is not the truth of the present day, and yet it may have been as genuine. Truth at Rome is not the truth of London, and both of them differ from the truth of Constantinople. For my part, I believe everything,' said Lord Cadurcis.

'Well, that is practically prudent, if it be metaphysically possible,' said Herbert. 'Do you know that I have always been of opinion, that Pontius Pilate has been greatly misrepresented by Lord Bacon in the quotation of his celebrated question. "What is truth?" said jesting Pilate, and would not wait for an answer. Let us be just to Pontius Pilate, who has sins enough surely to answer for. There is no authority for the jesting humour given by Lord Bacon. Pilate was evidently of a merciful and clement disposition; probably an Epicurean. His question referred to a declaration immediately preceding it, that He who was before him came to bear witness to the truth. Pilate inquired what truth?'—('Herbert') *Venetia.*

A A 2

It is dishonest to blush when you speak the truth, even if it be to your shame.—('Winter') *Contarini Fleming.*

Time is precious, but truth is more precious than time. *Speech at Aylesbury, Royal and Central Bucks Agricultural Association, September 21, 1865.*

TU QUOQUE.

A *tu quoque* should always be good-humoured, for it has nothing else to recommend it.—*Speech in House of Commons (Prosecution of the War), May 24, 1855.*

TURF.

That vast institution of national demoralisation.—*Endymion.*

Even the jockeys were civil to him, and welcomed him with a sweet smile and gracious nod, instead of the sour and malicious wink with which those characters generally treat a stranger ; those mysterious characters, who in their influence over their superiors, and their total want of sympathy with their species, are our only match for the oriental eunuch.—*The Young Duke.*

The ring is up ; the last odds declared ; all gallop away to the Warren. A few minutes, only a few minutes, and the event that for twelve months has been the pivot of so much calculation, of such subtle combinations, of such deep conspiracies, round which the thought and passion of the sporting world have hung like eagles, will be recorded in the fleeting tablets of the past. But what minutes ! Count them by sensation, and not by calendars, and each moment is a day and the race a life.—*Sybil.*

TUTOR.

Mr. Dallas was a clergyman, a profound Grecian, a poor man. He had edited the 'Alcestis' and married his laundress ; lost money by his edition, and his fellowship by his match.—*Vivian Grey.*

UNCONSTITUTIONAL.

I admit the immense difficulty of encountering any argument that is based on 'unconstitutional' objections. I never yet have found any definition of what that epithet means, and I believe that, with the single exception of the word 'un-English,' it baffles discussion more than any other in our language.—*Speech in House of Commons* (*Government of India* [*No.* 3]), *April* 26, 1858

UNFORTUNATE.

The unfortunate are always egotistical.—('Agrippina') *Endymion.*

UNHAPPINESS.

There is no such thing as unhappiness.—('Winter') *Contarini Fleming.*

UNOBTRUSIVENESS.

He (Premium) was an object of observation for his very unobtrusiveness.—('Ernest Clay') *Vivian Grey.*

VACATION.

To the world in general—the mighty million, to the professional classes, to all men of business whatever, the end of the season is the beginning of carnival. It is the fulfilment of the dream over which they have been brooding for ten months, which has sustained them in toil, lightened anxiety, and softened even loss. It is air, it is health, it is movement, it is liberty, it is nature—earth, sea, lake, moor, forest, mountain and river. From the heights of the Engadine to Margate Pier there is equal rapture, for there is an equal cessation of routine.—*Endymion.*

VARIETY.

Variety—that divine gift which makes a woman charming.—*Tancred.*

Variety is the mother of enjoyment.—(' Essper') *Vivian Grey.*

VEGETARIAN VIEW OF ANIMAL FOOD.

The heresy of cutlets.—('Herbert') *Venetia.*

VEHEMENCE.

Whatever they did, the Elysians were careful never to be vehement.—*The Infernal Marriage.*

VENETIA.

The beauty of the young Venetia was not the hereditary gift of her beautiful mother. It was not from Lady Annabel that Venetia Herbert had derived those seraphic locks that fell over her shoulders and down her neck in golden streams, nor that clear grey eye even, whose childish glance might perplex the gaze of manhood, nor that little aquiline nose, that gave a haughty expression to a countenance that had never yet dreamed of pride, nor that radiant complexion, that dazzled with its brilliancy, like some winged minister of Raffael or Correggio. The peasants that passed the lady and her daughter in their walks, and who blessed her as they passed, for all her grace and goodness, often marvelled why so fair a mother and so fair a child should be so dissimilar, that one indeed might be compared to a starry night, and the other to a sunny day.—*Venetia.*

VENICE

As our gondolas glided over the great Lagune, the excitement of the spectacle reanimated me. The buildings that I had so fondly studied in books and pictures rose up before me. I knew them all; I required no cicerone. One by one, I caught the hooded cupolas of St. Mark, the tall Campanile red in the sun, the Moresco Palace of the Doges, the deadly Bridge of Sighs, and the dark structure to which it leads. Here my gondola quitted the Lagune, and, turning up a small canal, and passing under a bridge which connected the quays, stopped at the steps of a palace.

I ascended a staircase of marble, I passed through a gallery crowded with statues, I was ushered into spacious apartments, the floors of which were marble, and the hangings satin. The ceilings were painted by Tintoretto and his scholars, and were full of Turkish trophies and triumphs over the Ottomite. The furniture was of the same rich material as the hangings, and the gilding, although of two hundred years' duration, as bright and burnished as the costly equipment of a modern palace. From my balcony of blinds, I looked upon the great Lagune. It was one of those glorious sunsets which render Venice, in spite of her degradation, still famous. The sky and sea vied in the brilliant multiplicity of their blended tints. The tall shadows of her Palladian churches flung themselves over the glowing and transparent wave out of which they sprang. The quays were crowded with joyous groups, and the black gondolas flitted like sea-serpents over the red and rippling waters.

I hastened to the Place of St. Mark. It was crowded and illuminated. Three gorgeous flags waved on the mighty staffs, which are opposite to the church in all the old drawings, and which once bore the standards of Candia, and Cyprus, and the Morea. The coffee-houses were full, and gay parties, seated on chairs in the open air, listened to the music of military bands, while they refreshed themselves with confectionery so rich and fanciful that it excites the admiration of all travellers, but which I since discovered in Turkey to be Oriental. The variety of costume was also great. The dress of the lower orders in Venice is still unchanged; many of the middle classes yet wear the cap and cloak. The Hungarian and the German military, and the bearded Jew, with his black velvet cap and flowing robes, are observed with curiosity. A few days also before my arrival, the Austrian squadron had carried into Venice a

Turkish ship and two Greek vessels, which had violated the
neutrality. Their crews now mingled with the crowd. I
beheld, for the first time, the haughty and turbaned Ottoman,
sitting cross-legged on his carpet under a colonnade, sipping
his coffee and smoking a long chibouque, and the Greeks,
with their small red caps, their high foreheads, and arched
eyebrows.

Can this be modern Venice ? I thought. Can this be
the silent, and gloomy, and decaying city, over whose dis-
honourable misery I have so often wept? Could it ever
have been more enchanting? Are not these indeed still
subjects of a Doge, and still the bridegrooms of the ocean ?
Alas ! the brilliant scene was as unusual as unexpected, and
was accounted for by its being the feast day of a favourite
Saint. Nevertheless, I rejoiced at the unaccustomed appearance of the city at my entrance, and still I recall with pleasure the delusive moments, when, strolling about the Place
of St. Mark, the first evening that I was in Venice, I mingled
for a moment in a scene that reminded me of her lost light-
heartedness, and of that unrivalled gaiety which so long
captivated polished Europe.

The moon was now in her pride. I wandered once more
to the quay, and heard for the first time a serenade. A
juggler was conjuring in a circle under the walls of my hotel,
and an itinerant opera was performing on the bridge. It is
by moonlight that Venice is indeed an enchanted city. The
effect of the floods of silver light upon the twinkling fretwork
of the Moresco architecture, the total absence of all harsh
sounds, the never-ceasing music on the waters, produce an
effect upon the mind which cannot be experienced in any
other city. As I stood gazing upon the broad track of brilliant light that quivered over the Lagune, a gondolier saluted
me. I entered his boat, and desired him to row me to the
Grand Canal.

The marble palaces of my ancestors rose on each side,
like a series of vast and solemn temples. How sublime

were their broad fronts bathed in the mystic light, whose
softened tints concealed the ravages of Time, and made us
dream only of their eternity ! And could these great creations ever die ? I viewed them with a devotion which I
cannot believe to have been surpassed in the most patriotic
period of the Republic. How willingly would I have
given my life to have once more filled their mighty halls
with the proud retainers of their free and victorious nobles !

As I proceeded along the canal, and retired from the
quarter of St. Mark, the sounds of merriment gradually died
away. The light string of a guitar alone tinkled in the
distance, and the lamp of a gondola, swiftly shooting by,
indicated some gay, perhaps anxious, youth, hastening to
the general rendezvous of festivity and love. The course
of the canal bent, and the moon was hid behind a broad,
thick arch, which black, yet sharply defined, spanned the
breadth of the water. I beheld the famous Rialto.

Was it possible ? was it true ? was I not all this time in
a reverie gazing upon a drawing in Winter's studio ? Was
it not some delicious dream ? some delicious dream from
which perhaps this moment I was about to be roused to
cold, dull life ? I struggled not to wake, yet, from a
nervous desire to move and put the vision to the test, I
ordered the gondolier to row to the side of the canal,
jumped out, and hurried to the bridge. Each moment, I
expected that the arch would tremble and part, and that
the surrounding palaces would dissolve into mist, that the
lights would be extinguished and the music cease, and that
I should find myself in my old chamber in my father's
house.

I hurried along ; I was anxious to reach the centre of the
bridge before I woke. It seemed like the crowning incident
of a dream, which, it is remarkable, never occurs, and
which, from the very anxiety it occasions, only succeeds in
breaking our magical slumbers.

I stood upon Rialto ; I beheld on each side of me,

rising out of the waters, which they shadowed with their solemn image, those colossal and gorgeous structures raised from the spoils of the teeming Orient, with their pillars of rare marbles, and their costly portals of jasper, and porphyry, and agate ; I beheld them ranged in majestic order, and streaming with the liquid moonlight. Within these walls my fathers revelled !—*Contarini Fleming*.

If I were to assign the particular quality which conduces to that dreamy and voluptuous existence which men of high imagination experience in Venice, I should describe it as the feeling of abstraction which is remarkable in that city and peculiar to it. Venice is the only city which can yield the magical delights of solitude. All is still and silent. No rude sound disturbs your reveries ; Fancy, therefore, is not put to flight. No rude sound distracts your self-consciousness. This renders existence intense. We feel everything. And we feel thus keenly in a city not only eminently beautiful, not only abounding in wonderful creations of art, but each step of which is hallowed ground; quick with associations that, in their more various nature, their nearer relation to ourselves, and perhaps their more picturesque character, exercise a greater influence over the imagination than the more antique story of Greece and Rome. We feel all this in a city, too, which although her lustre be indeed dimmed, can still count among her daughters maidens fairer than the orient pearls with which her warriors once loved to deck them. Poetry, Tradition, and Love, these are the graces that have invested with an ever charming cestus this Aphrodite of cities.—*Contarini Fleming*.

Venice by Night.—How beautiful is night in Venice ! Then music and the moon reign supreme ; the glittering sky reflected in the waters, and every gondola gliding with sweet sounds ! Around on every side are palaces and temples, rising from the waves, which they shadow with their solemn forms; their costly fronts rich with the spoils of kingdoms, and softened with the magic of the midnight beam. The whole city too is poured forth for festival. The people lounge on the quays and cluster on the bridges ; the light barks skim along in crowds, just touching the surface of the water, while their bright prows of polished iron gleam in the moonshine, and glitter in the rippling wave. Not a sound that is not graceful : the tinkle of guitars, the sighs of sere-, naders, and the responsive chorus of gondoliers. Now and then a laugh, light, joyous, and yet musical, bursts forth from some illuminated coffee-house, before which a buffo disports, a tumbler stands on his head, or a juggler mysti-. fies ; and all for a sequin !

The Place of St. Mark, at the period of our story, still presented the most brilliant spectacle of the kind in Europe. Not a spot was more distinguished for elegance, luxury, and enjoyment. It was indeed the inner shrine of the temple of pleasure, and very strange and amusing would be the annals of its picturesque arcades. We must not, however, step behind their blue awnings, but content ourselves with the exterior scene ; and certainly the Place of St. Mark, with the variegated splendour of its Christian mosque, the ornate architecture of its buildings, its diversified population, a tribute from every shore of the midland sea, and where the noble Venetian, in his robe of crimson silk, and long white peruque, might be jostled by the Sclavonian with his target, and the Albanian in his kilt, while the Turk, sitting cross-legged on his Persian carpet, smoked his long chibouque with serene gravity, and the mild Armenian glided by him with a low reverence, presented an aspect under a Venetian moon such as we shall not easily find again in Christendom, and, in spite of the dying glory and the neighbouring vice, was pervaded with an air of romance and refinement, com-pared with which the glittering dissipation of Paris, even in its liveliest and most graceful hours, assumes a character alike coarse and commonplace.

It is the hour of love and of faro ; now is the hour to press your suit and to break a bank ; to glide from the apartment of rapture into the chamber of chance. Thus a noble Venetian contrived to pass the night, in alternations of excitement that in general left him sufficiently serious for the morrow's council. For more vulgar tastes there was the minstrel, the conjuror, and the story-teller, goblets of Cyprus wine, flasks of sherbet, and confectionery that dazzled like diamonds. And for everyone, from the grave senator to the gay gondolier, there was an atmosphere in itself a spell, and which, after all, has more to do with human happiness than all the accidents of fortune and all the arts of government.— *Venetia.*

VICE.

There is a great deal of vice which really is sheer inadvertence, and there are many who pursue a course which cannot be commended merely because an opportunity is not given of following one which is laudable, and which they will find conducive to their content and happiness.—*Speech at Westminster Industrial Exhibition Prize-giving, July* 13, 1879.

VICTORIA.

In a palace in a garden, not in a haughty keep, proud with the fame but dark with the violence of ages ; not in a regal pile, bright with the splendour, but soiled with the intrigues, of courts and factions ; in a palace in a garden, meet scene for youth, and innocence, and beauty, came a voice that told the maiden that she must ascend her throne !

The council of England is summoned for the first time within her bowers. There are assembled the prelates and captains and chief men of her realm ; the priests of the religion that consoles, the heroes of the sword that has conquered, the votaries of the craft that has decided the fate of empires ; men grey with thought, and fame, and age, who are the stewards of divine mysteries, who have toiled in secret cabinets, who have encountered in battle the hosts of

Europe, who have struggled in the less merciful strife of
aspiring senates ; men too, some of them, lords of a thousand
vassals and chief proprietors of provinces, yet not one of
them whose heart does not at this moment tremble as he
awaits the first presence of the maiden who must now ascend
her throne.

A hum of half-suppressed conversation which would
attempt to conceal the excitement, which some of the
greatest of them have since acknowledged, fills that brilliant assemblage ; that sea of plumes, and glittering stars,
and gorgeous dresses.   Hush ! the portals open ; she
comes ; the silence is as deep as that of a noontide forest.
Attended for a moment by her royal mother and the ladies
of her court, who bow and then retire, Victoria ascends
her throne ; a girl, alone, and for the first time, amid an
assemblage of men.

In a sweet and thrilling voice, and with a composed
mien which indicates rather the absorbing sense of august
duty than an absence of emotion, the Queen announces
her accession to the throne of her ancestors, and her humble
hope that Divine Providence will guard over the fulfilment
of her lofty trust.

The prelates and captains and chief men of her realm
then advance to the throne, and, kneeling before her, pledge
their troth, and take the sacred oaths of allegiance and
supremacy.

Allegiance to one who rules over the land that the great
Macedonian could not conquer ; and over a continent of
which even Columbus never dreamed : to the Queen of
every sea, and of nations in every zone.

It is not of these that I would speak ; but of a nation
nearer her footstool, and which at this moment looks to her
with anxiety, with affection, perhaps with hope.   Fair and
serene, she has the blood and beauty of the Saxon.   Will it
be her proud destiny at length to bear relief to suffering
millions, and, with that soft hand which might inspire trou-

badours and guerdon knights, break the last links in the chain of Saxon thraldom?—*Sybil.*

VIGO (MR.),

He was by birth a Yorkshireman, and gifted with all the attributes, physical and intellectual, of that celebrated race. At present he was the most fashionable tailor in London, and one whom many persons consulted. Besides being consummate in his art, Mr. Vigo had the reputation of being a man of singularly good judgment. He was one who obtained influence over all with whom he came in contact, and as his business placed him in contact with various classes, but especially with the class socially most distinguished, his influence was great. The golden youth who repaired to his counter came there not merely to obtain raiment of the best material and the most perfect cut, but to see and talk to Mr. Vigo, and to ask his opinion on various points. He was neither pretentious nor servile, but simple and with becoming respect for others and for himself. He never took a liberty with anyone, and such treatment, as is generally the case, was reciprocal.—*Endymion.*

VIRTUE.

It has been well observed, that no spectacle is so ridiculous as the British public in one of its periodical fits of morality. In general, elopements, divorces, and family quarrels pass with little notice. We read the scandal, talk about it for a day, and forget it. But, once in six or seven years, our virtue becomes outrageous. We cannot suffer the laws of religion and decency to be violated. We must make a stand against vice. We must teach libertines that the English people appreciate the importance of domestic ties. Accordingly, some unfortunate man, in no respect more depraved than hundreds whose offences have been treated with lenity, is singled out as an expiatory sacrifice. If he has children, they are to be taken from him. If he has a profession, he is to be driven from it. He is cut by the higher orders, and hissed by the lower. He is, in truth, a sort of whipping boy, by whose vicarious agonies all the other transgressors of the same class are, it is supposed, sufficiently chastised. We reflect very complacently on our own severity, and compare, with great pride, the high standard of morals established in England with the Parisian laxity. At length, our anger is satiated, our victim is ruined and heart-broken, and our virtue goes quietly to sleep for seven years more.—*Venetia.*

The beautiful cannot be obtained without virtue, if virtue consists, as I believe, in the control of the passions, in the sentiment of repose, and the avoidance of all things in excess.—(' Mr. Phœbus') *Lothair.*

Voice.

There is no index of character so sure as the voice. There are tones, tones brilliant and gushing, which impart a quick and pathetic sensibility: there are others that, deep and yet calm, seem the just interpreters of a serene and exalted intellect. But the rarest and the most precious of all voices is that which combines passion and repose; and whose rich and restrained tones exercise, perhaps, on the human frame a stronger spell than even the fascination of the eye, or that bewitching influence of the hand, which is the privilege of the higher races of Asia.—*Tancred.*

Hark ! a voice softer and sweeter than the night breaks upon the air. It is the voice of his beloved ; and, indeed, with all her singular and admirable qualities, there was not anything more remarkable about Henrietta Temple than her voice. It was a rare voice ; so that in speaking, and in ordinary conversation, though there was no one whose utterance was more natural and less unstudied, it forcibly affected you. She could not give you a greeting, bid you an adieu, or make a routine remark, without impressing you with her power and sweetness. It sounded like a bell, sweet and clear and thrilling ; it was astonishing what influence a little word uttered by this woman, without thought, would have upon those she addressed.—*Henrietta Temple.*

VOLTAIRE.

Now I had never read any work of Voltaire's. The truth is, I had no great opinion of the philosopher of Ferney ; for my friend, the Professor, had assured me that Voltaire knew nothing of the Dorians, that his Hebrew also was invariably incorrect, and that he was altogether a superficial person : but I chanced to follow my father's counsel.

I stood before the hundred volumes ; I glanced with indifference upon the wondrous and witching shelf. History, poetry, philosophy, the lucid narrative, and the wild invention, and the unimpassioned truth, they were all before me, and with my ancient weakness for romance I drew out Zadig. Never shall I forget the effect this work produced on me. What I had been long seeking offered itself. This strange mixture of brilliant fantasy and poignant truth, this unrivalled blending of ideal creation and worldly wisdom, it all seemed to speak to my two natures. I wandered a poet in the streets of Babylon, or on the banks of the Tigris. A philosopher and a statesman, I moralised over the condition of man and the nature of government. The style enchanted me. I delivered myself up to the full abandonment of its wild and brilliant grace.

I devoured them all, volume after volume. Morning, and night, and noon, a volume was ever my companion. I ran to it after my meals, it reposed under my pillow. As I read I roared, I laughed, I shouted with wonder and admiration ; I trembled with indignation at the fortunes of my race ; my bitter smile sympathised with the searching ridicule and withering mockery.—*Contarini Fleming.*

VOLUNTEERS.

The British army is the garrison of our Empire, but the volunteer force is the garrison of our hearths and homes. Patriotism never had a better inspiration than when it established that effective and powerful institution.—*Speech at Aylesbury, Royal and Central Bucks·Agricultural Association, February* 18, 1879.

WALDERSHARE.

He was a young man of about three or four and twenty years : fair, with short curly brown hair and blue eyes ; not exactly handsome, but with a countenance full of expression, and the index of quick emotions, whether of joy or of anger. Waldershare was the only child of a younger son of a patrician house, and had inherited from his father a moderate but easy fortune. He was one of those vivid and brilliant organisations which exercise a peculiarly attractive influence on youth. He had been the hero of the debating club at Cambridge, and many believed in consequence that he must become prime minister. He was witty and fanciful, and, though capricious and bad-tempered, could flatter and caress. Waldershare was profligate, but sentimental ; unprincipled, but romantic ; the child of whim, and the slave of imagination so freakish and deceptive that it was almost impossible to foretell his course. He was alike capable of sacrificing all his feelings to worldly considerations or of forfeiting the world for a visionary caprice. . . . Waldershare talked the whole way. It was a rhapsody of fancy, fun, knowledge, anecdote, brilliant badinage—even passionate seriousness. Sometimes he recited poetry, and his voice was musical ; and when he had attuned his companions to a sentimental pitch, he would break into mockery, and touch with delicate satire every mood of human feeling. All this time, what was now and ever remarkable in Waldershare were his manners. They were finished, even to courtliness.

Affable and winning, he was never familiar. The bow of Waldershare was a study. Its grace and ceremony must have been organic ; for there was no traditionary type in existence from which he could have derived or inherited it.—*Endymion.*

WAR.

I hear of peace and war in newspapers, but I am never alarmed, except when I am informed that the sovereigns want treasure : then I know that monarchs are in earnest. ('Sidonia') *Coningsby.*

If there be a greater calamity to human nature than famine, it is that of an exterminating war.—*Speech at Mansion House, November* 9, 1877.

To lay down as a principle that the leading Powers of Europe should never engage in a war unless they are certain and predetermined to achieve victories which may figure among what are called the decisive battles of the world, is really one of the most monstrous propositions that were ever addressed to the intelligence of a nation. To suppose, for instance, that France or England is never to go to war unless they can be certain of achieving victories like Rocroi or Blenheim, Austerlitz or Waterloo, is totally to misunderstand the object for which great States should go to war. Instead of their being the vindicators of public order, you degrade them into the gladiators of history, and their brilliant achievements would only be crimes which might accomplish the ruin of this country.—*Speech in House of Commons (Address in answer to the Queen's Speech), January* 31, 1856.

WEALTH.

After all, wealth is the test of the welfare of a people; and the test of wealth is the command of the precious metals.—('Neuchatel') *Endymion.*

Nonsense !—Great wealth is a great blessing to a man

who knows what to do with it ; and as for honours, they are inestimable to the honourable.—(' Neuchatel ') *Endymion*.

In a commercial country like England every half-century developes some new vast source of public wealth which brings into national notice a new and powerful class.— *Sybil.*

WELLINGTON, DUKE OF.

He has been called fortunate, but fortune is a divinity which has never favoured those who are not at the same time sagacious and intrepid, inventive and patient. It was his own character that created his career—alike achieved his exploits, and guarded him from every vicissitude ; for it was his sublime self-control alone that regulated his lofty fate.—*Funeral of the Duke of Wellington, November* 15, 1852.

The Duke of Wellington has left to his country a great legacy, greater even than his fame : he has left to them the contemplation of his character. I will not say of England that he has revived in her the sense of duty—that, I trust, was never lost. But that he has inspired public life with a purer and more masculine tone I cannot doubt ; that he has rebuked by his career restless vanity and regulated the morbid susceptibility of irregular egotism, is, I think, no exaggerated praise. I do not believe there is one amongst us who may not experience moments of doubt and depression, when the image of Wellington will occur to his memory, and he finds in his example support and solace.— *Speech in House of Commons (Funeral of the Duke of Wellington), November* 15, 1852.

The Duke's government—a dictatorship of patriotism.— *Endymion.*

The Duke of Wellington has ever been the votary of circumstances. He cares little for causes. He watches events rather than seeks to produce them. It is a characteristic of the military mind. Rapid combinations, the result of a quick, vigilant, and comprehensive glance, are generally triumphant in the field : but in civil affairs, where results are not immediate, in diplomacy and in the management of deliberative assemblies, where there is much intervening time and many counteracting causes, this velocity of decision, this fitful and precipitate action, are often productive of considerable embarrassment, and sometimes of terrible discomfiture. It is remarkable that men celebrated for military prudence are often found to be headstrong statesmen. In civil life a great general is frequently and strangely the creature of impulse; influenced in his political movements by the last snatch of information; and often the creature of the last aide-de-camp who has his ear.—*Coningsby*.

The Duke of Wellington brought to the post of first minister immortal fame; a quality of success which would almost seem to include all others. His public knowledge was such as might be expected from one whose conduct already formed an important portion of the history of his country. He had a personal and intimate acquaintance with the sovereigns and chief statesmen of Europe, a kind of information in which English ministers have generally been deficient, but without which the management of our external affairs must at the best be haphazard. He possessed administrative talents of the highest order.

The tone of the age, the temper of the country, the great qualities and the high character of the minister, indicated a long and prosperous administration. The only individual in his cabinet who, from a combination of circumstances rather than from any intellectual supremacy over his colleagues, was competent to be his rival, was content to be his successor. In his most aspiring moments, Mr. Peel, in all probability, aimed at no higher reach; and with youth and the leadership of the House of Commons, one has no reason to be surprised at his moderation. The conviction that the Duke's government would only cease with the termination of his public career was so general, that, the moment he was installed in office, the Whigs smiled on him ; political conciliation became the slang of the day, and the fusion of parties the babble of clubs and the tattle of boudoirs.

How comes it, then, that so great a man, in so great a position, should have so signally failed ; should have broken up his government, wrecked his party, and so completely annihilated his political position, that, even with his historical reputation to sustain him, he can since only reappear in the councils of his sovereign in a subordinate, not to say equivocal, character ?

With all those great qualities which will secure him a place in our history not perhaps inferior even to Marlborough, the Duke of Wellington has one deficiency which has been the stumbling-block of his civil career. Bishop Burnet, in speculating on the extraordinary influence of Lord Shaftesbury, and accounting how a statesman, so inconsistent in his conduct and so false to his confederates, should have so powerfully controlled his country, observes, ' His strength lay in his knowledge of England.'

Now that is exactly the kind of knowledge which the Duke of Wellington never possessed.—*Sybil.*

WHIGS.

It is in the plunder of the Church that we must seek for the primary cause of our political exclusion, and our commercial restraint. That unhallowed booty created a factitious aristocracy, ever fearful that they might be called upon to regorge their sacrilegious spoil. To prevent this they took refuge in political religionism, and paltering with the disturbed consciences, or the pious fantasies, of a portion of the people, they organised them into religious sects. These became the unconscious Prætorians of heir ill-gotten domains. At the head of these religionists, they have continued ever since to govern, or powerfully to influence, this country. They have in that time pulled down thrones and churches, changed dynasties, abrogated and remodelled parliaments ; they have disfranchised Scotland, and confiscated Ireland. One may admire the vigour and consistency of the Whig party, and recognise in their career that unity of purpose that can only spring from a great principle ; but the Whigs introduced sectarian religion, sectarian religion led to political exclusion, and political exclusion was soon accompanied by commercial restraint.—*Coningsby.*

I look upon an Orangeman as a pure Whig; the only professor and practiser of unadulterated Whiggism.—*Coningsby.*

WHISPER.

A whisper of emphasis.—*Lothair.*

WILL.

Everything in this world depends upon will.—('Lady Montfort') *Endymion.*

WILLIAMS (FENWICK) OF KARS.

I wish the House had proposed a vote of thanks to General Williams and expressed its indignation at the manner in which he had been supported. But we were stopped by routine. There was no precedent. I think it would have been wise if we had made a precedent. There would have been something noble in an exile and a prisoner receiving the homage of an applauding Senate and an admiring country. I think it is well, sometimes, that we should show our sense of the conduct of men who, though not successful, are at least triumphant. Sir, there are heroes in adversity ; there are prisoners—not to say it profanely— who lead captivity captive. We have not been able to express those feelings ; but at least we have done this : we have not taken refuge in a shameful silence ; we have had the satisfaction of expressing our sympathy with heroic merit and with national honour.—*Speech in House of Commons.*

WOMAN.

The action of woman on our destiny is unceasing.—*Sybil.*

A reputation for success has as much influence with women as a reputation for wealth has with men.—*Coningsby.*

Where there are crowned heads, there are always some charming women.—*Endymion.*

Our strong passions break into a thousand purposes; women have one. Their love is dangerous, but their hate is fatal.—*Alroy.*

In the present day, and especially among women, one would almost suppose that health was a state of unnatural existence.—*The Young Duke.*

Woman alone can organise a drawing-room: man succeeds sometimes in a library.—*Coningsby.*

Male firmness is very often obstinacy. Women have always something better, worth all qualities. They have tact. ('Lord Eskdale') *Coningsby.*

The woman who is talked about is generally virtuous, and she is only abused because she devotes to one the charms which all wish to enjoy.—*The Infernal Marriage.*

There is no mortification, however keen, no misery, however desperate, which the spirit of woman cannot in some degree lighten or alleviate.—*Coningsby.*

Talk to women as much as you can. This is the best school. This is the way to gain fluency, because you need not care what you say, and had better not be sensible.—('Baron Fleming') *Contarini Fleming.*

I believe women are loved much more for themselves than is supposed. Besides, a woman should be content, if she is loved; that is the point; and she is not to inquire how far the accidents of life have contributed to the result.— ('Myra') *Endymion.*

A woman loses
In love what she may gain in rank, who tops
Her husband's place.

('Solesa') *Count Alarcos.*

Women are generous, but not precise in money matters.—
('Queen Agrippina') *Endymion.*

Women are the priestesses of Predestination.—*Coningsby.*

Perhaps he (Baron Fleming) affected gallantry, because
he was deeply impressed with the influence of women
both upon public and upon private opinion.—*Contarini
Fleming.*

The conversation of men, when they congregate together,
is generally dedicated to one of two subjects : politics or
women.   In the present instance the party was not political ;
and it was the fair sex, and particularly the most charming
portion of it, in the good metropolis of England, that were
subject to the poignant criticism or the profound speculation of these practical philosophers.   There was scarcely a
celebrated beauty in London, from the proud peeress to the
vain opera-dancer, whose charms and conduct were not
submitted to their masterly analysis.   And yet it would be
but fair to admit that their critical ability was more eminent
and satisfactory than their abstract reasoning upon this
interesting topic ; for it was curious to observe that, though
everyone present piqued himself upon his profound knowledge of the sex, not two of the sages agreed in the constituent principles of female character.   One declared that
women were governed by their feelings ; another maintained
that they had no heart ; a third propounded that it was all
imagination ; a fourth that it was all vanity.   Lord
Castlefyshe muttered something about their passions ; and
Charley Doricourt declared that they had no passions
whatever.   But they all agreed in one thing, to wit, that the
man who permitted himself a moment's uneasiness about a
woman was a fool.—*Henrietta Temple.*

When Sidonia felt a disposition to be spell-bound, he used

to review in his memory all the charming women of whom he had read in the books of all literatures, and whom he had known himself in every court and clime, and the result of his reflections ever was, that the charming woman in question was by no means the paragon, which some who had read, seen, and thought less, might be inclined to esteem her. There was, indeed, no subject on which Sidonia discoursed so felicitously as on woman, and none on which Lord Eskdale more frequently endeavoured to attract him. He would tell you Talmudical stories about our mother Eve and the Queen of Sheba, which would have astonished you. There was not a free lady of Greece, Leontium and Phryne, Lais, Danae, and Lamia, the Egyptian girl Thonis, respecting whom he could not tell you as many diverting tales as if they were ladies of Loretto ; not a nook of Athenæus, not an obscure scholiast, not a passage in a Greek orator, that could throw light on these personages, which was not at his command. What stories would he tell you about Marc Antony and the actress Cytheris in their chariot drawn by tigers ! What a character would he paint of that Flora who gave her gardens to the Roman people ! It would draw tears to your eyes. No man was ever so learned in the female manners of the last centuries of polytheism as Sidonia. You would have supposed that he had devoted his studies peculiarly to that period if you had not chanced to draw him to the Italian middle ages. And even these startling revelations were almost eclipsed by his anecdotes of the Court of Henry III. of France, with every character of which he was as familiar as with the brilliant groups that at this moment filled the saloons of Madame de R——d.—*Coningsby*.

One should always make it a rule to give up to them, and then they are sure to give up to us.—('Lord Eskdale') *Coningsby*.

Few great men have flourished, who, were they candid, would not acknowledge the vast advantages they have experienced in the earlier years of their career from the spirit and sympathy of woman. It is woman whose prescient admiration strings the lyre of the despondent poet, whose genius is afterwards to be recognised by his race, and which often embalms the memory of the gentle mistress whose kindness solaced him in less glorious hours. How many an official portfolio would never have been carried, had it not been for her sanguine spirit and assiduous love! How many a depressed and despairing advocate has clutched the Great Seal, and taken his precedence before princes, borne onward by the breeze of her inspiring hope, and illumined by the sunshine of her prophetic smile! A female friend, amiable, clever, and devoted, is a possession more valuable than parks and palaces; and, without such a muse, few men can succeed in life, none be content.—*Henrietta Temple.*

WORDSWORTH.

Gentlemanly man—but only reads his own poetry.—('Alhambra') *Vivian Grey.*

WORKING CLASSES.

The honourable gentleman, the member for Birmingham, talks of the working classes as if they were paupers. I protest against these descriptions. The working classes are not paupers; on the contrary, they are a very wealthy class—they are the wealthiest in the country. Their aggregate income is certainly greater than any other class; their accumulations are to be counted by millions—and I am not speaking merely of the deposits in savings banks, but of funds of which I am aware they are in possession, and which are accumulated to meet their trade necessities and to defend their labour and rights, which can also be counted by millions—and therefore I protest against that language that the great body of the working classes in this country are in a state of pauperism.—*Speech in House of Commons (Elections Bill), July* 31, 1871.

The progress and elevation of the working classes have been wonderfully aided and assisted by three causes, which are not so distinctly attributable to their own energies. The first is the revolution in locomotion, which has opened the world to the working-man, which has enlarged the horizon of his experience, increased the knowledge of nature and art, and added immensely to the salutary recreation, amusement, and pleasure of his existence. The second cause is the cheap postage, the moral benefits of which cannot be exaggerated. And the third is that unshackled press which has furnished him with endless sources of instruction, information, and amusement.—*Speech at Manchester, April 3, 1873.*

WORLD.

Strange power of the world, that the moment we enter it our great conceptions dwarf. In youth, it is quick sympathy that degrades them ; more advanced, it is the sense of the ridiculous.—*Tancred.*

In a couple of years you will enter the world. It is a different thing to what you read about ; a motley, sparkling multitude, in which you may mark all forms and colours, and listen to all sentiments and opinions, but where all you see and hear has only one object—plunder.—('Lord Monmouth') *Coningsby.*

The great world—society formed on anti-social principles.—('Horace Grey') *Vivian Grey.*

To the great body, however, of what is called the world—the world that lives in St. James Street and Pall Mall, that looks out of a club window and surveys mankind, as Lucretius from his philosophic tower—the Duke and Duchess of Bellamont were absolutely unknown.—*Tancred.*

End of World.—All that I said was that the action of the sun had become so irregular that I thought the chances were in favour of the destruction of our planet. At least if I were a Public Office, I would not insure it.—('Baron Gozelius') *Lothair.*

YOUTH.

Youth is, we all know, somewhat reckless in assertion, and when we are juvenile and curly one takes a pride in sarcasm and invective.—*Speech in House of Commons (Her Majesty's Speech, Amendments), June 7, 1859.*

The two greatest stimulants in the world are youth and debt.—('Fakredeen') *Tancred.*

You know too little of life to think of death.—('Winter') *Contarini Fleming.*

Oh! what is wisdom, and what is virtue, without youth ! Talk not to me of knowledge of mankind ; give, give me back the sunshine of the breast which they o'erclouded ! Talk not to me of proud morality ; oh ! give me innocence ! *The Young Duke.*

The blunders of youth are preferable to the triumphs of manhood, or the successes of old age.—('Princess of Tivoli') *Lothair.*

Almost everything that is great has been done by youth. (Sidonia') *Coningsby.*

Youth, glittering youth ! I remember when the prospect of losing my youth frightened me out of my wits ; I dreamt of nothing but grey hairs, a paunch, and the gout or the gravel. But I fancy every period of life has its pleasures, and as we advance in life the exercise of power and the possession of wealth must be great consolations to the majority ; we bully our children and hoard our cash.— ('Lord Cadurcis') *Venetia.*

There are few things more gloomy than the recollection of a youth that has not been enjoyed.—*Henrietta Temple.*

'For life in general there is but one decree. Youth is a blunder ; Manhood a struggle ; Old Age a regret. Do not suppose,' he added, smiling, 'that I hold that youth is genius ; all that I say is, that genius, when young, is divine. Why, the greatest captains of ancient and modern times both conquered Italy at five-and-twenty ! Youth, extreme

youth, overthrew the Persian Empire. Don John of Austria
won Lepanto at twenty-five, the greatest battle of modern
time ; had it not been for the jealousy of Philip, the next
year he would have been Emperor of Mauritania. Gaston
de Foix was only twenty-two when he stood a victor on
the plain of Ravenna. Every one remembers Condé and
Rocroy at the same age. Gustavus Adolphus died at thirty-
eight. Look at his captains : that wonderful Duke of
Weimar, only thirty-six when he died. Banier himself,
after all his miracles, died at forty-five. Cortes was little
more than thirty when he gazed upon the golden cupolas of
Mexico. When Maurice of Saxony died at thirty-two, all
Europe acknowledged the loss of the greatest captain and
the profoundest statesman of the age. Then there is Nelson,
Clive ; but these are warriors, and perhaps you may think
there are greater things than war. I do not : I worship
the Lord of Hosts. But take the most illustrious achievements of civil prudence. Innocent III., the greatest of the
Popes, was the despot of Christendom at thirty-seven.
John de Medici was a Cardinal at fifteen, and, according to
Guicciardini, baffled with his statecraft Ferdinand of Arragon
himself. He was Pope as Leo X. at thirty-seven. Luther
robbed even him of his richest province at thirty-five. Take
Ignatius Loyola and John Wesley, they worked with young
brains. Ignatius was only thirty when he made his pilgrimage and wrote the "Spiritual Exercises." Pascal wrote a
great work at sixteen, and died at thirty-seven the greatest
of Frenchmen.

'Ah ! that fatal thirty-seven, which reminds me of Byron,
greater even as a man than a writer. Was it experience
that guided the pencil of Raphael when he painted the
palaces of Rome? He, too, died at thirty-seven. Richelieu
was Secretary of State at thirty-one. Well, then, there were
Bolingbroke and Pitt, both ministers before other men left
off cricket. Grotius was in great practice at seventeen, and
Attorney-General at twenty-four. And Acquaviva : Acqua-

viva was General of the Jesuits, ruled every cabinet in Europe, and colonised America before he was thirty-seven. What a career!' exclaimed the stranger, rising from his chair and walking up and down the room. 'The secret sway of Europe! That was indeed a position! But it is needless to multiply instances! The history of Heroes is the history of Youth.'—('Sidonia') *Coningsby.*

Wealth is power, and in youth, of all seasons of life, we require power, because we can enjoy everything that we command.—*Henrietta Temple.*

The youth of a nation are the trustees of posterity.— *Sybil.*

Extreme youth gives hope to a country : coupled with ceremonious manners, hope soon assumes the form of confidence.—('Bertie Tremaine') *Endymion.*

LONDON : PRINTED BY
SPOTTISWOODE AND CO., NEW-STREET SQUARE
AND PARLIAMENT STREET

NOVEMBER 1883.

GENERAL LISTS OF NEW WORKS

PUBLISHED BY

Messrs. LONGMANS, GREEN, & CO.

PATERNOSTER ROW, LONDON.

———•o›•‹o•———

HISTORY, POLITICS, HISTORICAL MEMOIRS, &c.

Arnold's Lectures on Modern History. 8vo. 7s. 6d.
Bagehot's Literary Studies, edited by Hutton. 2 vols. 8vo. 28s.
Beaconsfield's (Lord) Speeches, by Kebbel. 2 vols. 8vo. 32s.
Bramston & Leroy's Historic Winchester. Crown 8vo. 6s.
Buckle's History of Civilisation. 3 vols. crown 8vo. 24s.
Chesney's Waterloo Lectures. 8vo. 10s. 6d.
Cox's (Sir G. W.) General History of Greece. Crown 8vo. Maps, 7s. 6d.
Doyle's English in America. 8vo. 18s.
Dun's American Food and Farming. Crown 8vo. 10s. 6d.

Epochs of Ancient History :—
    Beesly's Gracchi, Marius, and Sulla, 2s. 6d.
    ⁃ Capes's Age of the Antonines, 2s. 6d.
    — Early Roman Empire, 2s. 6d.
    Cox's Athenian Empire, 2s. 6d.
    — Greeks and Persians, 2s. 6d.
    Curteis's Rise of the Macedonian Empire, 2s. 6d.
    Ihne's Rome to its Capture by the Gauls, 2s. 6d.
    Merivale's Roman Triumvirates, 2s. 6d.
    Sankey's Spartan and Theban Supremacies, 2s. 6d.
    Smith's Rome and Carthage, the Punic Wars, 2s. 6d.

Epochs of English History, complete in One Volume. Fcp. 8vo. 5s.
    Browning's Modern England, 1820–1874, 9d.
    Creighton's Shilling History of England (Introductory Volume).
    Fcp. 8vo. 1s.
    Creighton's (Mrs.) England a Continental Power, 1066–1216, 9d.
    Creighton's (Rev. M.) Tudors and the Reformation, 1485–1603, 9d.
    Gardiner's (Mrs.) Struggle against Absolute Monarchy, 1603–
    1688, 9d.
    Rowley's Rise of the People, 1215–1485, 9d.
    Rowley's Settlement of the Constitution, 1689–1784, 9d.
    Tancock's England during the American & European Wars,
    1765–1820, 9d.
    York-Powell's Early England to the Conquest, 1s.

Epochs of Modern History :—
    Church's Beginning of the Middle Ages, 2s. 6d.
    Cox's Crusades, 2s. 6d.
    Creighton's Age of Elizabeth, 2s. 6d. [Continued on page 2.

———

London, LONGMANS & CO.

Epochs of Modern History—*continued*.
 Gairdner's Houses of Lancaster and York, 2*s.* 6*d.*
 Gardiner's Puritan Revolution, 2*s.* 6*d.*
 — Thirty Years' War, 2*s.* 6*d.*
 — (Mrs.) French Revolution, 1789–1795, 2*s.* 6*d.*
 Hale's Fall of the Stuarts, 2*s.* 6*d.*
 Johnson's Normans in Europe, 2*s.* 6*d.*
 Longman's Frederick the Great and the Seven Years' War, 2*s.* 6*d.*
 Ludlow's War of American Independence, 2*s.* 6*d.*
 M'Carthy's Epoch of Reform, 1830–1850, 2*s.* 6*d.*
 Morris's Age of Queen Anne, 2*s.* 6*d.*
 Seebohm's Protestant Revolution, 2*s.* 6*d.*
 Stubbs's Early Plantagenets, 2*s.* 6*d.*
 Warburton's Edward III., 2*s.* 6*d.*
Fronde's English in Ireland in the 18th Century. 3 vols. crown 8vo. 18*s.*
 — History of England. Popular Edition. 12 vols. crown 8vo. 3*s.* 6*d.* each.
 — Julius Cæsar, a Sketch. 8vo. 16*s.*
Gardiner's History of England from the Accession of James I. to the Outbreak of the Civil War. 10 vols. crown 8vo. 60*s.*
 — Outline of English History, B.C. 55–A.D. 1880. Fcp. 8vo. 2*s.* 6*d.*
Greville's Journal of the Reigns of George IV. & William IV. 3 vols. 8vo. 36*s.*
Lecky's History of England. Vols. I. & II. 1700–1760. 8vo. 36*s.* Vols. III. & IV. 1760–1784. 8vo. 36*s.*
 — History of European Morals. 2 vols. crown 8vo. 16*s.*
 — — — Rationalism in Europe. 2 vols. crown 8vo. 16*s.*
Lewes's History of Philosophy. 2 vols. 8vo. 32*s.*
Longman's Lectures on the History of England. 8vo. 15*s.*
 — Life and Times of Edward III. 2 vols. 8vo. 28*s.*
Macaulay's Complete Works. Library Edition. 8 vols. 8vo. £5. 5*s.*
 — — — Cabinet Edition. 16 vols. crown 8vo. £4. 16*s.*
 — History of England :—
 Student's Edition. 2 vols. cr. 8vo. 12*s.* | Cabinet Edition. 8 vols. post 8vo. 48*s.*
 People's Edition. 4 vols. cr. 8vo. 16*s.* | Library Edition. 5 vols. 8vo. £4.
Macaulay's Critical and Historical Essays. Cheap Edition. Crown 8vo. 2*s.* 6*d*
 Student's Edition. 1 vol. cr. 8vo. 6*s.* | Cabinet Edition. 4 vols. post 8vo. 24*s.*
 People's Edition. 2 vols. cr. 8vo. 8*s.* | Library Edition. 3 vols. 8vo. 36*s.*
Maxwell's (Sir W. S.) Don John of Austria. Library Edition, with numerous Illustrations. 2 vols. Royal 8vo. 42*s.*
May's Constitutional History of England, 1760–1870. 3 vols. crown 8vo. 18*s.*
 — Democracy in Europe. 2 vols. 8vo. 32*s.*
Merivale's Fall of the Roman Republic. 12mo. 7*s.* 6*d.*
 — General History of Rome, B.C. 753—A.D. 476. Crown 8vo. 7*s.* 6d.
 — History of the Romans under the Empire. 8 vols. post 8vo. 48*s.*
Porter's Knights of Malta. 8vo. 21*s.*
Rawlinson's Ancient Egypt. 2 vols. 8vo. 63*s.*
 — Seventh Great Oriental Monarchy—The Sassanians. 8vo. 28*s.*
Seebohm's Oxford Reformers—Colet, Erasmus, & More. 8vo. 14*s.*
Short's History of the Church of England. Crown 8vo. 7*s.* 6*d.*
Smith's Carthage and the Carthaginians. Crown 8vo. 10*s.* 6*d.*
Taylor's Manual of the History of India. Crown 8vo. 7*s.* 6*d.*
Trevelyan's Early History of Charles James Fox. Crown 8vo. 6*s.*
Walpole's History of England, 1815–1841. 3 vols. 8vo. £2. 14*s.*

London, LONGMANS & CO.

General Lists of New Works. 3

BIOGRAPHICAL WORKS.

Bagehot's Biographical Studies. 1 vol. 8vo. 12s.
Bain's Biography of James Mill. Crown 8vo. Portrait, 5s.
— Criticism and Recollections of J. S. Mill. Crown 8vo. 2s. 6d.
Carlyle's Reminiscences, edited by J. A. Froude. 2 vols. crown 8vo. 18s.
— (Mrs.) Letters and Memorials. 3 vols. 8vo. 36s.
Cates's Dictionary of General Biography. Medium 8vo. 28s.
Froude's Luther, a short Biography. Crown 8vo. 1s.
— Thomas Carlyle. Vols. 1 & 2, 1795-1835. 8vo. with Portraits and
    Plates, 32s.
Gleig's Life of the Duke of Wellington. Crown 8vo. 6s.
Halliwell-Phillipps's Outlines of Shakespeare's Life. 8vo. 7s. 6d.
Koestlin's Life of Martin Luther, translated from the German, with 40 Illus-
    trations. Large crown 8vo. 16s.
Lecky's Leaders of Public Opinion in Ireland. Crown 8vo. 7s. 6d.
Life (The) and Letters of Lord Macaulay. By his Nephew, G. Otto Trevelyan,
    M.P. Popular Edition, 1 vol. crown 8vo. 6s. Cabinet Edition, 2 vols. post
    8vo. 12s. Library Edition, 2 vols. 8vo. 36s.
Marshman's Memoirs of Havelock. Crown 8vo. 3s. 6d.
Memoir of Augustus De Morgan, By his Wife. 8vo. 14s.
Mendelssohn's Letters. Translated by Lady Wallace. 2 vols. cr. 8vo. 5s. each.
Mill's (John Stuart) Autobiography. 8vo. 7s. 6d.
Mozley's Reminiscences of Oriel College. 2 vols. crown 8vo. 18s.
Newman's Apologia pro Vitâ Suâ. Crown 8vo. 6s.
Overton's Life &c. of William Law. 8vo. 15s.
Skobeleff & the Slavonic Cause. By O. K. 8vo. Portrait, 14s.
Southey's Correspondence with Caroline Bowles. 8vo. 14s.
Spedding's Letters and Life of Francis Bacon. 7 vols. 8vo. £4. 4s.
Stephen's Essays in Ecclesiastical Biography. Crown 8vo. 7s. 6d.

MENTAL AND POLITICAL PHILOSOPHY.

Amos's View of the Science of Jurisprudence. 8vo. 18s.
— Fifty Years of the English Constitution, 1830-1880. Crown 8vo. 10s. 6d.
— Primer of the English Constitution. Crown 8vo. 6s.
Bacon's Essays, with Annotations by Whately. 8vo. 10s. 6d.
— Promus, edited by Mrs. H. Pott. 8vo. 16s.
— Works, edited by Spedding. 7 vols. 8vo. 73s. 6d.
Bagehot's Economic Studies, edited by Hutton. 8vo. 10s. 6d.
Bain's Logic, Deductive and Inductive. Crown 8vo. 10s. 6d.
    PART I. Deduction, 4s. | PART II. Induction, 6s. 6d.
Bolland & Lang's Aristotle's Politics. Crown 8vo. 7s. 6d.
Grant's Ethics of Aristotle; Greek Text, English Notes. 2 vols. 8vo. 32s.
Hodgson's Philosophy of Reflection. 2 vols. 8vo. 21s.
Jefferies' Autobiography, The Story of My Heart. Crown 8vo. 5s.
Kalisch's Path and Goal. 8vo. 12s. 6d.
Leslie's Essays in Political and Moral Philosophy. 8vo. 10s. 6d.
Lewis on Authority in Matters of Opinion. 8vo. 14s.
Macaulay's Speeches corrected by Himself. Crown 8vo. 3s. 6d.
Macleod's Economical Philosophy. Vol. I. 8vo. 15s. Vol. II. Part I. 12s.
Mill on Representative Government. Crown 8vo. 2s.
— on Liberty. Crown 8vo. 1s. 4d.

London, LONGMANS & CO.

Mill's Analysis of the Phenomena of the Human Mind. 2 vols. 8vo. 28s.
— Dissertations and Discussions. 4 vols. 8vo. 48s. 6d.
— Essays on Unsettled Questions of Political Economy. 8vo. 6s. 6d.
— Examination of Hamilton's Philosophy. 8vo. 16s.
— Logic, Ratiocinative and Inductive. 2 vols. 8vo. 25s.
— Principles of Political Economy. 2 vols. 8vo. 30s. 1 vol. crown 8vo. 5s.
— Subjection of Women. Crown 8vo. 6s.
— Utilitarianism. 8vo. 5s.
Miller's (Mrs. Fenwick) Readings in Social Economy. Crown 8vo. 5s.
Müller's (Max) Chips from a German Workshop. 4 vols. 8vo. 36s.
Sandars's Institutes of Justinian, with English Notes. 8vo. 18s.
Seebohm's English Village Community. 8vo. 16s.
Seth & Haldane's Philosophical Essays. 8vo. 9s.
Swinburne's Picture Logic. Post 8vo. 5s.
Thomson's Outline of Necessary Laws of Thought. Crown 8vo. 8s.
Tocqueville's Democracy in America, translated by Reeve. 2 vols. crown 8vo. 16s.
Twiss's Law of Nations in Time of War. Second Edition, 8vo. 21s.
Whately's Elements of Logic. 8vo. 10s. 6d. Crown 8vo. 4s. 6d.
— — Rhetoric. 8vo. 10s. 6d. Crown 8vo. 4s. 6d.
— English Synonymes. Fcp. 8vo. 3s.
Williams's Nicomachean Ethics of Aristotle translated. Crown 8vo. 7s. 6d.
Zeller's History of Eclecticism in Greek Philosophy. Crown 8vo. 10s. 8d.
— Plato and the Older Academy. Crown 8vo. 18s.
— Pre-Socratic Schools. 2 vols. crown 8vo. 30s.
— Socrates and the Socratic Schools. Crown 8vo. 10s. 6d.
— Stoics, Epicureans, and Sceptics. Crown 8vo. 15s.

MISCELLANEOUS AND CRITICAL WORKS.

Arnold's (Dr. Thomas) Miscellaneous Works. 8vo. 7s. 6d.
— (T.) Manual of English Literature. Crown 8vo. 7s. 6d.
Bain's Emotions and the Will. 8vo. 15s.
— Mental and Moral Science. Crown 8vo. 10s. 6d.
— Senses and the Intellect. 8vo. 15s.
Beaconsfield (Lord), The Wit and Wisdom of. Crown 8vo. 3s. 6d.
Becker's *Charicles* and *Gallus*, by Metcalfe. Post 8vo. 7s. 6d. each.
Blackley's German and English Dictionary. Post 8vo. 7s. 6d.
Contanseau's Practical French & English Dictionary. Post 8vo. 7s. 6d.
— Pocket French and English Dictionary. Square 18mo. 3s. 6d.
Farrar's Language and Languages. Crown 8vo. 6s.
Froude's Short Studies on Great Subjects. 4 vols. crown 8vo. 24s.
Grant's (Sir A.) Story of the University of Edinburgh. 2 vols. 8vo. 36s.
Hobart's Medical Language of St. Luke. 8vo. 16s.
Hume's Essays, edited by Green & Grose. 2 vols. 8vo. 28s.
— Treatise on Human Nature, edited by Green & Grose. 2 vols. 8vo. 28s.
Latham's Handbook of the English Language. Crown 8vo. 6s.
Liddell & Scott's Greek-English Lexicon. 4to. 36s.
— Abridged Greek-English Lexicon. Square 12mo. 7s. 6d.
Longman's Pocket German and English Dictionary. 18mo. 5s.
Macaulay's Miscellaneous Writings. 2 vols. 8vo. 21s. 1 vol. crown 8vo. 4s. 6d.
— Miscellaneous Writings and Speeches. Crown 8vo. 6s.
— Miscellaneous Writings, Speeches, Lays of Ancient Rome, &c.
Cabinet Edition. 4 vols. crown 8vo. 24s.

London, LONGMANS & CO.

Mahaffy's Classical Greek Literature. Crown 8vo. Vol. 1. the Poets, 7s. 6d.
   Vol. II. the Prose Writers, 7s. 8d.
Millard's Grammar of Elocution. Fcp. 8vo. 3s. 6d.
Milner's Country Pleasures. Crown 8vo. 6s.
Müller's (Max) Lectures on the Science of Language. 2 vols. crown 8vo. 18s.
   —   —   Lectures on India. 8vo. 12s. 6d.
Owen's Evenings with the Skeptics. 2 vols. 8vo. 32s.
Rich's Dictionary of Roman and Greek Antiquities. Crown 8vo. 7s. 6d.
Rogers's Eclipse of Faith. Fcp. 8vo. 5s.
   —   Defence of the Eclipse of Faith. Fcp. 8vo. 3s. 6d.
Roget's Thesaurus of English Words and Phrases. Crown 8vo. 10s. 6d.
Saltoun's (Lord) Scraps, or Memories of my Earlier Days. 2 vols. cr. 8vo. 18s.
Selections from the Writings of Lord Macaulay. Crown 8vo. 6s.
Simcox's Latin Literature. 2 vols. 8vo. 32s.
White & Riddle's Large Latin-English Dictionary. 4to. 21s.
White's Concise Latin-English Dictionary. Royal 8vo. 12s.
   —   Junior Student's Lat.-Eng. and Eng.-Lat. Dictionary. Sq. 12mo. 12s.
            Separately { The English-Latin Dictionary, 5s. 6d.
                        { The Latin-English Dictionary, 7s. 6d.
Wilson's Studies of Modern Mind &c. 8vo. 12s.
Wit and Wisdom of the Rev. Sydney Smith, Crown 8vo. 3s. 6d.
Witt's Myths of Hellas, translated by F. M. Younghusband. Crown 8vo. 3s. 6d.
Yonge's English-Greek Lexicon. Square 12mo. 8s. 6d. 4to. 21s.
The Essays and Contributions of A. K. H. B. Crown 8vo.
         Autumn Holidays of a Country Parson. 3s. 6d.
         Changed Aspects of Unchanged Truths. 3s. 6d.
         Common-place Philosopher in Town and Country. 3s. 6d.
         Counsel and Comfort spoken from a City Pulpit. 3s. 6d.
         Critical Essays of a Country Parson. 8s. 6d.
         Graver Thoughts of a Country Parson. Three Series, 3s. 6d. each.
         Landscapes, Churches, and Moralities. 3s. 6d.
         Leisure Hours in Town. 3s. 6d. Lessons of Middle Age. 3s. 6d.
         Our Little Life. Essays Consolatory and Domestic. 3s. 6d.
         Present-day Thoughts. 3s. 6d.
         Recreations of a Country Parson. Three Series, 3s. 6d. each.
         Seaside Musings on Sundays and Week-Days. 3s. 6d.
         Sunday Afternoons in the Parish Church of a University City. 3s. 6d.

ASTRONOMY, METEOROLOGY, GEOGRAPHY, &c.

Freeman's Historical Geography of Europe. 2 vols. 8vo. 31s. 6d.
Herschel's Outlines of Astronomy. Square crown 8vo. 12s.
Keith Johnston's Dictionary of Geography, or General Gazetteer. 8vo. 42s.
Merrifield's Treatise on Navigation. Crown 8vo. 5s.
Nelson's Work on the Moon. Medium 8vo. 31s. 6d.
Proctor's Essays on Astronomy. 8vo. 12s. Proctor's Moon. Crown 8vo. 10s. 6d.
   —   Larger Star Atlas. Folio, 15s. or Maps only, 12s. 6d.
   —   New Star Atlas. Crown 8vo. 5s. Orbs Around Us. Crown 8vo. 7s. 6d.
   —   Other Worlds than Ours. Crown 8vo. 10s. 6d.
   —   Sun. Crown 8vo. 14s. Universe of Stars. 8vo. 10s. 6d.
   —   Transits of Venus, 8vo. 8s. 6d. Studies of Venus-Transits, 8vo. 5s.
Schellen's Spectrum Analysis, translated by J. & C. Lassell. 8vo. 28s.
Smith's Air and Rain. 8vo. 24s.
The Public Schools Atlas of Ancient Geography. Imperial 8vo. 7s. 8d.

The Public Schools Atlas of Modern Geography. Imperial 8vo. 5s.
Webb's Celestial Objects for Common Telescopes. Crown 8vo. 9s.

NATURAL HISTORY & POPULAR SCIENCE.

Allen's Flowers and their Pedigrees. Crown 8vo. Woodcuts, 7s. 6d.
Arnott's Elements of Physics or Natural Philosophy. Crown 8vo. 12s. 6d.
Brande's Dictionary of Science, Literature, and Art. 3 vols. medium 8vo. 63s.
Decaisne and Le Maout's General System of Botany. Imperial 8vo. 31s. 6d.
Dixon's Rural Bird Life. Crown 8vo. Illustrations, 5s.
Edmonds's Elementary Botany. Fcp. 8vo. 2s.
Evans's Bronze Implements of Great Britain. 8vo. 25s.
Ganot's Elementary Treatise on Physics, by Atkinson. Large crown 8vo. 15s.
  — Natural Philosophy, by Atkinson. Crown 8vo. 7s. 6d.
Goodeve's Elements of Mechanism. Crown 8vo. 6s.
  — Principles of Mechanics. Crown 8vo. 6s.
Grove's Correlation of Physical Forces. 8vo. 15s.
Hartwig's Aerial World. 8vo. 10s. 6d. Polar World. 8vo. 10s. 6d.
  — Sea and its Living Wonders. 8vo. 10s. 6d.
  — Subterranean World. 8vo. 10s. 6d. Tropical World. 8vo. 10s. 6d.
Haughton's Six Lectures on Physical Geography. 8vo. 15s.
Heer's Primæval World of Switzerland. 2 vols. 8vo. 12s.
Helmholtz's Lectures on Scientific Subjects. 2 vols. cr. 8vo. 7s. 6d. each.
Hullah's Lectures on the History of Modern Music. 8vo. 8s. 6d.
  — Transition Period of Musical History. 8vo. 10s. 6d.
Keller's Lake Dwellings of Switzerland, by Lee. 2 vols. royal 8vo. 42s.
Lloyd's Treatise on Magnetism. 8vo. 10s. 6d.
Loudon's Encyclopædia of Plants. 8vo. 42s.
Lubbock on the Origin of Civilisation & Primitive Condition of Man. 8vo. 18s.
Macalister's Zoology and Morphology of Vertebrate Animals. 8vo. 10s. 8d.
Nicols' Puzzle of Life. Crown 8vo. 3s. 6d.
Owen's Comparative Anatomy and Physiology of the Vertebrate Animals. 3 vols.
  8vo. 73s. 6d.
  — Experimental Physiology. Crown 8vo. 5s.
Proctor's Light Science for Leisure Hours. 3 Series, crown 8vo. 7s. 6d. each.
Rivers's Orchard House. Sixteenth Edition. Crown 8vo. 5s.
  — Rose Amateur's Guide. Fcp. 8vo. 4s. 6d.
Stanley's Familiar History of British Birds. Crown 8vo. 6s.
Text-Books of Science, Mechanical and Physical.
    Abney's Photography, 3s. 6d.
    Anderson's (Sir John) Strength of Materials, 3s. 6d.
    Armstrong's Organic Chemistry, 3s. 6d.
    Ball's Astronomy, 6s.
    Barry's Railway Appliances, 3s. 6d.
    Bauerman's Systematic Mineralogy, 6s.
    Bloxam & Huntington's Metals, 5s.
    Glazebrook's Physical Optics, 6s.
    Gore's Electro-Metallurgy, 6s.
    Griffin's Algebra and Trigonometry, 3s. 6d.
    Jenkin's Electricity and Magnetism, 3s. 6d.
    Maxwell's Theory of Heat, 3s. 6d.
    Merrifield's Technical Arithmetic and Mensuration, 3s. 6d.
    Miller's Inorganic Chemistry, 3s. 6d.   [Continued on page 7.]

London, LONGMANS & CO.

Text-Books of Science, Mechanical and Physical—*continued.*

    Preece & Sivewright's Telegraphy, 3*s.* 6*d.*
    Rutley's Study of Rocks, 4*s.* 6*d.*
    Shelley's Workshop Appliances, 4*s.* 6*d.*
    Thomé's Structural and Physiological Botany, 6*s.*
    Thorpe's Quantitative Chemical Analysis, 4*s.* 6*d.*
    Thorpe & Muir's Qualitative Analysis, 3*s.* 6*d.*
    Tilden's Chemical Philosophy, 3*s.* 6*d.*
    Unwin's Machine Design, 6*s.*
    Watson's Plane and Solid Geometry, 3*s.* 6*d.*

Tyndall's Floating Matter of the Air. Crown 8vo. 7*s.* 6*d.*
  —   Fragments of Science. 2 vols. post 8vo. 16*s.*
  —   Heat a Mode of Motion. Crown 8vo. 12*s.*
  —   Lectures on Light delivered in America. Crown 8vo. 7*s.* 6*d.*
  —   Lessons in Electricity. Crown 8vo. 2*s.* 6*d.*
  —   Notes on Electrical Phenomena. Crown 8vo. 1*s.* sewed, 1*s.* 6*d.* cloth.
  —   Notes of Lectures on Light. Crown 8vo. 1*s.* sewed, 1*s.* 6*d.* cloth.
  —   Sound, with Frontispiece & 203 Woodcuts. Crown 8vo. 10*s.* 6*d.*

Von Cotta on Rocks, by Lawrence. Post 8vo. 14*s.*

Wood's Bible Animals. With 112 Vignettes. 8vo. 10*s.* 6*d.*
  —   Common British Insects. Crown 8vo. 3*s.* 6*d.*
  —   Homes Without Hands. 8vo. 10*s.* 6*d.* Insects Abroad. 8vo. 10*s.* 6*d.*
  —   Insects at Home. With 700 Illustrations. 8vo. 10*s.* 6*d.*
  —   Out of Doors. Crown 8vo. 5*s.*
  —   Strange Dwellings. Crown 8vo. 5*s.* Sunbeam Edition, 4to. 6*d.*

CHEMISTRY AND PHYSIOLOGY.

Buckton's Health in the House, Lectures on Elementary Physiology. Cr. 8vo. 2*s*

Jago's Inorganic Chemistry, Theoretical and Practical. Fcp. 8vo. 2*s.*

Miller's Elements of Chemistry, Theoretical and Practical. 3 vols. 8vo. Part I. Chemical Physics, 16*s.* Part II. Inorganic Chemistry, 24*s.* Part III. Organic Chemistry, price 31*s.* 6*d.*

Reynolds's Experimental Chemistry. Fcp. 8vo. ∵ Part I. 1*s.* 6*d.* Part II. 2*s.* 8*d.*

Tilden's Practical Chemistry. Fcp. 8vo. 1*s.* 6*d.*

Watts's Dictionary of Chemistry. 9 vols. medium 8vo. £15. 2*s.* 6*d.*

THE FINE ARTS AND ILLUSTRATED EDITIONS.

Dresser's Arts and Art Manufactures of Japan. Square crown 8vo. 31*s.* 6*d.*

Eastlake's (Lady) Five Great Painters. 2 vols. crown 8vo. 16*s.*
  —   Notes on the Brera Gallery, Milan. Crown 8vo. 5*s.*
  —   Notes on the Louvre Gallery, Paris. Crown 8vo. 7*s.* 6*d.*

Hulme's Art-Instruction in England. Fcp. 8vo. 3*s.* 6*d.*

Jameson's Sacred and Legendary Art. 6 vols. square crown 8vo.
    Legends of the Madonna. 1 vol. 21*s.*
  — — —   Monastic Orders. 1 vol. 21*s.*
  — — —   Saints and Martyrs. 2 vols. 31*s.* 6*d.*
  — — —   Saviour. Completed by Lady Eastlake. 2 vols. 42*s.*

Longman's Three Cathedrals Dedicated to St. Paul. Square crown 8vo. 21*s.*

Macaulay's Lays of Ancient Rome, illustrated by Scharf. Fcp. 4to. 10*s.* 6*d.*

The same, with *Ivry* and the *Armada*, illustrated by Weguelin. Crown 8vo. 6*s.*

Macfarren's Lectures on Harmony. 8vo. 12*s.*

Moore's Irish Melodies. With 161 Plates by D. Maclise, R.A. Super-royal 8vo. 21*s.*
  —   Lalla Rookh, illustrated by Tenniel. Square crown 8vo. 10*s.* 6*d.*

New Testament (The) illustrated with Woodcuts after Paintings by the Early Masters. 4to. 21*s.* cloth, or 42*s.* morocco.

Perry on Greek and Roman Sculpture. With 280 Illustrations engraved on Wood. Square crown 8vo. 31*s.* 6*d.*

London, LONGMANS & CO.

THE USEFUL ARTS, MANUFACTURES, &c.

Bourne's Catechism of the Steam Engine. Fcp. 8vo. 6s.
—   Examples of Steam, Air, and Gas Engines. 4to. 70s.
—   Handbook of the Steam Engine. Fcp. 8vo. 9s.
—   Recent Improvements in the Steam Engine. Fcp. 8vo. 6s.
—   Treatise on the Steam Engine. 4to. 42s.
Brassey's British Navy, with many Illustrations. 5 vols. royal 8vo. 24s. 6d.
Cresy's Encyclopædia of Civil Engineering. 8vo. 25s.
Culley's Handbook of Practical Telegraphy. 8vo. 16s.
Eastlake's Household Taste in Furniture, &c. Square crown 8vo. 14s.
Fairbairn's Useful Information for Engineers. 3 vols. crown 8vo. 31s. 6d.
—   Mills and Millwork. 1 vol. 8vo. 25s.
Gwilt's Encyclopædia of Architecture. 8vo. 52s. 6d.
Kerl's Metallurgy, adapted by Crookes and Röhrig. 3 vols. 8vo. £4. 19s.
Loudon's Encyclopædia of Agriculture. 8vo. 21s.
—   —   — Gardening. 8vo. 21s.
Mitchell's Manual of Practical Assaying. 8vo. 31s. 8d.
Northcott's Lathes and Turning. 8vo. 18s.
Payen's Industrial Chemistry Edited by B. H. Paul, Ph.D. 8vo. 42s.
Piesse's Art of Perfumery. Fourth Edition. Square crown 8vo. 21s.
Sennett's Treatise on the Marine Steam Engine. 8vo. 21s.
Ure's Dictionary of Arts, Manufactures, &, Mines. 4 vols. medium 8vo. £7 7s.
Ville on Artificial Manures. By Crookes. 8vo. 21s.

RELIGIOUS AND MORAL WORKS.

Abbey & Overton's English Church in the Eighteenth Century. 2 vols. 8vo. 38s.
Arnold's (Rev. Dr. Thomas) Sermons. 6 vols. crown 8vo. 5s. each.
Bishop Jeremy Taylor's Entire Works. With Life by Bishop Heber. Edited by the Rev. C. P. Eden. 10 vols. 8vo. £5. 5s.
Boultbee's Commentary on the 39 Articles. Crown 8vo. 6s.
—   History of the Church of England, Pre-Reformation Period. 8vo. 15s.
Bray's Elements of Morality. Fcp. 8vo. 2s. 6d.
Browne's (Bishop) Exposition of the 39 Articles. 8vo. 16s.
Calvert's Wife's Manual. Crown 8vo. 6s.
Christ our Ideal. 8vo. 8s. 8d.
Colenso's Lectures on the Pentateuch and the Moabite Stone. 8vo. 12s.
Colenso on the Pentateuch and Book of Joshua. Crown 8vo. 6s.
Conder's Handbook of the Bible. Post 8vo. 7s. 6d.
Conybeare & Howson's Life and Letters of St. Paul :—
     Library Edition, with all the Original Illustrations, Maps, Landscapes on Steel, Woodcuts, &c. 2 vols. 4to. 42s.
     Intermediate Edition, with a Selection of Maps, Plates, and Woodcuts. 2 vols. square crown 8vo. 21s.
     Student's Edition, revised and condensed, with 46 Illustrations and Maps. 1 vol. crown 8vo. 7s. 6d.
Creighton's History of the Papacy during the Reformation. 2 vols. 8vo. 32s.
Davidson's Introduction to the Study of the New Testament. 2 vols. 8vo. 30s.
Edersheim's Life and Times of Jesus the Messiah. 2 vols. 8vo. 42s.

London, LONGMANS & CO.

Ellicott's (Bishop) Commentary on St. Paul's Epistles. 8vo. Galatians, 8s. 6d.
Ephesians, 8s. 6d. Pastoral Epistles, 10s. 6d. Philippians, Colossians and
Philemon, 10s. 6d. Thessalonians, 7s. 6d.
Ellicott's Lectures on the Life of our Lord. 8vo. 12s.
— Antiquities of Israel, translated by Solly. 8vo. 12s. 6d.
Ewald's Christ and His Time, translated by J. F. Smith. 8vo. 16s.
— History of Israel, translated by Carpenter & Smith. 6 vols. 8vo. 79s.
Gospel (The) for the Nineteenth Century. 4th Edition. 8vo, 10s. 6d.
Hopkins's Christ the Consoler. Fcp. 8vo. 2s. 6d.
Jukes's New Man and the Eternal Life. Crown 8vo. 6s.
— Second Death and the Restitution of all Things. Crown 8vo. 3s. 6d.
— Types of Genesis. Crown 8vo. 7s. 6d.
Kalisch's Bible Studies. PART I. the Prophecies of Balaam. 8vo. 10s. 8d.
— — — PART II. the Book of Jonah. 8vo. 10s. 6d.
— Historical and Critical Commentary on the Old Testament; with a
New Translation. Vol. I. *Genesis*, 8vo. 18s. or adapted for the General
Reader, 12s. Vol. II. *Exodus*, 15s. or adapted for the General Reader, 12s.
Vol. III. *Leviticus*, Part I. 15s. or adapted for the General Reader, 8s.
Vol. IV. *Leviticus*, Part II. 15s. or adapted for the General Reader, 8s.
Keary's Outlines of Primitive Belief. 8vo. 18s.
Lyra Germanica : Hymns translated by Miss Winkworth. Fcp. 8vo. 5s.
Manning's Temporal Mission of the Holy Ghost. Crown 8vo. 8s. 6d.
Martineau's Endeavours after the Christian Life. Crown 8vo. 7s. 6d.
— Hymns of Praise and Prayer. Crown 8vo. 4s. 6d. 32mo. 1s. 6d.
— Sermons, Hours of Thought on Sacred Things. 2 vols. 7s. 6d. each.
Mill's Three Essays on Religion. 8vo. 10s. 6d.
Monsell's Spiritual Songs for Sundays and Holidays. Fcp. 8vo. 5s. 18mo. 2s.
Müller's (Max) Origin & Growth of Religion. Crown 8vo. 7s. 6d.
— — Science of Religion. Crown 8vo. 7s. 6d.
Newman's Apologia pro Vitâ Suâ. Crown 8vo. 6s.
Sewell's (Miss) Passing Thoughts on Religion. Fcp. 8vo. 3s. 6d.
— — Preparation for the Holy Communion. 32mo. 3s.
Seymour's Hebrew Psalter. Crown 8vo. 2s. 6d.
Smith's Voyage and Shipwreck of St. Paul. Crown 8vo. 7s. 6d.
Supernatural Religion. Complete Edition. 3 vols. 8vo. 86s.
Whately's Lessons on the Christian Evidences. 18mo. 6d.
White's Four Gospels in Greek, with Greek-English Lexicon. 32mo. 5s.

TRAVELS, VOYAGES, &c.

Baker's Eight Years in Ceylon. Crown 8vo. 7s. 6d.
— Rifle and Hound in Ceylon. Crown 8vo. 7s. 6d.
Ball's Alpine Guide. 3 vols. post 8vo. with Maps and Illustrations :—I. Western
Alps, 8s. 6d. II. Central Alps, 7s. 6d. III. Eastern Alps, 10s. 6d.
Ball on Alpine Travelling, and on the Geology of the Alps, 1s.
Brassey's Sunshine and Storm in the East. Crown 8vo. 7s. 6d.
— Voyage in the Yacht 'Sunbeam.' Crown 8vo. 7s. 6d. School Edition,
fcp. 8vo. 2s. Popular Edition, 4to. 6d.
Freeman's Impressions of the United States of America. Crown 8vo. 6s.
Hassall's San Remo Climatically considered. Crown 8vo. 5s.
Miller's Wintering in the Riviera. Post 8vo. Illustrations. 7s. 6d.

London, LONGMANS & CO.

The Alpine Club Map of Switzerland. In Four Sheets. 42s.
Three in Norway. By Two of Them. Crown 8vo. Illustrations, 6s.
Weld's Sacred Palmlands. Crown 8vo. 10s. 6d.

WORKS OF FICTION.

Arden. By A. Mary F. Robinson. 2 vols. crown 8vo. 12s.
Aut Caesar aut Nihil. By the Countess von Bothmer. 3 vols. crown 8vo. 21s.
Because of the Angels. By M. Hope. 2 vols. crown 8vo. 12s.
Brabourne's (Lord) Higgledy-Piggledy. Crown 8vo. 3s. 6d.
— 　　— 　　Whispers from Fairy Land. Crown 8vo. 3s. 6d.
Cabinet Edition of Novels and Tales by the Earl of Beaconsfield, K.G. 11 vols.
　　crown 8vo. price 6s. each.
Cabinet Edition of Stories and Tales by Miss Sewell. Crown 8vo. cloth extra,
　　gilt edges, price 3s. 6d. each :—

Amy Herbert. Cleve Hall.
The Earl's Daughter.
Experience of Life.
Gertrude. Ivors.

A Glimpse of the World.
Katharine Ashton.
Laneton Parsonage.
Margaret Percival. Ursula.

Novels and Tales by the Earl of Beaconsfield, K.G. Hughenden Edition, with 2
　　Portraits on Steel and 11 Vignettes on Wood. 11 vols. crown 8vo. £2. 2s.
The Modern Novelist's Library. Each Work in crown 8vo. A Single Volume,
　　complete in itself, price 2s. boards, or 2s. 6d. cloth :—

By the Earl of Beaconsfield, K.G.
Lothair. Coningsby.
Sybil. Tancred.
Venetia. Henrietta Temple.
Contarini Fleming.
Alroy, Ixion, &c.
The Young Duke, &c.
Vivian Grey. Endymion.

By Bret Harte.
In the Carquinez Woods.

By Mrs. Oliphant.
In Trust, the Story of a Lady
　　and her Lover.

By Anthony Trollope.
Barchester Towers.
The Warden.

By Major Whyte-Melville.
Digby Grand.
General Bounce.
Kate Coventry.
The Gladiators.
Good for Nothing.
Holmby House.
The Interpreter.
The Queen's Maries.

By Various Writers.
The Atelier du Lys.
Atherstone Priory.
The Burgomaster's Family.
Elsa and her Vulture.
Mademoiselle Mori.
The Six Sisters of the Valleys.
Unawares.

Novels and Tales of the Earl of Beaconsfield, K.G. Modern Novelist's Library
　　Edition, complete in 11 vols. crown 8vo. price £1. 13s. cloth extra.
In the Olden Time. By the Author of ' Mademoiselle Mori.' Crown 8vo. 6s.
Messer Agnolo's Household. By Leader Scott. Crown 8vo. 6s.
Thicker than Water. By James Payn. 3 vols. 21s.
Under Sunny Skies. By the Author of ' Robert Forrester.' 2 vols. 12s.
Whom Nature Leadeth. By G. Noel Hatton. 3 vols. 21s.

POETRY AND THE DRAMA.

Bailey's Festus, a Poem. Crown 8vo. 12s. 6d.
Bowdler's Family Shakspeare. Medium 8vo. 14s. 6 vols. fcp. 8vo. 21s.
Cayley's Iliad of Homer, Homometrically translated. 8vo. 12s. 6d.

London, LONGMANS & CO.

Conington's Æneid of Virgil, translated into English Verse. Crown 8vo. 9*s.*
— Prose Translation of Virgil's Poems. Crown 8vo. 9*s.*
Goethe's Faust, translated by Birds. Large crown 8vo. 12*s.* 6*d.*
— — translated by Webb. 8vo. 12*s.* 6*d.*
— — edited by Selss. Crown 8vo. 5*s.*
Ingelow's Poems. New Edition. 2 vols. fcp. 8vo. 12*s.*
Macaulay's Lays of Ancient Rome, with Ivry and the Armada. 16mo. 3*s.* 6*d.*
The same, Cheap Edition, fcp. 8vo. 1*s.* sewed, 1*s.* 6*d.* cloth, 2*s.* 6*d.* cloth extra.
Southey's Poetical Works. Medium 8vo. 14*s.*

RURAL SPORTS, HORSE AND CATTLE MANAGEMENT, &c.

Dead Shot (The), by Marksman. Crown 8vo. 10*s.* 6*d.*
Fitzwygram's Horses and Stables. 8vo. 10*s.* 6*d.*
Francis's Treatise on Fishing in all its Branches. Post 8vo. 15*s.*
Horses and Roads. By Free-Lance. Crown 8vo. 6*s.*
Howitt's Visits to Remarkable Places. Crown 8vo. 7*s.* 6*d.*
Jefferies' The Red Deer. Crown 8vo. 4*s.* 6*d.*
Miles's Horse's Foot, and How to Keep it Sound. Imperial 8vo. 12*s.* 6*d.*
— Plain Treatise on Horse-Shoeing. Post 8vo. 2*s.* 6*d.*
— Remarks on Horses' Teeth. Post 8vo. 1*s.* 6*d.*
— Stables and Stable-Fittings. Imperial 6vo. 15*s.*
Milner's Country Pleasures. Crown 8vo. 6*s.*
Nevile's Horses and Riding. Crown 8vo. 6*s.*
Ronalds's Fly-Fisher's Entomology. 8vo. 14*s.*
Steel's Diseases of the Ox, a Manual of Bovine Pathology. 8vo. 15*s.*
Stonehenge's Dog in Health and Disease. Square crown 8vo. 7*s.* 6*d.*
— Greyhound. Square crown 8vo. 15*s.*
Wilcocks's Sea-Fisherman. Post 8vo. 12*s.* 6*d.*
Youatt's Work on the Dog. 8vo. 6*s.*
— — — — Horse. 8vo. 7*s.* 6*d.*

WORKS OF UTILITY AND GENERAL INFORMATION.

Acton's Modern Cookery for Private Families. Fcp. 8vo. 4*s.* 6*d.*
Black's Practical Treatise on Brewing. 8vo. 10*s.* 6*d.*
Buckton's Food and Home Cookery. Crown 8vo. 2*s.* 8*d.*
Bull on the Maternal Management of Children. Fcp. 8vo. 1*s.* 6*d.*
Bull's Hints to Mothers on the Management of their Health during the Period of
  Pregnancy and in the Lying-in Room. Fcp. 8vo. 1*s.* 6*d.*
Burton's My Home Farm. Crown 8vo. 3*s.* 6*d.*
Campbell-Walker's Correct Card, or How to Play at Whist. Fcp. 8vo. 2*s.* 6*d.*
Johnson's (W. & J. H.) Patentee's Manual. Fourth Edition. 8vo. 10*s.* 6*d.*
— — The Patents Designs &c. Act, 1883. Fcp. 8vo. 1*s.*
Longman's Chess Openings. Fcp. 8vo. 2*s.* 6*d.*
Macleod's Elements of Banking. Fourth Edition. Crown 8vo. 5*s.*
— Elements of Economics. 2 vols. small crown 8vo. VOL. I. 7*s.* 6*d.*
— Theory and Practice of Banking. 2 vols. 8vo. Vol. I. 12*s.*

London, LONGMANS & CO.

M'Culloch's Dictionary of Commerce and Commercial Navigation. 8vo. 63*s.*
Maunder's Biographical Treasury. Fcp. 8vo. 6*s.*
— Historical Treasury. Fcp. 8vo. 6*s.*
— Scientific and Literary Treasury. Fcp. 8vo. 8*s.*
— Treasury of Bible Knowledge, edited by Ayre. Fcp. 8vo. 6*s.*
— Treasury of Botany, edited by Lindley & Moore. Two Parts, 12*s.*
— Treasury of Geography. Fcp. 8vo. 8*s.*
— Treasury of Knowledge and Library of Reference. Fcp. 8vo. 6*s.*
— Treasury of Natural History. Fcp. 8vo. 6*s.*
Pewtner's Comprehensive Specifier; Building-Artificers' Work. Crown 8vo. 6*s.*
Pole's Theory of the Modern Scientific Game of Whist. Fcp. 8vo. 2*s.* 6*d.*
Quain's Dictionary of Medicine. Medium 8vo. 31*s.* 6*d.* or in 2 vols. 34*s.*
Reeve's Cookery and Housekeeping. Crown 8vo. 7*s.* 6*d.*
Scott's Farm Valuer. Crown 8vo. 5*s.*
Smith's Handbook for Midwives. Crown 8vo. 5*s.*
The Cabinet Lawyer, a Popular Digest of the Laws of England. Fcp. 8vo. 9*s.*
Ville on Artificial Manures, by Crookes. 8vo. 21*s.*
Willich's Popular Tables, by Marriott. Crown 8vo. 10*s.*

MUSICAL WORKS BY JOHN HULLAH, LL.D.

Hullah's Method of Teaching Singing. Crown 8vo. 2*s.* 6*d.*
Exercises and Figures in the same. Crown 8vo. 1*s.* sewed, or 1*s.* 2*d.* limp cloth; or 2 Parts, 6*d.* each sewed, or 8*d.* each limp cloth.
Large Sheets, containing the 'Exercises and Figures in Hullah's Method,' in Five Parcels of Eight Sheets each, price 6*s.* each.
Chromatic Scale, with the Inflected Syllables, on Large Sheet. 1*s.* 6*d.*
Card of Chromatic Scale. 1*d.*
Grammar of Musical Harmony. Royal 8vo. price 3*s.* sewed and 4*s.* 8*d.* cloth; or in 2 Parts, each 1*s.* 6*d.*
Exercises to Grammar of Musical Harmony. 1*s.*
Grammar of Counterpoint. Part I. super-royal 8vo. 2*s.* 6*d.*
Wilhem's Manual of Singing. Parts I. & II. 2*s.* 6*d.* each or together, 5*s.*
Exercises and Figures contained in Parts I. and II. of Wilhem's Manual. Books I. & II. each 8*d.*
Large Sheets, Nos. 1 to 8, containing the Figures in Part I. of Wilhem's Manual, in a Parcel, 6*s.*
Large Sheets, Nos. 9 to 40, containing the Exercises in Part I. of Wilhem's Manual, in Four Parcels of Eight Nos. each, per Parcel, 6*s.*
Large Sheets, Nos. 41 to 52, containing the Figures in Part II. in a Parcel. 9*s.*
Hymns for the Young, set to Music. Royal 8vo. 8*d.* sewed, or 1*s.* 6*d.* cloth.
Infant School Songs. 6*d.*
Notation, the Musical Alphabet. Crown 8vo. 6*d.*
Old English Songs for Schools, Harmonised. 6*d.*
Rudiments of Musical Grammar. Royal 8vo. 3*s.*
School Songs for 2 and 3 Voices. 2 Books, 8vo. each 6*d.*
A Short Treatise on the Stave. 2*s.*
Lectures on the History of Modern Music. 8vo. 8*s.* 6*d.*
Lectures on the Transition Period of Musical History. 8vo. 10*s.* 8*d.*

London, LONGMANS & CO.

Spottiswoode & Co., Printers, New-street Square, London.